Waterfoals!

Two of the watery beasts pulled up alongside the shore, training their bright eyes on the blood-red Heart in Logan's hands. One of them released a snort, relaying to the young man in unspoken words that there was a task that needed fulfilling. In awe, Logan paused. The waterfoals were all a shade of blue, their manes frothing silver bubbles. How any creature made up of water could support him, Logan did not know, but the waterfoals certainly seemed to indicate they wanted him to mount up.

Nightwalker drew his empty eyes from the waterfoals. "You have . . . caused this?" he wondered, hesitating.

Logan nodded, then shrugged. "Yeah, well . . . I don't know." He stepped into the waves and stared at the magical beasts. "Are they safe to ride?" he questioned.

Nightwalker cast his empty eyes on the young man. "You wield the Bloodstone," he replied. "You tell me."

Ace Books by Steven Frankos

THE JEWEL OF EQUILIBRANT
THE HEART OF SPARRILL

THE HEART OF SPARRILL

STEVEN FRANKOS

ACE BOOKS, NEW YORK

This book is an Ace original edition,
and has never been previously published.

THE HEART OF SPARRILL

An Ace Book / published by arrangement with
the author

PRINTING HISTORY
Ace edition / September 1993

ISBN: 0-441-32137-2

ACE®
Ace Books are published by The Berkley Publishing Group,
200 Madison Avenue, New York, NY 10016.
ACE and the "A" design
are trademarks belonging to Charter Communications, Inc.

10 9 8 7 6 5 4 3 2 1

To Janis Sartin,
who's been waiting nearly as long as I have;

To the memory of my father,
who never could read a trilogy in the proper order;

And to Angela,
who put up with the neuroses, paranoia,
and all the "guess whats"

·1·

Wind

An empty, sorrowful feeling lurked deep within, drowning out the disturbing sense of discordance that hovered in the late afternoon air. Matthew Logan glanced up from where he was seated upon his horse and tried to spy the invisible emotions fluttering about him. He seemed to focus in on that remorse and stare silently at it. Gradually, layers of his sorrow began to peel away until its very roots were revealed, and Logan saw that they stretched far off into the sky—winding back toward the real world . . .

His world. Earth. Santa Monica. The world that surrounded Logan now was not his. It was a world where magic worked and men used weapons to discuss business transactions. It was a world where invading Reakthi warriors continuously strived to beat the people of Sparrill into submission. And it was a world that sensed Logan's difference, and, therefore, detested his presence. But Logan's difference gave him the odd ability to sense magic and/or magical items, and that made many people eager to sway Logan to their cause.

A Demon, a priestess, the Reakthi, King Mediyan, and Cyrene— all of them had lusted after Logan because of his ability—many of them had already paid for that folly. Of course, Logan thought foully, this would never have happened back in my world. I'm no different from anybody else in Santa Monica. It's the goddamn magic here that makes me different—that makes me what I am: an instant magic-detector and magic-sucker. Oh, yeah. Don't forget that aspect! Each day I stay, the more magic I take in. Each week I remain, the more desperate the Reakthi and Mediyan get.

Why was I ever pulled out of my world in the first place?

A rasping whisper of a memory sprouted in Logan's mind: *Why not?* was the reply. The very words spoken by the Smythe, the only spellcaster sane and powerful enough to send Logan back to his rightful world, who was, oddly enough, from that very world himself. Now, however, the Smythe was dead, and so was Logan's surest route home.

Logan tore his gaze away from the sky and blinked. He could feel his contact lenses swirling under his eyelids as he turned to peer at the shrubbery around him. The sun was slowly setting behind him, casting a blood-red glare upon the greenness, and shadows stretched themselves lazily across the soil. A few insects began to chirp in anticipation of the night, and a cool breeze sprang up from the north.

A portion of shadows came alive and a grey-and-black horse burst free of the brush. Its rider was similarly cloaked in darkness, his grey cape billowing out behind him like the night sky turned to cloth. Flickering grey eyes burned within his lean face, and a sneer and a trim mustache were both drawn on his upper lip. Silver flashed as the sun's dying rays glinted off the strap of daggers slung across the grey-clothed chest.

"We shouldn't be detected here," the stranger declared, "if Thromar doesn't alert them with all the noise he's making."

A second horse broke free of the forest, arrogantly tossing its crimson mane into the evening sky. Its rider towered upon its crude saddle, grinning with yellowing teeth that lurked within a heavy, reddish-brown beard. A vest of rusting chainmail clad the muscular chest, and a bloodied but still sharp sword dangled at his side.

"When Nature calls, Murderer," Thromar responded good-naturedly, "one must act—or else things become very uncomfortable."

Moknay the Murderer sneered again in reply, bringing a gloved finger across his mustache. "And judging from the way you smell, you've learned that through past experience," he retorted. The Murderer turned to face Logan and his eyes gleamed. "Well, friend," he commented, "it seems when you start an adventure, you leave nothing out. The town's been completely surrounded by Mediyan's Guards; we'll have to sneak in under cover of the night."

Thromar leapt off his red-and-black mare, Smeea, and snorted. "Don't see why we're sneaking around in the first place!" He shoved a massive hand into one of the many saddlebags hanging by Smeea's flanks and withdrew a few pieces of fruit. "The four of us are more than enough to wipe out a few of Mediyan's buffoons!"

Four, mused Logan, that's right! They were still missing the fourth member of their band.

Thromar released a startled shout as a light blue hand suddenly snatched one of his pieces of fruit away.

"Foooooooood!" the enormous ogre roared happily.

Moknay flinched at the resounding boom. "Between the two of you, it's a wonder Mediyan himself doesn't know we're here!"

"Let 'im come!" Thromar remarked, his mouth full. "I've got one or two things to stick up that bugger's ass!"

Moknay nodded dourly, dismounting and surveying the forest about them. "I'll say this for the fat Shagshooter, it's the fastest he's ever moved his backside. He didn't make a move when the Reakthi first came; he didn't try to help when Agasilaus conquered practically all of Denzil . . . but when Logan pops in with his magical ability . . . old Mediyan moves faster than a chomprat on skelmp! I've never seen so many Guardsmen in Sparrill at one time."

"How the hell are we supposed to get into the town if it's crawling with Guards?" Logan wanted to know.

"By being extremely cautious," the Murderer replied. His grey eyes flicked to Thromar. "And quiet." A grim expression set on his face. "It's a pity Thromar and I got rid of our uniforms—we could have used them as a disguise."

"Not me!" Thromar boomed indignantly. "I'm not about to dress up as one of Mediyan's dungheads!"

"Duuuuuungheeeeeeads!" the ogre agreed.

The Murderer twirled on the two, eyes ablaze. "The two of you seem to have forgotten it is quite important we get into Debarnian and get to Barthol. Or have you forgotten that lovely little gemstone Logan has in one of his saddlebags?"

Logan turned away from his friends to glare at the leather saddlebags hanging at his horse's sides. Hidden within one of the pouches was the gleaming, golden Jewel of Equilibrant . . . one of Logan's many "mistakes" from his previous journey. It was the very source of Balance for the Wheel and one of the most powerful magical items in all of Sparrill . . . which also made it very easy for Logan and his magic-sensing ability to "stumble" across it.

The young man slowly drew his eyes away from his green and yellow mount and focused back on his companions. It suddenly became clear to him why Moknay was so upset as to their present situation: The Murderer had a very real fear of magic. For all his stealth and cunning, magic was the one thing that could trip him up—for that reason, he feared and mistrusted it.

"The way I remember it," Logan decided to say to ease Moknay's tension, "Debarnian had no walls—only Eadarus did. So can't we just sneak in from any direction?"

Moknay nodded his head of black hair. "You're right there, friend, but Mediyan's men are *everywhere*. They're swarming more than fuzzbugs in a tavern cellar. They've had time to stretch all the way from Magdelon to Semeth by now! Remember how many of them there were in the Hills?"

Logan nodded grimly. He wouldn't forget that incident!

"In Imogen's name, Murderer!" Thromar protested. "Who cares how many of them there are? They're inept dunderheads! We shouldn't have any problem creeping past them!"

"*I* know *I* won't!" Moknay snapped. "It's you I'm worried about!"

The large fighter clamped a massive hand on the Murderer's shoulder and smiled. "Don't waste your worry on me, Murderer," he declared. "I was the one who crept into Agasilaus's castle and killed the bastard. I can move about just as quietly as you can."

Moknay's eyes flickered uneasily as he gave Logan's horse an unpleasant look. Gradually, the Murderer drew away from his giant companion and faced the northeast. Somewhere, Logan knew, through all that greenery, the town of Debarnian was waiting for them.

"I'll scout ahead into the town," Moknay told his friends. "Maybe I can learn exactly where the Guards are stationed. You three, wait." He gave a second glance at Thromar and the ogre. "Quietly," he added. Then, with a flap of his cape, the Murderer ducked into the shadows and melded with the blackness.

Matthew Logan felt a shock of panic yank at his heart as he feared for Moknay's welfare. So many people had gone out of their way for him, and all of them had been hurt—or killed. Once before this trait had plagued the young man's conscience, but Moknay had explained it as how the people of Sparrill acted. "I told you before the *people* have kept the Reakthi out, not the Guards," the Murderer had said. "That's the way we are here. We will gladly help anyone who opposes the invaders . . . even if it means laying down our lives."

The memory helped console Logan's aching spirit and he turned to his remaining companions as his fear diminished. Thromar, he saw, had settled himself on the grass, his brawny arms folded behind his head. The light blue ogre had imitated the fighter's position, grinning with crooked teeth.

Fatigue seeped into Logan's own limbs and muscles as he watched, and he soon joined the pair on the ground. Abruptly, the blades of grass seemed to shrink back in disgust at the young man's touch, and, like a skunk, penetrated Logan's pores with the feeling that he was unwanted.

As soon as the familiar buzz of disharmony began, Logan jumped back to his feet with an enraged curse. God, how he hated this place! He had never asked to be brought here! Some damn wind had singled him out! Some damn wind from the land itself, and, still, the land abhorred his presence.

Angrily, the young man strode across their small, makeshift campsite and peered into the darkness where Moknay had gone. Overhead, stars began to twinkle as the blackness deepened.

The cool breeze from the north offered no soothing caress as it passed gently over Logan. His black hair slightly ruffled in the wind's playful touch, but it did not calm him. Sparrill's colossal moon had risen into the night sky, a mere crescent, but still bright enough to spatter the forest with beams of moonlight. Grimly, Logan wondered how much light was cast upon Debarnian.

As worry ate through his innards, Logan pulled back the torn left sleeve of his sweat jacket and glanced at his wrist watch. A faint red light dotted with silver glimmered back at him from the watch's display screen; Logan cursed. He had forgotten that since his arrival in Sparrill, his digital watch no longer functioned properly. Instead of LED readouts, his timepiece flashed a crimson-and-silver glow upon his arm.

Turning away from the sparkling watch, Logan gazed into the heavens. None of the constellations above him were familiar—none were of his universe—but from the height of the moon, Logan knew it was well into the night. That meant Moknay had been gone a long time.

Too long.

Tormenting the young man, the cool breeze rustled through the shrubbery, trying its very best to sound like a man. For a moment, Logan was fooled. Moknay was coming back! he exclaimed to himself. Then he realized the wind's trick and scowled unhappily.

Matthew

Logan froze. Out of the dying breeze, a voice had called to him.

Matthew Logan, help

This was no prank the wind was playing, the young man decided. The only other time a wind had talked to him had been back in Santa Monica. The very wind that had carried him to Sparrill had first, mysteriously, carried Thromar's voice to him.

Matthew Logan, please

Confusion overwhelmed the young man as he turned to his sleeping companions. Both Thromar and the ogre were sleeping peacefully, their usually fierce features softened in slumber. So faint was the feeble cry for help that it did not alert Thromar's keen warrior senses.

As his confusion rapidly surged into an electrical terror, Logan started toward his slumbering friends. Unexpectedly, a shriek dissolved the quiet of the night followed by a thunderous roar of anger that shattered the stars. The cool night breeze howled into a fiery tornado that struck Logan full in the face. Blinded and stunned, the young man felt his feet leave the ground and experienced a brief moment of weightlessness. The sturdy trunk of a tree rudely reminded him he was in the forest, and bright lights erupted behind his eyelids.

Thromar heaved himself to his feet, his blood-caked weapon in his hands. "By Brolark!" he cried.

The trees of the forest had come alive, quaking and shivering as though something threatened their very existence. No wind or gale caused this flurry of motion, yet the foliage itself was fitfully writhing.

"Friend-Logan!" Thromar boomed above the din. "Are you hurt?"

Logan unsteadily pulled himself out of the quivering brush and tried to clamber to his feet. "No," he gasped, "I should be all right." Abruptly, all sense of balance deserted the young man and he crashed to his knees. He crawled to where his oaken staff lay and endeavored to prop himself up.

A deafening squeal pierced the woods and green flame exploded from Logan's staff. Logan could only open his eyes wide in response as another concussion knocked him backwards into the shrubbery. Only this time, the serpentine movement of the forest stopped.

Silence hovered over the trio like a thundercloud. They neither moved nor spoke, warily eyeing the greenery around them. Once before they had seen the brush of Sparrill come to life, Logan recalled, but it had been under the control of Druid Launce and the staff Logan now possessed. Now they had just been witness to the very trees shaking with a terror as real as any of them might feel, and they had no idea as to the cause.

"Friend-Logan!" Thromar roared. "Your arm!"

Fearing the absolute worst, Logan jerked his head down. Severed at the shoulder! Maimed beyond healing! Broken in four different places! his mind suggested.

As the young man looked, a brilliant beam of power stabbed into his contact-covered eyes. Red and silver blazed beneath his sweat jacket, glittering from the fabric-covered face of his digital watch. This time shielding his eyes, Logan squinted through the glare. Never before had he seen his watch flare so brightly, yet, gradually, there was a change . . . something that made a knot form in the young man's stomach.

An impending sense of doom seeped into Logan's brain as all the silver specks swirling within the red flame grew black.

The beacon winked out.

Stunned into silence once more, Logan cast a bewildered look at Thromar. The fighter returned the gaze with a shrug and cautiously inspected their campsite. The ogre, its massive arms drawn over its head, remained on the ground.

"What the hell was that?" Logan muttered, finally forcing his quivering legs to support him.

"The very question I was about to ask," Thromar said, prodding the bushes with his sword. "I think, however, we can assume it was not Groathit."

Groathit! Logan's mind exclaimed. They had not been attacked by the Reakthi spellcaster since their battle in the Hills. So used to the wizard's constant attacks, Logan had almost forgotten he still lived . . . and still lusted after Logan's ability.

Thromar sheathed his sword and peered at Logan's green-and-yellow horse. "And it doesn't seem to be the Jewel," he went on. "We've kept that in check ever since we learned how!"

Logan scanned their clearing, his blue eyes jumping from bush to bush. "If it wasn't Groathit and it wasn't the Jewel, what else is there?"

"I do not know," Thromar admitted. Thoughtfully, the massive fighter stroked his beard. "Perhaps it *was* Groathit . . . I wouldn't put it past that scumcaster to try something like this! Make the forest shudder in a demonstration of his powers, maybe? Brolark only knows how the mind of a wizard works . . . if Groathit has one, the bugger!"

Logan's fear began to intensify as he continued scanning, stopping every so often at his wooden staff. "If it was Groathit," he replied, "he's certainly grown a lot more powerful. Somehow . . ."

The young man trailed off as he took a cautious step toward his staff.

"Somehow what, friend-Logan?" queried Thromar.

"Somehow I think it's bigger than that," the young man answered, tentatively reaching out for his staff. "There was . . . I heard a voice . . . on the wind. I don't know who it was, but I swear I heard them. They were asking for help . . . *my* help."

Thromar placed a meaty hand upon his sword hilt. "Then we must help them!" he declared. "From which direction did this plea arise?"

Logan's fingers curled about the oaken staff and a disconcerting numbness filled his hand. It felt as if his fingers had gone to sleep, but as soon as he lifted a digit away from the wood, the numbness ceased.

"There was no direction," he muttered, detached, staring at the oak pole. "It was on the wind."

"Well," rumbled Thromar, "from which direction was the wind coming from?"

As the insensibility faded from his hand, Logan turned away from the staff and peered at Thromar. "North or so."

"North, hmmmmm?"

Curiously, Logan watched the huge warrior wander across their campsite and peer northward into the blackness of the forest. There was a churning in the young man's gut as he suddenly recognized the area Thromar stood beside. It was the very shrubbery Moknay had disappeared into well over three hours ago!

"Moknay," Logan breathed.

Thromar glanced at him. "Hmmmm?"

"Moknay's still not back, and Debarnian's north of here!" Logan cried.

"Somewhat northeast, but you have a point," the fighter agreed. "It's not like that conniving footpad to be late."

"We've got to do something!" Logan exclaimed, his fear and concern mounting.

"But what, friend-Logan?" Thromar asked back. "How can we fight a menace when we don't know who—or what—that menace is?"

Logan threw some provisions into his horse's saddlebags and extracted a leather pouch. A faint tingling of disunity found its way to Logan's nerves as the young man hugged the bagged Jewel and tin of powder to his chest. "Whatever caused that wind isn't important right now!" he remarked. "What's important is if it was this bad here, how much worse was it farther north of here?" He gave the dark forest a frenzied look. "We've got to make sure Moknay's all right."

Bushy eyebrows raised above Thromar's black eyes. "What are you going to do with that thing?" he queried, jabbing a finger at the Jewel.

"Take it with me," Logan responded, uneasily juggling the bag. "I'm going to go to Barthol's so I might as well bring the Jewel. I've got to know if Moknay's alive or not."

"It may prove to be slightly dangerous," Thromar stated, tugging heroically at his sheath, "and fun; I'll come with you."

Logan's own urgency frightened him. "No!" he ordered. "You've got to stay here—with the horses! Our original plan was to take the ogre and leave him there as guard. He'll be sufficient protection."

Thromar plopped himself down on the ground, wearing a frown that made his beard droop. "Phoo!" he complained. "Friend-Logan, you're starting to think just like Moknay! You go traipsing back to that Church and leave me here in absolute boredom!"

Logan jogged toward the edge of the clearing. "You can look for whoever caused that wind," he suggested, "but stay near the horses! We'll need you once we get back."

If we get back, added the young man's pessimism.

Logan tried to ignore his negative thoughts and dashed headlong into the night-cloaked shrubbery, the ogre thundering behind him. The darkness and tangles of foliage were nightmarish, but Logan's concern blinded him from the scene. Moknay! his mind raced. Not Moknay! So many people so willing to sacrifice themselves for Logan—so many people getting hurt because of it! It was so hard for Logan here—so very, very hard! He did not belong here and could not shake the feeling of burdening everyone with his dilemma. Back in Santa Monica he knew where he was, what he had to do, and how he had to go about doing it. Here? Here he fairly needed directions how to relieve himself properly while traveling!

Preoccupied by his thoughts, Logan hardly noticed the forest thin out to his left, where a dirt road wound its way through the brush. Structures and buildings loomed up into the night sky, outlined by the moon's greenish-yellow glare. If the ponderous steps of the ogre had not stopped behind him, Logan might have foolishly bolted directly into the town of Debarnian without even realizing it.

The young man halted and cast a swift glance over his shoulder at the ogre. "This is it," he mumbled just to quell his own fears.

His light blue companion silently stared at the odd area. The ogre obviously preferred the forest to civilized regions, and this strange portion of distorted lumber and stones perturbed the large creature. Something was wrong with this piece of forest, the ogre's simple mind understood, and it knew the beasts that inhabited this section were most unfriendly . . . at least, to him anyway.

Eyes wide, the ogre watched Logan begin a slow, meticulous crawl toward the town. A wave of his arm told the ogre Logan wanted him to follow, so the light blue creature complied. Imitating its companion, the ogre bent forward and crept through the remaining foliage. A crooked grin spread across its squarish features as it took a liking to this new game Logan had concocted.

Thinking this was hardly a game, Logan took another step forward. A branch that snapped beneath his foot rang like an explosion in the young man's ears and he immediately ceased all movement. Streams of moonlight splashed the forest floor and gleamed off the cobblestone streets of Debarnian. Sweat dribbled its way down Logan's forehead as a silhouetted troop of men marched past his sight and vanished around the corner of a night-shrouded building.

Now or never, the young man concluded, throwing himself forward with a sudden burst of speed.

Darkness and moonlight mixed to make a blur of black and green as Logan bolted into Debarnian. From the deep chuckling behind him, he knew the ogre trailed, and together the two broke free of the forest and edged up alongside a dark building. The cobblestones felt odd beneath Logan's Nikes, as he had grown so used to the rough forest soil, and Logan blanched as he tried to peer around the corner. With a defeated groan, the young man sank to the street, clamping his hands to his face.

Grinning, the ogre did likewise.

"Oh, shit," Logan cursed, giving the ogre an imploring look. "Why didn't I let Thromar come? I can't find my way around this town during the day, let alone at night!" The young man knocked the palm of his hand against his skull. "Stupid! Stupid! Stupid!" he moaned.

The ogre cheerfully copied the motion.

"Oh, cut it out!" snapped Logan.

Blue eyes narrowed at his own stupidity, Logan turned away from the town and stared at the moon. It had risen even higher now, he noted, and its simple crescent was grinning down at him—mocking him with its toothless smile. *I've messed up again, and even the moon knows it this time!* whimpered Logan's mind. *Why did I even try at all? All I ever do is make things worse. Helpless.*

A slight vibration from the leather sack in his hands pulled Logan from this worthlessness. A smoking anger began to spark within his breast as he stared at the Jewel in his grasp and then turned to confront those thoughts. *Mess up, do I?* he snarled to himself. *Only make things worse? I kept the damn Jewel, didn't I? I finally got the powers under control! Why, I even kicked Vaugen's ass back to his fortress! Helpless, my backside!* Agellic's Church was a real tall, fancy-looking structure, he remembered. It shouldn't be too difficult to find—even in the dark. The only thing he really had to watch out for were the Guardsmen.

As quietly as he could manage, Logan got to his feet and crept around the side of his hiding place. The street was deserted and dark, a lone lamp flickering a few yards to his left. Unlike Eadarus, Debarnian was not an extremely active village at night, although he could hear voices and laughter coming from a nearby tavern.

The tavern! Logan mused. Thromar had entered a tavern as soon as they had entered Debarnian. Could Logan's luck have changed so that this was the very pub the fighter had ducked into? If so, Agellic's Church was only two streets down, he recalled.

The shadows gave Logan ample cover as he and the ogre forked across the street and snaked into a blackened alcove. Cautiously, Logan poked his head out to gaze about the roadway and satisfied himself that the street was clear. He sprang out of the alcove and zigzagged around a tethering post, slipped between two houses, and vanished behind a silversmith's shop.

Its grin even wider now, the ogre followed.

Logan gave the grinning creature a glance and grinned himself. It was somewhat exciting, he realized. Matthew Logan and the Temple of Debarnian! *Dum da dum dum, dum da dum!*

An unexpected glint of moonlight flashed upon one of Logan's contacts and the young man turned. He extended his neck slightly and caught sight of a titanic, castlelike rooftop towering above the other buildings. Triangular windows captured the glimmering moonbeams and sent them spewing across the town.

"The Church!" the young man gaped, awed by the apparent ease of his search.

Eyes locked onto the castlelike battlements, Logan stepped out into the cobblestone street and headed down the block. The sudden clatter of hooves upon stone pulled Logan's eyes away from the Church and back to earth. With a frenzied leap, Logan flew behind a merchant's tent, the ogre once again duplicating his actions. Logan's heart beat wildly as he spied a troop of mounted Guards canter around the corner, their leader brandishing a torch that flared like a miniature sun.

"The two of you," Logan could barely make out, "station yourselves further up this street . . . alert the other troop should anyone else try to enter the town tonight. The rest of you, go to the southern end. I will remain here should anyone else happen to sneak by you. The King wants no one entering or leaving any town without first being verified . . . tonight you almost bungled it!"

Hooves struck the cobblestones as the Guardsmen carried out their leader's orders, but Logan was not watching them. His eyes had dropped to the ground as words played over and over again in his mind. "Tonight you almost bungled it!" That meant someone had tried to sneak into this town and had failed.

Moknay?

So wrapped up in his fears, Logan failed to see that the tent they hid behind specialized in groceries.

The blue ogre's nostrils flared. "Foooooooooood!" it roared, plunging a monstrous hand through the tent's fabric to grab a piece of fruit.

His thoughts burst like a soap bubble as Logan stared first at the ogre, then at the torch that rode straight for their place of concealment.

"Smooth move, ace," Logan grumbled, scrabbling out from behind the tent.

The sound of steel chafing against leather was all too familiar to Logan's ears by now. Even through the darkness of the night, he knew the Guard had his sword free.

"You, there!" came the cry. "You are to remain where you are by order of His Majesty's Guardsmen!"

Uncertain which way to turn—blocked from the Church by the soldier—Logan skidded to a confused halt in the middle of the street. The Guardsman's horse slowed, its rider confident he had stopped the lone figure. To Logan's bewildered eyes, a torch and a sword tip were suddenly very near to him.

"Why were you skulking in the shadows?" the Guardsman queried as he neared. "We frown upon common thieves here. Perhaps you . . ."

There was a sudden blur of fire, steel, and light blue flesh as the ogre completed its simple snack and resumed imitating Logan's moves. Its skid into the street was much more purposeful than Logan's, but the grinning ogre had to contend with a mounted Guardsman who had gotten in the way.

With a shriek, the Guard's horse was knocked off its feet, spilling to the cobblestones. The Guard felt his mount topple, realized the town was flipping over, and suddenly crashed to the street. The hilt of a sword cracked against the back of his skull before he even had time to clamber to his knees.

Logan resheathed his Reakthi sword and scampered down the dark road. There was no doubt in his mind that others must have heard the abrupt commotion and would soon be on hand to investigate. It was now a race against time to see if Logan could reach the Church before someone else caught up with him.

Running in what he hoped was the direction of the Church, Logan clutched the Jewel tightly to his chest. It was unfortunate he had decided to leave the horses behind, he cursed. If he had known so many of the Guards would be on horseback . . .

A small band of about three men rounded a corner and Logan made a wild dive to his right. The trio released startled shouts but did not pursue. They were only townsfolk and had no concern for the young man's business, but Logan did not know that. Through the darkness and winding streets of Debarnian, anyone who stood in his way should be considered an enemy, the young man resolved. It was the only way he could reach Barthol.

Another flash of moonlight struck Logan as he wheeled about a corner and found himself staring directly at Agellic's Church. Even hidden in the night, Logan could see the massive pillars and elaborate architecture that built up the place of worship.

Giving the cobblestone street an inquisitive glance, Logan flung open the immense ivory door and disappeared inside. As soon as the ogre trailed, Logan slammed the portal shut and attempted to catch his breath. Unbelievable as it seemed, the young man had actually escaped the Guardsmen and was safely inside the Church. All that was left was to find out if Moknay had had similar fortune.

A powerfully large hand clamped itself upon Logan's shoulder. Questioningly, the young man turned to eye the ogre and suddenly discovered his light blue companion was off to one side, curiously inspecting a crystal goblet on a nearby table. At once the young man's relief fled and he whipped about. An enormous human being—almost as monstrous as the ogre—towered behind him, its thick hand resting close to Logan's neck. Huge, bushy eyebrows were the only hair on the tremendous head, and they villainously knitted together in anger.

"Oh . . . um . . . uh . . . hi," Logan sputtered. "I . . . I'm a friend of Barthol's . . ."

The bald giant lifted its free hand and made a fist that was larger than Logan's skull. "Goar kill!" it boomed, and the titanic fist descended.

·2·

Church

Stones exploded and skittered across the tile floor as Matthew Logan swung about and dodged the gargantuan fist. Releasing an enraged bellow, the hairless giant lifted its mammoth hands and flailed them through the air.

"Goar smash!" the creature yelled, bringing its fists down.

"No, you don't understand . . ." Logan started.

The young man was cut short as the ground beneath his tennis shoes bucked violently and he was heaved into the air. The foyer of Agellic's Church reeled as Logan scrambled back to his feet and uncertainly withdrew his Reakthi sword.

"Goar pulverize!" Goar thundered, charging.

Logan threw the light blue ogre a glance. The creature was still inspecting the crystal dinnerware on a nearby table, completely oblivious of Logan's predicament and the infuriated Goar. Finding it quite difficult to believe anyone could be oblivious of Goar's resounding threats, Logan darted sideways, grasping his sword in one hand, the Jewel in the other.

"Goar decimate!"

Fortunately, Logan noted, this Goar was not too swift. The young man had managed to move twice and Goar was just now striking where he had been two moves ago. Still, the rubble and debris that shot from the walls pelted Logan with such a ferocity he may well have been standing beside them. Unexpectedly, the bald Goar wheeled around, his tiny eyes flaring.

"Goar dismember!" it roared.

Move! Logan's brain screamed, and Logan's muscles reacted. Insanely, Logan propelled himself forward, narrowly escaping the piledriver fists that crashed through the tile behind him. Steel clattered as his sword dropped out of his hands, and, for a second, Logan's life began to play behind his eyelids. Before he saw too much of his past, Logan's thoughts backflipped as he ducked another swing from those prodigious hands.

What did I do? he wondered. Get the wrong Church? No . . . the black-and-white pattern on the floor marked this church as the one Moknay had taken him to before. So had someone taken it over? Had this Goar charged in and killed everyone?

There was an odd moment of what felt like no activity within Logan's mind. Gradually, almost reluctantly, a memory forced its way through Logan's consciousness. A memory that Logan cherished, and yet, feared. A memory of a beautiful, dark-haired priestess with the greenest eyes in all of Logan's two worlds. An attractive young girl who had confessed her interest concerning Logan, but one who had been injured because of him. Wounded by another girl of her order when she tried to protect Logan.

Mara.

Logan's blue eyes flared as he fixed them upon Goar.

Had this brute killed Mara?

"Goar annihilate!" the bald giant thundered.

A maddening fury overtook Logan as the immense Goar lumbered closer. Adrenaline surging, the young man launched forward, slamming his skull into Goar's solar plexus. As the bald head pitched forward, Logan followed through with a wicked kick. His right fist completed the barrage, lashing out and knocking the titanic creature to the floor.

The anger had not yet started to fade as Logan made a menacing step toward the downed Goar. Once before this creature had feigned sluggishness and had almost smashed Logan; the young man would take no chances now.

Goar looked up slowly, his colossal hands clamped about his face. A huge tear welled up in one eye. "Why you hurt Goar?" it pitifully queried. "Goar no mean it."

His fury deserted him and Logan was helpless before the overwhelming guilt that bombarded him. The large beast had not purposely meant to kill Logan, only to scare him. Blast it! The light blue ogre had probably sensed that and that's why it had made no move to help. Logan, it knew, would not need help since there was no danger.

While Logan was kicking himself, a small portion of self-righteousness rose up to defend him from his guilt. "If you didn't mean it, why the hell were you smashing everything?" he demanded. "And where is everybody?"

"Watching the show, friend," came the amused reply.

Logan spun about as the darkness near Barthol's workroom door sparked to life and Moknay sauntered out. "Most impressive," the Murderer mused. "You've got some moves I'd be hard pressed to make."

As the darkly clad Murderer neared, Logan could only gape, dumbfounded. Wearing a similar expression, Barthol stumbled out of his doorway, his hands holding the sides of his head.

"Look at this mess!" the priest moaned. "You and your idea of fun, Moknay! Goar's made an absolute shambles of my Church!"

A huge tear dribbled down Goar's cheek. "Goar sorry."

Logan snatched up his fallen sword and turned on Moknay. "This was your idea?" he barked. "Letting this overgrown son of King Kong try to beat me to a pulp?"

Moknay grinned and slapped a gloved hand across Goar's back. "Goar doesn't mean anything," he explained. "Just think how boring it must be working for Barthol."

Logan flung up his hands and entertained the nasty thought of throwing the Jewel at the Murderer. *Scares the shit out of me and tells me afterward Goar was just playing!* the young man fumed. Still muttering, Logan turned as the stumpy Barthol came to his side.

"Moknay's told me something of what you plan," the priest said, "but not all of it."

Motioning for the two to follow, Barthol headed back toward his workroom, his head still shaking at the state of his foyer. Moknay scampered behind the priest, mischief leaking from his pores. Somewhat numbed from his strenuous night, Logan trailed them in silence. *A nervous wait at camp, a frenzied charge through the town, and now a game of dodgeball with a bald giant!*

A frown crossed the young man's lips as he followed the Murderer and priest into the other room. "Just where the hell were you, Moknay?" he questioned. "You were just supposed to scout ahead."

Moknay leaned up against a wall. "Ah, yes, that," he replied. "I'm sorry about that. It seems I wasn't expecting quite as many Guards as there are and I got a little cocky. Fortunately, someone else was trying to sneak into town at about the same time. Drew all the attention to himself and left me free to reach Barthol. Unfortunately, they doubled the amount of Guards and I decided I shouldn't risk trying to leave. I was going to try just before morning, though."

"Doubled the amount of Guards?" sputtered Logan, collapsing into a chair. "And I . . . ?"

The Murderer grinned. "Like I said—some moves that I'd be hard pressed to make." Moknay's grey eyes flashed toward Barthol. "Now, to the matter at hand. As I was saying, Logan wants to try again, this time searching for the Heart of the Land."

Barthol nodded uneasily, running a hand through his hair.

Moknay continued: "Since the Heart has always been confused by myths, we'll have some trouble locating it . . . even with Logan's talent. In the meantime, we'd like you to look after the Jewel."

"Me?" Barthol exclaimed. "I'm no spellcaster!"

"Neither are we, Barthol," the Murderer responded, "but we've done quite well once we found out how to keep its powers in check. We'll even leave Logan's ogre-friend to help guard it."

The plump priest waved his hands frantically through the air. "But I don't . . . I mean, I can't keep . . . What will my . . . By Harmeer's War Axe, Moknay! You're asking me to look after an object more powerful than anything else in the multiverse!"

"There'll be no danger if you use the powder Zackaron created for Pembroke," Moknay explained. "It's magical stuff so it never runs out. All you'd have to do is sprinkle some on the Jewel every ten days or so. *We* certainly can't carry it around! Mediyan and the Reakthi still want Logan."

"But what if they find out it's here?" Barthol asked, worried.

"You've got . . ." Moknay began.

"And what if they come to get it?" the priest added.

"There's still . . ." the Murderer tried again.

"And what if they should threaten me with bodily harm?"

"They shouldn't . . ."

Barthol rapidly shook his head. "No, no, no," he argued. "I couldn't undertake such a task. I'm an insignificant little priest who just . . ."

"Consider it a way of paying us back for not helping us the first time we came to you," interrupted Moknay. "Logan needs your help, Barthol." The grey eyes flashed. "*I* need your help."

Barthol's eyes jumped from Moknay to Logan to the bagged Jewel. So long was the priest's silence that night sounds began to creep into the workroom, and Logan thought he heard hurried footsteps of Guardsmen rush unsettlingly close to the Church. Finally, Barthol fixed his gaze on his two guests.

"I guess it's the least I can do for you," he said, "since I didn't help you get to the Smythe the first time."

Moknay clamped a hand upon the chubby man's shoulder and smiled. "I knew we could count on you, Barthol," he said. "Now, there's a few more things we'll need to ask you to . . ."

The stumpy man sprang out of his chair. "No, you can't have any money! The collection box is still empty!"

Moknay frowned. "That's not what I was going . . ."

"Already agree to take care of the damn Jewel and now they want more from me!" Barthol complained.

"But we don't need any . . ." Moknay attempted.

"It's not bad enough you take advantage of my kind heart and generosity by forcing this Jewel upon me, but now you want my few paltry gold pieces as well!"

"Barthol," Moknay snarled, losing his composure, "I wasn't going to . . ."

"Money! Money! Money!" the priest went on. "Always demanding my money!"

Moknay's grey eyes flamed as a rigid finger extended under Barthol's nose. "Stop aggravating me, Barthol," he growled. "You know you're very good at it."

"Yes," Barthol replied, "you say that every time you visit me and ask for money."

Déjà vu! Logan noticed, holding back a snicker. Barthol and Moknay practically had routines when they bargained! It's too bad I missed the Murderer's entry into Barthol's Church. I wonder what trick he had pulled on him this time around.

When Logan turned back to the bickering two, Moknay had Barthol by the collar of his tunic. "If you do not stop your whining, Barthol, I shall personally give you something to whine about," he threatened. "There should not be any danger from Reakthi or Mediyan since no one knows we are here. Besides, we've already told you we'd leave the ogre here with you—if you feel your own hired help isn't enough. Other than that, the only other thing we need from you is some information concerning the Bloodstone."

"Information?" Barthol brightened. "Why didn't you say so? I am a veritable fountain of knowledge, brimming over with tales and facts concerning all!"

"Wonderful," sneered Moknay. "Enlighten us, O spewing one."

Ignoring the Murderer's sarcasm, Barthol rummaged through the number of leatherbound volumes littering the many tabletops of his workroom. He finally came across a larger book than the rest and flipped through its pages, leaning closer to see the words.

"Well," he started, "as you well know, the Bloodstone—more popularly known as the Heart of Sparrill—was always said to control and fluctuate the magic of our land. It is believed that from the Heart, beauty and magic flowed. Even today it is a well-known fact that no other land is as magically endowed or as lush as Sparrill. Magdelon itself, only some eighty leagues from Sparrill, is mostly harsh desert.

"Although this fact seems to indicate such an object as the Bloodstone exists, there is still some doubt as to its actuality. I mean, no one can deny that, out of all our neighboring lands, Sparrill is unparalleled, but is this because of some magical gemstone? Well, regardless whether this Bloodstone exists or not, it would still be considered the most powerful item in the entire world."

Logan, listening intently, raised his eyebrows in curiosity. He gave the bagged Jewel in his lap an inquisitive glance. "Since when did the Bloodstone become the most powerful jewel in the world?" he asked. "I thought the Jewel was."

Barthol smiled at the young man's query. "Well, yes and no. By all means, the Jewel of Equilibrant is the most powerful item in the world—in the entire multiverse—but too powerful for the likes of us. Look at Zackaron. He only released a small portion of the Jewel's energies and it drove him mad. What little power he took from the Jewel gave him control over Nature herself. Can you imagine what would happen if someone tapped into even more power? Perhaps godhood; who can say? But at what risk? What with the Bloodstone—if it exists—its magicks would be controllable by the human will. And, since it directly links with Sparrill's magic, would give its owner immediate command over the entire land, extending the user's powers as far as the Bloodstone's powers extended. Not only would all the magic and nature of Sparrill be at your fingertips, but that of surrounding lands as well. And it would not have the damaging effects of the Jewel. So, on to the myth.

"According to the many tales of Sparrill's birth, all have agreed upon the fact that three sprites guarded our land: Roana, Salena, and Glorana. They regulated the Bloodstone's irregular flow and made sure the land remained pure and beautiful and that all of Sparrill's inhabitants lived full and happy lives. It was then that the Voices of the Dark surfaced.

"Perhaps I should explain to Matthew that it is believed two Forces exist outside the forces of the Wheel: Light and Dark. Of course, the power and vastness these two Forces have over our world is plain enough, since they meet directly in our plane of the multiverse as shadows. Now, according to these tales, the Voices of the Dark were always 'longing for the final destruction of Light and the consumption of all that is Pure and Untainted.' When they sensed the beauty and magic of Sparrill, they sent one of their foulest servants, a *Deil* called Gangrorz. Gangrorz's task was to destroy the Heart of Sparrill, thereby ending the glorious life of our land. 'And so was the *Deil* sent by his Masters to pierce the Heart of the Land and to Taint that which was Untainted.'

"What follows has been called the Time of the Worm, for, although Gangrorz failed to even find the Heart, he did succeed in injuring the land itself and corrupting some of the beasts and magic of Sparrill—such as the creation of the Demons." Barthol pulled the book he had been skimming through up to his nose. "'And did come the Time of the Worm, He who was called the Wreaker of Havoc. And did the Foul *Deil*, the Shatterer, He whose Masters were the very Voices of the Dark, set upon our Land with Tooth and Nail. And there did come a Time when the Lifefluid of Sparrill ran low, and Abomination did spread like Fire upon the Winds. Remember, Gangrorz the Worm did lurk in each Night's Darkness. Remember, the Wreaker of Havoc did wound greatly the Beauty and Power of Sparrill. Remember, the Shatterer did await the Time when all things would Decay, and the perfume of Death would fill his nostrils.'

"So, you see," Barthol explained, "although Gangrorz never directly found or wounded the Heart, he indirectly damaged it by damaging the land. And when he awaited 'the Time when all things would Decay,' he knew sooner or later the Heart would succumb to his merciless pounding of Sparrill and die. However, after seeing Sparrill's plight, the oldest of the sprites, Roana, became determined to do something. They were, after all, the guardians of Sparrill and of the Heart. So, without telling her sisters, Roana removed the Bloodstone from where it was kept and set out to find the *Deil*. 'Eldest of the three, did Roana seek out He who was called the Wreaker of Havoc. And did the pulsing of the Heart grow ever stronger as she called upon its Magicks to aid her in casting out He who was the Shatterer.' "

Interesting, Logan mused. This book makes it sound like Gangrorz was some kind of infection that needed to be removed.

"Anyway," Barthol continued, "a battle followed in which *Deil*, sprite, and Bloodstone were all lost. 'So did Roana, She who was the eldest of the three, invoke the Powers of the Heart. Such was the blow that Gangrorz, Foul *Deil* of the Voices, was torn high into the Air. And did He who was the Shatterer fall, ablaze with the cosmic fire of the Air, and strike the Land with a thousand thunderclaps. And did the Land give way, suffering a grievous sore from the Worm, and did Foul and Putrid waters fill this sore. And, alas, was Roana likewise lost, thrown into the very Beauty she swore to protect.' " Barthol looked up from his book, gently closing the leather volume. "I'm afraid that's all it says. It doesn't say anything more about the Heart."

The priest noticed the depressed expression that crossed Logan's face. Hastily he added, "But this whole ordeal may just be myth. No one's ever seen the sprites, a *Deil*, or the Bloodstone."

Moknay pushed himself away from the wall and strode behind Logan. "And what would you say if I told you Logan's seen the sprites?" the Murderer inquired.

"I'd say you were being sarcastic again," retorted Barthol.

Moknay only smirked in reply as he looked down at Logan, his grey eyes sparkling. Understanding Moknay's unspoken suggestion, Logan declared: "Roana had violet hair, Salena had green hair, and Glorana had blue hair."

Barthol's mouth dropped open as he peered at the young man seated across from him.

"Roana, of course, guards her river," Logan went on. "Salena guards the Ohmmarrious, and Glorana guards the Lephar."

Barthol's mouth remained wide as rapid blinking began to accompany the gape. "How do you know . . . ?" he gasped.

"They acted more like mischievous girls than magical guardians, though," Logan finished.

Silence filtered into the workroom once more as Logan stopped talking and faced Barthol. Stunned, the priest could only continue blinking at the young man, his open mouth trying frantically to form words yet failing.

"So now what do you say to the existence of the Bloodstone?" smirked Moknay.

"Well, it must have existed!" Barthol exclaimed. "Nonetheless, there's no telling what happened to it after Gangrorz's defeat. What makes you think that it can get you back to your world?"

Logan scratched at the stubble on his chin. "The Smythe told me that Sparrill itself had something to do with my being brought here, so, since the Heart is directly linked to Sparrill's magic, we figured it could get me back."

Barthol vigorously began nodding his head. "Hmmmm, yes. It might just work. Still, the Bloodstone could be anywhere."

"Isn't there some way we could pinpoint it?" Moknay queried.

"Afraid not," Barthol replied. "No one knows what kind of energies the Heart radiates, so it's beyond us to trace it. However, there is someone who should know of its position."

"Who?" both Moknay and Logan asked.

"Why, the sprites, of course!" the priest told them. "All you need to do is contact the sprites again and ask!"

It was Logan's turn to blink in stupefaction. "It's as simple as that?"

"It should be," Barthol shrugged. "After all, they are still Sparrill's guardians."

Moknay's gloved hand fell upon Logan's shoulder. "Well, there you have it, friend," he proclaimed. "You're as good as home. Now let's say we get some sleep? We'll have to make some intricate moves tomorrow to get us out of here." The Murderer faced Barthol. "You're sure you can handle the Jewel?"

Barthol gave the leather pouch an uneasy glance but nodded. "I suppose so," he muttered. "Goar will keep me and it safe. Besides, who's going to miss a fat little priest if he accidentally blows himself up?"

There was a brief flash of seriousness in Moknay's steely eyes. "I might," he admitted. The emotion faded. "But only if I'm standing too close to you at the time."

A smile came to Barthol's cherubic face as he led his guests out of his workroom and directed them to an empty chamber. Sleep began to overtake Logan as he settled himself down in the feather bed and heaved a thankful sigh at the simplicity of his forthcoming journey. No unstable Jewels and greedy spellcasters to worry about this time!

When Logan's mind finally recalled the odd wind that had brought him to Debarnian in search of Moknay, sleep embraced him tightly and refused to let go.

It could wait until morning.

Chunk! Chunk!

Logan's eyes slowly pried themselves open, allowing in a small stream of sunlight. With a disturbed groan, the young man pulled himself into a seated position and wearily blinked the sleep from his contact lenses.

Chunk! Chunk!

Logan's eyes popped open. What the devil was that? he wondered. Sounded like someone chopping wood, but who would be out so early in the morning chopping wood in a churchyard?

His interest aroused, Logan heaved himself out of bed and washed. He surprised himself by surviving his dagger-shave without a cut and started toward the grounds behind the Church. Half way down a hall, Logan noticed the emptiness of the building and guessed everyone was outside—making those strange noises.

Clang!

Logan flinched. His right hand swiftly sprang to his sword hilt and jerked the weapon free. There could be no mistaking the sound he had heard as steel on steel! He had been in Sparril long enough to know that! Abruptly, there was another clang, Barthol's muffled voice, and Moknay's laughter. Then there was silence.

Dead silence.

Logan's stroll down the hall transformed into a run as he hurried around a corner and shoved open the double doors leading to the Church's yard. Dazzling sunlight beamed down upon him and a carpet of grass flourished beneath his feet. Squinting into the rising orb of flame, the young man saw Barthol sitting on an iron-wrought bench. Nearby there was a sturdy wooden pole pierced by slender shoots of wood and iron. Even through the sun's blinding glare, Logan could make out Moknay's dark form beside the post but had trouble seeing the third figure standing outside.

"He awakes!" Moknay jested. "We were afraid you were going to sleep the whole day through!"

Confused, Logan replaced his sword and blinked. "I heard some noises," he said hesitantly. "Just wondering what was going on."

Moknay motioned toward the figure beside him. "We're going to have some help finding the Bloodstone for you," he announced.

Logan stared as Mara stepped out of the sun's light and smiled at him. The young man instantly felt his legs melt, and a warmth raced throughout his body at the sight of the priestess. She is so beautiful! his mind told him. The sun gleaming off her dark hair . . . and her eyes! Those gorgeous green eyes!

"Welcome back, Matthew Logan," Mara greeted him.

Logan could not keep his eyes from roving across the slender form before him. The slim priestess was clad in a black tunic and red pants. Black boots similar to Moknay's hugged her calves, and a black belt and sword sheath dangled from her waist. It was certainly a different outfit from her previous robe, but no article of clothing could ever make Mara look bad, Logan concluded.

"She's been practicing ever since you left the first time," Barthol was saying at Logan's elbow. "Gave up Lelah's teachings that very afternoon!"

Logan turned a quizzical eye on the priest. The three around him, he saw, knew full well what they were talking about . . . and acted as if Logan should too.

Abruptly, Moknay's words repeated themselves in his mind: "*We're going to have some help* . . . "

Logan blanched. "No! Oh, no!" he cried. "She can't come!"

The trio gave each other puzzling looks.

"Why not?" Moknay asked, raising an eyebrow.

Because I think I might fall in love with her! Logan's mind screamed. There's something so very special about her I couldn't bear to see her get hurt because of my stupid journey! I already hurt her once before—I couldn't do it again!

Logan gazed at the three, wondering how he could put these personal fears into words. How could he tell them how he felt? He didn't go around professing his emotions to everyone . . . not even his close friends needed to be burdened in his opinion. How the devil could he tell them he feared for Mara's safety more than his own?

"It . . . It might be dangerous," he finally stated.

"I've prepared myself for that," Mara answered, tapping the sword at her hip.

"But . . . people have gotten killed!" Logan protested.

"They do every day," Moknay grimly reminded him. "Look, friend, I wouldn't have agreed to Mara's coming unless I knew she could take care of herself." The Murderer turned on the dark-haired priestess. "Mara, calm Logan's fears, will you?"

Mara smiled pleasantly at both the Murderer and Logan as she picked up an odd-looking device from the grass. It appeared to be a compact crossbow, Logan noted, with a strange box on top of the stock. Swiftly, Mara's slim hand threw a lever forward and drew the same handle back. Two iron-tipped quarrels shrieked from the front of the weapon and lodged in the wooden pole with twin *chunks*!

"A Chu-Ko-Nu," Logan breathed, thoroughly amazed.

"Excuse me?" Barthol questioned. "That's a Binalbow."

Whatever they call it, it's a repeating crossbow! Logan's
mind reeled. The Chinese used them as late as the Chinese-
Japanese war in 1894 . . . or was it 1892? Anyway, that one lever
worked the whole bow. Throwing it forward and back drew the
bow, slipped the quarrel into place, and discharged the bolt. And
Mara had mastered it!

"It appears our friend is reasonably impressed," said Moknay
with a grin. "And that's not all she can do. She just knocked
the very sword from my hand with a nice little dagger-sword
combination. I believe she'll make a nice little addition to our
band since we're losing your ogre."

"You're not losing your ogre," Barthol piped up. "I've got
enough problems with Goar. Two of those brutes would be worse
than the Reakthi that attacked last time you visited! I found Goar
after that just in case that spellcaster got any ideas about attacking
me again. One monster's enough to protect the Jewel."

"Well, then," Moknay replied, nodding in satisfaction, "it looks
like there'll be four of us helping you find the Heart, Logan. Now,
Barthol, about those provisions you were going to give us . . . ?"

The chubby priest was taken aback as Moknay draped an arm
about his shoulder. "Provisions? What provisions? I never said
anything about . . ."

The man's voice trailed away as he and the Murderer disappeared back inside Agellic's Church. Of their own will, Logan's
eyes turned back to Mara, drinking in every detail about the
priestess-turned-fighter. Why? his mind cried. Why does Mara
want to expose herself to these dangers?

The dark-haired priestess could not read the chaotic thoughts
churning through Logan's mind but sensed something was wrong.
"Is something the matter?" she asked gently.

Embarrassed, Logan shook his head.

Mara smiled faintly at the young man and seated herself on
the iron bench. She motioned for Logan to do likewise, and,
awkwardly, he did so. "You don't have to worry about me," she
informed him. "I've been practicing every day since you first left
the Church. Somehow I knew you'd come back."

I care about this girl, Logan admitted to himself. For some
unknown reason, I know there's something unique about her—
to me, anyway. Why can't she understand I don't want to see
her hurt?

"I've gotten quite good with my sword although I haven't fully
perfected the Binalbow," Mara commented.

A laugh escaped Logan's lips. "That's the best shooting I've ever seen anyone do with a Chu-Ko . . . uh, a Binalbow," he said. Nervously, like a kid out on his first date, Logan peered up at the sky. "Uh . . . Mara, you know that looking for the Heart may not be that easy?"

"Of course," the priestess replied.

The young man could not bring himself to look at her as he went on. "And that there's no guarantee that we'll find it."

"Yes."

It was becoming increasingly difficult for Logan to find the proper words. "So if you don't want to come, feel free to say so . . ."

"Matthew," Mara said softly, "I want to come."

Protests formed and died all in the same breath as Logan gazed into those emerald eyes. He could not deny the priestess her rights. She wanted to come; Logan could not demand she stay behind because of his own selfishness. If it were Mara's problem, he would certainly want to do everything in his power to help her. No, he would not be hypocritical with the young woman.

"If you're sure . . . ?" He finally gave in, eyebrows raised.

"Positive," Mara answered with a smile. "Perhaps now you'll have time to tell me about your world?"

Helpless to prevent it, Logan felt a smile forming on his face. "Maybe."

·3·

Funerary

Logan glanced up from under the hood of his heavy, priestly robes and gave the real priest beside him an annoyed glare. Without speaking, Barthol waved at the young man to lower his head and be silent as he directed the horse-drawn cart through the cobblestone streets of Debarnian. Mara rode behind them, also disguised in a heavy robe that concealed her new adventurous garb and weaponry. In the back of the cart itself, hidden by a tarpaulin, were Moknay and the light blue ogre.

Sweat formed under his hood and robe, and Logan tried to ignore the heat by inspecting his surroundings. They weren't doing a very good job of being inconspicuous, he realized. Everyone along the road seemed to stop and stare at the cart, including the mounted Guardsmen dotting the village. All Logan would need was one accidental ruffle of his robe and his sweat suit would be seen by an entire town.

The cart proceeded on down the cobblestone path, torturously bouncing off the rounded rocks. Hot, sore, and apprehensive, Logan could feel an inexplicable anger coming on—the kind of irritability he experienced when a phone call would get him up too early in the morning back in Santa Monica. He had no true reason to become mad, yet his discomfort needed a means of escape, and anger was as good as any.

Not that their means of escape from Debarnian was any bit more sensible.

Peering up from under his heavy hood, Logan's stomach twisted as he spied the line of Guardsmen blocking the path out of town. The lead Guardsman had his hand up, implying Barthol should rein in his mounts. Anxiety gnawing at his innards, Logan ducked his head down so that fabric and shadows obscured his face.

"And what may I do for you?" Barthol pleasantly asked the Guard.

The Guardsman peered down his nose at the priest, arrogant as one of his rank tended to be. "What is your purpose for leaving town, priest?" he snorted.

"The demise of poor Cavill," Barthol responded, motioning toward the still forms in the back of the cart.

Logan saw the dread scrawl across the features of the other Guardsmen. It was almost as if the people of Sparrill accepted death in battle but feared the natural passing away of someone. Perhaps in one of their myths they feared that whatever took away one's life might not have any qualms about taking theirs away as well.

The lead Guardsman, however, refused to be balked. "Why does there appear to be more than one body?" he interrogated.

Barthol gave the back of his cart a swift glance and leaned closer to the mounted Guard. "Cavill's wife," he whispered as if telling some horrible secret. "They both died from the . . ." He gave Logan a sideways glance. " . . . fandango."

The dread turned to absolute terror as the troop of Guardsmen pulled their horses away from the old-fashioned hearse. A smirk drew across Logan's face under his screen of shadow and cloth. Maybe this wild plan might just work after all, he mused.

A flurry of apprehension sparked to life within the leader's eyes, but his conceit forbade him to back away. "And where are you taking these corpses?" he demanded.

"Far into the forest," Barthol replied, "to bury them. We must make sure this horrid affliction does not descend upon anyone else."

The anxiety diminished in the eyes of the lead Guardsman as he finally pulled his mount away from the horse-drawn cart. "Carry on," he ordered, sweeping his hand imperiously past them.

As compliant as ever, Barthol nodded his thanks and clicked his horses forward. The awed and horrified stares of the Guardsmen trailed after the small procession, their leader's gaze mixed with misgiving and suspicion. Logan was just about to wipe the perspiration beading under his hood when there was a muffled thump from the back of the cart. The young man swung around just in time to see the ogre's massive leg jerk underneath the heavy tarpaulin and hear Moknay's muttered curse.

Ice water cascaded down Logan's back as a shout split the air.

"Halt!"

Pale-faced, Barthol turned a fearful look on Logan and whipped about to meet the Guards galloping out of Debarnian after them. The sweat returned to Logan's brow in a sheet as hooves slowed and stopped.

The lead Guardsman gave the pair of priests a sardonic sneer. "It seems there is some movement in the back of your cart," he snarled, his confidence and arrogance restored in force. Threateningly, he half freed his sword. "I think, perhaps, that your cargo is not quite dead yet." The blade slid completely free of its scabbard.

"Common action," Logan piped up, his voice cracking in terror.

The leader eyed the hooded figure expectantly. "What?" he growled.

"Common reflex action," Logan continued, trying to keep his head down and not be too obvious about it. "It is a well-known fact that corpses have been known to twitch or even sit up after death. Gases and bodily fluids settling, don't you know?"

A skeptical mien clouded the leader's face as he scrutinized the shrouded form. Eyebrows narrowed dubiously, the Guard pivoted on Barthol. "Who's he?" he questioned haughtily.

"Necromage," the chubby priest hurriedly replied.

This time the trepidation was clear in the leader's pupils. Appalled, he began to jerk his horse back, eyes still trained on the cloaked form hunched at the front of the cart. Unexpectedly, one of his men released a terrified scream as the tarpaulin sprang to life and leapt out of the cart. The heavy cloth engulfed the lead Guardsman, entwining about him and pulling him to the ground. Before the small squad of soldiers could see the grey-and-black blur, silver flashed in the afternoon sun and two more men went down.

"Now we've done it," Barthol cursed under his breath as he urged his horses into the forest.

Startled by Moknay's sudden movement and the abrupt lurch of the cart, Logan tried to get a clear picture of the battle. His vision blurred as the rapid bouncing of the cart made his teeth clatter, but he could vaguely see the Guardsmen regroup, their weapons raised into the air. Two high-pitched whines severed the afternoon air, and blood splattered. Another Guard went down, two crossbow bolts slicing into his rib cage.

Through the rumbling of the cart, Logan glanced downward and saw the light blue ogre still lying in the back of the cart, motionless in mock-death. With an exasperated look skyward, Logan cuffed the ogre across the head and pointed a rigid finger back toward Debarnian.

"Fight, you idiot!" he yelled, springing from the moving cart.

The young man released a curse as he hit the uneven forest floor and promptly crashed to the ground. They make it look so damn easy in the movies! he muttered to himself, picking himself up and doffing his heavy robe.

Sword free, Logan charged back toward the brawl, a growing expectation ablaze within him. Battles like this were not uncommon in Sparrill, he thought, and yet, each one he was a part of increased the chance that that one possible blow might get through and kill him. So why was he now running back to join? Why hadn't he remained with Barthol?

The young man's eyes fell upon Moknay and Mara, and he knew why.

A war cry spilled from Logan's lips as he made a dashing leap for the closest Guardsman. His Reakthi blade plunged up through the mounted soldier at an angle, and the coppery odor of blood rose through the air like a fog. There were disgusting gushy noises as Logan jerked his weapon free, but he tried to ignore them and keep his thoughts locked on the danger surrounding him. They were but three against a small squad of soldiers.

"Fiiiiiiiight!" The forest reverberated as the ogre bellowed, and three horses rammed into one another.

Four, Logan corrected himself, watching the ogre hurl a Guard into the forest. That made things just about even.

There was something akin to thunder behind him, and Logan wheeled around. Silver flashed before his eyes and he instinctively lunged backwards, hearing the slash of the air before his face. His own weapon acted, leaping up and skewering the Guardsman's leg. The uniformed soldier screamed, but Logan felt no compassion for the man as his arm snapped about, cracking down against the Guardsman's neck. Groaning, the Guard toppled from his mount and landed with a dusty thump on the ground.

A stream of someone else's blood wound its way down Logan's arm as he turned to face his companions.

"Nicely done." Moknay was nodding, retrieving his daggers.

Logan wiped the crimson droplets from his sweat jacket with a shudder. "Why'd we do that?" he wanted to know. "They were going to let us by."

The grim expression so familiar to Moknay's face appeared.
"True," he admitted, "but too risky. You had them fooled with
that comment of yours, but I promised Barthol safety so long as
he had the Jewel. If rumors spread that Barthol had been seen
with a necromage, too much attention would have been drawn to
him . . . and his Church . . . and the Jewel."

Matthew Logan ran a hand through his black hair and cursed
his ignorance of Sparrill. "Why?" he asked. "What the hell is a
necromage?"

"Necromages are unique spellcasters trained only in the magical
workings of our bodies," Mara explained. "All they do is aid
healers and prepare bodies for burial, but some have been known
to go mad."

Magical morticians, Logan concluded. The way the body works
was deemed magical to the people of Sparrill . . . so necromages
honed their skills to operate these "body magicks." A memory sparked in Logan's mind: like Groathit's animated dead! he
recalled. In order to speak—and partially to think—Farkarrez's
corpse had been animated with the ability to breathe. Necromagic
was that grotesque combination of sorcery and physiology.

"I thought I was just getting them off our case," Logan mumbled.

Moknay shrugged. "Don't worry about it, friend," he advised.
"Only a few Guardsmen." The Murderer gave the forest a perturbed glance. "Now where has Barthol run off to?"

"That direction," Mara declared, pointing as she trailed the cart
tracks from atop her red-and-gold horse.

Moknay's eyes locked in on one of the furrowed marks in the
dirt and he began into the woods. As his companions entered the
forest, Logan could not fight off the feeling of disturbance that
rose within him concerning the squad of Guards. True, they would
not have hesitated to kill him, but still . . . Logan was so unused
to the way of life in Sparrill. Gradually, the young man was able
to pull his eyes away from the corpses staining the soil red and
trail his companions. Leaves and branches closed in around him
and obscured the already distant town of Debarnian.

When his companions halted, Logan gave the surrounding foliage a cursory look. Situated in the center of a small clearing was
Barthol's cart. The stumpy priest sat at the front of the vehicle,
his eyes transfixed on something before him. Obstructed by the
wooden cart, Moknay moved to attain a better view. His grey eyes
flickered.

"Odd," he said under his breath.

"Odd?" Barthol shot back. "I should say it's downright sickening!"

Mara sprang from her mount and approached the pair. Logan remained behind, his thoughts still jumbled by the fight that lingered in his mind.

Mara's eyes narrowed as she rounded the side of Barthol's cart. "What . . . Why?" she asked in bewilderment.

The priestess's confused query succeeded in pulling Logan from his reverie and piquing his interest. With the light blue ogre shadowing him like a puppy, Logan stepped up behind the three and peered over their shoulders.

Before his blue eyes found anything of interest, a horrid, fetid smell wafted into the young man's nostrils. So malodorous was the fetor it was warm, Logan noted. Warm? Yes, a foul, putrid horridness that caused the very air to warm around it. A smell vaguely recognizable to the young man as that of decomposition. It was then his blue eyes froze.

Off to one side of the shrubbery lay a twisted, fur-covered corpse. The large hindquarters of the small form told Logan it may have once been a rabbit, but the young man could not be sure—since it had no head. Jagged tears in the decaying flesh indicated that the head had been bitten off and the rest of the body had been left to decompose.

Logan blinked. "Its head . . ." was all he could gag.

"Completely unnatural," stated Moknay. "Whatever did this doesn't know a thing about survival. Most predators *leave* the head."

The decapitated corpse stole the color from Barthol's face. "What kind of creature would do such a thing?" he wondered in revulsion.

Moknay, Logan, and Mara all remained silent, unable to answer the priest's question. Nonetheless, the low rumble of a voice beside them afforded them the solution.

"Baaaaaad," the light blue ogre whispered. "Deeeeeemon."

The quiet lingered as disgusted comprehension tinged the faces of the four surrounding the headless corpse. Demons, Logan remembered. Skinny, toad-eyed creatures that—according to Moknay—were an uncommon sight. The one they had encountered on their previous journey had been easily defeated, but its scream . . . Logan could never forget that soul-wrenching scream that had issued from its small, round mouth.

"A Demon?" Barthol breathed. "So close to Debarnian?"

Moknay grimaced. "Either it's extraordinarily stupid or over-whelmingly courageous," he quipped. "Demons are not physically strong."

"But their magical potential . . ." Mara began.

"Please, Mara," Barthol begged out of fear, "do not remind us of their magic capability. It's unnerving enough to find Demonic traces so near to home, not to mention to recall the fact that they can consume and use infinite magicks."

"Only if they find a proper source," Moknay put in. The Mur-derer pulled his eyes away from the small cadaver and looked back toward the obscured town of Debarnian. "Barthol, I suggest you head back to the Church. A Demon this close might be able to sense the Jewel we left behind—even though it is kept in check. Mara, Logan, and I will head off toward the Roana and contact the sprites." His grey eyes flashed. "Just to be on the safe side, you might even want to draw this . . . incident to the Guards' attention."

Barthol bobbed his head up and down in vigorous agreement. "Indeed!" he exclaimed. "If there are Demons about, let the Guards handle them!"

Numbed by the flurry of information and suggestions passing around him, Logan gazed at the twisted corpse. As if over-whelmed by curiosity, he took a step closer to the headless form and felt a sudden electric jar disrupt his entire system. So intense was the abrupt pain, the young man experienced none of it. His body reacted violently, deadening his nerves and causing the world to evaporate around him. When his mind finally agreed to make sense of what he saw, Logan spied the ground rush up before him and felt soft dirt break his fall.

There were no sensations in his body, but a piercing whine stabbed through the young man's cranium like a white-hot rod.

With startled exclamations, Logan's companions hurried to his side. Logan himself was oblivious of the number of helpful hands aiding him, mesmerized by the flashes of pain accompanied by color. Faceless eyes glared down at the young man within his turgid thoughts, and the overpowering agony took on familiar features. It was a destructive buzz, loud and abrasive to the point of injury. A buzz that was rimmed with disharmony, and yet, consisted of helplessness. Overlapping and mixed emotions raced through both buzz and Logan as the young man's deadened nerves finally sparked back to life, and unbearable pain gripped his body.

Soothing, calm blackness engulfed Logan, and he succumbed.

A foul odor escaped the stony chamber, fleeing out into the corridor. Strands of serpentine smoke coiled upward, striking the ceiling and spiraling back down. Grotesquely shaped artifacts lined the many bookcases, and thick volumes with yellowed pages lay strewn about the floor. Unrecognizable sludge seeped between the huge stones of the floor, and the stench grew worse as the chestplated soldier neared.

A gnarled, black-robed form sat hunched over a leatherbound volume, a shriveled, bony finger tracing across the strangely printed words. Only the right eye followed the print; the left eye was glazed and unmoving. A silver chestplate protected the scrawny figure, an odd contrast to the ebony robe. The form refused to move; only its finger and eye trailed down the page.

Clearing his throat nervously, the soldier stepped into Groathit's chambers and tried to face the spellcaster. "Imperator Vaugen wishes to inform you that he is ready and awaiting your presence," the Reakthi announced, his voice quaking.

The wisps of smoke hissed as the eye and finger ceased all movement. Beads of sweat broke out across the soldier's brow as the black-robed figure froze.

Silence engulfed the wizard's chambers.

Parchment crackled as Groathit's gnarled hand turned the page and resumed reading.

The Reakthi standing in the doorway felt the muscles of his legs betray him and he almost collapsed. The room reeked of magic, and the silence surrounding the twisted spellcaster indicated his foul mood. Still, Vaugen had requested the sorcerer himself.

"Sir?" the soldier attempted once more. "Vaugen requests your presence . . ."

The eye and finger stopped again, only this time the head of spiky, blue-grey hair slowly swiveled on the soldier. The man in the doorway fought down the urge to turn and run once the eyes—both living and dead—trained on him. A hideous scowl drew across the wrinkled face, and shadows danced and convulsed upon the lean features of the sorcerer.

"Vaugen requests?" came the scratchy, sarcastic reply. "You may tell Vaugen I shall not be accompanying him this time. I have no more time for the petty little games he likes to play."

The spellcaster's head returned to its original position, and eye and finger resumed their task. The Reakthi uneasily stood at the entrance, befuddled. He had been commanded by his Imperator to summon Groathit to the stables—there was another hunt on for the stranger who could sense magic. Vaugen's hideous disfiguration inferred Groathit's knowledge would be necessary on this journey, but the sorcerer refused. Should he report this to Vaugen and face his wrath, or try once more to persuade the wizard . . . ?

"But sir," the soldier pressed, "Vaugen requires . . ."

The hunched, gnarled form slashed about with astonishing speed. Streaks of raw energy erupted from the skeletal fingers, crackling with murderous delight as they struck the chestplated warrior and instantly dissolved his flesh. Internal organs, muscles, and bone charred and cindered in a blinding burst of sorcery that left only a melted bronze chestplate smoldering in the doorway.

Groathit took three menacing steps toward the heap of slag, his right eye ablaze. "I believe you are hard of hearing," the spellcaster snarled. "I am through playing games with Matthew Logan. If Vaugen so desires to chase him to the ends of the world, so be it! I have found more . . . permanent means of dealing with him." Bony fingers clenched into a tight fist. "He shall not gain ascendancy! When the Darkness speaks, Matthew Logan shall *die!*"

"We are dying."

The voice arose from the eddying tidepools of red-and-black light, piercing the stillness with its deep, resonating tone.

"Can you not feel the magic and vitality ebbing away?"

Matthew Logan blinked his eyes repeatedly, staring at the spiraling vortex of blood and velvet that encircled him. Red and black paled as the churning rush slowed to a gurgling whirl—a slow and painful waltz of death.

"There was a time once before when Darkness reared its foul head above the waves of our Cosmic ocean, caring not of the damage and havoc they wreaked. Their only purpose was to destroy that which they loathed. And now that time has come again, but more than Purity is at stake. Before we faced a battle betwixt two Forces—since then more have come into play; the danger has increased a thousandfold."

The ominous, low-pitched voice slowly sank into the vacuum of lights and colors. Logan blinked as the ground beneath his feet heaved, and the shadows came alive to create a humanlike form. Shadow-streams billowed out behind the humanoid figure as pale eyes turned their gaze upon Logan.

"We are witnessing the death of all that is Nature, Matthew Logan," the shadow-form warned. *"We are seeing it corrupted and tainted by the same, shapeless Evil as before."*

The red-and-black glare brightened momentarily around the shadowy figure until the blackness began to seep into the red and overwhelm it.

"We shall die, Matthew Logan, and, should that happen, there will be no one left to attend our funeral."

Sensation returned to Logan's body, and the young man felt hard wood beneath him. He was lying supine, staring up at the clusters of treetops that draped above him. The low-pitched voice of the shadow-form was fading from his mind.

Funeral, his subconscious rasped.

All traces of the shadow-thing's voice vanished as Logan was seized by the horrendous fear of being in an uncovered coffin. He sat up with a fearful shout, sweat dribbling down his face. A number of heads turned toward him, and a soft touch fell upon his shoulder.

"Matthew?" Mara queried beside him, her concerned hand on his shoulder.

Logan focused his wild gaze on the priestess, droplets of sweat flying from his hair. "Mara?" he exclaimed, and swung about to face the others. "Moknay? Thromar?"

The Murderer and fighter rose from where they were sitting and approached the young man. Worry gleamed in both their eyes as they neared. A nervous smile drew beneath Thromar's reddish-brown beard as he stretched out a meaty hand toward Logan.

"You certainly gave me a shock," he declared. "Here I am, waiting around for you and Moknay, and in rumbles this cart! And who's lying in the back as still as death but you! I thought Brolark had taken you from me."

Logan turned his bewildered gaze away from the fighter and glanced down at the wood platform below him. He sat in Barthol's cart, he realized, and the priest himself stood slightly behind the ogre. Concern still lurked upon Barthol's chubby face, but a forced smile stretched across his lips when he spotted Logan's confused stare.

"Barthol . . . ?" mumbled Logan.

"Right here, my boy," the priest answered, coming nearer.

"I thought you were leaving . . ."

Barthol's smile grew into a true expression of beneficence. "I couldn't leave you," he announced. "I was the only one with transportation to take you back to your horses."

The facts were slowly beginning to seep into Logan's cloudy brain and assume an understandable structure. Still, befuddlement and fear traced Logan's mind, and his jerky, frightened glimpses around him persisted. Abruptly, he became aware of Mara's hand resting on his shoulder and felt the terror abate.

Steel-grey eyes fixed onto Logan's blue eyes. "How are you feeling, friend?" Moknay inquired.

Logan drew a shaky hand across his forehead, gathering the streams of perspiration that trickled down his face. "Okay, now . . . I guess."

"Any idea what happened to you?" the Murderer queried.

Logan tried to formulate a response but could not find the proper words. Defeated, he shook his head.

"It certainly wasn't any illness I have seen," Barthol commented.

"Nor I," agreed Mara.

Logan shook his head in convinced negation and almost lost his faulty grip on consciousness. "No," he gasped, trying to catch his breath, "I'm not sick. Something just . . . Something just bowled me over."

Thromar scratched his heavy mane of hair. "Do you mean like a soup bowl, friend-Logan?" he questioned.

"No," Logan corrected, "like a bowling ball. You know, it knocked me over."

"I've never heard of anyone being attacked by a soup bowl before," Thromar muttered in wonderment.

"Logan was not attacked by a soup bowl," Moknay said, "but something certainly did something to him. I haven't seen him this shaken since he destroyed the Blackbody."

Logan's eyes popped open. Moknay's right! he thought. When I fell through the Blackbody, I received a jolt combination of pain and Sparrill's feeling of disharmony. It practically short-circuited my brain for a minute, and I just sat there. The sensations were almost the same, but there was no Blackbody this time! No magical talisman! Not even the Jewel! So if we're missing these aspects, what caused me to black out . . . certainly not the feeling of disharmony. That's bothered me ever since I was zapped here . . . Or . . . wait a minute! All the time I was in Debarnian, I wasn't pestered once. Why was that so?

Examining the experience from every side, Logan was suddenly interrupted as Thromar questioned, "Do you think it had anything to do with that wind?"

The wind! Logan kicked himself mentally. *I'd forgotten all about it!*

"Wind?" repeated Moknay. "What wind?"

"Friend-Logan heard a voice calling for help on the wind," Thromar explained. "Then we all felt a veritable explosion of wind that . . . soup-bowled us all over."

Moknay turned his gaze on Logan, his steely-grey eyes flickering. In response to the Murderer's puzzling gaze, Logan nodded.

"Foreboding," Barthol murmured. "Demonic activity and ill winds. Very foreboding."

Puzzlement came to Logan's eyes now. "Why?" he wanted to know.

"The wind is Sparrill's essence," Mara answered for the priest. "It was believed the sprites regulated the Heart's magicks through the wind. Certainly, your own arrival here corresponds to the wind's activity. To suddenly have the wind be the bearer of ill tidings is a very foul sign indeed."

"That and the headless corpse," Moknay said with a frown. "Not to mention your odd collapse."

The three events inscribed themselves in Logan's brain and the young man went back to pondering their significance. Unexpectedly, the tiny door leading to his subconscious creaked open, and a low, ominous voice whispered:

We shall die, Matthew Logan, and, should that happen, there will be no one left to attend our *funeral.*

An arctic breeze sailed over the six centered around the wooden cart.

·4·

Gone

There was no gleeful chirp of unseen birds, nor any rustle in the foliage from an unfelt breeze, but, most disconcerting to Logan, there was no trace of disharmony plaguing his senses. The young man frowned, cocking his head in an attempt to pick out the disorienting sensation, yet no matter how intently he listened, no twinge of discordance sparked within his system.

The sun started its slow plunge behind the Hills of Sadroia as Logan raised his head. It had been more than a day since his unexplained collapse and Barthol's departure. Since then things had been quiet . . . much too quiet. No birds sang, no forest animal accidentally scampered out in front of the horses, no familiar barb of disagreement speared the young man's mind. Something, Logan mused with grim certainty, was brewing. It was like that same feeling of impending disaster that had accompanied the young man back in the Hills when dark clouds had converged overhead. Only this time, there were no clouds . . . only the absolute stillness of everything natural around them.

Shadows played across the forest as the western Hills obscured portions of the sun. Smeea suddenly drew back under Thromar's command, tossing her blood-red mane back in annoyance. The mare's red eyes flamed in the rays of the setting sun as her rider turned to face his companions.

"We've made good time," Thromar stated, "so we're not that far from the Roana. If we keep going, we should reach the river as the first stars come out of hiding."

Moknay's head instantly swiveled to face Logan behind him. Confronted by the Murderer's gaze, Logan held up his hands in an expression of helplessness.

Moknay's eyes flickered in replication. "It's your journey, friend," he commented. "You're the one who has to contact the sprites."

The question in the young man's eyes faded as he realized the veracity in the Murderer's words. It was—as much as Logan loathed the idea—his own notion to search out the sprites and the Bloodstone. Thromar had suggested the quest, but it had been Logan's final okay that sent them on this already foreboding trek. None of his companions had seen the sprites, nor did any of them have the desire to uncover and use the Heart of their land. The final decisions made on this journey would rest with Logan.

The young man's blue eyes fixed on the lowering sun, and his thoughts pieced together. Logan had only seen the sprites that night beside the Ohmmarrious, and it had been only in a seemingly real dream. Since Logan lacked the proper means to summon up the sprites, perhaps sleeping by the river would increase his chances of seeing them.

Keeping his voice purposely low, Logan instructed, "Keep going."

Feeble, his mind snarled at him. If something awful happens, I'll still be the cause . . . whether or not I give the command loudly.

The four horses resumed their leisurely pace through the darkening forest, and Logan felt the silence and portentousness expand. Sparrill should not be like this, he told himself. Sparrill was a land alive with magic and beauty, just like in their myths. Logan disliked the world because it was not his own, but he had admitted to himself that Sparrill had things Santa Monica lacked. Now, however, the stillness made him uneasy, burrowing under his skin and striking blows at his raw nerves. Even the constant buzz of disunity was better than this!

Fortunately for the young man, Thromar's calculations were correct, and the gurgling rush of the Roana sounded before them as the blue in the sky deepened to black. A cool breeze began to blow as the blackness thickened, but no night sounds commenced. As mysterious as the birds, the creatures of the dark remained mute.

The group of five made their way through the darkened greenery and arrived on the banks of the Roana. The large moon gleamed above them, its pale rays striking the crystal surface of the river. No matter how silent the rest of the forest life remained, the Roana retained its breathtaking beauty. Small, rounded water plants bobbed calmly atop the clear water, and the moss-covered rocks standing guard at the water's edge flared in the yellow-green moonlight. For a moment, Logan was taken in by the natural splendor of the scene, but then visions of his previous visit to the river clouded his mind. Arrows shrieked around him and his companions, Vaugen and Groathit cursed them from within the forest, and Druid Launce was already dying from an arrow wound. Even then the beauty of the Roana had hit Logan hard, yet he had had little time to appreciate it. Instead, the elegance of the water became a deathtrap that blocked him and his friends from the opposite bank . . . and finally caused the untimely demise of Druid Launce.

An uncontrollable anger erupted the young man's thoughts—a grim playback of his fury after that battle. Oh, he had been determined to see Vaugen dead, Logan remembered. If there had been any way to avenge Launce's death, Logan would find it . . . and he had. Imperator Vaugen was surely dead by now, struck full in the face by a magical blast pulled from the very center of the Jewel by Logan himself.

A morbid smile crossed Logan's face: The young man had perhaps done Sparrill some good by disposing of the only man capable of conquering her.

The beauty gradually seeped back to the river as Logan's guilt and anger abated.

Heavy footsteps sounded in Logan's ears as Thromar dismounted and lumbered toward the clear waters of the Roana. His tiny eyes flicked across the river surface; a meaty hand stroked his beard. "I certainly don't see any sprites," he proclaimed. He glanced up toward Logan. "Are you sure they're in there?"

Thromar's strange aura of innocence brought another type of smile to Logan's face as the young man dismounted. "I don't know where they are," he admitted. "Magic doesn't work in my world."

"And sometimes I wish it didn't work here either," murmured a disgruntled Moknay.

Thromar remained perplexed. "But if you don't know where they are, friend-Logan, how can you contact them? You keep telling us you're not a spellcaster."

"I am *not* a spellcaster!" Logan remarked, the ire he felt when reminded of that fact drawing up once more. "I don't want to become one either! It's just that, last time, the *sprites* contacted *me*. I figure all I have to do is hang around here for a while."

"You mean from the trees?" exclaimed Thromar.

Logan blinked. "What?"

The large fighter scratched his head in bewilderment. "You said you were going to hang here," he repeated.

"Not hang hang!" Logan yelled, frustrated. "I mean wait!"

A sardonic smirk spread across Moknay's face as he threw a few provisions to the ground. "Perhaps we should leave Logan in peace, Thromar," he suggested. "He is the only one who can contact the sprites." The Murderer unrolled a blanket and peered up into the night sky. "I think it would best suit our needs if Logan took the first watch; if you haven't contacted the sprites by the time I come on watch, we'll just try again in the morning."

A sense of misfortune bloomed inside Logan as he watched his friends lie down to sleep. They counted on him to take them on the next step of their journey, he noted, and he had no idea how to establish contact. What if the sprites didn't contact him? Or what if they could only contact him at the Ohmmarrious? Logan had not been the active party beforehand, and his passivity in this instance could cause quite a deal of delay—and embarrassment.

When the dark sky was fully dotted by the stars, Logan sat alone. His eyes roved from the sparkling river at his right to his slumbering companions on his left. On numerous occasions, Logan's eyes stopped on Mara, drinking in every minute detail about the slender priestess. He still did not have the faintest idea how such strong emotions had exploded within him concerning her, but they were there. Never before had he felt in such a way toward any other woman—Cyrene had been a senseless infatuation. Merely physical from the start! Okay . . . so maybe I did start to like her—grow fond of her—but my major interest in her had been of the flesh.

Logan's thoughts soured. No, he scolded himself, that's a lie and I know it. I had met Cyrene based on her physical appearance—I thought she was a whore!—but my liking for her had been due to her betrayal.

A sharp wrench ran through Logan's senses. Cyrene had purposely flirted with and made love to Logan in the hopes of winning him over: first filling his head with false love, then intending to use him as a tool against Vaugen, Mediyan, and whomever else the girl disliked. In that sense, she had been no better than those men she wanted dead.

Logan blinked away those thoughts. But Mara, his mind went on. There was something special about her. Logan had been attracted to her immediately, not to say she was magical, but, speaking in romantic terms, maybe she was.

There was a faint rustle further down the river and Logan jerked about. His vision had improved since his arrival in Sparrill, but the young man failed to find anything lurking in the darkness along the riverbanks. Sometimes a few stones seemed to take on aspects of bizarre, slouched creatures, but that, Logan knew, was his imagination.

Sighing, Logan leaned back and gazed up into the black heavens. Stars twinkled down at him, yet no sensation of disagreement maligned their glitter. As hard as Logan found it to believe, the feeling was gone. That irritating buzz of disunity had up and left. After that, the hours seemed to flow together, and Moknay joined the young man on watch. Logan refused to turn in, figuring it best to contact the sprites at night. Gradually, however, sleep forced its way past his contact lenses and began to inject its drowsiness into his limbs. It was as Moknay's watch was coming to a close that Logan finally slid into sleep.

Logan's eyes flickered open as a freezing wind moaned overhead, sending flakes of ice skittering across the river's shores. The crystal waters of the Roana churned expectantly, increasing their flow toward the Sea. Silver-and-black beacons sparkled in the red night sky, each struggling for dominion over the firmament. Curiously, Logan propped himself up and looked behind him. His companions and their horses were not there.

The young man beamed proudly. Contact!

Logan turned an anticipatory look toward the surging waters of the Roana. Silver-and-black glitters rebounded off the turbulent river and the freezing, polar wind made Logan glad he wore his sweat jacket. The young man's blue eyes narrowed as the clear waters refused to slow and still as they had done at the Ohmmarrious. Instead, the rushing waters intensified, sending droplets of liquid spewing into the night air. The flow of agitated water grew deafening, like the enraged growling of a wild beast. Wonder and trepidation mingled in Logan's eyes as pillars of water shot skyward, ignoring the whirlpool of activity beneath them. No tiny figure stepped through the columns of liquid, and Logan's wonder increased. This was surely the same type of sequence he had experienced at the Ohmmarrious—why did the waters churn so violently?

The strange numbness Logan had felt before entered the young man's form. Logan guessed it was the muted sensation of disharmony—similar to the feeling he had when he had grasped Launce's staff. But what in the world was dampening the magic of Sparrill? And why hadn't the sprites appeared yet?

The rocketing fountains joined the rapidslike Roana with a harmonious growl of power. Misgiving arose in Logan that forced him to get to his feet, staring at the river. Abruptly, the streams of water shooting skyward turned a deep red, and, at first, Logan thought it was the intense reflection of the reddish night. Then he caught the coppery scent that wavered on the freezing wind and noticed how thick the fluid had become.

The roar of rushing water was drowned out by a second roar, one of extreme anger and indignation. A pair of faceless eyes Logan had seen before sprouted amidst the fountain of blood, blazing with a fury that sent ripples of energy through its ebony irises. Logan could only gape in surprise at the sudden manifestation. Sizzling blasts of energy forked out from the eyes hovering in the blood, and Logan's reflexes refused to kick in. An unexpected tug from the shadows behind the young man sent him sprawling to the ground and out of harm's way. Instantly, the pillars of blood vanished, taking the black-filled eyes with them.

Logan whipped a curious gaze on his savior and saw only restless shadows writhing around him on the forest floor. The numbness fled Logan's frame and confusion took its place.

The arctic wind moaned once more.

A sudden ruckus broke through the veil of sleep encasing Logan, and the young man opened one eye. Faint light drizzled upon the grassy bank of the Roana, and a fine, white mist hovered in the air. Voices pierced the fog, cries of uncertainty and surprise. The neighing of horses joined in and Logan was fully roused out of slumber.

Trying to blink away the thickness of sleep about his contact lenses, Logan turned away from the river. His sleepy vision focused on the bulky figure of Thromar scurrying back and forth, the green of the forest as a backdrop. A grey form wavered beside Thromar, almost hidden in the early morning light. The red and black clothing of Mara indicated the priestess also sat on the ground, rudely awakened by the shouting.

There was also a great deal of movement from where the horses were tethered.

"Just suddenly!" Thromar boomed. "I'm sitting here, minding my own business, then . . . !" The huge man's voice trailed off. "See for yourself!"

The tiredness was seeping from Logan's eyes as his mind began to pick up the conversation.

"I don't like this," came Moknay's reply. "There was no point of emission?"

"There was no point to it at all!" Thromar returned. "I'm just fortunate I was not standing up!"

As his conscious mind took full control, Logan suddenly saw the smoking, sizzling tree trunks at the edge of the forest. Bark and branches had been burned away, as if some massive bolt of energy had struck the foliage from the opposite side of the Roana.

Or from the center of the river itself, Logan thought with a gasp.

The stunned look on the young man's face must have been obvious as he staggered unsteadily to his feet. Moknay's peering grey eyes instantly fixed on him, demanding without a voice of their own an explanation.

"What happened?" Mara asked, rescuing Logan from the Murderer's stare.

"The trees exploded!" Thromar howled.

Moknay's grim visage clouded his face. "The trees did not explode, Thromar," he corrected, his voice unsettlingly calm. "There was magic involved."

"Magic?" Mara questioned. "Whose? From where?"

"And why hit the trees and not one of us?" wondered Thromar.

"Maaaaaagic," the light blue ogre echoed, staring fearfully at the charred tree trunks.

Logan's eyes glanced away from the massive creature and started back toward Moknay. Abrupt motion caught his attention and his sight fixed on the magically ruined trees. The foliage was writhing, painfully shrinking in on itself. Thick, viscous sap swelled up from around the scorched portions of trunk, and leaves withered and browned. The healthy bark, untouched by the blast, went black and wrinkled inward like elderly flesh. The earth supporting the trees also turned dark, and hideously malformed blades of grass sprouted in place of healthy turf.

Numbness made its way up Logan's legs and into his stomach. The sensation of disagreement was trying to reach him again, he speculated. This event, as Moknay had surmised, originated in magic.

The young man turned his bewildered gaze on the Murderer. Moknay, however, paid no attention. A look of absolute horror changed the Murderer's face, and fear sparked wildly in his steel-grey eyes.

"Maaaaaagic," the ogre repeated, shying away from the mutating brush.

Thromar's meaty hand rested upon his sword hilt. "Must we stay here much longer?" he queried. "Perhaps it's safer farther upstream?"

"Magic as powerful as that could track us wherever we went," Mara declared. "It's managed to weaken and corrupt a portion of Sparrill's own magic."

"But where can magic that powerful come from?" Moknay demanded, his fear swiftly transformed to anger. "The only thing I can come up with is the possibility of more Demonic activity, but a blast that large with those kind of results . . . ? It would mean the Demon had come across something like the Jewel itself!"

"What if your friend Barthol didn't get back to town in time?" Thromar worried.

"It's not the Jewel," Logan suddenly found himself saying.

All eyes—as was expected—fell on him.

Logan could only stare back.

"What do you mean?" Moknay probed, sensing the knowledge the young man held. "Did you contact the sprites?"

The numbness settling in Logan's belly became dread. "No . . . well, sort of," he stuttered. "There's something wrong. I almost contacted them, but, then . . . well, they're not there."

"What do you mean they're not there?" Thromar inquired.

"They're gone!" Logan shouted angrily, furious that the fighter had touched upon the reason for his fear. "Something did something with them!"

"What kind of something?" Mara wondered. "A Demon, as Moknay said?"

Logan gave the tangled and warped shrubbery a nervous glance and shook his head. "It's not a Demon," he answered. "It's something else . . . I guess."

"You guess?" Moknay sneered, eyebrows raised.

The young man's rage erupted again. "Yeah!" he roared. "I guess! Look, I'm not from this world! I don't know what could have taken the sprites! All I know is that—in my dream—some-thing tried to kill me from the center of the river. It hit the forest rather than me! Dreams don't make sense, I know that, but this one suddenly sprouts an explosion and disfigured trees? It has to mean something, but what it means I have to guess at!"

The Murderer's own disquiet quelled as he saw the sympathetic emotions mirrored in Logan. "Calm down, friend," he soothed. "No one's blaming anyone for their ignorance. We're as far in the dark as you are, except you're the only one with any kind of information."

"Maybe the sprites aren't gone," Mara suggested. "Maybe some-thing is just blocking them from you."

Thromar nodded. "Perhaps this very something that tried to blast us doesn't want friend-Logan to meet them."

Logan felt his own head bob up and down in agreement. Some-thing *was* dampening the usual sensations he experienced. Maybe it was purposeful. "But who would be doing this?" he queried.

"That's something to be deciphered later," replied Moknay. "Whoever it is, we've never met them before. I'd recognize that kind of magic."

Logan looked back at the withered and black trees and shud-dered. True, he thought, I'd remember magic like that if I saw it before too.

Thromar untied Smeea and stood ready beside her. "Now where?" he wanted to know.

Moknay turned on the fighter and frowned. "I was hoping you might tell us," he said. "You're the only one out of all of us who's been all across Sparrill and Denzil."

Thromar shrugged in response. "Any other time I would have suggested the Smythe, but we all know what happened to him."

Logan flinched.

"Because the Roana is still flowing, I'm positive the sprites are alive," Mara put in. "Since they are a vital part of Sparrill's nature, maybe we should seek out someone in tune with Nature herself?"

"Too true," Moknay agreed, "and I'd suggest Druid Launce at that—but he's taken the same route as the Smythe."

Logan flinched again and averted his gaze. His companions weren't purposely reminding him of all those who had died aiding the young man from Santa Monica, but it hurt nonetheless.

A blur of motion rustled a few bushes further down the river and broke the young man's train of thought. The strange, slouched beasts he imagined the night before had returned to haunt the day. Small, dark forms leapt in the forest, perhaps trying to spy the distorted and twisted vegetation nearby.

"Moknay," Logan said through clenched teeth, "we're being watched."

The Murderer cast a quick but casual glance over his caped shoulder. Silver immediately flared in his gloves and rocketed for the half-obscured creatures. There was a tortured shriek from the brush as Moknay's blade connected, and instant panic swept the unseen animals. Mara swiftly dived for her Binalbow, drawing it up and facing the forest. Thromar's blood-caked sword gleamed in the rays of the rising sun, and Logan realized with a grumble that he was the last to react to his own discovery.

"What is it?" Mara whispered, Binalbow aimed at nothing in particular.

Moknay sneered and his mustache lifted. "Don't know," he murmured, one of his three-bladed throwing knives in his hand.

The numbness building in Logan's stomach unexpectedly screeched toward his spine and brain. A searing burst of pain caught the young man by surprise as the beat of leathery wings echoed from the forest.

With a terrified bellow, the light blue ogre sprang to its feet and thundered away from the woods. Its massive arms draped over its squarish head, and its eyes were wide with terror.

The ogre's abrupt flight knocked Logan's composure off balance. The young man's start was doubled by the hideous mockery of animal life that launched itself out of the bushes, fused and twisted beaks releasing anguished cries. Featherless wings propelled the monsters through the air, and jagged, gnarled spines created sharp prongs that lined the backs.

Logan blinked as he saw the flock of unnatural birds freeze his friends where they stood. All of his companions seemed uncommonly terrified by the misshapenness of the fowl, and, although prepared, none moved to defend themselves.

The lurch of pain coursed through Logan's bloodstream once more and Logan gritted his teeth. In reply to the painful throb, Logan's Reakthi blade slashed through the early morning mist and cut one of the mutated birds out of the sky. Blood as crimson as normal blood splashed to the dew-draped floor, the twisted carcass crashing beside it. The remaining birds acted with one mind and directed their aerial attack on Logan. The young man's blade chopped two more of the featherless beasts out of the air before a razor-sharp beak struck his hand.

Flaring pain crackled up Logan's right arm from the gash that raced across his knuckles. Another beak jabbed for his eyes, but a wild blow from Logan's arm saved his sight. Unexpectedly, a sharp, resonating twang split the mist and two of the flying monsters went down. Mara hurriedly jerked forward and back the lever on her bow and speared a third beast.

"Friend-Logan!" Thromar boomed. "Get your head down!"

Curiosity was a fatal mistake in brawls such as this, so Logan obeyed. Almost simultaneous with his duck, Thromar's heavy blade sliced the air in half, catching and killing a number of the transformed birds. Cut down to less than half their fighting force, the remaining fowl banked sharply and fled.

Logan wiped the blood dribbling about his fingers. "What the hell were they?" he swore.

"Birds," Mara responded, reloading the casing of her Binalbow.

"Ugliest looking birds I've ever seen!" declared Thromar.

"Perhaps they were caught in the same blast that changed the trees," Moknay mused, heading toward the forest to retrieve his dagger.

Mara glanced up from studying a gnarled corpse. "No," she answered, "they've been like this for a while. You can see the structure of their flesh is changing to accommodate their flying. Without feathers, they're developing strange points at the edges of their wings."

"To act as the propeller function," Logan muttered.

Mara looked up at him with a knowing look in her eyes but Thromar remained very much confused.

"A bird is supported mainly by the base of its wings," Logan explained, not knowing all that much about the aerodynamics of flight but unable to ignore Thromar's perplexed gaze, "but the wing tip gives it its propelling force forward. By spreading and closing the feathers on the wing tip, a bird can steer. Without feathers, these things are molding their own flesh." The young man frowned. Even though, he added to himself, I thought birds were grounded if they lost just their flight feathers.

"And they must have had a few days in which to shape their own wings." Mara was agreeing with Logan's spoken statement.

Moknay returned, brandishing his dagger. The first bird still dangled from the blade, skewered clean through the breast. "I give up," the Murderer snarled. "Whoever is doing this has enough power to alter and disrupt Nature."

"And keep the sprites from us," Mara added.

Moknay flicked the warped body from his dagger and cleaned the blade on the dew-and blood-spattered grass. "Magic is bad enough," he growled, "but magic from an unknown source is the worst kind."

"Maaaaaagic," the light blue ogre breathed, cowering beside the river.

"So now what do we do?" Logan sighed, cleansing his wounded hand in the Roana's clear water.

"I'd still say our best bet is to contact the sprites and ask them what the *Deil*'s going on," Moknay frowned. "Imogen knows we won't find out by ourselves!"

"But that still leaves us the problem of who to turn to," Thromar reminded.

Another flicker of movement invaded Logan's line of vision and his head jerked upward. Relief washed over him like the river water when he realized it was just the breeze batting at a strand of moss dangling from a stone, yet a memory and idea materialized.

"Munuc," the young man breathed.

"What?" queried Moknay.

Logan pulled himself away from the Roana. "Munuc and his people lived below the ground," he exclaimed. "One of the rocks was the entrance."

Moknay stroked his chin, flickers of possibilities darting across the greyness of his eyes. "Hmmm, you may have something there," he said, nodding. "The little fellow would know more about Nature than we would; Launce was his companion." The Murderer's eyes flashed away from Logan and scanned the length of the Roana. "All right, Thromar," he ordered, "you're the tracker. Where were Munuc and his people hiding?"

The brawny fighter scratched his titanic tuft of hair. "If I knew that, Murderer, they wouldn't be hiding, would they?" he retorted.

"Don't attempt to get intellectual now, Thromar," Moknay quipped. "You've had all your life to do that and shouldn't go wasting Logan's time trying to make up for it now."

Thromar turned his massive back on the Murderer and faced Logan. His beady black eyes were filled with regret. "Were I capable of such a feat, friend-Logan, I would gladly comply," the large Rebel apologized. "Unfortunately, an attempt to find one rock out of the many leagues of riverbank would be . . ."

"Like trying to find a needle in a haystack," Logan finished, nodding in understanding. "Don't worry about it, Thromar. It was just an idea."

"But it was the best one so far," Moknay mumbled gravely.

Thromar could not help but feel guilty as his tracking ability failed his friends. "Although I can not promise anything, I don't think it would hurt if we followed the river northward. Maybe we'll recognize something."

Moknay and Logan nodded their approval, Mara and the ogre unfortunately left helpless. Only three of the five could spot the opening to Munuc's world, and the feeling of incapability strengthened in the small group.

A slow trot brought the band northward. They had not gone more than a mile when Logan's improved vision noted an object lying slightly right of the Roana. So narrow was the weapon, anybody else would have been hard pressed to see it, yet Logan's roving eyes caught and held fast. Its brownish color caused it to blend expertly with the yellow-brown dirt about the river, but Logan knew his contact-covered eyes were not playing tricks on him.

A Reakthi bow lay just beyond the forest.

"But does it mark the opening?" Moknay questioned the young man's find.

It marked more than the opening, Logan's mind ached. The Reakthi who had carried this bow had been the one who had seen Munuc's opening. He was the reason Launce ran back. An unarmed Reakthi, flailing an empty bow above his head, had caused the druid to run from protection and be struck down.

Logan nodded to himself. Yes, this bow marked much more than Munuc's home.

Thromar released a victorious whoop as he pushed aside the moss-veiled stone that led to Munuc's world. A grim smile played across Moknay's features as he neared the entrance.

"It seems luck is with us," he said, then added, "this time."

Thromar threw the Murderer a puzzled glance. "Don't swing your sword until it's forged, Murderer," he warned. "I can't hear anything from inside and there aren't any fresh tracks. From the way those little fellows liked to hop about, you'd think there'd be more noise."

The memory of Launce's last moments fled Logan's mind as he approached the opening. Moknay curiously lowered his head through the hole and looked. His eyes were filled with mystery as he looked back up, a gloved finger smoothing his mustache.

"They're not there," he informed the others.

Logan felt despair gnaw at his gut as he poked his head into Munuc's hidden portal. Like Moknay, he found the underground cavern devoid of life, unlit and unlived-in. Something had happened to the little, monkeylike creatures, and guilt blossomed up around Logan as he already started blaming himself.

"They're gone," the young man repeated, stunned. "They're gone too."

"But what could have happened to them?" Thromar questioned. "They were a feisty little band of buggers!"

As if in answer to Thromar's query, a scream reverberated from across the river, striking Logan to the very heart. Startled, half-curses escaped their lips as the five wheeled about to spy a humanoid figure lope its way into the sky above the Roana. The early morning sun glistened off the needle-sharp fangs that lined the tiny, rounded mouth, and leathery wings unfolded, turned all but transparent by the sun's rays.

"Demon!" Mara shouted, scrambling toward her horse.

A murderous grin spread across the circular mouth and toadlike eyes flamed with the magical energy brewing within the gangly form. Sticklike arms jabbed accusingly at the five grouped together on the opposite bank and sorcerous flames spat from the iron talons.

Moknay blanched at the sight of magic. "Thromar, I don't think we should bet on this one."

·5·

Medallion

Thromar snorted contemptuously at the oncoming Demon. "By Harmeer's War Axe, Murderer! Don't tell me these things still give you the shakes?"

Moknay snatched two daggers from his chest strap and glared at the shrieking beast above the river. "It's using magic, Thromar," he grated.

The fighter released another disdainful grunt. "So what?" he retorted. "I don't remember magic upsetting you so much beforehand."

The Murderer's grim sneer replaced his anxiety. "That was before I saw what magic could do if given the chance," he answered. "That Jewel almost blasted all of us into so many magical motes."

"That's the key word, Murderer," Thromar replied. "*Almost.* You don't kill a Reakthi if you *almost* hit him." The fighter threw Moknay a yellowing grin. "You've got to stop thinking about that Jewel; it's ruining your concentration. Not all magic is that powerful—and this skinny little Demon certainly can't compare to the Jewel!" The massive fighter cocked his head toward the hovering Demon. "Magic may have its mystery and danger, Murderer, but so do you."

An inquisitive eyebrow raised above a steel-grey eye. Logan could almost see the thoughts forming in the Murderer's mind as he glanced at the daggers he held and at the sorcery sparking from the Demon's claws. Magic, Logan recalled, had not frightened Moknay when they had first met. Sure, he had always been uneasy around it, but he had rescued Logan from a transformed Groathit back in Eadarus. Anyone fearful of magic would never have attempted such a thing! Perhaps the danger that the Jewel presented heightened the Murderer's mistrust to a greater degree.

Thunder burst in Logan's ears and the air above the Roana crackled with energy. A searing blast of power howled from the Demon's taloned fingers and screeched with magical fury toward Thromar. The large fighter hastily sprang to one side. Pebbles and sparks screamed into the air as the ray of thaumaturgy splintered and exploded against the riverbank.

In reply, Mara's Binalbow twanged and caught the Demon on the shoulder. Reeling under the blow, the Demon almost plunged into the river beneath it, yet its thin, leathery wings beat against the updraft and held it aloft. Rage and magic boiled in its toadlike eyes as the gangly creature wheeled on Mara, saliva dribbling from its mouth. Lights erupted from its claws, and magic speared the air once more.

Mara dodged to her left, her long hair billowing about her.

Frustration and fear built up around Logan as he glared at the hovering Demon. The damn thing purposely stayed over the Roana! he growled to himself. It probably hopes to pick us all off from there! And it has a good chance, too! I can't hit it with my sword; Thromar can't hit it with his. Mara's the only one with a long-range weapon—Moknay's still uncertain . . . He probably won't be able to hit it thinking it's going to turn its magic on him.

A resounding boom shattered Logan's thoughts. "*Deeeeeemon!*" the light blue ogre roared, clapping its hands together.

Invisible shock waves sundered the air as the ogre's titanic palms crashed together. The Demon emitted a startled shriek, its huge, frail-looking wings beating frantically to keep it above the river. It performed a bizarre dance across the sky, its limbs and wings flailing erratically.

Yellow-white blood spurted from the Demon's chest, released by a pair of golden hilts abruptly lodged in its rib cage. With an agonized screech, the Demon splashed into the crystal waters of the Roana, its murky blood clouding the river.

Moknay freed two more daggers and trained his eyes on Thromar. "If I can force myself to go back to fighting spellcasters, Thromar, I'll expect you to get over your fear of tight places," he wagered, steel gleaming in his gloves and in his eyes.

Water spread out in umbrellalike fashion as the Demon erupted from the Roana. Streams of energy rocketed from both its lanky arms, instantly transforming droplets of water to steam. Moknay easily somersaulted away, evading the blast as if it were nothing more than a normal weapon. Logan narrowly escaped the other blow.

As the Demon dragged itself toward the shore, Thromar slashed the air above his head and charged. "I'll dance on your corpse, Demon!" he bellowed, throwing an odd gesture in Moknay's direction.

The toadlike eyes of the Demon targeted the enormous fighter and magic coiled about its iron claws. Two daggers unexpectedly lodged themselves in the Demon's thin neck, defiling the Roana with more yellow-white fluid.

Thromar laughed triumphantly. "Haven't used that one since we first met!" he roared. "Nice throwing, Murderer!"

"Get your head down, oaf!" Moknay demanded.

Magic streaked over Thromar's right shoulder, singeing a few of his shoulder-length hairs. The fighter's small eyes went wide as the smell of his own burnt hair forced its way into his nostrils.

Mara sprinted around Thromar, trying to draw her bow on the floundering Demon. Logan and the ogre, however, stood across from it. Should she miss, her twin quarrels could strike either of them, and she certainly didn't want to show her worth by injuring Matthew Logan.

"It's getting out!" cried Logan, instinctively backing away.

The injured Demon pulled itself from the river and rose into the air, mystical beacons glimmering in its large, amphibian eyes. A war cry from Thromar jerked the bulbous head about, but the fighter was forced to dodge before reaching the magically endowed Demon. Wild bolts of power sizzled through the air, spinning insanely across the riverbank. None of the five could strike, preoccupied as they were with avoiding the random streaks of sorcery. No sooner would Moknay or Mara aim than a sudden eruption of energy would send them rushing for cover.

Pretty damn hopeless, Logan said to himself.

A scream split the morning air as the Demon jerked spasmodically, yellowish-white blood fountaining from its forehead. A golden hilt protruded from the creature's skull, sending rivulets of lifefluid streaming down its face. Its muscles twitched, and the lights and colors of magic dimmed from its hands.

Devoid of life, the Demon spiraled out of the air and lay still upon the bank.

Thromar neared the corpse, a distasteful frown under his beard. "Did you have to go and kill it so quickly, Murderer?" he complained. "I didn't even get in a decent shot!"

Moknay replaced the daggers he held and smirked. "I'm sorry to disillusion you, Thromar," he replied, "but I didn't kill it. I was too busy trying to keep my rump from getting scorched."

The frown beneath Thromar's beard grew as he glanced at Logan.

Logan made every negative move he knew. "I didn't do it," he confessed, indicating the dagger he still wore at his belt.

In reply, both Logan and Thromar looked to Mara. "My dagger is not for throwing," the priestess declared.

Quizzically, Logan directed his gaze to Moknay and saw the admiration and awe that filled the Murderer's eyes. "Whoever threw that," Moknay murmured, "pierced bone. The strength and skill required . . ."

Grey eyes came alive as the Murderer wheeled around, his cape flapping about him. So abrupt was the move, Logan flinched in surprise and attempted to follow the Murderer's glare. Only because of his improved vision did Logan catch sight of the dark, slouched form that stood at the forest's edge. Tiny, black eyes glittered in the morning light and a wicked grin spread across the fanged mouth.

"What did I tell you?" bellowed Thromar. "Feisty little buggers!"

Munuc scuttled toward the large fighter, bobbing his furry head enthusiastically up and down. His long arms dangled behind him as his stumpy legs brought him closer to the five gathered on the riverbank.

"It appears not all of them have disappeared," Moknay remarked. He turned to the monkeylike creature. "You have our thanks, Munuc . . . uh . . . you are Munuc, aren't you?"

Munuc continued to nod, ripping his dagger from the Demon's forehead. He gave the yellow-white blood a disgusted look and wiped the blade clean. Then, his zeal returning, he peered up at Logan. The young man could not be sure, but there was a hint of comradeship glowing in the creature's beady eyes, like the look old friends might give one another.

"He remembers us," noticed Moknay.

"What is he?" Mara questioned, smiling at the furry anthropoid.

"Not quite sure," Thromar answered. "His name's Munuc . . . likes to throw food around."

As if he understood, Munuc grinned broadly, his fangs glinting in the sunlight. Then, concerned with other matters, he turned back to face Logan.

His blue eyes filled with wonder, Logan could only stare down at the small form. The look in Munuc's eyes was now unmistakable. It was like the little beast wanted Logan for his new friend, having finally gotten over the loss of Launce.

Momentary sorrow burned through Logan's skull. How undeserving he felt to be regarded by Munuc as Launce's successor. Launce had been a loyal, peace-loving man of the forest who cared more about others than about himself; Munuc had been his companion. Together the two had "taken care" of the forest around them.

Logan blinked as a brilliant flash of understanding flared to life. That look in Munuc's eyes also gleamed with secretive thoughts, as if the little creature knew something devilishly important. And, perhaps, Munuc did.

"Munuc," Logan said, bending down, "we need your help."

Munuc nodded, not in answer, but curtly, as if more pressing matters needed to be discussed. The motion greatly disturbed Logan as his properly phrased questions suddenly disintegrated. Munuc seemed to be saying he needed their help as much as they needed his.

Did it have something to do with the rest of his people?

"Is something wrong?" Logan asked, his inquiries and statements thoroughly fragmented. "Where's the rest of your people?"

Munuc's constant nodding halted instantly and he turned his back on the five. His loping gait toward the forest was a mixture of urgency and dread, but there was an exasperated spark in his eyes.

"I think you've offended him," Thromar muttered.

Logan gave the fur-covered creature a questioning stare. "I don't know what I did," he grumbled. "I think he wants something."

"What could he want from us?" Moknay wanted to know. "We're the ones seeking information from him."

The monkeylike Munuc suddenly disappeared into the forest and silence controlled the riverbank. Curious glances rebounded about the five, and a horse snorted impatiently. Branches rustled as Munuc dangled from a tree limb, waving his gangly arms frantically at the group. In an instant, the small beast was gone again and swiftly reappeared elsewhere in the trees.

"Maybe he wants us to follow him," Mara suggested.

Munuc released a sharp bark at the priestess's comment that startled Smeea. For a moment, no one moved; Moknay strode toward the Demon's corpse and withdrew his daggers. "We've nowhere else to go," he shrugged.

Logan could not help grumbling to himself at the Murderer's statement. Things were going so badly for them. I must be a jinx! the young man decided. What else could be the explanation? Find the sprites, sounds easy enough! Then something mutes Sparrill's magic, we stumble over a headless corpse, a Demon acquires some magic from God knows where, and, most importantly, the sprites aren't where they should be! How the devil can I contact them if they're not at their rivers? All I want to do is go home.

The four colorful horses trailed the swinging Munuc for over an hour, Logan grimly reminding himself of his many misfortunes. So wrapped up in his despair, Logan almost bumped into the horse ahead of him as the line of horses halted. The light blue ogre questioningly stepped up beside Logan and cocked its head in one direction.

"Cliiiip clooooop!" the beast informed them.

Thromar looked over a chainmailed shoulder and nodded to those behind him. "He's right," he declared. "Riders from the north."

Moknay's hands went to his daggers. "Guards?"

Thromar's reddish-brown head of hair shook. "I don't think so," he replied. "We've been heading east—back toward Debarnian—so they aren't coming from there."

The five went silent; even Munuc dropped out of the trees onto Smeea's back. The hoofbeats echoing from the foliage grew louder until three horses broke free of the trees, their riders greatly surprised by the four horses and the ogre suddenly blocking their route. Each, Logan noted, wore a vest of chainmail, the links set in a hexagonal pattern with wide center links. Other than that, they appeared to be nothing more than travelers or adventurers, armed only with familiar-looking swords.

Sweat began to dribble down the lead horseman's face as he licked his lips nervously. "Ho, journeyers," he croaked. "Pleasant day, is it not?"

Moknay cocked an eyebrow high onto his forehead as Thromar responded, "I've yet to find out for certain. Why? Has it been so for you?"

The lead rider nodded and attempted a friendly smile, yet the perspiration trickling down his face marred his benevolence. "Indeed it has," he answered, giving his two companions a swift glance. "We should . . . uh . . . be thankful for these days before the cold of winter falls upon us."

"Indeed we should," Thromar returned. "Forgive us, but we must be off. We have some pressing business to the east."

Relief washed over the lead horseman's face. "Oh, yes! Of course!" he cried cheerfully. "Don't let us delay you!"

Thromar nodded—half amicably, half suspiciously—before waving his companions onward. Curiosity swirled inside Logan as he started back into the forest, throwing the trio of riders a backward glance. Logan's mind puzzled about the three. Their actions reeked of nervousness, and their friendly banter had been quite forced, but there was something else plaguing the young man's suspicion and he could not put his finger on it.

Another half-hour passed as the five trailed the tree-swinging Munuc through the woods. The little creature abruptly dropped heavily to the forest floor and ivy rustled about him. A roiling sense of déjà vu grumbled like hunger in Logan's stomach as he peered about the ivy-strewn clearing and the half-obscured hillock of grass. The faint sound of water babbling in the distance only increased the feeling that Logan had been here before.

"Launce," Thromar realized, startling Logan out of his thoughts.

The large fighter saw the puzzled stare thrown at him from Logan's direction. "This is where Druid Launce lived," Thromar explained. "Don't you remember?"

Logan's blue eyes flicked across the clearing once more and memories began to click into place. The toppled tree that blocked the hillock, the outcropping of rocks looming on their right—all of these finally reminded Logan of the faintly smiling druid that gave his life to help them.

"But why did we come here?" Moknay asked Munuc.

The Murderer's question was answered when the forest came alive with furry, dark shapes that poured out of the shrubbery. A grey-furred Munuc suddenly climbed atop Launce's hillock, surveying his people as they led the four horses to the hidden stable around the side of the grassy knoll. Barks and yaps greeted the five as the monkeylike creatures swarmed around them, welcoming them to their new home.

"A suitable move," Thromar approved. "Probably much better for their health than that damp little cave under the Roana."

A malicious grin spread below Moknay's mustache. "Tight spaces, Thromar," he snickered. "I *did* fight that Demon."

The conversation passing between Rebel and Murderer went unheard by Logan. Thoughts and past emotions clouded the young man's brain, and mental pain played across his nerves. Why had he not trusted Launce? he wondered. Because of his mistrust, Launce felt it necessary to prove his friendship . . . it cost him his life.

A soft, yet hairy hand touched Logan's and the young man glanced down. Eyes filled with wisdom peered up at him from the grey-haired face of the eldest of Munuc's people. The gentle touch on Logan's hand instructed him to follow.

Moknay, Thromar, and Mara trailed the young man toward the ivy-hidden staircase beneath the toppled tree. Munuc abruptly bounded in before them, grasping the oaken staff that had once belonged to Launce. With almost reverent actions, Munuc handed the staff to Logan and scampered down the hidden steps.

Gripping the staff, Logan could not fight off the memories that surrounded him. Your fault, his mind accused. Launce is dead; your fault. The force of the memories strengthened when the four stepped into Launce's main chamber. The hidden window, the table and bowl of fruit, the chairs and moss-filled pillows . . . the sorrow was almost more than Logan could bear.

"This is incredible," Mara breathed, awed by the natural formation of Launce's home.

"Struck us pretty much in the same way," Moknay told her. "Launce said something about taking care of the forest, so the forest took care of him."

Mara nodded in astonishment. "Yes," she replied. "I've read where men of nature are able to survive in the forest with every conceivable comfort of town."

Logan caught the voices of his friends, but they were foggy, almost dreamlike. Loud barks and screeches began to rebound about the chamber as Munuc conversed with his elder, their lean arms flailing about their heads. Somehow Logan knew the creatures discussed the young man's plight and tried to come up with a solution. Munuc and his kind were in tune with nature and had already discovered the disappearance of the sprites.

The barking died down and the grey-haired Munuc took the staff from Logan's hands. The word *sprite* seemed to resonate within the young man's mind the instant the monkeylike thing touched the oak, yet the sensation passed almost immediately. In its place, faint light began to radiate from the wooden staff. The chamber full of anthropoids grew silent as the shimmer of magic burned within the oak. Sparks crackled and scorched the air, yet no one spoke. Blurry images took on substantial form above the upraised staff, their outline made up of crystal-blue geometric angles. For a moment Logan thought his imagination was playing tricks on him when he spied three slender figures hovering through the magical mist. However, the geometric shapes suddenly exploded with a violent concussion of power that knocked everyone to the ground. Flashing black eyes winked into being above the glimmering staff, and panic swept over the chamber of furry creatures. Horrified screams and barks penetrated Logan's ears, and an earth-shuddering roar of anger shook Launce's home. Clods of dirt dropped from the ceiling, and furniture overturned. Flaring black points of energy leapt from the ebony eyes peering down at Logan, yet the glister of humor replaced the hatred and fury the young man had seen in his dream. As if enjoying some wicked joke, the night-filled eyes gleamed sadistically.

A faint voice reached Logan's ears.

Matthew Logan, help

The sorcerous glitter winked out from around Launce's staff, and the ebony eyes vanished as well. The frightened barks of Munuc's people continued for many minutes after.

"Agellic's Gates," said Moknay. "What in Imogen's name are we up against?"

The hushed comment died amidst the turmoil of Munuc and his kind as they raced frantically about the chamber. Only the grey-furred creature kept its composure, ordering another beast with a rigid arm. Obediently, the black-haired creature loped out of the chamber, scrabbling down a darkened hallway. Through the chaos, the monkey-thing returned, bearing a golden medallion. The elder Munuc accepted the golden necklace and turned its aged eyes on the real Munuc. Without spoken words, Munuc nodded, picked up Launce's staff, and bounced toward Logan. The young man from Santa Monica could only stare down at the monkeylike creatures in puzzlement as Munuc pointed the staff in his direction, urging him to take it. Stunned, Logan complied and his eyes went wide.

Failed, Munuc told him, still gripping the staff. *Something . . . has them. Need other. We . . . no strong enough.*

"You can talk!" Logan exclaimed out loud.

Munuc smiled, shaking his head. *Not your language,* he explained. *Staff let us speak . . . you. You must . . . earn staff power. Help, will do. We can no help.*

The grey-haired Munuc lifted the medallion toward Logan. It was a circular plate of bronze, an eight-sided piece of amber mounted in the center. Red and blue ink of some sort decorated the edges with foreign script.

Take, Munuc told him. *Help find sprite, be-may.*

"I can't take it," Logan protested. "It wouldn't be right."

Danger magnitude, Munuc replied. *Must take. Must take. Was Launce. We can no help. Need other.*

"Other what?" Logan questioned, ignoring the looks his companions gave him.

Other help . . . find sprites, explained Munuc. *We no enough.* A hairy finger jabbed at the medallion. *That help. Keep you live.*

"But I . . ." the young man started, but his voice caught in his throat. Keep you live? "Just what the hell are we up against?"

Fear seeped into Munuc's black eyes. *Can no name!* he apologized. *No name! For kill sure! Need other!* Munuc offered Logan the medallion. *Must take. Launce. Magic good.*

Magic, Logan mused to himself. Now I don't want it for certain! The more magic I'm around, the faster I suck it up!

But must take! Munuc answered. *Help will! Help! Sprites die!*

Die? Logan repeated, knowing now Munuc could read his thoughts through the staff as he could read Munuc's. This thing will kill the sprites?

And Heart! And Heart! Munuc nodded, the fear still in his eyes.

Sweat coated Logan's palm as he slowly took the medallion from the hairy hand that held it. No buzz of Sparrill's magic filled the young man's mind, yet that odd sensation of numbness deadened the nerves in his hand.

All right, he told Munuc, I'll take it. Hopefully, it'll help speed things up. But who do I go to now? Who else can help me?

Nature, Munuc declared. *Need Nature! More strong!*

Logan nodded. Yeah, Mara was right when she suggested that, but who? I don't quite know the population around here like you might.

Thing cause . . . pain, Munuc tried to explain. *Kill land. Kill Heart! Wants do. Take first sprites! Hurt land! Need Nature! Power Nature! Madman!*

Madman? Logan echoed, his thoughts turned inward. What in the world did Munuc mean by that? Where was there a Nature-linked, powerful madman?

Logan blanched.

"Uh, guys," he sputtered out loud, almost losing his weak hold upon the medallion and staff. "Munuc and his people did their best to help us but they're not strong enough. Still, I know who we've got to go to next."

"Who?" Thromar wanted to know.

Logan wiped the sweat that formed on his brow. "Uh . . . um . . . would you believe, Zackaron?"

Moknay's face paled. "I can see it's going to be one of those days."

Logan's eyes remained locked on the medallion dangling about his neck and the oaken staff strapped to his horse's side. Both were magical—or so Munuc said—and both could be used by Logan. The idea of magic certainly did not thrill the young man, since it had been magic that had gotten him here in the first place. However, Munuc and his people had been so terrified of those black-filled eyes—and that whispering plea for help from the sprites—how could Logan refuse? He could not bring himself to be *that* selfish! Using a little bit of magic would not, as the Smythe had told him, make him an instant spellcaster. It took time, thank God!

Logan cast a swift glance at the Roana that faded in the west. A pang of guilt swept through the young man at the thought of the sprites, imprisoned by some hulking monster with flaring black eyes. With the Smythe dead, the sisters had called upon Logan for help, and he didn't even recognize them! Some help he was!

A delicate hum began to pierce the afternoon air, and the guilt churning in Logan's stomach transformed into a painful, numbing distortion. Perspiration splashed across the young man's face, and an overpowering desire to be sick gripped Logan by the kidneys. The muted buzz of disharmony tried to force its way through, yet was blocked by some invisible force. Nonetheless, Logan's newly acquired medallion began to glisten, its red and blue lettering twinkling like miniature stars.

Unable to steady himself, Logan pulled his yellow and green mount to a halt and wiped a line of sweat from his forehead. The ogre, stomping behind him, noticed the young man's sickness and hurried to help him. Unexpectedly, its ears picked up the soft hum radiating from the forest and it backed away, eyes wide.

"Maaaaaagic," it gasped.

The three riding ahead slowed their mounts and looked back. The sight of Logan drenched in sweat, swaying weakly in his saddle, alarmed Mara. The priestess swiftly jerked her red-and-gold horse around and reached the young man's side. It appeared to be a relapse of his odd collapse outside Debarnian, she noted. Then she too heard the consistent buzz fluttering in the afternoon sky.

Moknay pulled his horse around, violently whacking a gloved hand across Thromar's back. "Demon dung!" he cursed. "Let's get out of here!"

"What?" Mara queried, trying to steady Logan. "What is it?"

In answer to her question, a flare of man-shaped blackness stumbled out of the forest, its white eyes wide on its otherwise featureless face.

"Blackbody!" Moknay cried, the electric charge he experienced on a previous run-in replaying itself for his nerves.

"Blackbodies can be destroyed," Thromar calmed his companion. "Friend-Logan did so to the last one that dared cross our path."

"Logan had the talisman!" Moknay yelled furiously. "Let's get out of here!"

Mara's green eyes flicked from the pale and sweaty Logan to the stumbling figure of energy. The helplessness in both Logan's eyes and the Blackbody's was unquestionable. Each needed medical attention of one kind or another. Of course the priestess had heard of the vast powers Blackbodies held, but there was something definitely . . . unnatural here.

The Blackbody advanced, staggering a few paces to the right.

"I'll never understand why creatures of Cosmic proportions always seem to bump into us," Thromar muttered, stroking his beard.

Moknay's terror was mounting as he noticed the glimmering medallion about Logan's neck. "Did Munuc say just how powerful that necklace is?" he asked.

"It was magical," Logan gasped. "That's all."

"Maaaaaagic," whimpered the ogre.

Moknay delved into his cape and extracted his katar. "It's not bad enough we're on our way to see the most powerful, *mindless* spellcaster in all of Sparrill, but we've been interrupted now by a magical Demon and another Blackbody! Brolark, sometimes I wonder why I get up in the morning!"

Soft boots crunched the foliage underfoot as Mara dismounted. Wide-eyed, Moknay could only stare as the dark-haired priestess

neared the stumbling Blackbody. Thromar hurriedly jerked free
his sword and tried to move forward, yet Smeea refused to get
near the crackling form of black energy, remembering all too well
the Cosmic power bursting about it.

Concern fought down the illness storming within Logan's frame.
The sight of Mara approaching the Blackbody freed the young man
from his sickness, and he leapt off his horse, his legs almost giving
out beneath him.

"Mara!" Thromar boomed. "Don't touch it!"

Mara looked back at her companions. "It's hurt," she announced.

Such a simple comment, and yet, the shock was evident on
Thromar and Moknay's faces. Somehow, something other than
Logan had done damage to a Blackbody! That very fact stunned
both Rebel and Murderer equally.

Logan tried to follow after Mara, but the queasiness refused
to leave him. Almost mirroring the Blackbody's moves, Logan
staggered toward the creature while it staggered toward him.

"*You,*" the Blackbody croaked, its eyeless white orbs focusing
on Logan. "*Once again you bring out the Macrocosm. Know you
not what havoc is wreaked?*"

There was no forbidding, condescending tone to the Blackbody's words, Logan realized. It was only stating what it knew
to be obvious.

Mara, meanwhile, had frozen between Logan and the Blackbody, her emerald eyes wide with fear.

"*I place my existence in your hands, you who hold sway to the
entire multiverse,*" the Blackbody declared, almost falling to the
forest floor. "*I am a Being of the Megacosmos, yet still feel the
shattering of this world.*"

Mara took a step back.

The plight Logan and his friends faced was also faced by the
Blackbodies, Logan understood. Oh, what was it Moknay had
said? Blackbodies were responsible for the very fundamental
nature of matter? Now that Nature was being distorted, so were
the Blackbodies themselves!

The wounded form of energy took a limping step forward.
"*Please,*" it rasped, "*you must set the Balance of Nature aright.*"

A shrill scream suddenly ripped through the forest as the Blackbody crumpled to the ground in a convulsion of agony. Black
flames shot from the creature's humanlike shape as a grotesque
monster sprang out of the brush. Pale, sickly whitish flesh glistened under the matted and sparse coating of fur, and melted,

warped eyes turned on the horses and their riders. Contorted, irregular rows of teeth protruded from its mouth and lower jaw, and serpentine tentacles writhed from the twisted and unnatural torso. A ridged, snaillike organ coiled itself about on the monster's forehead, a third eye blinking from its stump. At one time it may have been a forest animal not uncommon to Sparrill's woods, Logan considered, but now it was a complete and utter perversion of nature.

The Blackbody screamed again as the malformed creature lunged forward, its tentacled arms weaving through the trees. Thromar jammed his heels into Smeea's flanks, but the red-and-black horse balked, terrified of both Blackbody and beast. Moknay fumbled with his weapons, trying to replace his katar and withdraw a throwing weapon, yet his still persistent apprehension of magic made his usually steady hands shake.

An intense eruption of fear hit Logan as he saw how near Mara was to the hulking, bearlike monstrosity. The priestess had her sword out, yet the mass of the beast was immense. The jagged rows of teeth, the winding, snakelike tentacles—Mara alone could not battle this thing!

Logan ripped free his Reakthi blade and darted to the priestess's side. Mara gave him a curt glance, smiled briefly, and pointed her sword toward the Blackbody.

"We've got to help it out of here," she said.

Logan shook his head, never taking his eyes off the mockery before them. "We can't touch it," he informed her. "Our hands pass right through them."

"But there's got to be some way to help it," she protested.

"Kill this thing," Logan replied, wishing his legs would stop quivering. "Both Blackbody and this Nature-distorting magic are linked to some kind of Balance."

"The Balance of the Wheel," Mara nodded.

Leaves cascaded to the ground as the bearlike monster roared. The bellow rang in Logan's ears as a squall of both fury and pain. Whatever lurked at the bottom of this took natural animals and twisted them, driving them insane with rage and agony.

"*Use the Forces of that which is natural,*" the Blackbody wheezed. "*Mere weapons alone can not quench the horror of what is happening.*"

Mara nodded at the Blackbody's words, and Logan blinked. "You seem to know what's going on," he observed.

Mara gave the struggling Blackbody a fear-filled glance. "I may," she whispered, and the terror in her green eyes deepened.

A mucus-lined limb thrashed overhead, and Logan jumped back, bringing his sword up. Blood leaked from a slight wound in the monster's tentacle as it released an anguished howl, its three eyes ablaze. Mara drove in, her sword piercing the creature's breast. Thundering, the beast knocked the priestess's sword aside, unbalancing Mara herself.

"*Nature*," the Blackbody urged, grasping out for Logan's Nikes. "*Only the natural can balance the unnatural.*"

Speak in English, goddamn it! Logan snarled mentally, hating every second of this mystery-enshrouded conflict. What the hell natural things could he use?

As Logan looked around him helplessly, the warped creature sprang forward in an enraged charge, blood oozing from its wounds. Trees shivered and branches broke free as the titanic beast pushed its way toward the young man and the priestess.

A tree branch rebounded off of Logan's shoulder and knocked the young man to the forest floor. The sudden shock of pain was dimmed by a golden flicker of light at Logan's chest, and the young man lifted Munuc's medallion. It belonged to Launce, Logan hurriedly thought, therefore the chances of its being a natural object are very high. But how the hell do I use it?

Logan lifted the medallion off his chest and raised it toward the bear-thing. Instantly, the third eye widened, and the maddening rush ceased. A grim smile played across Logan's face as he turned the medal on one side, the glittering chunk of amber flaming like gold. The bear-thing unexpectedly howled, its fury overcoming its initial hesitation.

Great! Logan muttered to himself. It knows I can't use the damn thing!

"Matthew!" Mara shouted, scrambling out of the beast's way.

Logan saw how near the creature came to the priestess and wanted to throw down the medallion. Come on, goddamn it! he cursed silently, strangling the bronze plate. If you're gonna do something, do it now! Work! Work!

A painful blast of light caught Logan on the side of the head, and numbness worked its way into every crevice of his body. When he reopened his eyes, the battle scene was gone. In its place was a thoroughly different kind of world. Logan could see the myriad molecules that made up the shambling creature that menaced him and Mara. Mara herself had become a glittering form of yellow-gold lights, as had Thromar and Moknay. The Blackbody had simply vanished, and in its place there lay a man-shaped portion of universe—a titanic gyroscope whirling around at its center. Green, brown, and silver lights flickered in the millions of atoms and molecules that formed the trees and bushes around him, and all else was red.

Logan returned his gaze to the hideous mockery of nature and studied its structure. Among its naturally colored molecules, ebony pinpricks of energy pushed into the natural order. In fact, the tentacled third eye was made up completely of these black sparks, as were the extra rows of fangs. Logan could see the distortion clearly now and focused his mind on those ebony molecules of sorcery. Although the action was mental, the oozing touch of slime and sticky-dry fingers tingled across the young man's body each time he "touched" a black spot. Cautiously, he tried to cast the black formations out of the creature's makeup, yet the ebony dots gave little ground.

The sensation of a million parasitic worms burrowing through his intestines rattled Logan's concentration, and the black sparks regained their strength. A fury built up inside him as Logan once again tried to evict the invading molecules, yet there was a hideous roar from the bear-thing and its molecular form raced the concentrating Logan.

"Friend-Logan!" Thromar's voice reached his ears.

Logan panicked. Through the magically induced sight of the medallion, Logan grabbed hold of the bear-thing's molecules and pulled. An agonizing shriek split the afternoon air as the creature exploded, its molecules magically ripped apart and cast out into the red sky. Numbness washed over Logan's mind, and searing pain jolted his limbs. When he opened his eyes, he sat in the forest.

There was no sign of the bear-thing.

"What . . . Where'd it go?" the young man stuttered.

"You did it!" Mara exclaimed. "Somehow you destroyed it!"

Logan hung his head in both exhaustion and shame. "I didn't mean to," he mumbled.

Energy crackled as the Blackbody rose to its feet-shaped base, the whiteness of its eyes brightening. It nodded its thanks to Logan, sparkling shocks of black power leaping from its human-oid form.

Drained physically and mentally, Logan weakly returned the nod and stared at the medallion around his neck. One of the amber's eight facets still glittered dully, its sorcerous abilities stilling itself. In surprise, Logan wondered if all he had used was one facet, and, if such was the case, did the remaining seven each do something different?

"*You have soothed that which you search for,*" the Blackbody declared, "*yet there shall come a time when He will strike again. The Balance has been greatly distorted, and my existence and that of all my brethren lies in your hands. Only you who are an Unbalance in himself may set things right.*" The Blackbody retreated. "*Remember, only the natural can Balance the unnatural.*"

The flaring, man-shaped figure vanished into the forest.

Moknay leapt off his grey-and-black horse, gave Logan's medallion a sidelong glance, and sneered. "What I'd really like to know," he said, "is who is 'He'?"

Logan looked away from Moknay and gazed at Mara. The priestess lowered her eyes, reluctant to speak but fearful not to.

"I think I have an idea," she answered, her voice low.

"Who?" Thromar blurted.

Mara shook her long, dark tresses, formulating the proper words. "While I studied at Agellic's Church, I learned much more than just the Art of Lelah. Among such things, I was told of the creation of our land and the battle that took place shortly after Sparrill's birth."

Moknay nodded his head impatiently. "Yes, yes," he urged. "The one between Gangrorz and Roana. What about it?"

"In our myths," Mara went on, "Gangrorz is referred to by many different names, most commonly as the Worm. His other titles, however, were the Wreaker of Havoc and the Shatterer. Twice, the Blackbody made mention of those other names."

"You can't honestly think that we're up against someone who's been dead since Sparrill's youth, can you?" Thromar asked.

"Whoever said Gangrorz died?" frowned Moknay. "Roana survived, didn't she? So did the Bloodstone."

"But what of Gangrorz's Tomb?" the fighter argued. "What of Lake Atricrix?"

"What of it?" Moknay retorted. "Roana has a river named after her, doesn't she?"

Mara pursed her lips grimly. "The distortion of Nature, the missing sprites, the Demonic activity—all of it easily relates back to the Worm himself," she declared.

Logan sat off to one side, silently soaking in all the information. Of course, his rationale reminded him, this was only speculation . . . and yet, the young man could not help but feel Mara had hit the nail on the head. Only someone as powerful as the myths said the Worm was could do such horrors to Sparrill in such a short time. But what really frightened Logan—what truly struck him to the very bone—was Gangrorz's initial task: to find and destroy the very object Logan searched for . . . the Heart of the Land!

·6·

Enemies

Quick, purposeful footsteps resounded off the marble flooring, leaving hollow, ominous echoes to fade softly behind them. A dark robe swirled arrogantly about legs that appeared too thin to support the human body. Gnarled hands clenched and unclenched reflexively, and an unseen light source gleamed dimly off the foggy left eye.

The marble hallway enlarged, filling out into a squarish chamber of marble. Large pillars of stone stood erect, their tops fading into a gloomy blackness that was not shadow. Here and there damp clumps of water plants lay strewn across the floor, brackish waters trickling from their stems. Jerkily, Groathit's right eye trailed the line of plants into a corner and a scowl drew across his skull-like features.

A dark shape billowed upward from the corner, pliable flesh folding and unfolding into a giant, maggotlike form. Evil, flaring black eyes glimmered down at the Reakthi spellcaster, and numerous rows of teeth stretched across the wormlike face.

"He knows my Name," a deep, accented voice rumbled.

Groathit's scowl grew, his bony hands clenched tightly. "So?" he snarled.

"My Name is known; my Powers are halved," the creature declared.

The gnarled sorcerer cast an accusing finger at the malleable beast rising and expanding in the corner. "You allowed him to learn your Name," Groathit barked. "I told you there were no games to be played here! Matthew Logan is to die!"

Another row of teeth formed as the creature spoke. "He is not my primary task." Nostrils gaped upon the wormlike face, then vanished. "Nor are you my Master."

Groathit's right eye flashed and the knuckles of his clenched hands turned white. "You dare?" he shrieked, the flesh of his face taut. "Without my aid you would still be lying dead, beast! Remember that!"

The flashing black eyes of Gangrorz sparkled. "I slept the Sleep of the Dead but did not die," the Worm responded. "You only awoke me from my Slumber."

"I recreated life that was extinguished!" Groathit snapped back. "Speak in whatever Cosmic terms you wish, beast, but, by the Voices that created you, you were inanimate!" Veins bulged grotesquely from the wizard's neck as his right eye fixed on the bubbling figure. "You will follow my commands now—not those of your long-gone Masters!"

A squirming tentacle writhed free of the shifting, ductile body and snaked toward Groathit. "Those whom I serve are not gone," replied the Worm. "They created me to wound and destroy that which is Pure and Untainted. Your cause is inferior."

Groathit extended a menacing finger at the *Deil*. "I have the power to see that you do as I say," he threatened, and energy leapt from his hands. "I want Matthew Logan dead, or you shall die in his stead."

The bursts of power crackling about Groathit's fingers dimmed as Gangrorz's black eyes sparked. "I acknowledge your persistence, yet it reeks of ignorance. Know you not what this one seeks?" The forming and vanishing rows of teeth pulled back into a horrid, leering smile. "He wishes to uncover that which I also desire. Although created for one task alone, I am unable to find that wretched Heart. Therefore, I shall continue my destruction, damaging that which is Pure by damaging the land, until this Matthew Logan finds what he and I both seek. Then my task shall be completed, and, perhaps, I shall comply with yours." The bulbous, ever-shifting head of Gangrorz turned and fixed on Groathit. "You fear this being."

Intense fury blazed in Groathit's good eye. "Groathit fears no one!" the wizard thundered indignantly.

Smiles formed and vanished across the glistening, maggotlike face of the Worm. "Then you are a greater fool than even I imagined."

The dark form slowly sank in on itself and silence filled the great mausoleum. The rage burned within Groathit as he stood glaring at the now-still bulk.

"He halved your Powers!" the spellcaster finally screamed. "He has not done so to mine! *You* should fear him! Play all the games

you like, beast! Vaugen did so as well, and he has paid dearly."
The wizard wheeled about, his robe billowing around his thin
frame. "You will learn, beast," he snarled, stalking away. "You
will allow Matthew Logan to live. In doing so you will allow
him to gain the upper hand and uncover the Heart before you
do . . . Tell me, who will wake you from the death *he* shall
deal you?"

Black eyes flicked back into being on the collapsed flesh of
the Worm. "I have the sprites," came Gangrorz's deep, accented
voice. "There exists no one else capable of stopping my task."

Now a leering smile crossed Groathit's wrinkled face. "Then
you do not know the capabilities of Matthew Logan," the spellcaster
sneered.

Silence reigned once again.

Thromar reined in his horse and peered through the forest. A
lone bird chirped—a solitary piping, yet it seemed to bring life
back to the otherwise still woods. Rooftops peeked above the
treetops to the west and Logan found himself longing for their
shelter. Home, his mind raced. A roof above my head. Indoor
plumbing. Refrigerator. Stereo.

"Plestenah," Thromar informed the group behind him. "Probably swarming with Guardsmen."

"Probably," Moknay agreed, dismounting, "but there's only one
way to find out for certain."

"Oh, no, you don't, Murderer!" protested Thromar. "Last time
you went sneaking off, I was left to guard the horses!"

"I'll go," Mara declared. "No one's looking for me."

Moknay grinned slyly. "You have a point."

Logan's eyes tore themselves away from the rooftops as an
icy lump of fear landed in his stomach. "No!" he could not help
exclaiming.

Even the ogre started at the emotion in the young man's voice.

"It's a logical choice," Moknay returned. "We're the three
fugitives. No one even knows Mara's traveling with us."

"Unless someone got a message from Debarnian," argued Logan,
his emotions in utter turmoil.

"Might be somewhat difficult seeing as we left all the Guards
for dead," Moknay responded, "and, besides, Mara had on a heavy
cloak like you did."

Mara threw Logan a trusting smile. "I'm a big girl now," she
said. "I know how to take care of myself."

As the priestess clucked her horse forward, Thromar called out: "Don't do anything foolish!"

"Like calling out so close to the town's outskirts," Moknay sardonically added.

The Murderer's joke was not at all funny to Logan as he watched Mara canter deeper into the forest. It wasn't the priestess he was worried about, it was the assortment of dangers that could be awaiting her. There could be Guards, or bandits, or any number of dangers. Mara might not even make it to the town! And how would we know she's okay? She might just disappear and we'll never hear from her again!

Like an explosive raincloud, Logan's emotions erupted. Even the young man's mind gave in to the outburst of feelings raging within him, and he spurred his horse forward. A startled shout from Thromar was all Logan caught as his green-and-yellow mount swiftly bolted past his companions. Green-and-brown blurs distorted the forest as Logan charged toward Plestenah, his concern and fear on Mara. An abrupt change in his horse's gallop—and the sudden harsh hoofbeats—told Logan he had left behind grass for cobblestones. Heads swung toward him in surprise, and Mara jerked around, her slim hand leaping for her sword.

"Matthew!" the priestess cried. "What's wrong? What's the matter?"

The intense emotions controlling him up and fled, leaving Logan completely without answer. Dumbly, he stared at the priestess, grateful she was safe. Then, unexpectedly, the young man cast a terrified gaze about him. Guards! his now rational mind reminded him. You fool! What about the Guards?

Although Logan's blue eyes roved up and down the small cobblestone streets of Plestenah, he could not spot a single uniform.

"Matthew," Mara said, "what's wrong?"

"Huh?" Logan replied, still peering down the streets. "What? Oh, nothing's wrong. Nothing."

"Then why did you follow me?"

Warmth crept across Logan's cheeks accompanied by a brilliant shade of red. "I—I was worried," he confessed, feeling quite idiotic.

There was a flash of kindness in Mara's green eyes before it was replaced by a very necessary anger. "Matthew Logan," she scolded, "you could have placed your entire quest in jeopardy. What if there had been Guardsmen here?"

Logan started to shrug when his curiosity halted the motion. "Where are all the Guardsmen?" he wanted to know.

"That's just what I was finding out when you came charging in," Mara stated, her angry concern fading. "It seems the Sparrillian . . ."

The priestess was cut off as the earth trembled beneath them and a thunderous voice rent the air: "Fiiiiiiight!"

The townsfolk drawn to the forest's edge by Logan's sudden entrance scattered. Cobblestones shook as massive feet pounded into town and light blue fists flailed through the air. Abruptly, the ogre skidded to a halt, its eyes nervously flicking back and forth. Its friends were here, but there was no fight.

Hooves clattered behind the massive creature as Thromar and Moknay charged headlong into Plestenah, their weapons drawn. Shocked expressions flashed on each of their faces as they drew in their mounts.

"Some stealth," Moknay grunted.

"Stealth doesn't seem necessary, Murderer," Thromar remarked. "Where are all of Mediyan's dungheads?"

Mara released an exasperated sigh. "That's what I've been trying to find out," she replied, "but I won't learn anything if you people keep charging mindlessly into town and scattering the townsfolk."

"Don't blame us," Moknay answered. "Logan charged first."

"A fat lot of good you did at staying behind!" the young man retorted.

The light blue ogre blinked at Logan and Moknay. "Fiiiiiight?" it queried.

"No," Logan snapped harshly at it, "there's no fight."

"Unfortunate, indeed," rumbled Thromar. "I'd like to know who would dare to rob me of my valor and victory today."

"A man named Fraviar," Mara returned. "He rallied the people together and forced the Guards out of town. That was all I was able to learn before certain people started interrupting me."

"Fraviar?" Thromar laughed loudly. "That old coot? *He* rallied the people?"

"And what if I did?" came a voice from the crowd.

Logan swung his head toward the gathered population of Plestenah and spied a large man of about Thromar's size force his way through the throng. Although slightly overweight, Fraviar's girth matched that of Thromar's and his bleary, light blue eyes held that same battle-thirsty gleam. Cropped black hair flecked with grey was tousled atop the tavern-owner's head, yet a thick, dangling mustache drooped across his upper lip. An ugly scar trailed down the left side of Fraviar's face, starting just above his left eye and winding its way to his mustache.

"What brings you back to Plestenah, Thromar?" the heavyset man questioned. "Come to check up on my handiwork?"

"Indeed, friend-Fraviar!" Thromar thundered, dismounting. "I've been wondering when we'd get around to chasing away Mediyan's men!"

Fraviar screwed up the right side of his mouth and spat. "Wouldn't have those whoresons in my town!" he declared. "We've taken care of ourselves for some time now—don't need the likes of them dirtyin' up our streets with their political claptrap!"

Logan suddenly realized his jaw dangled open and closed his mouth. But Plestenah is such a small town! his thoughts protested. How in the world could they have beaten back the Guardsmen? Most of Plestenah's inhabitants were merchants and shopkeepers. Not even Debarnian had chased away the invading Guards, and that was a much bigger town.

"You look shocked, friend," Moknay's voice came from behind the young man. "I told you about the people of Sparrill . . ."

Dazedly, Logan nodded. The people of Sparrill were indeed a force to be reckoned with when riled! Tavern-owners, thieves, and whores were capable of fighting back and chasing away trained Guardsmen with orders to hold and secure all towns! Unbelievable.

"Haven't been able to chase 'em away for good, though," Fraviar was saying. "They've got a troop stationed 'bout a league down the road. Tried plantin' one across the bridge, but we showed them but good! Wouldn't have 'em by our river, neither! Might kill the fish!"

"So they just kept running until you didn't bother them anymore," Thromar nodded. "Sounds like Mediyan's buffoons. A lot of good they're going to do there."

"A lot of good they're going t' do anywhere!" Fraviar corrected, chuckling. He clamped a meaty forearm about Thromar's shoulder. "You and I have to talk, friend-Thromar! What about my sister's talisman? Did that ever come in handy on your last adventure?"

Watching the two massive figures walk away, Moknay faced Mara and Logan. "Looks like we have lodgings for the night."

"But shouldn't we keep going?" Mara inquired. "We need every moment we can get."

"Too true," answered the Murderer, "but you're going to find it very difficult to separate Thromar and Fraviar until after they've talked. Then we'll need at least a night so Thromar can sleep off all the ale he'll guzzle. In the meantime, we'll get some more provisions, a full night's sleep, and, perhaps, some more help from Fraviar's sister . . . she's a sorceress of sorts. Gave Logan a real useful talisman last time we passed through here."

Mara reluctantly nodded. "I suppose a day won't make much of a difference with the Worm."

"Not unless he uses that time to find the Heart before we do," Logan muttered grimly, casting an uneasy glance around him and the town of Plestenah.

His right eye reflecting the magical glow of the chamber, Groathit swung about and faced the writhing, changing mass of Gangrorz.

"Do you hear that, beast?" the spellcaster snarled. "You have a day; what can you accomplish in a day?"

The flaming ebony eyes crackled with energies of unimaginable magnitude. "In a day I could create and destroy a world," the deep voice echoed. "Or swallow an entire ocean. Or twist and wrench the life out of one such as yourself."

"Do so!" Groathit shrieked impatiently. "Slay Matthew Logan *now*!"

A gnarled horn spiraled up out of the Worm's shifting mass and submerged just as quickly. "I do not so wish it," the creature stated.

"I do not care what you wish, beast!" Groathit snapped. "Only what I wish matters! Kill him! Kill him now!"

"You bother me, inferior organism," Gangrorz sighed, and an iron-tipped claw stretched out from the dark pillar of protoplasm. "You hold no sway over me . . . stop pretending that you do. I was placed on this world for one purpose and one purpose only. If you wish another task done, speak with my Masters."

Groathit fought back the insane rage that boiled within his gnarled frame and fixed his good eye on his floating cloud of magicks. Through the hazy portal, the wizard could see Logan and his companions making their way through the winding streets of Plestenah toward Fraviar's tavern, and the spellcaster's hatred amplified itself a hundredfold.

"Do something." Groathit's voice cracked. "Do not allow him such an easy victory." The sorcerer wheeled on Gangrorz, his robe fluttering. "If you will not kill him now, at least make his existence painful!"

A nefarious, ever-changing smile crossed the Worm's pliant features. "There is something I am curious about," Gangrorz rasped. "This being is an Unbalance, yet holds a very powerful object, Pure and Untainted like that which I seek. Perhaps I shall take that from him."

Gangrorz's smile was mirrored on Groathit's face. "Yes," the wizard wheezed, "do so. Teach Matthew Logan the folly of crossing Groathit's path."

The Worm's smile lengthened by a number of teeth as the insidious black eyes focused on Groathit and a deep, resonating laughter spouted from about the *Deil*. Snarling—yet keeping his anger in check—Groathit turned his back on the mocking laughter and peered into his misty spying orb.

"The Smythe is dead, Matthew Logan," the spellcaster sneered, "and I shall see that you do not take his place."

Matthew Logan gently shook the mug of ale before him and watched as the hops swirled and swam about in the dark liquid. Hops, the young man thought, blanching. Yuck! All around him people consumed this foul, hop-infested drink, gulping, refilling, getting plastered. Even Moknay sat off to one side, a mug of the darkly colored beverage in his gloved hand. In his other hand, Logan noted, was a slender whore, peering at the Murderer with lust in her eyes. Thromar and Fraviar were at another table, their deep, booming voices carrying the length of the enormous tavern. Logan had long since lost sight of Mara in the dimly lit and crowded barroom, and only the light blue ogre shared Logan's table, sharing also the young man's silent stares. Even without the constant buzz of disagreement, the young man still felt sadly alone and lost.

"So much for having a good time," he muttered.

"Gooood tiiiime," the ogre responded.

The young man nodded. "I really should be grateful for all of this," he decided. "They're practically throwing a party for me, and—after all that weird stuff in the forest—I need this."

"Weeeeeeird," agreed the ogre, staring at the townsfolk.

"You'd think I could at least use this time to talk to Mara," Logan sighed, propping his head up with his hands.

The ogre cocked its squarish head in Logan's direction, an unspoken question written upon its monstrous features.

Logan let out a small laugh. "Confuse you too, huh?" he queried. "You should see what it does to me. I mean, it was this town . . . this very town where I bumped into Cyrene. Remember her? The white girl?"

The ogre nodded its massive head, smiling crookedly.

"Yeah," Logan continued, "she sure as hell played me for the fool."

"Foooooool?"

"You can say that again," Logan snorted. The young man absentmindedly tapped the hops into another dance in the mug. "And what's really confusing," he went on, "is that I instantly felt so strongly for Mara. And so soon after Cyrene. It . . . It isn't like me to act like that. Christ! One girl split up with me back in L.A. and I ran away and hid to lick my wounds for about three years." Logan's vision blurred as he stared at the swimming, spiraling hops. "It's not like me to place my emotions in danger. Hah! It's not like me to get sucked up into another world and kill people either!"

"Weeeeeeird," the ogre repeated, its crooked smile almost one of understanding.

Shadows splayed across Logan's table in the poorly lit tavern, and the young man looked up. Mara and another woman approached his bench, the former's eyes still a glowing green even in the dim lighting. Mara's companion was a slim female clad in a flowing silver gown, light brown hair tinted by gold curled atop her head. Narrow, almost villainous-looking eyebrows arched above soft brown eyes, and a smile played across her thin lips.

"Matthew," Mara said, introducing them, "this is Danica, Fraviar's sister."

Logan nodded to the young woman, still overcome by his loneliness. True, Mara was here, but with someone else. Somehow that didn't make things quite right. Or else, Logan thought, I just don't want things right.

"I heard my talisman came in handy," Danica said. "I'm glad I could be of some help."

Logan forced a smile to cross his lips, trying to keep his gaze away from Mara. "Saved my life more than once," he said just to be polite. "It actually destroyed a Blackbody . . . did you know it was that powerful?"

"A magical instrument such as that talisman is only as powerful as the user," Danica replied, raising a narrow eyebrow at Logan.

A stab of anger wounded Logan as he watched the wizardess. Why did everyone have to remind him of his impending doom should he remain in Sparrill? He didn't want to be there, let alone be the next great spellcaster of the land! He wasn't like the Smythe—life in Sparrill was just too complicated and disorienting in comparison to the young man's life in Santa Monica. Earth was his home, not Sparrill. He was not staying.

The young man's eyes fell on Mara and his thoughts backflipped.

"Mara was telling me of your dilemma," Danica went on. "I wish I was more magically in tune with Nature to help. Going to see Zackaron is not something I envy you."

"He might not be much help at all," Logan replied, fixing his gaze back on his hop-filled mug of ale. "I met him once before. It wasn't until he recognized the Jewel that he really did something about it. If we waited that long now, we might just give the land over to Gangrorz."

"Gangrorz doesn't want the land," Mara gravely stated. "He wants to destroy it."

Danica's soft brown eyes trained on Logan. "And you're actually trying to stand up to him," she said, awed. "You have courage like a true Sparrillian."

"Well," Logan snarled, "I'm not. And it isn't all courage that's making me do this. It's selfishness too, don't forget that! I want to get back home—Gangrorz is just getting in my way."

"Whatever your reasons, it's a very brave thing to undertake," Danica answered.

"Braaaaaave," the light blue ogre parroted.

Danica placed her hands on the table and Logan saw how slender and delicate they appeared. These were the hands of a sorceress? "Why I really came over here was because Mara told me about a medallion you received," the wizardess declared. "We thought I might be able to tell you something about it."

Logan slipped the bronze plate from around his neck and passed the item to Danica. The ogre peered at the necklace quizzically and its gaze was almost duplicated by Fraviar's sister.

"I've never seen anything like this before," the sorceress admitted after a moment's inspection. "It certainly wouldn't bring in any money for its looks, would it?"

"Appearances aside," Mara stated, "Matthew destroyed one of the Worm's distortions with it."

Logan took a tentative sip of his ale, trying to strain the hops with his front teeth. "I think I only used one side," he said. "Is that possible?"

"You mean of the amber?" Danica asked back. "I suppose so . . . Imogen, I wish I knew more about Natural magicks."

"What's the difference?" Logan wondered. "Magic is magic, isn't it?"

Danica set the medallion down and faced Logan. "Not necessarily," she explained. "There are different sources of magic all across the spinning of the Wheel, thereby making different kinds of magic. Some magic is directly related to Sparrill—like the Heart and that medallion. Others originate from the many alternate planes of power existing here, but invisible to us—like mine and the talisman's. Some are a collection of all the Wheel's many worlds, and others stretch beyond the Wheel toward the outer Forces of Light and Dark—like Groathit's.

"I've heard it said that that Reakthi spellcaster is capable of transforming himself into some kind of Demon/*Deil* manifestation. Such an ability can only be possible through links subtle or unsubtle with the Voices or their servants."

Groathit's monster form! recalled Logan. The young man knew from first-hand experience that the spellcaster could indeed transform himself. And this could mean he had some kind of ties with the Voices. Did he also have some kind of tie-in with Gangrorz's unexpected resurrection?

The young man frowned. Or am I just getting overly paranoid?

Danica passed the medallion back to Logan and the ogre visibly shied away from the necklace this time. Logan ignored the ogre's apprehension and slipped the medallion over his head, tucking it into his sweat jacket. His eyes accidentally caught Mara's as the priestess watched him replace the necklace. Both gazes were quickly averted.

"I'm sorry I can't tell you its powers," Danica apologized, "but it's the kind of item that can only be understood through trial and error. My only advice would be that it seems to focus on Sparrill's natural magicks, so try to use it in that aspect."

I really don't want to use it at all, Logan muttered to himself.

The cheerful noises went on around him, yet Logan felt even farther away than before.

* * *

There was silence—even in this Manmade conglomeration of wood and stones. Dim lights kept the town aglow, and Human creatures strutted up and down their oddly-paved streets. Strange garments clad these bizarre beings, and weird, nonsensical sounds issued from their hideously straight mouths . . . yet that must not matter. Only the Unbalance mattered—the Unbalance and his Natural magicks.

Claws scrabbling on the cobblestones, the Demon made its way to Fraviar's tavern. Lanterns still flickered within, however, few people occupied the bar. Toadlike eyes blinked from one window to the next, peering in at the oddly proportioned and ugly Humans. How Natural their structure was. How utterly obscene were their Untainted forms. But the Creator was back . . . back from a deathlike Sleep to create new and more Demons. And it was the Creator that demanded the Unbalance's magic.

Leathery wings cut silently through the night sky and lifted the gangly Demon off the pavement. With the grace of a spider, the Demon latched its claws onto a window ledge of the second story and pushed its bulging eyes up to the glass. The room was dark, yet no Natural darkness could halt a Demon. Two WoMen slept within, but there was no sign of the Unbalance. Still, Human WoMen were so soft and tender . . . certainly the most delicious of meats should one happen to fall into a Demon's claws . . .

A painful twinge in the back of the Demon's mind reminded the creature that the Creator watched. "Bring me the object that the Unbalance wears around his neck," the Creator had commanded. "Bring me that object and its magicks shall be yours to devour." Such an order could not be turned down regardless that the Creator wanted neither the Unbalance nor his Brethren harmed.

Its slender tongue sliding out of its rounded mouth, the Demon leapt sideways from Mara's window and landed on the next ledge. Claws hooked into the wood and the lean monster held fast, glaring into the second upstairs room.

Darkness once again, yet a lone Human slept inside. The Unbalance! He slept here! Alone!

Quiet claws sliced into the pane of glass separating the Demon from Logan. Sleeping soundly, Logan did not even stir as the toad-eyed beast cut its way into the young man's room. Around him, the night swallowed the noises of Fraviar's tavern. Mara and Danica had retired to their chamber when Logan had, and Moknay had gone Imogen knew where with his handful of hookers. Thromar and Fraviar had both drunken themselves into a stupor downstairs in the tavern itself.

Clinking like a crystal bell, the glass slipped from its frame and the Demon gently set it aside. Silence, the Creator's voice told it. Absolute silence and stealth is Power. Strike from below. Let them not know your presence until it is already too late. *That* can make up half your Power alone.

Claws faintly raked the wooden flooring as the clumsy and malformed Demon lurched toward Logan's bed, its enormous eyes glinting in the moonlight. So weak and helpless these creatures were, the Demon sneered, glaring down at Logan's sleeping form. So absolutely ignorant to the dangers that lurked in the dark.

A long-clawed hand reached out for Logan's bare throat and the golden chain around his neck. An abrupt clump from one corner of the darkened room startled the Demon, yet it did not have time to turn around. Titanic light blue hands clapped shut on the creature's lean and fragile skull and splattered its brains across the bedsheets.

"Deeeeeeeemon!" the ogre boomed, hurling the quivering, shuddering corpse across the room.

Logan's eyes popped open as droplets of warm liquid splashed across his face and bed coverings. He sprang out of bed, strings of veins and arteries drenching the sheets. Logan, however, did not find time to care. He was blind in the darkness until he could get a candle lit.

The young man's door burst open and Mara hurried in. Danica stood behind her, a candle guttering in her delicate hands. At once the young man caught sight of the spattered brains and blood painting his bed and walls yellow-white, and his stomach heaved at the sight. The mashed skull of the Demon dangling atop its twitching cadaver didn't help much either.

Mara's arms entwined about Logan. "Matthew!" she cried.

The young man's queasiness failed to lessen even through the closeness he shared with the priestess. "How'd it get in?" he stuttered. "I . . . What did it want?"

Danica held her candle above the neatly opened window, a frown drawn on her thin lips. "These are not normal Demonic behaviors," she stated.

Yellowish-white lifefluid coated the ogre's hands as it pointed a huge finger at Logan's throat. "Maaaaaagic," it boomed. "Waaaaaant maaaaaagic."

Instinctively, Logan clutched the medallion. "What for?" he questioned.

"Demons consume magic," Mara reminded. "As much as they can get their hands on."

"But surely a Demon would have just broken in," Danica argued. "I've never known one to be so smart."

"Nooooot smaaaaart," the ogre corrected. "Baaaaaad."

Her dark tresses bouncing, Mara nodded. "The Worm," she breathed. "We know who our enemies are—he wants us to know that he knows his as well."

Beads of perspiration broke out along Logan's brow and beneath his palm as his grip tightened on the medallion. "Great," he gritted. "Just great!"

Hooves echoed dully from the wood beneath them as the four horses trotted across the bridge, the Lephar River rushing below them. Clouds fought the rising sun for possession of the sky, and the polar breeze wafted its way through the trees of the forest.

"We're going to have to be much more careful from now on," Moknay said. "It doesn't make sense why the Worm didn't just kill you, but it's obvious he wants that medallion."

"Why not just take it himself?" sneered Logan. "If it's such a great little trinket, why not come and get it?"

"He might be afraid of it," Thromar put in. "And of you."

"The one thing Gangrorz hates is the one thing that can doom him," Mara added. "Nature's own magic."

Moknay brought a gloved finger across his mustache. "And that's why I can't understand why he didn't kill you," he murmured.

"Lucky thing that ogre follows you around like a puppy," Thromar said, smiling his yellowish smile.

Yeah, Logan mused. Luck. Pure, stupid luck. It's a wonder my luck's held out for as long as it has! Every time I start out on some kind of search, my luck goes sour and causes the whole thing to become cataclysmic. I'm amazed my luck just doesn't change next time I'm in combat. One second of bad luck and—Wham! No more Matthew!

Through the silent forest the horses made their way, the light blue ogre keeping up with the animals' pace. The clouds gradually gained command of the heavens and blotted out the sun, splashing shadows across the woods. Thromar began to curse the cloudy sky, glaring unsettlingly at the dirt path that wound its way through the forest.

"Blasted weather," the fighter rumbled. "Can't tell the time of day if the sun isn't going to shine. Fraviar told me it would be safe to travel at least half a day before coming anywhere near Mediyan's Guards—can't tell the day from night if the sun's going to hide from us!"

"Perhaps we should leave the road now?" suggested Mara.

"No sense in running any risks," Thromar responded.

As the riders turned their mounts to the north, shrubbery parted and released three other riders. Questioningly, Logan glimpsed over his shoulder the trio of newcomers and recognized them as the same journeyers they had seen before. The only difference was that one now leveled a crossbow at the group.

"Greetings once again," the lead rider called, no trace of his previous anxiety twinging his expression or his voice. "I'm so glad we could have this second, more appropriately timed meeting."

"If you're common thieves, I've a word of warning to you," Moknay threatened, his gloved fingers flexing.

"Thieves?" the leader remarked sarcastically, seeming insulted. "You demean us, Murderer." The man withdrew his familiar-looking sword and pointed it at Moknay. "We're not just petty vagabonds and cutthroats. We're scouts—searching for three journeyers." A wicked grin stretched across the leader's face. "You three. You can imagine our surprise when we found you—or, should I say, you found us?—much sooner than we expected."

Let him talk, Logan growled. The three of them didn't seem a match for either Moknay or Thromar. And yet . . . there was something about those swords . . .

"So you're looking for us," snorted Thromar. "Many men have come looking for us. What's your business?"

The lead rider pointed his blade in Logan's direction. "Him," he replied.

Diamond-shaped point with a concave face, Logan thought, noticing the rider's blade. Just like my own sword . . .

The young man gave a terrified look at his sheathed weapon and then glared at the vests of chainmail worn by the trio. His hand leapt to withdraw his blade as his mind screamed: *They're not wearing their chestplates!*

"Reakthi!" the young man warned, freeing his sword.

The crossbow whined and a searing jolt of agony tore through Logan's hand. The young man gaped in amazement at the blood fountaining from his own palm and at the crossbow bolt embedded in his flesh. There was another retort from the weapon and Logan felt a painful blow knock him backwards, another quarrel slamming into his right shoulder. Blood raced across his sweat suit as the young man crashed to the ground, his Reakthi blade landing beside him.

What a rotten time for his luck to change . . .

·7·

Wounded

A flurry of thoughts streaked through Logan's mind, dimmed by an overpowering red haze.

Omigodimdead.

Pain coursed through the young man's nerves, and warm, cascading fluid trickled across his arm, soaking into the blue fabric of his sweat jacket. Confused, bewildering pictures flashed across his brain, all accompanied by the intense agony originating from his right side.

Not me, Logan protested. Happens to other people . . . not me. I can't . . . God, it hurts! What . . . ? Need help . . . Call an ambulance! Do something, goddamnit! At least let me pass out!

Mara's emerald eyes went wide with horror as she sprang off her red-and-gold mount. "Matthew!" she exclaimed, falling to her knees beside him. Her hands poised above the young man, almost hesitant to touch him. All that blood, she thought with a gasp. All that blood.

Silver flashed and Moknay held twin daggers. "You bastards," he said.

The crossbow trained on the steely-eyed Murderer and an arrogant smirk crossed the lead Reakthi's lips. "Don't do anything foolish, Murderer," the scout advised. "You might end up like your friend."

Rage boiled in Moknay's grey eyes as he glanced down at the injured form of Logan. Mara met the Murderer's gaze, uncertainty and concern alive in her eyes. Abruptly, heavy footsteps sounded behind the two as Thromar dismounted and headed toward them. The same fury blazing in Moknay's eyes surged in the fighter's, yet a determination not flaming in the former's strengthened in Thromar's.

The crossbow twanged, its quarrel lodging into the tree directly before Thromar's nose. Rage swirling in the fighter's eyes, he stopped, fixing the three Reakthi with a glare of intense hatred. Then, giving the warning shot a cursory look, Thromar resumed his walk.

The scouts did not attempt to stop him a second time.

Throughout all the pain, Logan felt gentle hands touch his wounded arm. Tears blurred his vision—and his contacts felt like they would slip out—but the young man could make out the faces peering down at him. The heavily bearded face of Thromar held lines of deep concern, and that concern echoed in Mara's eyes.

"You're not going to like this, friend-Logan," Thromar said, "but I've got to remove the quarrels."

Teeth clenched, Logan nodded his head. Instant agony speared through his arm as Thromar's callused fingers merely touched the wooden bolt protruding from the young man's shoulder. Then, all at once, the quarrels were gone. No sensations whatsoever stabbed Logan's body until the shock wore away; Logan screamed.

"That hurt . . ." the young man grated.

"That's a good sign," Thromar replied. "I'd be worried if you had lost all feeling."

Shock, Logan's pain-clouded mind understood. My luck hasn't gone all bad. At least I didn't go into shock or something.

Mara inspected the wound in Logan's hand. "Can you move your fingers?" she queried.

Logan stared down at his blood-drenched hand and flexed. A blast of pain exploded in his palm and rocketed up to his brain, yet his fingers were able to move. "Hurts like hell," he breathed, grinding his teeth together.

"He shot you between your thumb and forefinger," Mara informed him. "I was afraid he had hit a bone—he must have missed."

"Of course he missed," the lead Reakthi sneered, leaning forward on his horse. "Imperator Vaugen doesn't want his prisoner damaged beyond use."

"Vaugen?" snarled Moknay, his eyes glinting. "Is that who you're scouting for?"

"None other," the Reakthi scout answered, smirking. "The most successful of all searches, incapacitating and capturing the stranger and his friends. Our Imperator hardly has any need of the other men he brought along."

"Other men?" questioned Thromar, applying a piece of gauze to Logan's wounds.

"Yes," the Reakthi went on. "Imperator Vaugen felt he needed at least two troops of men for you people." A frown crossed the soldier's smug features as he glared at Logan. "Still, after what that scum did to Vaugen . . ."

"Vaugen's . . . dead," Logan strained, trying to sit up and being held down by Thromar and Mara.

"Hardly," the scout remarked, "but he should be. What you did to him . . . no one should have survived that."

"Spout all the information you want," whispered Thromar, bringing his head down to Logan's ear. "Friend-Logan, I hate to ask you this, but do you think you can ride? We need to get out of here before Vaugen and his other men find us."

Logan attempted to sit up once more. He succeeded, yet bright crimson stained the makeshift bandages wrapped about his shoulder. "I . . . I can try," he gasped. "Can't fight."

Thromar placed Logan's sword back in the young man's sheath and stood up. "Hopefully," the fighter whispered, "we won't have to."

Mara's green eyes glittered wonderingly. "What are you planning?" she asked in a hushed voice.

A smile spread beneath Thromar's reddish-brown beard, then was quickly erased as hoofbeats sounded. More men were coming this way, the fighter knew. Many men. If they were going to escape before Vaugen arrived, they had to move fast.

Thromar helped Logan into his saddle, where the young man swayed precariously. However, as the huge fighter mounted his own red-and-black horse, a line of horsemen appeared on the road, all clad in vests of chainmail. Only one figure wore a chestplate that gleamed a dull ebony.

Trying to ignore the throbbing pain in his shoulder and hand, Logan glared at the approaching Vaugen. Flakes of skin peeled off the scorched and scarred scalp, surrounded by the sparse remains of the Imperator's grey-black hair. Melted and fused flesh half closed Vaugen's lips, and three out of five fingers remained on his left hand, yet there was no mistaking the dull grey eyes flickering with presumptuous triumph.

"Matthew Logan," Vaugen sneered, his voice a rasping, rattling wheeze.

"Damn," Logan heard Thromar swear.

There were some twenty men now on the northern portion of the road, all battle-ready. Moknay's eyes flicked to Thromar, his daggers shimmering malevolently in the clouded sunlight. The large fighter turned away from the Murderer's gaze and glanced at the crossbowman. He then glanced southward.

"They can't be thinking of running," Mara whispered beside Logan. "They'd catch up with us for certain."

Logan shrugged and immediately regretted it as soul-wrenching agony blistered upon his right side. Damn! Damn! Damn! Damn! the young man cursed. What I wouldn't give for some codeine . . . some Tylenol . . . anything!

"You are finally mine," Vaugen wheezed, gesturing with his disfigured hand. "I do not take kindly to what you've done to me, but I'm certain—with your ability mine to control—you can undo what you've done."

"You wish," Logan spat, allowing the pain in his body to transmute into anger. This was the man who had killed Launce and the Smythe . . . Logan would sooner die than work for him.

Vaugen's maimed hand waved and the crossbow leapt from Moknay to Mara. "If I am forced, Matthew Logan," the Imperator rasped, "I shall persuade you by killing off your friends . . . and then you. True, you are valuable, but if you will not work for me, I shall see to it that you work for no one."

Logan's face paled as he stared at the crossbow bolt directed at Mara. The crossbowman was an expert, the young man surmised. He would not miss.

"We need a diversion." Moknay's whisper reached Logan's ears.

Logan's head jerked away from the Murderer, back to Mara, then down to peer at the medallion hidden under his sweat jacket. Is there some possible way to use the item without holding it or directing it? he wondered. I sure as hell can't pull it out, lift it up and use it. They'll shoot me down, Mara, and everyone else. Vaugen isn't kidding around this time . . . he really just might kill me.

A second chorus of hoofbeats heralded the arrival of Vaugen's second troop. Unexpectedly, a massive shadow draped itself across the roadway, as if a cloud had passed in front of the already obscured sun. Muted sensations of magic tingled their way into Logan's sore nerves as the veil of shadow bubbled into life, raising itself off the ground and forming a curtain between Logan and the Reakthi.

Vaugen and his men gaped in astonishment as living tendrils of shadow leapt off the forest floor and reached out for them.

"Now's our chance!" Thromar thundered. "Ride!"

The huge fighter wheeled Smeea about and galloped southward down the road. Still stunned by the sudden blockade of shadow, Logan trailed. Wind whistled past the young man's ears, and the harsh movements of his green-and-yellow mount brought sporadic bursts of pain into his right arm. Frantically, the four horses bolted down the dirt path, the forest green-and-brown blurs on either side.

Logan cast a worried glance over his right shoulder and flinched at the jab of pain he received. A lone figure on foot was slowly vanishing behind them, trying valiantly but failing to keep up with the quartet on horseback.

"The ogre!" the young man cried. "What about the ogre?"

"Leave him!" Moknay snapped, his cape billowing. "Whatever you did back there won't stop Vaugen for long! They'll soon be on our heels!"

"I didn't do anything!" Logan shouted back to be heard over the rushing wind and thunderous hoofbeats. "But we can't leave him!"

"We have no choice, friend-Logan!" Thromar called back.

A deep feeling of inability and guilt washed over the young man as he looked back to catch a last glimpse of the light blue ogre. Already the lone figure had disappeared behind them, and in its place was a charging cloud of dust spewed into the air by Vaugen and his twin troops of Reakthi.

"Holy shit!" Logan yelled. "They're right behind us!"

"I thought as much," Moknay nodded, his grim mien stretching itself across his face.

"What are we going to do?" Mara inquired. "We're going to be outrun and outnumbered!"

A strange grin came to Thromar's features. "Just a little bit farther," he urged his companions.

Pain coursing through his frame, Logan grasped tightly to his reins, his left hand feeling awkward and unsteady. Right-handed, Logan found great difficulty using his left hand. Now it was the only grip the young man could trust.

Pangs of sorrow streaked the pain as Logan took another glance over his wounded shoulder. Trust, he mused. The ogre should never have trusted me. Such an innocent, gentle creature. Satisfied by only a few handfuls of food, certainly it was one of the only people Logan could completely trust in this strange, alien world. Is this how I repay my friends? Logan asked himself. The ogre saved my life from that Demon just last night, and now I run off and leave him behind. No one should befriend me here—it's just too damn dangerous!

The air beside Logan's ear screamed as a crossbow bolt tore past him. Moknay also heard the shaft whizz by and wheeled about on his horse, his right arm flashing forward. The air screeched beside Logan's face a second time as Moknay's dagger streaked back toward the oncoming Reakthi. A hideous cry sprouted behind the four and Logan turned to see the crossbowman's horse crash to the dirt, tripping and toppling many of the soldiers behind it.

"There is no escape!" Vaugen screamed, his voice as brittle as a dry leaf. "You cannot escape me this time!"

The Imperator's curses were lost to the wind as the quartet bolted down the forest path. Dust and pebbles spumed into the air, and foam began to dot the horses' mouths. Hooves skittering on loose dirt, the colorful mounts rounded a slight bend in the road. Logan's eyes suddenly went wide and all thoughts of the throbbing in his arm vanished. He tried desperately to halt his mount, but his left hand felt clumsy and unused.

"Keep going!" Thromar boomed. "Keep going!"

Logan gritted his teeth and leaned forward on his yellow-and-green horse, digging his heels into the stallion's flanks. The ranks of Guardsmen scattered. Shouts and orders split the air, yet none of the uniformed soldiers reacted swiftly enough to halt the four fugitives. Men in charge screamed fierce commands, and the Guardsmen regrouped, leading a mounted attack on the oncoming Reakthi.

Thromar released a humorous whoop. "I'd never thought I'd see the day when I'd say the Guards could come to some good!" he roared.

Cape flapping, Moknay glanced behind them. "Lucky thing for us they heard us coming," he stated.

"I think it would be a little difficult to miss hearing two troops of Reakthi," Mara returned. The priestess brushed some of her long hair out of her face. "Why weren't they wearing chestplates?" she questioned.

"Vaugen's ploy," answered Moknay. "Lets them sneak around without being noticed . . . much. Damn! I should have recognized their swords sooner. I'm sorry, Logan."

Logan waved the Murderer off. "Don't worry about it," he said. "I'm not dead." The young man attempted to blink some tears onto his contacts, yet the harsh speed of the wind whipped the fluid away. "Where to now?"

"Westward!" Thromar shouted.

Clumps of grass shot into the air as the fighter pulled Smeea off the road and darted into the forest. The trees were much closer now, and Logan ducked instinctively every time his mount galloped too close to an overhanging branch. The constant dodging of tree limbs helped keep the young man's mind off his bleeding shoulder, and, when no trees loomed near enough to worry, Logan mourned the loss of the light blue ogre.

"We can't ride all day!" protested Mara. "Matthew's wounds need time to heal!"

Thromar screwed up his face, his beady eyes glistening. "To the Ohmmarrious, then!" he exclaimed. "Brolark knows Smeea's going to want a drink after this ride is through!"

Thromar led the quartet through a mossy clearing, leaping his red-and-black horse over fallen trees and patches of mushrooms. Without trees, Logan tried to occupy his mind by spotting the sun. Clouds still clustered in the air, swallowing and filtering the sunlight. Undaunted, Logan glanced at his watch and cursed. The constant red-and-silver glare continued to luminesce from its face. So how the hell are we supposed to know what time it is? the young man wanted to know.

As deep red lights flickered in the west, Logan and his friends arrived at the Ohmmarrious. Only by the blood-red glare above the Hills could Logan tell it was early evening, yet Thromar did not stop. The fighter directed the small band northward along the river, actually entering the water itself so that Smeea left no prints on the bank. The maddening pace the horses had held all afternoon died to a slow trot, and the silent relief was obvious in all of the mounts' eyes.

"What now?" Moknay queried.

"We stop," Thromar curtly responded. "Fording the river at this time of day with the weather growing colder is not what I'd call ideal. And we certainly don't want to build a fire."

Moknay nodded. "No, I suppose we don't." He quietly dismounted, giving the forest to their east a grim stare. "How far do you think Vaugen'll get?"

Thromar raised his bushy eyebrows. "You mean if he hasn't lost the trail by now?" he asked back.

The Murderer nodded swiftly.

In reply, Thromar leapt off Smeea and waved a meaty hand at the trees in dismissal. "He won't come within a league of the river," he declared proudly. "Even though we spent a day in

Plestenah, he and his troops still needed time to catch up with his scouts. That means they've been riding for a while."

"Two troops means he has men to spare—horses, too," Mara put in. "Maybe we should camp in the forest tonight in case Vaugen sends out a horde of scouts."

"Good idea," said Moknay, "and tomorrow we'll ride into the Hills and lose him for good."

As his companions talked, the pain in Logan's arm returned. The muscles of his right side felt stiff and rigid, no longer flexible, and dried blood cracked along the sleeve of his sweat jacket. Each beat of his heart seemed to drive an invisible stake of suffering into his shoulder, and a thin line of perspiration crossed his brow.

"Don't you guys have anything to stop the pain?" the young man questioned, clenching his teeth at the increasing fire in his arm.

"Friend-Logan," Thromar apologized, "I forgot all about you. Quickly, let's get your wounds properly washed."

Logan sneered to himself. Yeah, forget all about me like we forgot all about the ogre. God, how could I just ride off and leave him there? He must have been instantly cut down by that damn crossbowman.

Delicately, Logan tried to remove his jacket and instantaneous agony burst upon his shoulder. The pain, he knew, was going to get much worse before it got better . . .

I ain't even got a bullet to bite on! Logan cursed, the aching in his arm and hand still blazing like a wildfire. Already evening again and it hasn't gotten any better! Damn! It's times like this when you really begin to miss the things you took for granted. I hate the stuff, but what I wouldn't do for a glass of brandy right now . . . !

Logan tried to shut out the throbbing pain in his right arm and glanced behind him. Greenery stretched out below him, dusty brown rocks immediately behind him. The four horses all bobbed their heads in exhaustion, Smeea arrogantly tossing her red mane into the evening air. Once again they had pushed their horses to the limit. They must have forced their mounts up to speeds of some fifty miles an hour . . . since that was around a horse's maximum speed, Logan tried to recall. Usually a horse doesn't run that fast, but they tended to go faster when goaded by a rider.

Logan appreciatively patted his yellow-and-green horse's neck

and looked up at the Hills before him. The area was a mixture
of colors. Here and there lush patches of grass sprouted on every
available ledge, but large boulders broke into this greenery with
their drab browns and greys. Few trees grew in the foothills, yet
what ones existed grew to tremendous heights, their gnarled roots
twisting and coiling above as well as below ground.

Thromar motioned his companions to follow him and took the
three over a slight incline that blocked the eastern portion of Sparrill
from sight. The sun gradually dipped behind the Hills themselves,
spreading shadows of different values across the stones and carpets
of grass. Logan warily eyed the flowing rivulets of shadow as they
covered the hilly regions and beyond.

With an ungraceful thump, Thromar leapt off his horse and
looked over the western mountains. The fighter's bearded face
wrenched into a frown as his tiny eyes caught hold of something
and held fast.

Moknay instantly noticed the fighter's gaze. "What is it?" the
Murderer queried.

"More distortions," Thromar muttered, pointing westward.

Logan cocked his head and tried to catch sight of the warped
area before the sunlight was gone for good. Prodded on by his
own curiosity, Thromar led Smeea toward the mutated portion of
Sparrill, and his friends trailed. Rocks gradually became grotesque,
bulbous structures, appearing more yielding than of stone—like
rotting fruit or something, Logan noted. The grass had turned
black, unnatural, jagged blades stabbing upward. Slopes and
inclines made up of loose dirt had taken on brownish-grey hues,
and the entire scene was marred by an enormous inverted cone
at its center.

Thromar released Smeea's reins and stepped up to the edge of
the conical depression. "I don't get it," the fighter said. "This
crevice looks almost natural."

Recognition glittered in Mara's eyes as she dismounted and
approached the fighter. "Maybe it is," she said. "I've read something about ealhdoegs digging out depressions like this to catch
rainwater, but I didn't think they made them this large."

Moknay smiled briefly. "Their own water barrel," he laughed.
"I bet they won't be too happy about what Gangrorz has done to
their water flask."

Logan pulled his eyes away from the massive crater. "Wait a
minute," he responded. "What's an ealhdoeg?"

"They're about the size of a wolf," Mara explained, "with large forepaws and claws for digging. Exceptionally intelligent and relatively harmless. Still, I didn't think their holes were quite so big . . ."

Unexpectedly, Thromar let out a startled shout and disappeared over the edge into the inverted cone. Her dark hair flying, Mara whipped about to spy a pinkish-grey tentacle coil outward from the crater and entwine about her leg.

"Carrioncreator!" she shrieked, also vanishing down into the cone.

Stunned, Logan gaped from atop his horse. Moknay, however, sprang out of his saddle, daggers glinting in his hands. More writhing, twisting limbs sprouted from the pit like bizarre plants. There was a garbled scream from deep within the earth as one of Moknay's daggers sank deep into the creature's pinkish-grey tentacle. Hands clutched at the edge of the cone as Mara tried to pry herself away from the monster's grip, kicking futilely at the limb grasping her foot.

Logan jumped down from his horse, his right arm instinctively reaching for his sword. Agony exploded up and down the length of the young man's right side as the wound on his shoulder broke open, spilling blood down the front of his jacket. Bursts of pain clouded his mind, and Logan crashed to his knees, trying to shut out the unbearable sensations blistering on his arm. He clenched his teeth, glancing up through tears of agony. A number of twisting, coiling pink limbs thrashed out of the inverted cone. Grasped in one of the flailing tentacles was Thromar, his blood-caked sword hacking at the very limb that held him prisoner.

"Let go of me, you overgrown mucksnake!" the fighter threatened.

"It regenerates!" Mara cried out, her own sword flashing silver.

Moknay's eyes gleamed as he replaced his daggers. "We need something other than weapons," he mused. "What about fire?"

"Brilliant idea," Thromar returned. "Kill this thing but attract Vaugen!"

The Murderer cast Thromar a snide glance. "I don't think you're in any position to argue," he quipped.

"I'm in no position to do anything!" the fighter exclaimed. "And I wish *you'd* hurry up and do something, Murderer! I've been embraced by much nicer-looking creatures than this thing!"

Moknay gave the distorted hillsides a swift glance. "Oh, I don't know," he replied. "This creature has your looks."

There was an abrupt scream from Mara as the priestess lost her grip on the edge of the cone and was lifted into the air along with Thromar. The warped and discolored dirt around and in the crater shifted, and a faceless mouth appeared near the bottom of the cone, fangs inches long glistening with a thick sheet of yellowish saliva.

"Acid!" Mara shouted.

Logan's head jerked up at the priestess's frightened cry and the pain in his shoulder subsided briefly. Mara is in dire danger! the young man's pain-befuddled brain understood. Something in that region of perverted nature had hold of both the priestess and Thromar, and Logan was serving no purpose kneeling off to one side.

The young man went for his sword again and an invisible lightning bolt of misery electrified his right arm. A half-stifled scream broke through his lips, and he grabbed at his bleeding shoulder. Fuck that idea! he cursed. I'm out! Forget it! I'm going to bleed to death and Mara and Thromar are going to be eaten!

Holding tightly to his wounded shoulder, Logan felt something other than blood briefly touch his hand. It was cold, his pain-numbed mind informed him. Cold and metallic . . . the medallion!

Clumsily, Logan's left hand jerked the bronze medallion free of his bloodstained jacket and held it up to his face. His vision blurred as crimson fluid dribbled down his right side, but the young man could see the eight-sided piece of amber twinkling faintly in the diminishing sunlight.

Magic! Logan shouted to himself. You're *not* helpless! You can do something to save Mara! Magic!

Concentrating on the medallion rather than on the pain erupting from his shoulder, Logan closed his eyes. A sudden feeling of nausea gripped him by the throat and a slight sense of weightlessness forced the young man's eyes to pop open. Nothing around him had changed—the creature still gripped Mara and Thromar, and Moknay stood off to one side thinking—yet another world had been added. Perhaps it was like Danica had told him, Logan recalled. Those other planes of power that existed in Sparrill . . . perhaps this was one of them.

Logan wonderingly peered up at the millions of streaks of color and lights that zoomed around him. Like a thousand renegade rainbows, Logan and the Hills were surrounded by an array of beams, all flashing certain colors and all arcing insanely across and through Logan's physical world. These were bolts of energy, Logan comprehended. Beams as yet unused and usually invisible . . . as Danica had explained. Now, however, the medallion enabled Logan to see this other plane—this secondary world of magic—and made its power accessible.

Logan reached out a tentative finger toward a line of reddish streaks. One of the flashes touched his hand and halted, going limp like a piece of string. Pins and needles tingled the young man's left hand as the strand of red energy dangled from his fingers, and the muted feeling of disharmony swarmed up from below him. Then, still not fully understanding, Logan tossed the twine toward his captive friends.

Energy crackled and the bolt came alive, re-forming itself into a blazing streak of magic. The only difference was—it now existed on both planes.

The carrioncreator shrieked as the crimson bolt slashed a tentacle in half, simultaneously cauterizing the wound. No new limb could grow through the fused flesh, and the remaining limbs whipped into a frenzy of anger.

Logan reached out and plucked another red slash out of its course. With a backward wave of his left hand, the young man sent the second arrow of sorcery howling toward the monster, this time aiming more accurately.

Mara crashed to the distorted ground outside the crater, hurriedly unraveling the severed tentacle still gripping her boot. Her green eyes were wide with wonder and admiration as she looked at Logan.

Moknay ducked a flailing tentacle and rolled backwards. Red beams of energy were erupting from Logan's hands! The Murderer blinked. The medallion and amber were glimmering, so Logan must be using that . . . but they were shooting right out of Logan's hands!

Logan pulled another beam into his hand and sent it hurtling into the physical world as magic. Thromar released a shout as the tentacle holding him split in half and he started to plunge toward the carrioncreator's acid-filled maw. Fear welled up inside Logan as he saw what he had done, and his mind raced for a way to save the fighter. Obediently, four streaks of golden light left their designated route and sped to Thromar's aid, holding him aloft. Gradually, Logan realized he held full control over this plane while here, and the spells reacted instantly to his thoughts and needs. " . . . it seems to focus on Sparrill's natural magicks,"

Danica had guessed, and these planes of power were as natural as Sparrill itself. Just how powerful was this medallion?

Logan gently levitated Thromar away from the carrioncreator's pit and set him down beside Moknay. Then, blue eyes gleaming, Logan turned to examine the shooting bolts of power surrounding him. A purplish strand of energy obeyed his unspoken command and leapt into his hand. Although left-handed, Logan's aim was true.

Moknay, Mara, and Thromar watched in stupefaction as a blazing quarrel of purple sorcery soared out of Logan's hand and arced into the carrioncreator's cone. A hideous scream went up from the hidden monster as the blast sent clouds of dirt and blood spuming into the air. Warped rocks careened sideways, crashing into the pit and burying the beast beneath them. The maimed and injured tentacles retracted, seeking the shelter of the warped and distorted ground once more.

Logan smiled and blinked away the alternate plane; the single facet of the amber faded.

The young man threw his companions a weak grin before the loss of blood, pain, and sudden exertion finally caught up with him, and he collapsed.

Cool, misty white clouds floated about him as Matthew Logan opened his eyes. Only the refreshing coolness played itself upon the young man's skin, and it wasn't until he rolled over that a flash of pain reminded him of his previous evening.

Letting out a groan, Logan drew himself into a sitting position and blinked. The sun peeked back at him from the east and an odd, almost pulling sensation awoke from the west. Questioningly, Logan turned to look behind him and found Mara watching him, a smile of greeting on her lips.

"How are you feeling?" she queried.

Logan felt a stab of pain lance through his right side as he flexed his hand. "Sore," he replied, clearing the sleep from his voice.

The priestess nodded, her eyes sparkling in the early morning light. "That's to be expected," she answered. "You're not giving yourself time to heal."

"It's not me who's stopping it," the young man returned, pleased to be conversing with the young woman, "it's things like that carrionwhatchamacallit." Logan gave the area around him a curious look and noticed the scenery had changed overnight.

"Hey," he wondered, "where'd it go?"

Mara's smile remained. "We moved a little farther west," she explained. "Moknay didn't want to camp so close to that thing's lair. Especially since you seemed so badly off."

"Well," the young man remarked, "I certainly got enough sleep."

Mara nodded in response, her smile never faltering.

A sense of well-being began to seep into the constant aura of gloom and despair enshrouding the young man as he locked onto Mara's green eyes. Silence lingered between the two, yet they shared a gaze both had been longing for for weeks.

An abrupt tug of displacement broke Logan's thoughts and he glanced into the hills.

As suddenly as the feeling arose, it vanished. Confused, Logan turned away from the mysterious tugging and looked down at his jacket. He could feel fresh bandages gently covering his wounds, yet dried blood caked along the front of his sweat suit. Self-consciously, the young man began to wipe the brittle flakes of lifefluid away, flinching when his brushing came too close to his injuries.

"I must look like I'm half-dead," he murmured.

"Better to look half-dead than to be that way," answered Mara. The priestess curled her slim legs underneath her and faced Logan. "There's something I've wanted to ask you," she said. "Yesterday . . . how did you do that?"

Logan threw her an awkward grin. "The medallion," he admitted. "I wanted so badly to help you I even let myself use magic."

And probably took in a good portion of it, the young man's pessimistic side snarled. What are you doing, ace? Trying to suck up all the magic like the Smythe said you would?

"I must admit," a third voice shot up, "there are times when that magical claptrap comes in handy. At least using that medallion doesn't tax your wounds."

Logan swung about and saw Moknay propping himself up on one arm, smirking mischievously at the pair. "How long have you been up?" the young man demanded.

The Murderer's grey eyes twinkled. "Oh, from about 'How are you feeling?' 'Sore.' "

Logan felt the redness spreading across his cheeks. His embarrassment was foolish, his mind tried to tell him. You didn't say anything *really* personal, you know. So what if you acted like life is grand and everything's cheery in the world. Can't you be a little friendly with your friends?

Logan's blush only deepened.

"Leave it to a man without a heart to do something utterly heartless," Thromar put in, rolling over to face his companions.

"Better to be heartless than brainless," Moknay retorted, scampering to his feet and putting on his cape.

"Are you insinuating something, Murderer?" Thromar growled playfully, raising his bushy eyebrows.

Moknay's eyes widened in mock horror. "Me?" he asked. "Never!"

Mara pulled herself to her feet, dusting off her backside. "Since we're all up," she stated sarcastically, "shall we start?"

The humor dispersed from Moknay's eyes and voice as he glanced at Logan. "That's up to Logan," he declared. "Thromar and I weren't the ones who met Zackaron in his home; Logan was. He'll have to lead—if he's up to it."

As the burdening of continuing the quest once again fell upon Logan's shoulders, another brief twinge of strangeness tapped the young man's mind. It almost seemed to be a distortion of wind . . . and yet, throughout the forced silence of Sparrill's magic, it became almost natural.

A wicked grin stretched across Logan's face as he recognized the flow of Unbalance. Zackaron, like the land itself, radiated a sort of magical pulse about him. Logan had felt it before while in the Hills. In fact, it had helped him find the insane spellcaster the first time.

It would work a second time.

"I'm up to it," Logan stated, pushing himself to his feet with his left hand.

The four swiftly mounted and began a casual trot through the Hills of Sadroia. Logan rode up front, his eyes and ears straining to pick out the odd disturbance that marked Zackaron's cavern. His companions rode behind him, silently watching the young man. Even though danger steadily grew elsewhere, Logan could not fight off the sense of triumph that swelled within him. It was almost as if that horrid experience with the crossbowman was all worth it. They had outrun Vaugen and the Guards, they had already reached the Hills, and they were about to find the only person powerful enough to help them.

Darkness roiled to life inside Logan's brain and forced its way into his thoughts. Be realistic, Matthew, the gloom reminded him in a jeering rasp. You've been wounded to the point of helplessness, only useful if you use magic. You rode off and left the ogre behind to die, and, although you're safe for now, both Reakthi and Guards know pretty much your whereabouts.

The glow of well-being started to fade as Logan steered his green-and-yellow horse through the Hills.

Through the cloud-obscured sky, the sun reached its zenith. Logan gave the flaming orb a disdainful stare and halted his mount. The abnormal wind had not touched the young man's senses for at least half an hour, and Logan hoped he had not been leading his friends in the wrong direction. The Hills had grown larger and almost identical, and the horses' footing was treacherous, yet Logan kept to wide ledges, following his instincts whenever the strange flow of irregularity struck him. Now, however, Logan stopped.

"Is something wrong, friend-Logan?" Thromar wondered.

The young man made no reply, then finally shook his head. "I don't get it," he grumbled. "Last time the feeling got stronger as I got closer."

"What feeling?" Mara queried.

"Zackaron's magic," Logan explained. "I can sense him with my . . . 'ability.' I suppose he's as much of an Unbalance as I am, but a more natural Unbalance. Right now I can't sense him."

Lost in a daze of bewilderment, Logan clucked his mount forward and rounded an outcropping of stone. The ledge he appeared on allowed a magnificent view of the southern Hills, and the young man cast his blue eyes across the mountain range. Simultaneously, the young man was bombarded by sensations. His contact-covered eyes abruptly noted slight movement within a mountain valley—a troop of mounted Guardsmen winding their way through the Hills. At the same instant, the tugging of Unbalance pulsated behind him.

Logan wheeled his horse away from the ledge so that he would not be spotted and galloped northward. The strange pull of Zackaron's magicks almost ripped the young man's stomach apart as he spied the narrow cavern hidden in the crook of a nearby mountain. Hurriedly, he spurred his yellow-and-green mount for the entrance, his friends trailing him in confusion.

A flash of pain in his shoulder accompanied the young man's dismount as he tried to unseat himself as quickly as possible. "There's a troop of Guards still in the Hills," he explained frantically. "Follow me."

Leading his horse, Logan walked directly into the irregular beat of magic and entered the cavern. An alien, green-colored glow illuminated the stone corridor, but Logan had seen it all once before. Without so much as a surprised glance, Logan bolted headlong into Zackaron's chamber and felt his jaw drop open.

The wizard's cavern home remained pretty much the same, Logan noted, filled with miscellaneous devices and books, magical inscriptions and pieces of furniture. Only it was the pale, half-slumped figure in a nearby chair that startled the young man. Brown hair streaked with grey was rumpled atop the form's head, but the wildness in the brown eyes had all but faded. A sickly tinted yellow glimmered from the spellcaster's magical orb situated in the center of the room, and a shaking, palsied hand stroked the trim beard and mustache of the lean face.

Zackaron pulled himself forward on his chair, peering at Logan with his dark eyes. "I . . . I know you," the spellcaster wheezed.

Zackaron! Logan's mind reeled. What's happened to you?

There was silence behind the young man as his companions also stared in shock at the deathly pale sorcerer.

"Speak up," Zackaron demanded. "Do I know you or not?"

Logan nodded, unsure at first, then vigorously. Nonetheless, he still could not find his voice.

Zackaron noticed the shocked stares of the quartet and smiled briefly. He forced himself out of his chair, swaying on unsteady legs. "Gape," he said. "You gape. All gape. Why do you gape?" The wizard's dark eyes narrowed. "Those who gape are seldom ever known."

There remained hints of the sorcerer's madness, Logan noticed, but not nearly the insanity the young man had experienced before. "I'm Matthew Logan," he said, befuddled. "I need . . . I need your help."

Zackaron barked a laugh. "Need my help, do you?" he answered. "Your help need I!" The lean spellcaster teetered precariously and allowed himself to slump back into his seat. "Your help," he whispered. "My help. Both are futile."

Logan could stand it no longer and neared the wizard's side, worriedly reaching out his left hand. "Zackaron, are you all right?" he inquired.

The insane wizard's head bobbed weakly upon his neck, yet the dark eyes peered vainly up at Logan. "I . . . I have been wounded," he declared, and a trembling finger pointed toward Logan's wounds. "Much like you, young man. Wounded, I have been. Wounded, you have been. Both wounded. Both dead."

"How?" exclaimed Logan. "Who did this?" The young man's eyes made a swift examination of Zackaron's robed form. "I don't see any wounds."

"Hardly physical," Zackaron croaked, another brief smile crossing his lips. "Physical, hardly." The sorcerer sighed. "Oh, the madness! Wish how I to take me away once again!"

Logan felt someone nearby and wheeled about. Mara stood behind him, her green eyes reflecting the same concern Logan felt.

"The lands feels much pain," Zackaron went on, sounding almost delirious. "I am the land. The land is I. What with wounds, what I feel. Feel the wounds! Pain! To the Heart!" The wizard slumped in his seat. "To the Heart."

A horrified expression came across Logan's features as his mind grasped what had happened. Gangrorz's attack upon Nature wounded Zackaron as much as it wounded the Heart, he realized. Zackaron's magical overflow from the Jewel had directly fixed him with Sparrill's nature; he only lacked the common sense to use it. Now, however, Zackaron felt Gangrorz's blows against the land as if they were against his very own body.

"It's the Worm," Logan told the wounded spellcaster. "Gangrorz. He's trying to destroy the Heart."

Zackaron's dark eyes fixed on the young man, and the approaching insanity fled. "Half his Power," the wizard whispered, and a permanent grin stretched across his face. "You know his Name. Half his Power!"

The wizard sprang victoriously to his feet, some of the color returning to his lean face. "I give you thanks, MatthewLogan. You have told me the Name of my enemy and have lessened the pain that I feel." Zackaron threw up his robed arms and glared at the roof of his stone chamber. "Oh, how the wounds cut deep! But the pain is fleeing!" Zackaron wheeled on the quartet, his eyes wild with triumph rather than madness. "How did you know to come to me?"

"I needed someone in touch with Nature," Logan replied, not knowing how to explain Munuc to the wizard. "You seemed to be the only sensible choice."

"Sensible? Sensible, I? Nonsensible, young man! Nonsensible!" Zackaron chuckled.

Logan gave his friends a look of perplexity and returned his gaze to Zackaron. The wounds Gangrorz had inflicted seemed to dampen Zackaron's madness . . . some, but not fully.

"I was looking for the Heart," Logan admitted. "Could you help us find it? Maybe it'll help us free the sprites so they can destroy Gangrorz again."

Zackaron nodded enthusiastically, his brown-and-grey hair flying. "Yesyesyesyes!" he cried. "Uncover the Heart! Use it! Slay the Shatterer!" The wizard unexpectedly turned on Logan. "Me?" he exclaimed. "Me help? I? Nonononono! Madness! Nonsensible! Not much help I'd be!"

"But the Heart," Logan protested. "We can't find it without the help of someone like you."

A wild grin bordering on the insane crossed Zackaron's lips, bringing his trim beard and mustache upward. "Perhaps it's not the Heart you seek, but someone who knows what dangers lurk in the Darkness," the spellcaster whispered dramatically. "You must search out and find Darkling Nightwalker. *He* will know how to silence the Voices that speak in the Darkness."

"Darkling Nightwalker?" Thromar repeated. "That's a name I don't like the sound of!"

Zackaron returned to his chair, his posture rigid and regal. "Listen not to sounds," he advised them. "Darkling Nightwalker is the man you wish to aid you. Consider this my help to you."

Logan felt his spirits drop. Zackaron himself was powerless to help them uncover the Heart so long as Gangrorz kept up his consistent pounding of the land. Instead, they were being sent off to find someone else. It seemed every time they reached someone, they were directed to someone new. "So where can we find this Darkling Nightwalker guy?" the young man questioned.

Zackaron smiled broadly, waggling a finger at the young man from Santa Monica. "He is as fleeting as the dawn, and as silent as the dusk." The spellcaster's dark eyes gleamed. "You will need a guide, MatthewLogan."

A sudden, abrasive chime rang out through Zackaron's chamber and the four horses started, their hooves beginning to paw nervously at the stone. An abrupt figure darted into sight, a tattered cape fluttering out behind him. Spiky black hair and rumpled, disheveled clothing covered the scrawny newcomer. A sharp, lengthy nose and fierce, pinpoint eyes completed the bizarre appearance of the form.

Logan felt his heart skip a beat as he glimpsed their guide and cried out: "Pembroke!"

·8·

Darklight

Black eyes blazing, Pembroke's lean features broke into a wicked grin as he wheeled on the young man. "Know you then of Pembroke?" he inquired.

Logan opened his mouth to speak, yet no sounds came forth. Fear churned through his bloodstream as Pembroke's disquieting aura of terror flittered about the stone chamber like an invisible bat, and the horses parroted Logan's unease.

Pembroke took an exaggerated step forward, craning his head closer until his beaklike nose almost touched Logan's. "So," the insane servant chuckled proudly, "Pembroke's fame succeeds him, eh? Verily the mightiest, he is."

Blue eyes wide, Logan cast his companions an apprehensive glance. A scowl twisted Thromar's beard downward, and Moknay wore his familiar grim visage, but neither moved or withdrew their weapons. For some odd reason, Pembroke did not recognize the three men as the thieves who had stolen both his horse and the Jewel placed in his care by his insane master.

"Pembroke," Zackaron declared, turning to face his servant, "this is MatthewLogan. He must get to Darkling Nightwalker. I have left it to you to aid him."

"MatthewLogan?" repeated Pembroke, cocking his head to one side as he peered at the young man. "Most intelligent is he who knows the greatness of Pembroke. How came you to know of him?"

Now what? Logan blanched. Somehow Pembroke's insanity has blotted out the fact that I stole his "Child." And I'm not about to remind him!

"Cannot the MatthewLogan speak?" the lean servant queried. "Can he but utter the name of he who is so greatly known?"

The unsettling dread that pervaded the air about Pembroke

caused Logan to throw an anxious glance at the servant's massive Triblade. Even in the magical glimmer of Zackaron's cavern, the three blades shimmered brightly, the razor-sharp barbs of the center blade's jagged tip glistening balefully.

"Ah!" Logan exclaimed, tearing his eyes away from the weapon. "Um . . . I heard about your Triblade . . . Only you can use one."

Pembroke gave the enormous sword at his wiry side a loving glance. "Ahhh, Pembroke's Triblade is his arm. Gives him great strength and power, it does."

"Talk not of your arm, Pembroke!" demanded Zackaron. "We must talk of knees! No! Curse me! Deformity! Freak! Outcast! Unclean! The time to talk of body parts must be held for later! Needs must we speak! Needs! Not knees or arms! Needs are great—knees are for bending!"

The wizard pulled himself from his chair, his dark eyes flaming with a vigor Logan had never seen before. "Bending, yes," Zackaron whispered. "Such is that which Gangrorz does . . . Bends, he does! Sunders that which is Nature! It is as he has told us. A rain of Darkness befalls us . . . the reign of the Worm impends! Duty calls! Call it duty! The talk must be of finding Darkling Nightwalker! He knows . . . indeed, he knows."

A suspicious eyebrow jerked upward on Moknay's brow as he turned toward the enthusiastic spellcaster. "Who told you?" the Murderer questioned.

Zackaron's eyes lost some of their glow, and madness swirled just beyond his pupils. "What?"

"You just said somebody told you about this forthcoming darkness," Moknay pointed out. "I want to know who."

"Perhaps he meant friend-Logan," Thromar suggested. "He did explain the enemy wounding Zackaron was Gangrorz . . . even though I still find it hard to believe the *Deil* could be alive."

"Logan said nothing about a rain of darkness," snarled Moknay in reply, his glare never wavering from the mad sorcerer and his servant. "There's something foreboding about this Darkling Nightwalker."

Thromar snorted. "You mean besides his name?"

Zackaron waggled a long finger in Moknay's direction. "You must go to Darkling Nightwalker," he advised. "Be not foolish. Doom not our world!"

"I will go to no one who knew of our coming," the Murderer

said, caution sparking in his steel-grey eyes.

Logan blinked, spinning about on his heel. "What?" he cried. "How could anyone know we were coming here? Even we didn't know where we were going next!"

"Exactly," Moknay replied.

The glittering orb in the center of Zackaron's chamber pulsed blue and sent reflective flashes through the wizard's dark eyes as he stepped behind the sphere. "You are cautious," the spellcaster stated.

The tone of voice caused Logan to wheel about once more, even sending a blinding burst of pain through his wounded shoulder. The voice! the young man blinked. Zackaron's voice sounded so steady and sure . . . no longer tainted by insanity.

"I will tell you this," Zackaron went on. "Darkling Nightwalker is not the enemy. He has aid to give and aid not given."

"That does it!" Thromar interrupted, throwing up his arms. "I think I'll wait until this dialogue straightens out before I attempt to follow it once more."

Glistening with flickers of blue, Zackaron's dark eyes trained momentarily on the fighter before turning away. "You have helped me, and I have offered my help," he said, matter-of-factly. "You need not pursue the task I set before you. That is your prerogative."

The mountain cavern was silent, broken only by the uneasiness of the horses around Pembroke. Even the dull throbs of pain in his shoulder weakened as Logan pulled his eyes away from Zackaron and looked at Moknay. For the briefest of instants, Zackaron's mind was whole . . . and his insistence to see Darkling Nightwalker remained. Surely he wasn't sending the quartet to their doom . . . ?

Moknay's finger clenched reflexively as he realized all eyes were on him, "But how did . . ."

"Power comes in all forms and shades," Zackaron broke in, "and Names." His dark eyes glittered as the magical orb twinkled silver. "You have uncovered the Name of our enemy, but you do not have a means to destroy him. The Heart? A desperate cause, that. Indeed, what should happen if you did find it . . . and the Worm snatched it away from you before you had the time to understand its magicks?"

Logan felt his head bob up and down in silent agreement.

"Only Darkling Nightwalker knows what may best be done to stop the time of the Worm from coming again," the gaunt spellcaster declared, "and to halt the death of all that is Nature. Go to him; save our worlds."

The quiet in Zackaron's chamber lingered as the sorcerous orb blinked from red to green. Oddly tinted shadows played themselves across the length of the rocky floor, and the muted sensations of disharmony tugged at Logan's nerves.

Maybe Zackaron's right, the young man mused. I sure as hell don't want to uncover the same thing Gangrorz is looking for. And have him take it away? For what? My own greedy desire to get back home? I'll wind up killing myself and everyone who's ever helped me in one fell swoop! Maybe this Darkling Nightwalker guy knows of another way to get rid of Gangrorz . . .

Another portion of the young man's mind burst into his silent speculations. So what? it demanded. This isn't your world. What do you care what happens to it? You want to go home—since when did your task become fighting Gangrorz? That's something for someone from Sparrill to do.

The logic was pressing, Logan noted, but he refused to be so selfish.

Somehow I'm to blame for this unexpected resurrection, Logan snapped at himself. Out of place or not, I've got friends here! Friends that I'm not about to let down! Earth'll still be there once Gangrorz is gone . . . so will the Heart. I can go back after I've finished what I've started!

But you're not to blame at all, his mind rasped back. This world is. That wind. You don't want to be here . . . you *shouldn't* be here. Why help at all? Have you taken some kind of liking to the excruciating pain in your shoulder? Or do you just like acting macho in front of Mara?

Shut up, you! Logan seethed. This world is in danger, and, since I am a pivotal point here, I'm going to do something about it!

The argumentative side toppled under the young man's determination, and he swung his gaze upward to catch Zackaron's. The words clogged in his throat when his gaze was interrupted by a glance of their guide, a wicked, dastardly grin of malice stretched across his lean, sunken features. Then, looking away from Pembroke, Logan staunchly faced Zackaron.

"I'll go," he said, and his legs trembled violently.

A heartbeat of silence followed as eyes throughout the chamber trained on Logan. Zackaron's dark pupils gleamed with achievement, and a slight portion of insanity returned; Mara's filled with concern and wonderment; a deathly stern flicker of steel continued to highlight the caution spinning in Moknay's eyes.

"Logan," the Murderer warned, his voice a throaty growl, "think this thing through. Whoever this Darkling Nightwalker is, he knew we'd come here. We're going to walk right to him."

The determination burning within him dwindled, and Logan felt fear well up around him. "No," the young man answered, "*I'm* going to walk right to him. None of you have to come. It might *just* be a trap."

Exclamations sprouted from Thromar, Mara, Zackaron, and Moknay so jumbled that Logan could understand none of them.

"I will not leave you, friend-Logan!" Thromar roared above the others.

"It could be a trap," Logan reminded the fighter.

"No trap! No trap!" Zackaron put in. "Darkling Nightwalker is not the enemy."

"And never once have you said he's a friend," Moknay retorted, grimly sneering. "Logan, I can't allow you . . ."

Logan fixed his eyes on the Murderer. "This is something I've caused," he stated. "Gangrorz would never have returned if my godforsaken entry into this world hadn't happened! Maybe even the Wheel's tilting did something, God only knows! Whatever the reason is, I'm sure I'm part of it." The young man lowered his voice. "I'm going to do my part—even if it means seeing this Darkling Nightwalker."

"I'm going with you," Mara declared, nearing Logan's side as if to punctuate her comment.

Concern for the dark-haired priestess amplified Logan's determination, and he slowly shook his head. "No," he replied, "you stay with Moknay."

The Murderer raised an eyebrow. "Who says I'm staying, friend?" A grave smile drew across his grim expression. "I can't say I like who we're going to see—or, for that matter, who's guiding us there—but I'm not about to turn tail and run. Moknay the Murderer was never one for such actions."

"His actions are more of the sneak-away-and-scamper attitude," remarked Thromar.

The Murderer's smirk grew. "All's well for you, Thromar," he returned. "*You* can walk headfirst into a trap—you've enough fat on your bones to stave off the sharpest of swords."

Zackaron's eyes scanned the quartet and a smile stretched beneath his trim mustache. "No trap, this," the spellcaster insisted.

"Darkling Nightwalker will give you aid where I could not. Pembroke, see that these people find Darkling Nightwalker at once. Gods know how much time is left before the Darkness descends and even Nightwalker's power is no more."

Logan had turned his eyes and ears away from the insane sorcerer and watched the lean Pembroke saunter toward them. Logan's green-and-yellow horse flinched as the crazed servant walked past it, and Logan felt the same jolt of fear enter his nervous system. An invisible shield of terror crackled outward from Pembroke's gaunt form as he stood directly in front of Logan, his ebony eyes glittering in the magical glow of Zackaron's chamber.

"Pembroke will get you there safe, he will," the servant chuckled. "But he will need a steed. Come."

A thin finger motioned for Logan to follow, and the young man fought down his unsensible feelings of anxiety. Leading his reluctant mount, Logan trailed Pembroke out of the stone cavern and stood waiting atop the ledge. Moknay, Mara, and Thromar crowded behind him, and the cloud-filled sky seemed to drop in upon them. Cautiously, Logan's eyes scanned the Hills blanketed by the dark clouds, searching for any movement that might mark Guardsmen or Reakthi. Unexpectedly, Pembroke leapt back into sight, a pale, sickly yellow creature dogging his heels. Magnified by Pembroke's aura of fear, Logan could not stop his face from drawing downward in a disgusted frown.

Pembroke's mount stared, unblinking, at the young man. It must have been one of Zackaron's creations, Logan surmised, meaning it was warped by the sorcerer's madness. Large, insectlike eyes protruded on either side of its head, and a deformed, slightly lopsided mouth held sharklike fangs rather than teeth. The hooves were squarish and seemingly metallic, supporting twisted, yet strong-looking, legs. No hair protected the creature's frame, nor did ears protrude from its head.

"Agellic's Gates," Mara whispered in revulsion. "What manner of creature is that?"

Pembroke affectionately patted the horse's twisted snout as he had earlier touched his Triblade. " 'Tis Pembroke's horse, she is," he cooed. "Pembroke's horse. Made for him by his master." The lean servant cocked his head to one side. "Had a horse once, Pembroke did. Stolen, it was. Taken from Pembroke by a foul and dastardly villain." The pinpoint eyes flared with hatred. "Horse! Horse and Child! Mine! My horse! *My Jewel!*"

Perspiration broke out across Logan's forehead and he knew it was not Pembroke's shielding of terror that caused his trepidation. Logan had seen Pembroke grow angered and use his Triblade—and he did not want to witness that sight again.

Pembroke's sudden fury died as abruptly as it started. "But Pembroke has been given a new horse . . . a better horse. Not scared of Pembroke, is she." With a wild, yet somehow graceful, leap, Pembroke landed astride his grotesquely formed horse. His tiny black eyes were unfocused, glaring far off into the mountains. "Fine horse, she is, but Child . . . dear, beloved Child. Gone. Stolen. Yet one day shall Pembroke recover his Child and find the thief who has taken her. Dead, the thief will be! Disemboweled, but not yet dead!" Pembroke's hand leapt to his Triblade in fury. "Then shall I strangle him with his very entrails."

The smile Pembroke flashed the quartet did nothing to settle the fears that churned within Logan. Unsteadily, Logan pulled himself into the crude saddle of his horse—his stolen horse—and swallowed hard. With sarcastic pessimism, the young man congratulated himself. Well, Matthew, he sneered, your quest seems to be coming along as smoothly as your last attempt. Not only are you wounded, you're not even trying to get home now, but instead put a stop to the Worm with the aid of someone who knew where you would be going and might possibly be setting a trap for you. Plus, the man taking you there is as nutty as a cashew and liable to rip out your guts and hang you by them at any time! A typical Matthew Logan screwed-up search party.

Logan pursed his lips and stared into the cloud-obscured heavens. Just what I need to top it all off, he grumbled. A sarcastic conscience.

A cold wind rushed through the Hills.

Arctic gusts of wind sent the edges of the black robe fluttering against the breeze. Pebbles and clods of dirt crunched underfoot as the gnarled form neared the makeshift camp, striding purposefully through the encampment. Unarmored soldiers gaped in silence at the lean newcomer, icy tendrils of fear wriggling down their spines. The newcomer's glazed left eye remained motionless, yet seemed to pick out and condemn every man seated about the camp. A silver chestplate reflected the eye's malevolent gleam, and bony, aged hands clenched and unclenched at his side.

Groathit stopped behind a black chestplated figure hunched over a poorly drawn map. Vaugen abruptly felt the wizard's one-eyed glare and spun about, his disfigured features tightened into an expression of rage.

"Now?" the Imperator tried to shriek, yet his injured throat would not raise his voice above a rasp. "Now you come? Where were you beforehand? I had him! In my grasp! Injured and unable to fight!"

Groathit smiled maliciously at the Reakthi leader. "And yet you let him slip right between your fingers," he mocked.

"It would not have been so if you had been there!" Vaugen accused, spittle dotting his half-closed mouth. "He used magic! Some kind of wall that held us off so they could make their escape!"

Groathit's hands tightened on air and his knuckles whitened. The whelp dared to use magic? the Reakthi sorcerer snarled to himself. Logan truly was intent on becoming the next Smythe.

"Matthew Logan would have been ours if you had been there," Vaugen finished.

Left eye glistening, Groathit fixed his gaze on the Imperator. "I am through playing your games, Vaugen," the spellcaster defiantly declared. "You and I do not see eye to eye on this matter, therefore, I no longer consider myself a part of your hunting party."

"You forget yourself, mage," Vaugen growled back, his dull grey eyes ablaze with indignation. "I am still the Imperator here . . . I command!" The Reakthi leader arrogantly turned his back on the spellcaster, holding up his map with his maimed left hand. "Thousands of trained men are at my command; enough men to quench your feeble bursts of sorcery."

There was a slight trace of morbid humor glinting in Groathit's eye as he allowed a smile to crack his wrinkled features. "Think you so, Imperator Vaugen?" he queried, making the title sound like an insult. "Incur not my wrath or you shall learn what powers I have been delving into. He who once served the Darkness now serves me . . . so tamper not with *my* anger."

Vaugen turned once more on the haughty spellcaster, inspecting the brash sorcerer with his piercing eyes. Then, spying no visible change in the wizard's physical appearance, the Imperator sneered back in contempt. "Why else would you be here unless it were in answer to my summons?" he asked.

The Reakthi spellcaster's right eye flamed. "I want the key to the third-floor library." A bony hand shot out, palm extended expectantly.

"What do you want that for?" the Imperator retorted. "There's only a few dusty old volumes up there. Certainly none of any use."

"You forget," Groathit corrected, smiling broadly. "There is one. The Darklight grimoire."

The puzzlement remained in Vaugen's drab grey eyes. "A worthless collection of tales and conjurations," he snorted. "Ancient powers that have faded into oblivion."

"So I thought myself," Groathit admitted, "yet I have been told otherwise. There are some conjurations that might yet be effective, and, should my ploy work, we will have no need of Matthew Logan, and Sparrill shall be ours."

The possible thought of victory cast a glitter through Vaugen's eyes. Somehow Groathit had learned of something, the Imperator mused. Something as powerful as the ancient energies mentioned in the Darklight grimoire. Why not let him trail this mysterious source of power? What harm could befall Vaugen should Groathit discover this magic? None, certainly. The spellcaster was still a Reakthi—only distraught over Matthew Logan's importance and possible power. Should he find some kind of energy strong enough to rival Logan's, why continue this accursed hunt for the stranger? And, due to the treacherous ways of the Darklight volume, Groathit may have an unforeseen accident, and Vaugen would be free of the insolent spellcaster. Either way, the Imperator came out ahead.

Vaugen's maimed left hand delved into a saddlebag and extracted a bronze key. He uncaringly tossed it over his armored shoulder at Groathit but kept his back to the one-eyed wizard. "Go," he commanded, "and report back should your attempts succeed."

Groathit clutched the key as if it were a golden idol of some great magical potency. "Oh, you will know," he chuckled nefariously. "Should my studies uncover that which I seek, you and Matthew Logan shall both know." The lean sorcerer drew the key up to his right eye and glared at it. "The Voices may yet speak again," he rasped to himself, "and I am eager to hear what they might say."

A glimmer of triumph flashed across the key's reflection in the spellcaster's eye, and heavy clouds blotted out the sun.

Matthew Logan gave nervous glances across the hillsides as he directed his yellow-and-green mount through the mountains. Ahead of him trotted Pembroke's horse-beast, its squarish hooves finding jagged and impracticable holds. Logan's own horse had little trouble keeping its balance, yet it was the eastward direction that caused the young man's blue eyes to flick from left to right.

"Uh, Pembroke," Logan said. "Do we have to go this way?"

The wiry Pembroke swung his head about, giving Logan the impression of an owl with its head turned all the way around. "Must go this way!" the insane servant replied. "Short cut Pembroke knows of! Oh, so clever is Pembroke! So clever."

Forthcoming doom sprang to life amongst Logan's anxiety at the servant's crazed advocacy. He threw his companions a helpless look, yet only Mara's eyes reflected the young man's worry. Thromar and Moknay both frowned.

Pembroke was taking them directly back toward the Reakthi, Logan mused. Wherever this Darkling Nightwalker was, the chance of finding him before Vaugen spotted them was slim. Already the Imperator should be within the Hills, or at least entering them. If he and his scouts were able to keep up the trail, they'd soon be in for a sudden surprise when their quarry walked right back into their waiting arms.

Much like we're doing with Darkling Nightwalker, Logan reminded himself, and frowned a frown quite similar to his friends'.

Pembroke drew in his malformed horse and pointed a rigid finger northward. "That way," the servant declared. "Pembroke must take you that way."

Thromar blinked and his frown grew. "The Sea's in that direction," he protested. "Just where in Imogen's name is this Darkling Nightcreeper?"

"That way," Pembroke repeated. "Darkling Nightwalker is as fleeting as the dawn and as . . ."

"And as silent as the dusk," Moknay interrupted, impatiently nodding. "Yes, yes, we've heard that one before. Now answer Thromar's question."

Pembroke clucked his mount forward. "This way," was all he said.

Logan gave Moknay a glance before following. The young man couldn't help but feel responsible for the well-being of his friends on this journey. If this Nightwalker was setting a trap, Logan was leading his friends directly into it. It made no difference that they came of their own free will—it had been Logan's insistence that he go that had persuaded them. Now, however, if things went wrong, all blame rested upon Logan's wounded shoulder.

The ogre was already dead—Logan could not bear to see anyone else meet their end.

The polar wind moaned audibly as it swept its way through the jagged Hills and ruffled Logan's black hair. The horses began a downward slant, winding through mountains that Logan had never seen before. Large, bluish hills rose up in the north, dotted by towering trees that were distant cousins of the pine. Wide, curling paths snaked across the northern Hills, and Pembroke's magically formed mare kept to them. The ceaseless echo of hooves resonated about the craggy peaks as the line of horses dropped downward even more and started out of the Hills. Greenery took over where rocks left off, and Logan's contact-covered eyes could barely make out thicker woods to the east. Few trees stood just east of the Hills, and a lush meadow stretched out before them on all sides.

Moknay's grim mien appeared as he glared at the expanse of grass warily. Such open spaces were not the kind of places men like Moknay appreciated.

Pembroke reined his distorted creature in and swung his head skyward. Though clouds hid most of the heavens, the lean servant seemed to sense the time of day nonetheless. "Must stop soon," he declared. "Night falls and your visions will be gone. Pembroke will wait with you. Your guide, he is."

"Guide or not," Logan heard Thromar mutter, "he's still a maggot."

The five horses cantered into the vast stretch of meadowland, the Hills of Sadroia looming behind them. Knee-high blades of grass bowed and swayed in the arctic breeze that steadily increased as night approached. The moans of the wind passing through the mountains behind them gradually faded, and Logan felt a slight stirring of Sparrill's muffled magic. Twinges of faint disunity reached the young man's nerves, yet vanished as if suddenly cut off.

"I don't like this," Moknay murmured, scanning the meadow.

"Just where *is* this Darkling Nightwalker?" Mara questioned Pembroke once more. "We don't have enough time to be running all over Sparrill."

"Near, he is," the insane servant-boy responded, "but far. Swift and fleeting, he is. Like Pembroke."

"If he's like Pembroke, we're probably wasting our time," Thromar snorted in a hushed voice.

Logan was about to scold the huge fighter for his whispered insults when an unexpected shriek shattered the young man's eardrums. His green-and-yellow mount released a startled cry as gangly arms jerked Logan out of his saddle and into the late evening sky.

"Matthew!" Mara screamed.

Pain blossomed anew across Logan's right arm as the sudden displacement ripped open the wound in his shoulder. The young man could feel the steady trickle of blood down the interior of the jacket as the winds fiercely beat at him. Tears whipped away, drying Logan's eyes and making his contacts feel quite uncomfortable. His body dangled high in the air, held aloft by viselike grips under each arm. Throughout the pain and surprise, Logan glanced down to see his friends and their horses diminishing in size, starting a frantic yet vain attempt to follow. Heavy, persistent beats broke through the currents of air behind Logan's head, and he tried to twist about. Pain splintered his thoughts, yet the young man strived to ignore the fire searing through his right side.

Half craning his neck about, Logan caught a glimpse of massive, rounded eyes, and hot, fetid breath was on the young man's cheeks.

Demons! his mind screamed. You're being abducted by Demons!

Logan's initial thought was for his sword, yet a rational section of his brain mentally kicked him. Weapons were out of the question, he concluded. Not only am I in no position to grab for them, I can't fight left-handed. My only other choice is . . .

Logan dropped his chin and felt the medallion dangling around his throat. Perhaps he would have time to grab the necklace and use it—even though it seemed to be what the Demons wanted— but then what would he do? Logan gave the distant ground a fearful glance and swallowed hard. There was a Demon on either side of him, one grasping each arm. If one or both were blasted, Logan would surely fall to his death.

Faint cries reached the young man's still-ringing ears and he attempted to twist his neck downward. Far below and behind him were his companions, madly pushing their horses eastward in their attempt to trail the kidnapped young man. It would be to no avail, Logan told himself. The clearing gave the Demons the perfect chance to snag me, and they took it. When that clearing ends, even Moknay won't be able to see me through the trees . . .

Unless I escape now.

Logan grunted. Sure, and fall to the ground. Unless . . . The young man's mind turned over a thousand possibilities . . . Unless I can use that piece of amber with the alternate plane of magic again, he decided. Mentally, I was able to levitate Thromar, surely I can levitate myself . . . Hey! I might even figure out how to fly!

Struggling against the iron grip of the Demon on his left, Logan brought his left hand across his chest and grabbed the medallion. Even under his sweat jacket, the amber responded almost instantly, exploding with a brilliant golden flame that startled the two Demons.

Instantly, Logan was elsewhere.

For a moment, the young man stood still, perplexed and unsettled by the abrupt change. Disagreement rose up around him, and the pins-and-needles sensation that accompanied the muted magic filled his legs and arms. Somehow the medallion had transported Logan to the ground—but where, he could not say.

Soul-wrenching shrieks split the evening air and Logan looked up. The Demons dive-bombed him from the left, their toadlike eyes narrowed in anger. They had what the Creator had sent them for, but it had escaped. They must not allow that to happen again.

Without thinking, Logan clamped his left hand over the medallion a second time. Another abrupt twist in reality took place, and Logan suddenly found himself standing ten feet to the side of where he had originally appeared.

The Demons halted in mid-dive, their large eyes blinking in confusion. Screams of unparalleled anger escaped their rounded mouths as they caught sight of the teleporting young man and redirected their dive.

Logan shifted again.

One of the Demons crashed headfirst into the forest, its leathery wings akimbo. Its partner screeched to a desperate halt and swung about, saliva spraying across the woods. The Unbalance was toying with them! Using the very object they had been promised to feast upon! He must be stopped! Caught and stopped, or the Creator would be most displeased!

The numbing sensation in his limbs did not disperse as Logan popped into the real world once more. He grinned victoriously as one of his would-be kidnappers rammed straight into the forest floor, sending a cloud of dirt and grass into the darkening sky. The other Demon, however, wheeled on him; Logan sensed the hunger

that swirled in the beast's amphibian eyes and felt sweat dribble
down the back of his neck. His left hand went for Moknay's
dagger, but his mind pulled his arm away.

Weapons are out of the question, the young man's brain repeated. Left-handed? Are you kidding? You've got to depend on the
magic until the others can get here. Just keep popping around and
confusing them.

Taking his hand away from his dagger, Logan touched the
bronze medallion again, readying himself for the abrupt pull
from one place to another. However, golden light flicked from
the small, eight-sided amber, and another facet burst into life.
Great! Logan cheered himself on grimly. That teleporting trick
only works three times!

As another section of amber filled the young man's eyes with
golden light, the world seemed to shift in different ways. A feeling
of weightlessness penetrated Logan's brain, lifting some heavy
weight off the young man's mind. Doors to other passages opened
within his cranium, and his blue eyes widened as he began to see
the world in another way.

Ebony sparks leapt and scurried about the Demon charging him.
A large collection of blackness filled the creature's skull, and the
millions of tiny impulses all sprouted from there. They followed
designated pathways, scrambling into the muscles of forearms and
wings, electronically inducing the rounded mouth to drop wider.
Somehow, Logan's fourth touch of the medallion opened up the
secret world of the mind—the natural workings of the human,
and not-so-human, brain.

Suddenly comprehending the vast powers at his control, Logan
projected a powerful blast of his own thoughts at the Demon.
Golden-white sparks spread out from Logan's frame, slamming
full force into the Demon. The electrical commands of its unnatural brain faltered, sending erratic impulses to any nerve that would
respond. Arms flailed and wings folded as the Demon flipped
backwards, knocked half-conscious by Logan's vicious mind-
blast. Unsteadily, it brought itself to its feet; and Logan saw each
spark and thought that burst from its unnaturally created brain.

Invisible discs of energy suddenly surrounded the Demon,
created by a single thought from Logan's freed mentality.
Frantically, the toad-eyed creature strained against the psychic
pressure, attempting to send back blows from its own mind.
Blackness, however, dimmed as Logan's flaring magicks pushed
in on the monster, weakening the ebony sparks that generated from

the Demon's mind. A hideous cry shattered the evening air as the Demon succumbed, its brain destroyed under Logan's unrelenting mental crush.

The amber blinked out and Logan crashed to his knees. Throbbing, pulsating agony rushed through his skull, and the heaviness returned to blot out the magicks he had just used. The Demon still twitched before him, its mind fragmented by Logan's psionic attack, yet the young man was left defenseless. The usage of those powers left him with an agonizing headache, and the pain in his right shoulder had not lessened either. And, somehow, the young man from Santa Monica knew he was not yet out of danger.

Smeared by dirt, the other Demon launched itself at the kneeling Logan. Tiny cuts marred its repellent face from its sudden impact with the ground, but it remained conscious and capable of fulfilling its task. Clawed hands stretched out and tore the medallion from Logan's throat, slicing the young man's flesh with its chain. Overcome by pain and the brutal theft, Logan toppled into the high grass of the woods. His ears caught the flapping of heavy wings, the triumphant flight of the Demon as it fluttered off toward the Worm, taking with it Logan's only weapon against Gangrorz.

As the sun dropped behind the Hills, the night that reached out across the land seemed to have a much more ominous darkness . . .

·9·

Tempest

An unexpected touch upon Logan's cheek liberated the young man from the blackness of unconsciousness. Like the softest of feathers, the touch trailed down Logan's jaw and tickled its way down his neck. Slowly, feelings began to be recognized: the dull ache in his head; the lingering fire on his right side; the burning pain encircling his throat.

A blue eye cracked open as another phantom touch tickled his left arm. Darkened blades of grass swayed before the young man's eye, and the night sky held a musty smell. When a third touch spattered Logan's forehead, the young man realized it was beginning to rain.

More and more droplets began to descend from the blackened sky, the wind scooping them up and throwing them southward. Lightning lit up the night, and Logan painfully drew himself into a sitting position. The few trees around him did little good at keeping the young man dry; the wind seemed to throw the rain in Logan's direction. So, trying to ignore the throbbing in his skull, Logan crawled forward and huddled beneath the closest tree. The branches of his makeshift umbrella trembled, and leaves were lost to the wind, flipping and fluttering out into the darkness. Logan's ears became filled with the plunking of raindrops on the land about him as he crouched beneath his tree, his knees brought up to his chest in an effort to block out the cold. Already small rivers of rainwater trickled down his face, and large droplets of cold water bombarded him from the tangle of branches overhead.

God, I hate this place, Logan said to himself, shivering from the cold. It's happened again. Everything goes wrong here—everything! Not only have I triggered off some ancient war between Gangrorz and Sparrill, what was supposed to be a real easy quest to get me home has become a matter of life and death for everything! I hate being the Cosmic champion! I just want to go home where the only thing I'd have to worry about was what I was going to watch on television! This is twice it's been up to Matthew Logan to save the day, and I'm getting sick of it! I mean . . . I'm lost again! How the hell is someone who keeps getting lost in this godforsaken place supposed to save the universe?

Logan cast his blue eyes across the rain-spattered night. There's definitely something about this place that has it in for me, he concluded dourly.

The musty woods lit up in a blue-white flash of lightning. Abruptly Logan stiffened, his contact-covered eyes possibly playing tricks on him. There had been something to his left. No, not just some*thing* . . . someone. There had been something undeniably human in shape off to Logan's left.

All thoughts of home, Gangrorz, and the cold fled Logan's mind. The young man fearfully leaned forward, trying to pierce the night with his gaze. He restrained the urge to cry out, uncertain whether the newcomer was friend or foe.

Logan snorted to himself. Or whether there really was someone out there! he reminded himself.

Thunder shattered the quiet of the rainfall. It might be a Reakthi or a Guardsman; Logan mentally checked off each possibility. Then again, it could be Moknay. No, no, no. It couldn't be Moknay—he'd be on horseback and the others would probably be with him. So what if it's Pembroke? He's a nutcase. Maybe he likes this kind of weather and came out looking for me. He is, after all, our guide.

Lightning flashed again and Logan felt an icy hand clutch at his wounded throat. The figure! It was gone! As suddenly as that!

Droplets of rainwater flew from Logan's hair as he jerked his head about frantically. Whoever had been standing out there—whoever had been towering in the rain—had vanished. They had used the momentary lack of light to scurry far away so that Logan could not see any trace of them at all.

Whoa, hold on a second, the young man told himself. You don't even know if there was anybody out there. It could have been nothing but the flickering of the lightning. You've got to be reasonable about this, Matthew. Who would be stupid enough to stand out in the middle of a forest, arms down at their sides, just peering in your general direction while they got soaked by the rain?

As thunder rumbled across the darkened clouds, Logan felt the tension and fear draw away from him. I'm just getting worked up over nothing, he told himself. The only thing I should be worried about right now is how I'm going to find my friends again.

Illumination forked across the night once more, and Logan went rigid. Among the briefly silhouetted trees and bushes, the figure had returned. Standing straight and tall, arms down at its sides, it was closer now and farther to Logan's right.

The night swallowed the lightning whole.

I've got a bad feeling about this, Logan thought, drawing himself to his knees. There *is* somebody standing out there, and they've no doubt seen me. Why else would they have gotten closer? But they sure as hell don't give a damn if I see them or not. So who would be so arrogant? And how were they able to find me?

The night sky seemed to rip apart as thunder shook the heavens, sounding sooner and louder after each flash of lightning. The rainfall began to quicken, turning the firm, fertile soil of Sparrill into swampy marsh. Logan, however, remained detached from his surroundings. Immediate danger lurked just beyond the trees . . . a danger that remained unknown, and, therefore, much more hazardous.

The lightning cracked a fourth time, and Logan pulled himself to his feet in a sudden burst of horror. The shape had disappeared again, he noticed. One flash, they're there! The next, they're gone! Whoever this is, they had the uncanny ability to slip away unseen and unheard and return just as mysteriously. But why? Why this game of Red Light, Green Light? And how the hell do they know where I am?

The roar of thunder sent a jolt of fear through Logan's system, and the young man hefted his sword out of its sheath. The weapon felt odd and heavy in his left hand, yet Logan tried to keep a firm grip on the blade. With his right side still aching, and his medallion lost to the Worm's minions, Logan was virtually defenseless. Nonetheless, perhaps with a weapon in his hand the young man might be able to scare away his nefarious prowler.

A noise that could have been a footstep—or perhaps a raindrop hitting the grass—sounded on Logan's right, and the young man swung about. Beads of perspiration joined the clinging droplets of rain on his forehead and hair, and the palm of his left hand felt slick and untrusting. Logan took a step out from beneath his protective tree and was instantly pelted by the wind-driven rain. Water splashed into his eyes and contacts, and he tried futilely to block the storm with his right arm. With every contraction and expansion of muscles on his right side, pain flared throughout the young man's body, yet Logan clenched his teeth and set about ignoring his discomfort.

Blue-white flame illuminated the forest, and Logan hurriedly surveyed the area; the form remained unseen.

The horror built up within the young man until it exploded like the clap of thunder above him. If they've been gone for two flashes now, think of how close they'll be to you the next time they do show up! his mind screamed in panic. You've got to get out of here! Run! You've got to! *Run!*

Logan's feet obeyed, and mud sloshed beneath the young man's Nikes. Wind shrieked past his ears and rain stung his face, yet he kept running. Several times he stumbled, losing his balance and faltering in the mire. All the trees appeared to be motionless forms, standing straight and menacing each time Logan neared them. Only sudden bursts of lightning informed the young man what was forest and what was not.

Rain cascading down his face, Logan gasped for breath. His head, shoulder, and throat still hurt, and the strength was gradually ebbing away from his legs. Perhaps he had lost the menacing shape in the darkness and forest, but somehow Logan doubted it. He had to keep on running. Running until he could run no more. Running blindly and insanely through the rain-drenched woods until he lost his nemesis forever in the gloom.

No longer knowing how far or for how long he had run, Logan felt his legs finally give way. All strength deserted him, and his next step sent him sprawling into the mud. Rain and muck splashed up into the night air. Logan lay there, unmoving, trying desperately to catch his breath.

The wind howled.

"We are dying."

Mud and rain streaking his face, Logan looked up. Trees and bushes wavered about him, their leaves splattered by raindrops. His sword lay somewhere in the muck. And, throughout it all, faintly, blown almost into silence by the wind, a deep, ominous voice had reached him.

"Can you not feel the magic and vitality ebbing away?"

Lightning split the darkness and Logan felt terror's skeletal hand tie his stomach into a knot. His own hand stretched out frantically for his fallen sword. Looming ahead of him was the same shape as before, still and statuelike. Yet . . . that voice Logan's mind pondered. Like something vaguely familiar . . . rimmed with twinges of recognition from his subconscious . . .

The wind shrieked as the rainfall slackened.

"The danger has increased a thousandfold."

My dream! Logan suddenly recalled. That same voice in his dream had mentioned death . . . and funerals.

Another fork of lightning splashed the forest, illuminating the dark figure that still towered before Logan. Wonderingly—his fear dampened by a sudden curiosity—Logan pulled himself to his feet, his muddied sword dangling in his left hand.

"That time has come again," the darkness whispered, fading gently into the screaming winds.

Logan's terror died to a weak flicker. "Who's there?" he challenged. "What do you want?"

Logan's answer was the rumbling of thunder.

The young man grew numb to the rivulets of water trickling down his face and frame. Standing out there in the blackness of the night was someone who had invaded his dreams. Someone who perhaps knew just what the hell was going on. Someone who might have some way of helping Logan destroy Gangrorz and return to his original task: finding some way of getting back home.

Another blue-white eruption of electricity littered the forest with light, and Logan saw that the dark figure had receded. There was no visible change in stance . . . only that the form had motionlessly drifted away from the young man.

An unexplainable panic rose in the young man's throat and he took three frantic steps toward the mysterious shape.

"No, wait!" he exclaimed. "Don't go!"

The wind moaned like a damned soul.

"We are dying," the low voice rasped.

"Wait a minute!" Logan cried. "I'm lost! I need some kind of help! Don't leave me here!"

Streaks of jagged electricity shrieked across the heavens, filling the world with blue-white fire. The fear returned to prance about Logan's mind, and his trepidation grew with each lightning flash. The mysterious form continued to drop away from him, gradually receding westward. The young man's frenzied steps had become a maddened run, a blind charge in the direction of the form when the lightning had flared last. As soon as Logan neared the area, blue-white light would explode, and the diminishing figure would be elsewhere.

The young man recalled the teleporting ability of his lost medallion and halted. His blue eyes narrowed as the darkness enclosed about him, suspiciously eyeing the general area of the shape. That isn't a Demon, he told himself, but they're popping around like they've found my medallion. How else could they be changing places so swiftly?

Lightning flared as the storm clouds began to disperse, and the curtain of rain grew weaker still. Through the blue-white flash, the form loomed on Logan's right. Logan caught sight of the shape, yet did not pursue, trying to catch his breath instead.

"Do not stop, Matthew Logan," the night advised in a deep whisper. *"Should that happen, we shall die."*

Logan's head swung upward at the mention of his name. "Who are you?" he cried out in frustration and fear. "How do you know my name?"

"A rain of Darkness befalls us," the low voice went on. *"The reign of the Worm impends."*

Lightning screamed as if to emphasize the words, and Logan saw that the figure continued to float backwards. Exhaling heavily, Logan forced his rain-heavy legs to follow, and his tennis shoes squished through the mud. The strength fueled by his fear and curiosity was almost depleted as the young man staggered a few paces toward the form and almost lost his balance. Throughout the storm-filled night, the lightning revealed the humanoid shape to be even farther away.

"Goddamnit!" Logan shouted at it. "Wait!"

"Halt! Who goes there?"

Logan froze. For the first time that night, the young man's weary eyes caught sight of a campfire, its flames leaping and shifting through the blackness.

"Halt! Who goes there?" the night repeated.

Logan took a fearful step backwards. Guardsmen? his mind suggested. Reakthi? Holy shit! Now you're in for it!

"Halt! Who goes there?"

The last droplets of rain spilled from the clouds and the night grew silent. An icy chill found its way up Logan's spine as the winds blew at his back.

"Halt! Who goes there?"

Logan gave the dark forest behind him an expectant glance. Thoughts of fleeing back into the trees crossed his mind just as a second voice queried: "Matthew? Is that you?"

Logan blinked. Mara . . . ?

"Halt! Who goes there?"

"Oh, shut up," a third voice commanded. "Friend-Logan? Is that you?"

"Brilliant," a snide, fourth voice commented, "and if it's a troop of Reakthi, I suppose we'll find out *after* our heads have been placed on a pike!"

Numbed from the cold, his injuries, and his exhaustion, Logan could not find his voice. A moving form abruptly appeared from a copse of trees on Logan's right. The figure halted, then broke into a run.

"Oh, Matthew!" Mara exclaimed, throwing herself at the young man. "It *is* you!"

Pembroke leapt into sight behind the priestess, his Triblade glistening with rainwater. "Halt! Who goes there?"

"Enough, already," Moknay sneered, suddenly appearing out of the night. "It's Logan."

The gaunt Pembroke cocked his head inquisitively, oblivious of the water that dribbled down his jagged features. "The MatthewLogan?" he inquired. "Dead, he must be. Eaten and surely digested by Demons, he was."

"Well, judging from the fact that he's here," Thromar stated, approaching and helping the young man toward a crude tent of blankets and tarpaulin, "I'd say he gave the Demons a bad case of indigestion."

Dazedly, Logan tore his blurry gaze away from Mara. "Did you see him?" he asked everyone at once, his voice dry.

"See who?" Mara wondered. "What happened to you out there?"

Logan sat down heavily under the cover of blankets. "The guy," he tried to explain, his words slurred by his weakness. "The guy I was following. Did you see him?"

Moknay raised a concerned eyebrow. "Friend, you're the only living thing that's been by here tonight."

The Murderer's statement pierced Logan to the very core of his mind, and doubts of mental instability began to flutter about his brain. Didn't I see somebody? Logan wondered. Didn't I hear somebody? Or did I make it all up? Images and voices conjured up by my injuries and predicament?

Mara's delicate fingers touched the red welts and cuts encircling Logan's neck. "The medallion," she said. "Where is it?"

"I lost it," Logan replied, and the defeat in his voice was obvious. "Gangrorz . . . has it . . ."

The shelter of Thromar's makeshift tent and the warmth of the small campfire forced Logan's eyes to close and the tiredness took control. But not even shelter, warmth, or the nearness of his friends could shut out the dreaded fact that the Worm had stolen Logan's one weapon against him.

And the rasping whisper of the night returned: "*A rain of Darkness befalls us; the reign of the Worm impends.*"

Groathit watched with something of a wry smile drawn across his wrinkled features at the pulsating, quivering mass before him. The aged Darklight grimoire rested in the wizard's lap, yet the spellcaster was more interested in the conversation going on between Gangrorz and a wounded Demon.

Ebony eyes flamed with energies blacker than the night. The oozing, coiling tentacle grasping Logan's medallion submerged back into the Worm's pliable flesh, dropping the bronze medal to the marble floor. "I have been tricked," the deep, accented voice snarled.

The Demon standing before the Worm cowered, fear glistening in its massive eyes. Its Creator was displeased. Although the Demon had faithfully carried out its task, the Creator was still enraged.

Gangrorz's black eyes shifted upward on the Worm's featureless face and fixed on the Demon. "You may take this . . . this worthless trinket and feast upon its magicks," the *Deil* instructed. "It does me little good."

Unable to contain his elation, Groathit stepped toward the writhing bulk of the Worm. "Is something amiss, beast?" he queried sardonically.

A long-clawed hand formed long enough to point at the medallion. "That is not what I detected," the creature snarled.

Smugly, Groathit stooped to pick up the bronze necklace and dangled it in Gangrorz's faceless face. "What?" the spellcaster mocked. "You mean to say that this is not what aroused your curiosity?"

The dark pillar of protoplasm shifted almost gracefully so that the malevolent black eyes trained on the Reakthi wizard. "It would serve you better not to mock me, inferior organism," the deep voice rumbled. "The creature you call Matthew Logan possessed something Pure and Untainted, like that which I have been sent to destroy. I felt for certain that this was that item. I see now that I am mistaken."

The sorcerer's bad eye gleamed dully. "So what shall you do?" he questioned, his scratchy voice twinged with eagerness.

The Worm glared at the medallion twirling from the spellcaster's fingers and snatched it away from him. "I exist here only because of the Task my Masters set me to perform," the creature growled. "Although created to destroy all that is Pure and Untainted, so is that my only weakness. Having ensnared the Guardians, I felt myself safe from any such attack; I was incorrect in making such an assumption." The jet-black eyes focused on the eight-sided piece of amber glinting from the center of the medallion. "Since this is not what I sensed, the threat must lie within the Unbalance himself."

His black eyes flickering with ebony flames, Gangrorz violently heaved the bronze medallion at the quaking Demon. "Take this out among your Brethren!" the Worm demanded. "Feast upon its magicks! Comsume its wretched, Natural energies! Then dispose of the only threat to my success." Rows of misshapen teeth stretched out across the beast's flesh. "Bring Matthew Logan to me."

Groathit could not stop the leering smile that drew across his aged face.

The musty odor of moisture still hung heavy in the air as Logan trailed his friends through the light forest. Droplets of rainwater continued to drip from the lush greenery, yet larger portions of blue sky forced their way through the clouds. Every now and again, Logan cast a cursory glance across the trees, hoping—and not hoping—to spot that strange figure from the previous night.

Maybe you didn't see anything at all, Logan thought, trying to console himself and quench any possible thoughts of insanity. Maybe the flickering of the lightning, your injuries, and your headache made you see and hear things that didn't exist. The only important thing was that you were able to find your friends.

Logan screwed up his face. Yeah, there was that, he mused. Insane or sane, how the hell did I happen to come across my friends? The chances of anybody finding anybody else in the darkness and rain were impossible . . . even standing a few yards apart. Still, I found my companions . . . or else that mysterious shape purposely led me there . . .

What shape? Logan asked himself, scrunching up his face again. I thought it was supposed to be tricks of the lightning.

The silence that hovered over Logan hovered over the others of his group as well. The same quiet also rested upon the forest, but Logan was steadily growing used to the stillness. By noon, the storm clouds had drifted away, and the rich smell of life wafted about the forest. The warming rays of the sun, however, only made things more uncomfortable for Logan as the mud that had soaked into his sweat suit dried and hardened. His discomfort suddenly became secondary when Pembroke halted ahead of him.

The young man peered over the shoulders of those before him and saw that the land gently sloped downward. Not far to the east ran a sparkling river, slightly overflowing from the rains. What could have been a dirt path emerged from the forest a few miles eastward, and the smell of salt was thick in the air. Although obscured by trees and distance, Logan could tell they were approaching the northern shore of Sparrill and that a sea lurked not too far away.

"Soon," Pembroke crooned to no one in particular. "Soon Pembroke will complete this journey so that he may once again search for his Child." He twisted his head around to smile at the four behind him. "Your quest nears its completion," he declared. "Appointed your guide, Pembroke was, and guide you he has done exceptionally well."

"That remains to be seen," Moknay answered. "You were to guide us to Darkling Nightwalker. I still don't see him."

A bony finger pointed northward. "There!" Pembroke cackled, his eyes blazing. "There did Nightwalker say he would await your coming! But haste! Haste! Not even the great Pembroke may halt the flow of Time. Only for a short while does Darkling Nightwalker wait. He is as fleeting as the dawn and as silent as the dusk."

"But where is he?" Mara asked, her green eyes scanning the northward region of Sparrill. "There's some six leagues stretched out before us."

Thromar, stroking his beard in thought, stopped and nodded understandingly. "Frelars," the large fighter comprehended. "It's just east of the Lephar on Sparrill's shore."

A grim frown crossed Moknay's face and stretched his mustache downward. "Mediyan has a port in Frelars," the Murderer said. "With all the activity Logan's stirred up, I'm sure he'll be using it."

"He is," Logan put in. The confidence in his voice faltered when everyone looked at him. "Well . . . he was when I got captured. They were going to take me there and sail to Magdelon . . . or wherever."

Moknay nodded gravely. "I thought as much," he murmured. "It's much faster sailing than marching. Since this Nightwalker is *waiting* for us, why couldn't he have picked a better place?"

Pembroke ignored the sarcasm and suspicion in the Murderer's voice. "Rain. Oh, rain," the servant grumbled back. "Wetness and muck shall slow down even the best of us. Eh? You fear something in the town? Pembroke fears nothing! Fear fears Pembroke! With Pembroke as your guide, you need not fear at all! Rather fear that the rains shall keep you from Darkling Nightwalker. The road would be swiftest, yet paths of mud they are now."

"And a good thing, too," Thromar retorted. "We couldn't take the road—we'd be spotted for sure."

"Pembroke is guide! Pembroke!" the insane servant screeched indignantly. "Imperative the road is taken, but what of the road not taken? That is a quest for questions. For how many alternate paths are created with each choice made and then recorded?"

A philosophical nutcase, Logan mused sourly to himself at Pembroke's ranting. Well, he went on, now it's been made public: Nightwalker *is* expecting us, but is he setting a trap? If he was, why would Zackaron have mentioned him? Was this Nightwalker offering Zackaron something in reply, or was Zackaron just acting out of his own insanity? No, the spellcaster had been very much sane—for that moment, at least—and still he had urged the four to go to this man with the ominous-sounding name. Why?

"Mud and muck!" Pembroke was cursing. "Swifter then *not* to take any road!"

"I don't see what you're complaining about," Thromar grunted, directing Smeea out in front of Pembroke's deformed mount. "If we keep riding, we should reach the Lephar River by nightfall. That's good enough for me."

Pembroke's beady little eyes went wide as the fighter's red-and-black mare replaced him as leader of the small band. With a furious shriek, the insane servant spurred his mount's disfigured flanks and charged ahead of Thromar. Instantly, the lean madman relaxed, grinning broadly to himself once he was once again in the lead. It didn't seem to matter to him that he now followed Thromar's suggested route; he was content with being first in line.

Logan turned his eyes away from the scrawny servant and shook his head dimly. A philosophical, childish nutcase, he moaned to himself. And it's up to him to finish *this* leg of the journey. Whatever it is here that doesn't like me does its damnedest to see that every little thing goes haywire.

Faint sensations were piercing the veil of Logan's subconscious mind: the mud encrusting his sweat suit, the persistent throb of pain in his shoulder, the bruises dotted along his throat, and the feathery touch of hair on his cheek.

The feathery touch of hair on his cheek?

Logan jerked himself rigid, sending a jolting blast of pain through his right side. A sudden hand clamped over his mouth before he could shout, and the young man's eyes went wide. There was a sort of numbing feeling from the hand over his mouth . . . the same kind of faint vibrations from Sparrill's magic. Wonderingly, Logan peered through the darkness of the riverbank at the form silencing him.

A slim, nude female knelt beside the young man, her slender hand placed firmly over his mouth. A finger of her free hand touched her full lips, indicating Logan should be silent. Even in the faint lighting of the moonless night, Logan could see the alarm ablaze in her light blue eyes. Slowly, the girl pulled her hand away from Logan's mouth and brushed at a strand of her long, light blue hair.

"Silence is of the utmost importance, Matthew Logan," she breathed, and her intake of breath neatly accented her perfectly sculptured breasts and their light blue nipples. "I only have a moment—Roana and Salena are concealing my escape from the Shatterer."

Logan's sleep-jumbled brain began to frantically slip pieces into place. Girl. Naked. Light blue. Roana. Salena.

Sprites!

"Wait . . . What . . . ? Uh . . ." Logan stuttered, trying to place all his questions together at once.

"Please, Matthew Logan," Glorana whispered, "I have so little time. It was only your nearness to my river and your growing strength that has allowed me to slip away unseen as of yet."

Logan cast a swift glance at the Lephar that gurgled and rushed just beyond a curtain of trees. Then he swung his gaze back to the blue-haired sprite.

"What do you . . . ?" he started. "Why didn't you come before?"

"The Shatterer has imprisoned us," Glorana told him. "We tried . . . oh, how we tried! Yet the first time you didn't even acknowledge us, and the second time the Worm tried to kill you. Only now, while the Wreaker of Havoc is concerned with other matters, have we had the chance to contact you."

"But . . . how . . . ?" the young man wondered.

Glorana gave the flowing river behind her a nervous glance as if expecting something to leap out at her from behind. "We're always here, remember?" she responded. "Even imprisoned, the Worm cannot fully stop our Natural task as Guardians. That, and your ever-increasing strength, has helped us. But that is not what I came to you about."

Logan found himself also glancing at the Lephar River as Glorana did so again. Then, secretively, the sprite whispered into his ear: "You have so much to learn, Matthew," she said, "yet many items have helped you up until now. The medallion . . . the Worm plans to use it against you. Its magicks are Natural, stemming from Sparrill . . . and us." She touched her naked breast. "Should you ever need those magicks again, remember us."

A shimmering silver line of energy radiated about Glorana's voluptuous frame, and the sprite dissolved into the night. Logan remained stunned for a brief second before shouting, "But the Bloodstone! What about the Bloodstone?"

Gentle proddings pulled Logan awake and he found Pembroke staring down at him, a wild, maniacal smirk on his face. "Is all well within, MatthewLogan?" the servant queried. "What makes you cry out from the depths of your sleep? Plagued by the wrongdoings of eons gone by?"

Logan ignored the crazed Pembroke and bolted upright, staring in silence at the dark river gurgling ahead of him. Stars twinkled through the moonless night, and Logan rose unsteadily to his feet, gaping. A dream, he repeated. A dream. Nothing but a dream.

And yet, a faint, hushed voice seemed to flow along with the river's waters: *Remember us, Matthew. Remember.*

·10·

Nightwalker

Mara turned away from the blue-grey sea on her left and fixed her eyes on the young man riding beside her. There was a faraway look on Logan's face as if the Sea of Hedelva brought back memories of his own home, yet the priestess could still see the tension built up in his muscles. The wistful, half-smile on his face could not detract from the anxiety that seemed to cover his body like sweat. To have lost your world, your people, and your hopes all in one blow, Mara sympathized, and then come to a place where things did not fare much better. She disliked seeing Logan so depressed—for it depressed her. It was odd, but never once in all her studying had she realized she might meet a man like Logan. There was something about him . . . something that told the priestess he was worth watching. Hidden deep under his protective outer shell, there was a man very sensitive to the unfairness and darkness that thrived on all worlds. A man whose sensitivity also longed to reach out and touch others, but feared their reaction, feared secretly what they might think of his actual self.

The young priestess forced her gaze away from Logan and returned to the sea. All the aromas of the shore drifted lazily about the late afternoon sky, and the continuous roar of the waves had kept the five company since that morning. Even seabeaks screeched and hovered over the waters, diving now and then at unseen fish. These were the first natural sounds Mara had heard in a long while, and she suddenly realized how greatly she missed them.

Her red-and-gold horse shifted uneasily beneath her and Mara drew her eyes away from the ocean. She gave the brightly colored horse a reassuring pat, then noticed Pembroke's own horse was reacting oddly. If it was not Pembroke's closeness that had frightened her beast, then what? the dark-haired priestess wondered. Pembroke himself, she noticed, had his sharp nose jutting skyward, a thoughtful frown on his features as he sniffed at the brine.

Mara turned and saw that Logan had noted the insane servant's animallike sniffing, and his own eyes were filled with confusion.

"Pembroke senses the nearness of danger," Pembroke abruptly declared. "While he would gladly rush headlong to meet it, your guide he was appointed. You must be cautious."

Thromar gave the lean servant a reproachful glare but caught the wary gleam in Moknay's eyes. Quizzically, the bearded fighter turned on the Murderer.

"He's right," Moknay responded, answering Thromar's unspoken question. "There's something wrong."

Mara surveyed the shoreline, swung her gaze eastward toward the path, then glanced behind her. "Are you sure?" she queried. "I don't see anything."

"Eyes are not the only senses for seeing," Pembroke stated, his beaklike nose still high in the air. "Trick you, they do. Tell you no danger abounds just because they cannot see it. *That* is when the danger attacks."

Moknay's right hand freed a dagger from his cheststrap. "I think it's safe to say this danger is not physical," he said, his eyes flicking from side to side. "It's more of a feeling . . . a sense of foreboding."

"Foreboding?" Thromar repeated. "The rains may have slowed us down, but we haven't seen hide nor hair of any Reakthi or Guardsmen. I would call that good fortune rather than foreboding."

Silver glistened as Moknay expertly spun the dagger in his right hand. "It's a feeling, Thromar," the Murderer explained. "And I've found it beneficial to my health to trust my feelings."

I used to feel things once, Logan thought, trying desperately to pinpoint the unrest in the air. Sparrill's magic used to warn me in lots of ways. Now I can't feel anything . . . Hell, I can't *do* anything! Whatever this danger is, I'm a handicap. I can't fight, physically or magically, and this is supposed to be *my* quest! So I'm just supposed to sit on the sidelines while my friends face possible death for something that I want? Somehow that just doesn't seem right.

Mara caught the despair etched on Logan's face and wished there was something she could do to relieve him of his depression.

If only there was some way that some of his burden could be given to her, she would gladly help him. But this was a problem that Logan felt only he alone could carry—there was no sense, to his mind, in burdening others with his woes. Couldn't he understand that sometimes others *wanted* to help? To them it would be no burden. Why couldn't Logan see that? So far along this journey, Mara had been of no real aid. Only her studies at Agellic's Church had allowed her to help Logan, but knowledge was not so much needed now as instincts and skill. Like Moknay had said, it was beneficial to trust your feelings, yet what did one do when those feelings had yet to be honed?

Mara frowned at her thoughts. You're being a self-pitying fool, she told herself. You've been an extra sword hand and you want more. You want to suddenly shine out so that Matthew will see how glorious and wonderful you are. Don't fool yourself, girl. You are who you are—an ex-apprentice priestess of Lelah's teachings so taken by a man from another world that you taught yourself archery and sword fighting. Up until now you've survived, and, in surviving, you've lived to help Matthew through another day. If that's all you're capable of doing without endangering the quest, so be it. Now stop feeling sorry for yourself and stay alert.

The sun began its westward descent as the five came into sight of Frelars. Larger, stone structures towered up from the shore, as grey and bleak as the sea itself. Logan had grown so used to the pleasant little villages in Sparrill, he had all but forgotten the dismalness and dark alleyways of towns like Eadarus. Frelars, it appeared, mirrored the flatness of the ocean. All the buildings were built out of stone, probably to survive the colder temperatures and constant moisture in the air. Logan could see where timber would swiftly be eaten away by the persistent spray of the sea. The pathway leading into Frelars remained a dirt road even within the town's borders. The smell of fish hung heavy in the air, mingled with the odor of dried seaweed. Wooden docks and ports extended out into the grey-blue waves, silver barnacles clinging to their support posts. A few of Sparrill's sea gulls—seabeaks, Mara said they were called—perched atop the roofs of some of Frelars's houses. Grey instead of the white Logan was familiar with, the birds appeared like an ill omen for some fateful occasion.

The stillness and solitude that radiated outward from the town unsettled Mara, and she felt prickly insect legs of fear crawl up her slim back. Her horse echoed her shudder of disquiet, and Logan's befuddled gaze toward Moknay also called out his bewilderment. There was an unhappy snarl on Thromar's heavily bearded mouth, and his meaty hand rested on his sword hilt.

"By Harmeer's War Axe," the fighter cursed. "What the *Deil* happened here?"

"Perhaps just that," Moknay returned solemnly.

The coastal town of Frelars was completely deserted, and the farther inward the horses went, the more desolate it became. Mara noticed with a sinking feeling in her stomach that some of the stone houses were damaged, their blocks shattered and littering the dirt street. Black scorch marks scarred the sides of other structures, and portions of ground had been shoveled away to leave gaping craters. A battle had taken place here, the priestess understood. But a battle between whom? And where had either party gone?

Moknay halted his grey-and-black stallion and dismounted, striding silently across the path. Thromar leaped off Smeea as well, his blood-caked blade flashing in his hand. The cries of seabeaks filled the bleak, empty town as the Rebel and the Murderer peered into a silversmith's shop.

"No one," Thromar muttered. "Not a single person."

Moknay drew his gloved hands away from a blackened section of rock. "This stone wasn't burned by any natural fire," he observed. "There was magic involved."

"Thought perhaps Reakthi and Guardsmen had had it out," Thromar murmured, replacing his weapon. "But that certainly wouldn't leave an empty town and no corpses."

Without a word, Pembroke leapt out of his saddle and scuttled crablike across the street, disappearing around a fragmented home. Thromar lumbered after the insane servant, Moknay a wisp of darkness on his heels. Quietly, Mara and Logan exchanged nervous glances before following.

Lost among the smells of the sea, a fetid, stomach-churning stench swelled up from the dirt roadway. Mara gagged as she turned the corner, her hand instinctively grasping Logan's left shoulder for support. Disgust twinged both Moknay's and Thromar's features, yet a wry, lopsided grin spread across Pembroke's lips. Blood slowly congealed, pooled around the massive corpse sprawled out across the street. A few seabeaks took to the air, startled by the sudden appearance of the five.

Logan turned away from the headless horse's cadaver and almost vomited.

Grinning his wild grin, Pembroke waded out into the puddles of blood, cupping some of the crimson fluid into his hands. "Such beauty," the madman sighed. "Such a sparkling glow found not in any wines made by human hands. But all has been wasted." The lean servant threw his handful of lifefluid back to the ground and glared malevolently at the decapitated corpse. "This is not the way!" he exclaimed, jabbing a rigid finger at the dead horse. "Pembroke knows the way! Pembroke does! They have taken the head! Who would do such a foul and evil thing? Pembroke must know their names so he may chew upon their beating hearts!"

"Demons," Moknay whispered, and his voice sounded like a church bell throughout the deserted village.

"Demons, indeed!" Pembroke ranted. "Demons! Pluck out their eyes, Pembroke shall! The expression of death is not to be taken! Where have they taken the head?"

"They've eaten it, you maggot!" spat Thromar, his ire growing at the scrawny servant-boy. "Like anything else that's unfortunate enough to fall into their claws, they've eaten the head and left the rest of the body."

"But the townsfolk?" Mara inquired. "What have they done to the rest of the people?"

"Magic was used," Moknay started.

"There'd be some bodies, wouldn't there?" Logan interrupted, an unbridled fury surging within him at the destruction of Frelars.

Thromar scanned the deathly still village, stroking his beard thoughtfully. "Fraviar has a secret chamber below his tavern cellar," the fighter declared. "Maybe that's where all the townsfolk have gone."

The five remained silent as they made their way through the empty town, Thromar leading the way. Rubble crunched underfoot, and shadows began to grow tall as the sun descended toward the Hills. Although not mounted, the horses nervously pawed at the dirt, the stench of Demon thick in their nostrils. Logan and Mara had to practically pull their mounts farther into town.

A numbing coldness overcame Mara as she followed the others down the dirt roads. Wintery winds swept inward from the Sea, and Mara folded her arms over her full breasts in an effort to block out the cold. So cold, lately, she mused. No doubt the work of the Shatterer and his Nature-corrupting magicks. His powers were obviously stronger at night; Darkness *was* his home. A way must be found to stop the Worm before the Heart gave in to his merciless pounding and warping of the land.

Hollow footsteps rang across Frelars as Thromar took three steps up a small flight of stairs toward a tavern. The fighter's expression was hopeful as he pushed the wooden door aside, his hand resting on his sheath. Moknay crept at his back, silver blades glittering in both of his hands. Pembroke trailed the pair, a childlike smile on his gaunt features and his hands uncaringly tucked into his belt.

Logan gave Mara a cautious look and nodded his head for her to go in first. The priestess nodded back, sliding her dagger free of its sheath. She didn't know why she had done that. If there were Demons still lurking about, they wouldn't spring an ambush. Stealth was not Demonic style, and yet, that one Demon that had first tried to steal Matthew's medallion had done so with the greatest of quiet and secrecy. With their creator back among the living, the Demons were no longer mindless, scrawny pests.

The priestess grimaced as her every footstep seemed to make the weathered floorboards groan in agony. The sunlight was fleeing from the sky and the tavern was rapidly filling with shadows. Mara glanced across the darkening structure with a puzzled frown on her lips. There's something very wrong here, she thought. Everything was in place . . . even mugs half-filled with ale rested atop the bar. No chairs were overturned, no tables smashed. When everyone left this place, they must not have been in a hurry to defend their town from Demons.

Logan gave the tavern a last, sweeping glance and plopped down in a chair, a distasteful sneer on his mouth. The sky grew ever darker outside the tavern windows, and the young man gave his searching friends a befuddled and angry glance.

"I give up," he stated, propping his elbow upon the table. "We've looked this place over at least three times and haven't come up with anything!"

"I'm afraid I have to agree with friend-Logan," Thromar answered, leaning up against the bar. "Brolark! I was so hoping they might have been here."

Moknay nudged a chair with his foot, his weapons glinting in the vanishing sunlight. "I've no further suggestions," he admitted in defeat.

Mara swung her gaze from the Murderer to Logan. So another mystery was added to their ever-increasing dilemma? she asked herself sourly. Enough problems didn't plague the small band already? They needed the entire population of a town to suddenly disappear?

The attractive priestess turned to see how Logan reacted to their failure and saw the darkness come alive. A man suddenly sat across from Logan, cloaked in the shadows of the tavern corner. He had not been there when the young man had sat down, nor had he been there when the five had entered.

"Matthew!" Mara called out in alarm.

Logan turned toward the priestess and stared directly into the pale, white eyes of the man sharing his table. The young man released a frightened yelp, almost spilling over backwards in his chair. Pain superimposed itself over his surprise as his right hand instinctively jumped for his sword, and his wounded shoulder jostled his memory sharply.

Thromar ripped free his sword, threateningly waving the blade at the newcomer. "Who are you?" the huge fighter demanded.

The stranger slowly—leisurely—turned toward the massive warrior and smirked. Through the dim light of the tavern, Logan could barely see the man's face. His skin was a glossy black—not Negroid, but a pure black, like polished onyx. He was clad in a grey tunic and a flowing black cowl, its hood down around his shoulders. The only thing that enabled Logan to see the stranger was his neatly groomed head of hair. Like the blackness of his flesh, the whiteness of his hair was an unnatural purity. Not silver or grey like aged hair, the newcomer's hair was as white as snow, a bizarre contrast to his nightlike skin.

Logan peered deep into the white, eyeless orbs set in the glossy face. There was no pupil, no iris . . . only the complete whiteness behind the cornea. And yet, Logan could feel the intense gaze with which the stranger fixed upon him.

"It is not like you to give up so easily, Matthew Logan," the stranger stated, his deep voice filling the emptiness of the tavern.

Daggers flickering, Moknay made a move to dart to Logan's side. "I'd advise you to move away from Logan and tell us how you got here, friend," the Murderer snarled, "or you'll be telling us from the slit in your throat."

"Threats ill become you, Murderer," the stranger remarked, smugly leaning back in his chair and almost vanishing into the darkness.

Logan cautiously backed out of his seat, keeping his blue eyes glued to the patch of shadows where the stranger lurked.

"We have a bit of a calamity on our hands and are all a bit on edge," Moknay went on, his daggers glistening with silver splendor. "Now if you'll be so kind as to tell us who you are and how you got here . . . ?"

The stranger stood up, a fluid, graceful motion which indicated the strength in his lean frame. Logan could now barely make out the black pants and boots that completed the newcomer's garb, fashioned in such a way that was both alien to Sparrill and to Logan.

An ebon smirk once again crossed the glossy features. "I am a friend," the stranger said with a grin, "and . . . perhaps . . . I am not a friend."

Thromar took a menacing step forward and the tavern floor-boards reverberated in their terror. "Well, I'm a dead shot," the fighter proclaimed, hefting his sword, "so you'd best not play word games with us."

Mara's emerald-green eyes roved up and down the darkly cloaked figure and saw no weapons of any kind dangled from his white belt. Even beneath the fabric of his cape there did not appear to be any sort of weaponry.

Odd, the priestess suddenly realized. A white belt? Certainly not the kind of clothing you wore if you were a skulker of the night like Moknay. Nor did a man of Thromar's profession wear such a color. It drew too much attention—even through the darkest of nights.

"He doesn't seem to be armed," the priestess said out loud.

"So I've noticed," Moknay responded, eyeing the newcomer suspiciously. The grim expression so familiar to Moknay's face appeared. "I'll ask you once more," he growled. "Just who in Imogen's name are you?"

The stranger spread out his ebony hands to show that they were empty and a faint smile drew across his face. "I am not the enemy," he said, his white eyes glittering.

Pembroke sprang off the top of the bar from where he was seated and waved his gangly arms at Moknay. "Put away the implements of war and death!" the servant commanded, bouncing about apelike. "Pembroke said he would lead you to him and lead you he has! Great is the power of Pembroke! Greater still is the power of his Child! Pembroke and his Child! Now I may search once again for her . . . infant of the multiverse and Pembroke, she is."

Thromar trained his dark eyes on the jet-black figure standing before them. "Are you saying that this is Nightcreeper, maggot?" he rumbled.

"Nightcreepermaggot?" Pembroke parroted, cocking his head to one side. "No! Darkling Nightwalker this is! Darkling Nightwalker! As fleeting as the dawn and as silent as the dusk!"

Logan saw Moknay lower his dagger but keep it well within throwing range of the white-and-black stranger. Once again a satisfied smirk crossed the gleaming black flesh as the eyeless white orbs singled out Logan.

Darkling Nightwalker returned to his chair and glared up at Logan. "We have much to talk about, Matthew Logan," he said in an ominous tone. "A rain of Darkness befalls us; the reign of the Worm impends."

Mara noticed the young man's mouth drop open as if his worst nightmare had just come true.

"You mean to say you knew that he was not yet in the town and yet you still sent your Demons in a day ahead of him?" Groathit shrieked, the veins bulging from the gnarled skin about his neck.

A foxlike ear formed on the left side of Gangrorz's featureless face as the black eyes focused on the spellcaster. "You have much to learn about the sources of Power," the accented voice grumbled. "Besides the many levels of pure, physical Power, there are other forms of strength. Ignorance is of the greater source. If your foe does not know of your existence, you may strike whenever and however you wish. Another source is display. Show what Power you have—let your foe quake in fear as he sees what you are capable of accomplishing, and let that terror grow. Let it plant the doubt that will spell his downfall when you are, at last, ready to strike the killing blow."

"Save me your senseless prattlings, beast!" Groathit barked, turning away from the writhing, shifting form. "You have a means to destroy Matthew Logan once and for all and still you play games!"

A smile pulled across the Worm's pliant flesh, then vanished. "You inferior organisms so amuse me when you demonstrate just how fully your emotions control your pitiful little lives," the monster mocked.

The wrinkled flesh around Groathit's ears grew red with anger as he snatched up the yellowed Darklight grimoire and wheeled once more to face Gangrorz. "I had thought you had recognized the danger that Matthew Logan posed," the wizard spat, his right eye ablaze with rage. "I see now I must return to my original task and find some other way to defeat him. In a few days time, you will be dead and gone, the loser of your own games."

The flaring black eyes of the Shatterer shifted to watch the gnarled sorcerer stalk out of the marble chamber. "No mere Unbalance may stop me," the deep voice boomed. "In league with the accursed Purity or not, I shall soon put him out of my destined path. You must force your small mind to comprehend this, inferior one: This is a battle between two Forces greater than your entire realm of existence. There is no one greater than I that you may turn to." The gleam in the coal-black eyes should have been accompanied by a sadistic grin. "Therefore, you must be pleased by what I intend to do . . . not by what you want."

Groathit's angered stride halted in mid-step, the wizard's bony hand enclosing tighter about the leatherbound volume at his side. For a moment he was tempted to scream out at the pliable monstrosity lurking at the center of its own tomb—tell it exactly what he planned to do and what good it would be to him once he had succeeded. But he restrained himself . . . Better to keep his intentions hidden from the shapeless creature until they bore fruit of their own.

Perhaps Groathit knew more about the different sources of strength and power than even Gangrorz imagined . . .

Darkling Nightwalker steepled his ebon fingers and leaned across the table to face Logan directly. "I have been with you from the very start, Matthew Logan," the bizarre figure said. "I have been the sixth member of your party throughout it all. It is now imperative we join forces."

Logan remained silently gaping, slumped in the chair he had narrowly found. Mara stood on his left side, her concern for the young man written in her face. Something about Nightwalker had so frightened or surprised Logan that he had almost collapsed, the priestess thought. What other tricks did this odd-looking man have in store for them?

"Sixth member?" Thromar grunted unpleasantly. "*We've* struggled through this entire ordeal, and *he* tries to take credit for it!"

Darkling Nightwalker may have given Thromar a snide glare, yet the glaring white orbs never once left Logan. "Think, Matthew Logan," the strange man prodded. "Your mind recognizes me; it knows who I am."

Dumbed, Logan slowly bobbed his head up and down. "You're the thing from my dream," he breathed, his eyes glazed from not blinking. "The one who made all the comments about dying."

"This world is dying," Nightwalker responded. "We are witnessing the death of all that is Nature. We are seeing it corrupted and tainted by the same, shapeless Evil as before. Yet I was with you even before then."

Logan made no response.

"Impossible," Moknay sneered. "That would have meant you were around before we had even gotten rid of the Jewel."

Darkling Nightwalker swung his head slowly about and fixed his empty orbs on the Murderer. "The night you entered Debarnian," he stated, calmly and methodically, "you were almost caught. That same night someone else crept into town and drew all the attention away from you. That was not accidental."

"You?" Moknay exclaimed. "But . . ."

"Your capture would have delayed my and Matthew Logan's quest," Nightwalker went on. "It was most important that that did not come to be."

As Nightwalker turned to face Logan, the young man blinked and feared that his contacts would pop out.

"And I was with you yet another time, Matthew Logan," the black-skinned man continued. "On the banks of the Roana—when the Worm attempted to slay you—*I* was that unexpected tug from behind. So too was I the cause that allowed your escape from the hordes of Reakthi hounding you."

The sudden answers to many of the young man's questions poured into his brain, and he had to close his eyes tightly in order to make any sense of them at all.

"The other night . . ." Logan attempted to query. "In the storm . . . was that . . . you?"

Nightwalker nodded.

"But . . . why . . . ?"

"Time is ever-changing," Nightwalker declared, the lanterns of the tavern flickering off his glossy flesh. "Delay cannot be tolerated. Before we faced a battle betwixt two Forces—since then more have come into play. You are one of these Forces, Matthew Logan. An Unbalance."

"I don't want to be . . ." the young man began.

Darkling Nightwalker nodded again. "Yes, I know full well of your reluctance, but such is the role you must portray while here in this world. Like the Wheel, you may tilt and change many times over throughout the course of your existence here. It is this inconstancy that may serve to destroy He who is called the Wreaker of Havoc."

An X-factor, the young man's bewildered brain registered. An integral, yet unstable, ace in the hole. The same aspect concerning his nature that made him different—his magic-detecting ability—now served as an unknown that could make or break the Worm's plans of conquest. But why him? Surely any person from Earth had this "difference" about them—why couldn't it have been the Smythe?

"Why did he have to come back now?" Logan vocalized, feeling the strain of an entire world's fate resting upon his shoulders. "This should have been a task for the Smythe. Someone who could do the job right. Not me."

"You play more of a part in this than you realize, Matthew Logan," corrected Nightwalker, his eyes flashing. "The Shatterer was dead, slain by the blast Roana delivered him eons ago. His resurrection was in the hopes that he would forsake his original task and slay you."

"What?" Mara gasped. "Someone purposely brought the Worm back to life just so they could murder Matthew?"

Nightwalker's nod was one of devastating finality.

"*Who?*" the dark-haired priestess cried when the strange figure gave no reply.

"The Reakthi spellcaster you know as Groathit."

Logan's head snapped upward at the name of the one-eyed wizard. How long had it been since the lean spellcaster's last attack? Weeks? Months! So long, in fact, that Logan thought himself safe from the Reakthi sorcerer. Now he learned how wrong he truly was. Groathit *did* have something to do with the Worm's resurrection as the young man had momentarily suspected back in Plestenah. Then why was he still alive?

His puzzlement obvious in his blue eyes, Logan wondered, "Original task? What do you mean?"

"The Worm feels himself above your kind," Nightwalker explained curtly. "He was created and sent for one Task: the destruction of Sparrill's Heart. He feels no sense of loyalty toward the Reakthi even though it was he who brought him back from the dead."

"But Demons have tried to abduct Matthew," Mara protested. "That means the Worm knows about him."

"Which brings us to the question of what happened here," Moknay said with a frown, indicating the empty town with a sweep of his arm.

Darkling Nightwalker gradually turned his head to face the Murderer, and Moknay sensed a sort of irritability swarming about the man as if such matters were too trivial to bother about at the moment. "Demons, as you already have deduced," he answered.

"And what became of them?" Moknay queried, irked at the stranger's indifference. "And the townsfolk?"

"The Demons left on their own accord," the sable-skinned man replied. "The townsfolk I sent elsewhere—for their own safety . . . and mine."

"You sent . . . ?" Thromar sputtered. "Where . . . ?"

"Where they will not intrude," Nightwalker interrupted, a trace of anger building in his voice. "This meeting must be of absolute secrecy."

"So you just 'send away' an entire town's populace so we can talk," Moknay sardonically stated. "Then why don't you just bring them back?"

"The Guardsmen as well, Murderer?" Nightwalker queried, smirking. "Although famed for your murderous prowess, I doubt if even you could defeat the four or five troops of Guards your King has stationed here."

"I have no king," Moknay snarled, unease glimmering in his eyes.

The unspoken indication of magically sending away an entire town was beginning to affect Moknay's composure, Logan noted. Nightwalker made himself sound like a very powerful sorcerer— one who had some interest in Logan's course of action. But there were no muted sensations of magic centering about the black-and-white figure . . . no pins-and-needles. How could he have done all the things he claimed to do if there were no magical tendrils reaching out and touching Logan?

Had the Worm's powers fully quenched all of Sparrill's magic, or was Darkling Nightwalker lying?

As silence settled over the darkened tavern, Mara studied the faces of her companions. Logan silently brooded on his own. Now and again flickers of anxiety drew across his features as his thoughts grew darker and more complex. Moknay remained in a battle-ready stance, his eyes faintly glittering with his distrust of magic. Thromar towered behind him, a perplexed and angry frown scrawled beneath his beard. Pembroke sat on the bar, cleaning under his fingernails with his massive Triblade.

Mara's eyes returned to the ebon-skinned figure at the table. "Zackaron said you would know best what needed to be done to stop the time of the Worm from coming again," she said, shattering the quiet of the barroom. She found it difficult to continue when Nightwalker's white eyes trained on her. "Do you?" she finally concluded.

The silence returned as Darkling Nightwalker leaned forward on his chair, briefly coming into the light of one of the lanterns. His movements were so slow and casual, one would have thought he was discussing the weather rather than the fate of everything Natural.

"A weapon must be found," the strange man declared. "A weapon as magically potent in Purity as the Heart of Sparrill."

"Even if such an object existed," Thromar snorted, "how are we going to find it?"

Nightwalker's blank eyes shifted to the large fighter and his malicious smirk appeared on his black lips. "You already know," he said.

There existed a moment of confusion on Thromar's face as he searched his brain. "I do not!" he finally retorted. "No one I know stoops to using magic in the midst of battle. Only a Reakthi or a Demon would stab a warrior in the back with a magical blow."

Nightwalker's smirk widened.

Thromar blinked as a name suddenly came to mind. "You don't mean Agasilaus?" he questioned.

"Imperator Agasilaus?" Mara cried back. "He's been dead for years!"

Thromar nodded. "Dead, yes, but he had the largest collection of magical items that I've ever seen. He brought every last piece with him to his fortress just west of Lake Xenois. To my knowledge, none of the surviving three Imperators wanted anything to do with his collection once he was dead. Oh, they split up his men, weapons, and provisions eagerly enough, but not a one touched Agasilaus's toys." The fighter turned on Nightwalker. "Are those the objects you mean?"

"If they are still there," Nightwalker declared, standing up, "one may be of the kind we seek."

Out of the corner of her eye, Mara caught Moknay stiffen. She spun about on her heel to see the Murderer glide to a window, his dark form hidden by the night. A tense hand was at his belt as he whipped around to face his companions.

"We've got company," he informed the others, hurriedly pulling free two daggers. "Vaugen's troops have found us."

"Impossible!" Thromar roared, glancing out the window himself.

Mara and Logan could tell from the expression on the fighter's face that Moknay had told the truth. "The bastard!" Thromar said. "They must not have entered the Hills at all! They gambled on the fact that we might come back out! That's the only way they could have found us."

Moknay extinguished the lanterns glowing in the tavern. "Or unless somebody informed them where we'd be."

Mara felt a sudden rush of fear clamp around her throat as she noticed that Darkling Nightwalker was nowhere to be seen.

·11·

Flight

"I knew we shouldn't have trusted him!" Thromar bellowed, his heavy sword shining faintly through the night. "There was something about his name!"

Matthew Logan threw a swift glance across the blackened tavern and felt despair swell in his throat. *Darkling Nightwalker is gone*, his mind snapped, *and there are two troops of Reakthi just waiting for you outside. And it's all your fault! You, Matthew! You were the one so determined to find Nightwalker. You were the one who had changed everyone else's mind about the possible dangers involved. And now you're the one who has trapped them in a deserted village with nothing to do except die!*

Moknay turned away from the window, his grim mien apparent even through the darkness. Over the Murderer's shoulder, Logan could see the fireflylike points of light from the Reakthi torches, fluttering and wavering in the distance. Amid the empty town of Frelars, the lights were like mournful will-o'-the-wisps searching for the missing villagers.

"What do we do?" Mara asked, the apprehension clear in her voice.

"We can't stay here," Moknay answered. "Our horses are tethered outside. We may as well place a large sign telling them where we are."

Thromar poked his head out and glared down the dark streets. "They look about as surprised as we were," he said. "Isn't every day an entire town up and disappears. So far they haven't seen our horses." The huge fighter scratched his reddish-brown beard. "Don't know, though. They'll hear and see us once we start untying our mounts."

"Damn," Moknay cursed. "It's either run for it and be seen, or hide here and be seen. I don't like either choice."

There was a sudden thump behind the four as Pembroke jumped down from the bar, the three blades of his weapon flaming silver. "Pembroke fails to see what causes such hesitation," the insane servant stated. "An enemy lingers outside, eh? Surely victory is not won by whisperings and curses in the dark? Victory is won by striding forth and confronting your foe. Watching as his blood pools about your feet and the gleam of death sparkles in his eyes."

"What you don't seem to understand," Moknay snarled at the servant in a hushed voice, "is that our enemy is some forty men strong. We can't face odds like that."

"What are men to the power of Pembroke?" the servant-boy asked back, yet he lowered his Triblade and made a thoughtful scratch of his nose. "But Pembroke understands you have the need for stealth. Well, is not Pembroke the greatest of the great? As silent as the hungry spider is Pembroke! Come, follow him. He shall get you away in the stillest of ways."

Thromar was about to grab the scrawny figure by the collar of his tattered cape when Pembroke suddenly dissolved into the darkness. Only by intense peering could Thromar even make out the dim outline of Pembroke as he crept toward the tavern door, his silence and stealth matched, perhaps, by only Moknay.

Logan was unable to find any outline of the servant when the tavern door slowly swung open. For a moment, a faint silhouette passed beneath the light of the moon, then Pembroke was outside. Moknay was a moving patch of darkness behind the madman.

Fear made Logan's stomach upset, and perspiration broke out along the young man's brow. Their survival depended on their absolute silence, and Logan feared being the one to give them away. Abruptly, cool sea air struck the young man's face, and he was outside. An instant chill rippled through his body as the cold breeze drew the sweat off his frame, and his worn and stained sweat suit did little to keep him warm.

The almost invisible Pembroke crept past the tethered horses and Logan felt his heart leap into his throat. Releasing a pitiful whinny as the madman flashed by, Logan's green-and-yellow horse instinctively backed away. Even Smeea shook her mane uneasily as the night-cloaked Pembroke streaked past, and Logan awaited the Reakthi warning at any second. His hands fumbled with the reins as his ears expected the sudden cries, yet none came . . . so far.

The anxiety eating away at Logan's stomach began to settle as the young man threw himself into his crude saddle and jerked his horse around. Just as the five were about to spur their mounts forward, more flickering torches rounded the street before them, blocking off their southeasterly escape route. What's more, the torches were heading right toward them! Logan realized in sheer terror. They were as good as dead!

An abrupt explosion sprouted somewhere off to the west, and the five Reakthi heading toward the group changed course. Confused shouts went up throughout the deserted village as all the various squads of warriors galloped westward, away from the tavern.

"They're leaving!" Thromar exclaimed in surprise. "What could have . . ."

Moknay pulled roughly on the reins and whipped his horse about. "It goes against my better judgement," the Murderer snarled, "but I think it was Nightwalker."

"What does it matter who it was?" Mara queried, her beautiful face flecked with beads of perspiration. "We've got a chance! Let's go!"

Clumps of dirt spumed into the air as the five horses charged insanely down the dirt path. Thromar and Moknay held the lead, casting careful glances to the right and left as they rode. Mara, Logan, and Pembroke all charged directly behind the pair. With all the Reakthi investigating the mysterious explosion at the west end of town, the hurried hoofbeats of the five would be lost amidst the rush.

Smeea released a terrified whinny as Thromar tugged hard on her reins, and Mara let out a curt shriek. A sudden squad of Reakthi had galloped around a darkened corner and had almost run headlong into the five. Logan felt his shoulder twitch in sympathetic agony as he caught sight of the crossbow strapped across the back of one of the soldiers.

"It's them!" one of the warriors cried. "Alert the others!"

Mara cursed as a shrill note from a bronze horn split the night before she could release the bolts of her Binalbow. Instant terror spurned Logan forward, digging his heels brutally into the flanks of his horse. The wounded crossbowman had lightning-swift reflexes, and his deadly weapon was already in his hands. Even as the five horses began to turn down another path, the Reakthi slid a quarrel across the tiller of his crossbow.

"I owe you, Murderer!" the Reakthi screamed vengefully, and the weapon in his hands twanged.

Moknay let out a shout that he wasn't quite able to stifle. Logan closed his eyes tightly, hearing the unmistakable "thwunk" of wood penetrating flesh. Tears came to his eyes as he could feel the pain Moknay must be suffering, but then he had no more time for sorrow. Another bolt slashed the night, screaming shrilly over Logan's wounded shoulder. The five horses charged maddeningly down the darkened streets, crossbow bolts filling the air about them. Logan could see Moknay tottering dangerously atop his mount, his left hand grasping somewhere near his heart. Nonetheless, the Murderer lashed about, silver glinting in his gloved hand. One of the Reakthi—the closest to the crossbowman—went down, screaming in agony at the blade that pierced his unarmored stomach.

A high-pitched scream filled the night, and Logan felt himself die. He watched in absolute horror as Mara's horse crashed to the dirt, two crossbow quarrels lodged in the beast's hindquarters. Almost in slow motion, Logan gaped as the red-and-gold stallion pitched forward, its legs buckling beneath its own weight. Mara felt the abrupt lurch and threw herself forward, trying to curl herself into a ball before striking the earth. She knew full well she could survive the fall, but she feared what would happen should her own horse fall on top of her.

Unable to instantly stop the crazed pace of his green-and-yellow mount, Logan stared in horror as he left the priestess and her fallen mount behind. His mind reacted violently, and adrenaline surged in his veins as he strangled the reins of his horse. Dirt spewed into the air as the young man ripped his horse around, agony sprouting through his wounded hand at his tight grasp. He had to reach Mara before the Reakthi came any closer! He had to!

Mara finished her roll and leapt to her feet, wheeling around to see if she was in any danger from her mount. She spied the Reakthi closing in on her, yet her horse was dead, its neck snapped by its own fall. Loud, harsh hoofbeats sounded behind her, and she spun about to see Logan. He looked like something out of a dream, her mind noted. Wind streamed through his black hair as he pushed his horse to its limit. The expression of pain on his face was obvious, but an overriding mien of determination scrawled over the agony. Heroically, he reached down his right arm to sweep the priestess off her feet and twist her into the saddle behind him.

Agonizing, searing, mind-numbing electricity speared through the muscles of Logan's right side as he tried to pull Mara up behind him. Scabs tore, flesh split open once more, and blood rushed free in a crimson tide. Unable to bear the pain and Mara's weight, Logan felt his center of gravity shift and he pitched out of his saddle. He heard Mara scream, then hard soil crashed into his face.

Stars played behind the young man's eyelids as he forced himself to stagger to his feet. Not even sure he was fully conscious, Logan pried open his eyes and spotted the Reakthi charging nearer. Mara was on his right side, her sword in her hands but looking ridiculously useless in the face of such odds. Still, Logan would not go down without a fight. A weapon! Any weapon! he demanded. For Mara! For me!

The nearing hooves grew like thunder in the young man's ears as he threw a frantic look around him. Mara on his right, his horse attempting to reorient itself on his left. Saddlebags . . . saddlebags! Logan muttered, his eyes scanning the flanks of his yellow-and-green mount. Sword . . . no. Dagger . . . no! Dammit to hell! Give me a weapon!

Throughout the pain in his right side and the confusion spiraling about his skull, Logan felt an unexplainable surge of triumph flow through his system. His bloodied right hand swiftly unstrapped the oaken staff from the side of his horse and held it out before him like a quarterstaff. Injured, Logan knew full well he could not use Launce's staff like a sword, yet it offered the young man the protection of a weapon . . . any kind of weapon!

A sudden force crashed into either end of the staff and almost knocked Logan to the ground. The crossbowman and the remaining Reakthi flipped off their horses, having caught either end of Logan's staff in the gut. Bewildered, Logan wondered how both had gotten so close, or why they didn't stop, but then those thoughts were gone. Logan had dismounted both foes!

As he charged the downed crossbowman, Logan heard a frenzied warcry shatter the night and realized it came from his own lips. Like an enraged animal, Logan pounced upon the stunned Reakthi, the blunt end of Launce's staff smashing into the soldier's skull. Blood sprinkled the oak, yet Logan brought the staff down for another blow. With every swing, pain flashed anew all across Logan's right side, and the staff dug cruelly into his injured palm, yet he ignored it. *This*! his mind screamed in total fury at the Reakthi crossbowman. This was the cause of his pain! *This*! He would see him die! *He would see him die!*

The sickening sound of bone fragmenting and scraping beneath flesh pulled Logan out of his pain-induced insanity. The Reakthi crossbowman lay sprawled out below him, his head a bloody pink pulp. Suddenly struck by the realization of what he had done, Logan failed to see the remaining Reakthi jump him from behind.

A scream sounded directly in Logan's ear as the last Reakthi spilled to the ground, Mara's dagger driven in between his shoulder blades. Angrily, the priestess ripped the weapon free of the corpse and grabbed Logan's left hand.

"Matthew," she warned, "there's more of them coming! We've got to get out of here!"

Logan turned away from her, wiping the blood and sweat from his face. Yes, he saw. More of them. More horses. Coming this way. Coming for them.

Smeea skidded to a halt beside the pair, and Thromar's meaty hand lifted Mara bodily into the air. He gently plopped her down behind him and swung his horse about. "Smeea doesn't like giving others rides," the fighter stated, "but she'll have to put up with it this time around. Mount up, friend-Logan! We've no time to lose!"

Logan turned toward his horse and saw that Moknay and Pembroke had also returned. The searing pain in his body grew intolerable, and the young man wanted to just lie down and die. Leave me, he wanted to croak. I can't go on. I just can't.

The young man's fury flared into life. Like hell you can't! it snapped fiercely. Move! Move your ass! Can't you see? There's more of them coming!

Inhaling deeply as if to add to his rapidly waning strength, Logan draped Launce's staff and his left arm over his horse's neck. It wasn't easy mounting from the opposite side, but his blue eyes had finally made his pain-clouded brain recognize the danger charging him from further down the road. More horses—some ten or so perhaps, torches flaring above their heads. And there was no mistaking the night-colored chestplate that led the troop.

"We'll never make it," Mara cried hopelessly.

Moknay wheeled his stallion about, and Logan could see the dark patches of blood staining the Murderer's gloves. "We might," he said. "If we hurry."

There was a sudden flurry of hooves and an insane scream of hatred as Pembroke launched himself toward the onrushing horde of Reakthi. The servant's flashing Triblade reflected the orange-red glare of the torches as he neared, and his scream echoed endlessly throughout the blackness.

Thromar jerked Smeea to a startled halt, looking backwards. "Pembroke!" he boomed. "Are you mad?"

Moknay clucked his horse back into a gallop. "Ask a stupid question, Thromar . . ." he retorted.

As his mount rode away, Logan watched in dumbed stupefaction as Pembroke neared the troop of soldiers. "You have the perfume of Pembroke's daughter about you!" the servant screeched at the deformed Vaugen. "You have been near Pembroke's Child! Where is she? Where is his Child? *Where is my Jewel?*"

Logan saw four Reakthi charge forward to halt the madman and then saw no more as his horse rounded a corner and left the Reakthi behind. From the continuing sounds of battle, Logan knew it would take far more than just a quartet of Reakthi to stop Pembroke and his Triblade.

As the quartet raced their way southward, another pair of Reakthi spotted their escape. Thromar barked a curse and swung Smeea about to the left, the cool night wind whipping through his reddish-brown mane. They were being cut off, Logan realized. With the sea at their backs, Vaugen's men only had to block three exits, two of which were the wrong direction that the four wanted to take. Already Vaugen had blocked the eastward route to freedom, and the other soldiers were returning from the explosion in the west. The four were being squeezed between squadrons.

Something that looked like black rope entwined itself about the necks of the Reakthi and jerked them off their horses. As the warriors crashed to the ground, a blazing white horse rode among them. Looking like some dark angel, Darkling Nightwalker caught up with the four, his pale eyes filled with some emotion Logan could not recognize.

"Where did you go?" Thromar roared at the stranger, his sword still in his hand.

"A distraction was necessary," Nightwalker simply stated, urging his white horse onward. "It is now possible to head in a southeasterly direction."

The small band steered their mounts through the town of Frelars and dashed free of the dirt roads. Trees fell back in around them, and they had reached the forest once more. Logan was sure he could hear the sounds of pursuit, yet every time he glanced over his wounded shoulder, he saw nothing. Trees and bushes became blurs, meaningless flashes of shapes surrounding him on either side. He knew his watch would not tell him the time, so the young man had to guess at the hundreds of hours that must have passed. The pain in his hand and shoulder grew worse, and there was a dizziness in his head that he had never gotten rid of since his fall from his horse. Foam flecked Smeea's reins as she struggled to maintain the breakneck pace Thromar forced upon her, struggled to support the weight of her owner, his many weapons, and the added weight of Mara. Moknay's right hand remained clamped about his chest, dark traces of blood trickling between his gloved fingers. His breathing sounded strained, and each gasp came through teeth clenched to fight off the pain. Nightwalker rode behind them, his white horse a fast-moving phantom through the shrubbery.

Wondering how the night had stretched to encompass so many years of pain and fear, Logan finally noted the pink glow in the eastern sky. The horses' pace began to slow until Thromar brought them to a complete stop just beyond a stretch of trees. Wearily, the fighter dismounted and wiped the streaks of sweat streaming down his face.

"I think . . ." he breathed, "I think we lost the bastards."

Logan felt no joy as he watched the sun rise above the Lathyn Mountains in the east. Hadn't they lost the Reakthi once before? he mused. Hadn't they thought themselves safe from the Imperator and his soldiers?

Using Druid Launce's oaken staff, Logan pulled himself down from his yellow-and-green horse. He gave the area a cursory glance and noticed their band numbered only four. Darkling Nightwalker had vanished again! When, who could say? Any time during the night the strange man could have veered off from the four. But why? Why answer questions that had been plaguing them for weeks? Why offer a solution to the Worm's demise? Why? Why? Why? Why? Why?

That was when Moknay collapsed out of his saddle from loss of blood, and Logan felt his own legs give out as he accompanied the Murderer into the oblivion of unconsciousness.

The first thing that touched Logan's conscious mind was the dull, muted throb of pins and needles that seethed within his right side. Questioningly, the young man cracked an eye open and stared into the greenness of the grass. Still no feeling other than the numbness coursed throughout Logan's right shoulder and arm, and, suddenly terrified at the lack of sensation, Logan bolted upright and grabbed at his limb. No, his left hand told him, his arm was still there, only there wasn't any feeling in it.

Perplexed, Logan wondered if that was good or bad.

"You are feeling well?" a voice behind him queried, and Logan turned to see Darkling Nightwalker.

"Huh? What?" the young man sputtered. "Hell! I'm *not* feeling!"

Nightwalker crouched down beside him, his white eyes emotionless. "That will pass," he declared. "A slight side effect of the spells."

"Spells?" Logan uneasily repeated. "What spells?"

"The ones I used to heal you and the Murderer," Nightwalker responded simply. "Your wounds were most grievous."

The previous night suddenly blossomed back into Logan's mind and the young man recalled the horror and pain vividly. Concerned, he wheeled around to see Mara standing a little ways behind him, anxious to approach him but not doing so. Nearby lay Moknay, a dark stain of blood smeared across the left side of his chest.

Thromar was nowhere in sight.

"Mara, where's Thromar?" Logan wondered. "And how's Moknay?"

"The Rebel is acting as guard should the Reakthi who are hounding you come within sight," Nightwalker answered for the priestess. "The Murderer sleeps still."

An intense anger suddenly built up inside Logan as he fixed his blue eyes on the pupilless orbs of Nightwalker. "And where were you?" the young man snapped. "Where the hell did you go last night? You're not much help to us if you keep running away!"

Darkling Nightwalker rose out of his crouch and turned his back on Logan. "I have my reasons for being here, Matthew Logan," the dark figure replied. "Reasons that I need not reveal to you. I suggest you grow used to my ways for I do not intend to change them for your gratification. Never once has Darkling Nightwalker explained his actions, nor will I begin now."

Logan watched and frowned as the ebon-skinned stranger stalked toward the woods. Fine, he grunted, be that way. Just don't expect any of us to help you out in a pinch either.

As Logan's fury grew, he glanced down once again at his right arm. I don't get it, the young man admitted to himself, clenching his fingers. Maybe Nightwalker *is* some help, but . . . how can we trust a man who might not be there when we need him? He may have healed me and Moknay, but . . . just how far can we trust him?

When Logan brought up his head, Mara was at his side. There remained traces of concern etched deep in her green eyes, but these gradually faded as she knelt beside the young man.

"You frightened me," she whispered, hanging her head as if ashamed of the emotions she felt.

Logan peered into the priestess's eyes, his mouth not knowing what words to form. "I did a pretty good job on myself," he responded flippantly.

"There was so much blood," Mara went on in a hushed voice. "I didn't know what to do."

Catching the ire in her voice, Logan raised his eyebrows. "Hey," he told her, "don't blame yourself. This whole thing's my fault."

"But it was my horse that was shot out from under me," protested Mara.

"Better your horse than you," Logan answered, tightly clasping the priestess's slim hand.

The move startled Logan as he realized how much of his feelings he was allowing through. This is the way to get hurt, Matthew, his mind informed him. Spill your guts and they turn on you. You've been there before. Now what the hell are you doing holding her hand?

Logan ignored the warnings until they became tiny whispers in the back of his mind. Never before had he felt so empty as when he had spied Mara's horse crash to the earth and thoughts of losing the dark-haired woman ran rampant in his brain. It had been a gut-wrenching stab of emotional agony, and Logan was no longer going to believe solely in what his thoughts told him—he would let his heart speak its piece as well.

"Mara, look," he said, "there are things that . . . just happen. If someone's to blame for all this, I am. It's my quest, my shoulder, my fault. Not you. If I wound up getting hurt, it's my own stupid fault . . . but I couldn't see anything happen to you. Not to you—can't you understand that? I don't know what I'm feeling—I don't know what I'm doing! I'm so damn confused in this world! All I know is that I'd never want anything to happen to you. Even if it meant never getting back."

There was a soft chuckle behind the two and Logan turned to see Moknay trying to prop himself up on his elbow. "It seems, my friend, you're beginning to acquire something of the Sparrillian spirit," the Murderer quipped, his voice dry with sleep. "Whether you want to or not."

Logan frowned, recalling Danica's similar statement, but then pushed these thoughts aside. "How are you feeling?" he queried.

"Like fat old Mediyan's been using my chest as his throne," Moknay tartly answered. "And speaking of fat, where in Agellic's Gates is Thromar?"

"Watching out for Reakthi," Mara explained. "You and Matthew needed time for Nightwalker's magic to take effect."

"Magic?" Moknay remarked, grinning feebly. "I've been healed by magic? Gods, is there no escaping that blight?"

Nightwalker's deep voice sounded at Logan's elbow: "It would appear not, Murderer. Even now such forces mass against us."

Logan swung about, gaping at the ebon-skinned man. How the devil did he get behind me? the young man wondered. How . . . ? When . . . ? Jesus!

A sneer had replaced Moknay's grin. "Speak in proper terms, Nightwalker, or I'll be thanking you for saving my life in more of a manner for one who bears the name Murderer."

Nightwalker either ignored or did not hear Moknay's threat. "A throng of Demons band in the west, the same that struck Frelars a day before your arrival. They have the stink of corrupted magic about them."

"Demons?" Mara exclaimed. "With magic? Matthew, your medallion . . . ?"

Logan shrugged. "Maybe . . . I don't know what they did with it."

With a grimace of pain, Moknay sat up. "What does it matter where they got their magic?" he snarled. "The question is, what are we going to do about it?"

"You must flee," Nightwalker instructed them. "Your wounds have already delayed my task by a day—I cannot afford any more interruptions."

"Forgive me," retorted Moknay. "Next time I'll try not to step in front of a flying crossbow bolt." The Murderer pulled himself to his feet, his expression betraying the pain that still lurked in his chest. "Magical Demons or not, I'll not leave without Thromar."

"I have already informed the Rebel of what transpires," replied Nightwalker, casually walking over to where his horse was tethered. "He should be joining us soon enough."

As if on cue, Smeea broke through the foliage and pranced to a halt before the four. Thromar's tiny black eyes scanned the quartet swiftly, a curious frown drawn beneath his beard.

"Friend-Logan? Moknay? Are you fit to ride?" the fighter questioned.

"No," Moknay answered sardonically, "but we'll ride nonetheless. Have you seen them, Thromar?"

The massive warrior nodded. "About twelve strong winging their way in from the Hills," he reported. "They're still some distance away, but I've never seen Demons move quite so fast before."

"If we can reach Greenwoods before they reach us, we should be all right," Mara stated.

"For a few days, at least," agreed Thromar, "provided we do reach Greenwoods."

"Then talk later," Darkling Nightwalker ordered from atop his mount. "Now you must flee or forever live in Darkness."

Logan clambered astride his horse, Mara swinging into the saddle behind him. Thromar, being the only one with horse and not wounded, rode alone should the Demons reach them before they found the safety of Greenwoods. Pins and needles continued to throb in Logan's right arm as he directed his yellow-and-green horse through the forest, throwing cautious glances skyward every now and again.

"Follow a southeasterly trail, friend-Logan!" Thromar shouted from the rear of the group. "We have to reach Greenwoods!"

Logan jabbed his Nikes into the flanks of his stallion as the wind tore through his hair. Mara's slim arms entwined about his waist sent myriad thoughts spiraling through his brain, but the young man forced them down. They were being trailed by Demons endowed with magical powers—or so Nightwalker said—and riding for their lives. Plus, the Reakthi still lurked somewhere behind them. Now was hardly the time to be thinking about Mara's arms around his middle.

Squinting against the winds, Logan threw Mara a look. "Where are these Greenwoods anyway?" he wondered, shouting to be heard.

"They should be just ahead of us," Mara called back, drawing herself closer to Logan's ear.

"What are they?" Logan asked.

"A denser portion of forest," the priestess explained. "Where the trees grow closer together. If we can reach them in time, there will be no way for the Demons to attack us from above."

Unless they blow the crap out of the forest, Logan mused sourly. If they are using the magicks of my medallion, they'll probably have the power to do it too. I'd only had time to use four out of the eight sides of that amber—God only knows what the other four did!

Time seemed to slip through Logan's fingers, and he hardly noticed the sun begin its westward descent toward the Hills of Sadroia. Blood-red light tinted the clouds as Mara caught sight of the dark shapes trailing the group, calling her discovery to everyone's attention.

"Not much farther!" Thromar bellowed back. "Greenwoods should be right ahead of us!"

Out of habit, Logan risked a glance at his watch and sneered at the flare of red that radiated in place of the digital readout. More black flecks had blotted out the silver, sending a shiver of unease down Logan's spine. Abruptly, trees closed in around him, and his yellow-and-green mount hurriedly slowed its pace, winding its way carefully through the maze of greenery.

"Hah!" roared Thromar. "Made it!"

Moknay's mien was one of foreboding. "Perhaps, but did anyone happen to notice when Nightwalker slipped away *this* time?"

Allowing his horse to trot through the dense forest on its own, Logan threw a bewildered glance over his left shoulder. He did it again! the young man cursed. One second, Nightwalker's alongside them—the next . . . poof! It was almost as if the dark-skinned creature *did* come and go with the dusk!

Pitiful shrieks sounded above the roof of leaves as the band of Demons hovered just outside the forest. Mara cringed inwardly at each soul-shattering screech that escaped the rounded mouths of the monsters fluttering unseen above them, and Logan felt a tingle of fear race through his own nerves. Claws raked at leaves, and branches shuddered fitfully, yet the dense forest of Greenwoods kept the airborne beasts away from their prey.

All at once, silence claimed the woods.

Mara looked up, her green eyes wide. "They've gone," she breathed.

"To probably wait for us to come out the other side," Moknay commented, fingering a dagger with his bloodstained gloves.

Logan eyed the closely knit trees before him. "I think we're going to have to walk," he declared. "The trees are getting even thicker."

"So we walk," Thromar answered. "A pity friend-Logan can't use Druid Launce's staff the way he could. We'd be out of here in a day."

Logan gave Launce's staff a sorrowful glance as he dismounted, his right side still numb from Nightwalker's spells. Mara stepped down beside him, leading his horse by its reins. Moknay and Thromar trailed.

"You're holding up quite well," Moknay suddenly complimented Thromar. "I thought an enclosed area like this would be fermenting your grapes."

"You underestimate me, Murderer," the fighter grinned with yellowing teeth. "But I must say you're doing quite well with a horde of magical Demons after us."

Moknay shrugged, wincing at the pain that lashed through his left side.

"But this doesn't really count," Thromar went on. "Forests and such can never be too small. There's always open spaces even if it's only through the branches."

Logan, listening to the fighter confess his fear of enclosed spaces, unexpectedly fell back into Mara as the boom of displaced air exploded before them. Momentarily deafened, Logan glanced up to see a Demon magically appear, a villainous smile drawn across its circular mouth.

"Matthew!" Mara cried out in warning.

Logan had already pulled himself to his feet, his numbed right hand drawing his Reakthi blade. "It's my medallion all right!" the young man yelled, swinging furiously at the gangly creature.

God, it was good to use a sword again!

Magic crackled as the Demon sidestepped the blade, its globular eyes glinting in the rays of the setting sun. Saliva drooled from its mouth as sparks of power leapt from its iron talons.

"Friend-Logan!" Thromar boomed. "Stand aside! Let me handle it!"

The young man disregarded the fighter's shouts, knowing there was little room to step aside and let Thromar through. He was caught between Mara and the Demon, and Logan was certainly not going to back away and leave Mara to handle the creature filled with his medallion's magic.

Although it was devoid of feeling, Logan directed his right hand for the Demon's middle and swung. Air rushed in to fill the gap left by the Demon, and more air erupted outward as the monster reappeared on Logan's left.

Silver whirled through the trees as Moknay released two daggers. Once again the frail, thin-limbed Demon sent its sorcerous energies into a magical leap through space, and, this time, emerged closer to Logan than before.

"I've got you now, you son of a bitch!" the young man swore. "That trick only works three times!"

Clenching his teeth, Logan swung erratically at the nearby Demon, sure to strike the coarse, leathery hide. Instead, the monster teleported a fourth time to Logan's right, a clawed hand slashing at the blade that now swung through empty air.

"Hey!" was all Logan could blurt before his numbed hand betrayed him and released its hold upon his weapon.

You idiot! the young man thought to himself. They're not using the medallion! They're using its magicks! That probably means they can do everything the medallion did as many times as they want to!

A victorious screech escaped the Demon's fanged mouth as it reached its bony hands out for Logan's throat.

·12·

Demons

Logan stumbled back as a reverberating twang beat upon his eardrum and Mara's Binalbow went off beside his right cheek. The Demon reeled backwards, yellow-white blood spuming from its grotesquely shaped face as the twin quarrels speared through its skull. The lean creature went down, limbs twitching, a garbled scream gurgling from the back of its throat.

"Good shot!" Thromar cheered from the rear of the band.

Mara smiled faintly, strapping her Binalbow back across her shoulder. Logan finally succeeded in pulling his eyes away from the Demon's corpse and gaped momentarily at Mara. Then, trying to shake the ringing from his ears, the young man retrieved his fallen sword and started forward.

"Damn things *are* using my medallion," he grumbled, stepping over the still body.

"At least we'll know some of the powers," Moknay replied.

"But not all of them," said Logan gravely.

The young man threw the dead Demon behind him a disgusted glance as Mara made her way over the motionless corpse. Unexpectedly, the priestess screamed as a taloned hand grazed her left leg. The fabric just above her boot tore as the Demon jerked back to life, energy crackling from its hands. The wooden bolts remained half lodged in the monster's face as it lunged again for the priestess.

Too shocked to react, Logan watched as Mara dived out of the way. The young man's yellow-and-green horse reared up in terror as the bloodied Demon staggered to its feet. Magic sparked from the Demon's iron claws as Moknay pulled free his katar, flinching at the burst of pain from his left side.

"It's beginning to seem things don't know just when to stay

dead anymore," the Murderer growled, slashing viciously with his twin blades.

The Demon leapt backwards, hissing in anger as it narrowly escaped Moknay's swing. A stream of sorcery flamed from the beast's claws and exploded into the trees behind the Murderer. Thromar ducked as a charred branch sailed overhead, sprinkling the fighter with splinters and magical flakes.

"By Brolark!" Thromar roared. "Let me through and I'll make sure this thing stays dead!"

Moknay avoided a sweeping claw and jabbed upward. "Right now, Thromar, it's trying to teach me the same thing," the Murderer remarked, his cape obstructing his movement in the dense forest.

Logan tightened his grip on his sword and started back. Immediately, the Demon turned on him, screaming its soul-wrenching scream. Undaunted, Logan plunged his Reakthi weapon forward, straightarming the sword directly into the Demon's rounded mouth. Yellow-white fluid sprayed as the Demon bit down on cold steel, yet it refused to die. Magical streaks danced up around the creature, and Logan narrowly dodged a yellow-orange blast thrown his way.

"Down! Get down!" the young man warned his friends. "It's using those rays!"

Trees cindered as red and black beams shot out from the Demon's arms. The beams, Logan knew, came from another plane that overlapped Sparrill. What made them so dangerous was that, when controlling these rays, the user practically had a mental control over the entire plane. By just thinking about it, Logan had saved Thromar.

Cringing as sorcerous knives of power flashed overhead, Logan noted an iron-tipped claw extending for Mara. Without thinking, Logan's muscles propelled him forward and his numbed right hand grabbed the gangly wrist and directed it downward. Surprised that a foe would dare hand-to-hand combat, the Demon grinned down at Logan, yellow-white lifefluid dribbling around its jagged and broken teeth.

Holy shit! Logan blanched. Just what the hell am I doing?

A sudden lance of white-hot pain arced up Logan's numbed right side and befuddled his thoughts. Blinking, Logan suddenly found himself in the same plane of power as the Demon. As if somehow sensing the young man's unexpected threat, the Demon tried to back away and shrieked as Moknay drove his katar in between its wings.

"Logan!" the Murderer shouted, unaware that the young man shared the Demon's stolen powers. "Get away from it!"

Logan ignored Moknay's advice, narrowing his eyes as he concentrated on the threads flashing about him. All the red ones, he commanded. Every single one of the red ones! Blast this sonuvabitch! *Blast him!*

Unable to see into the alternate plane, Logan's companions were startled when a brilliant aura of blood-red light surrounded the Demon and sank inward. The monster released a keening wail as the multitude of crimson beams drove downward, burning flesh from muscle and muscle from bone. The deadly nimbus of red light continued to pound at the Demon, leaving a pile of grey-brown ashes in its place before finally vanishing.

Logan blinked the overlapping plane away.

"How in Imogen's name . . . ?" Moknay started.

Logan shrugged, half-smiling. "My medallion," he answered. "Maybe I used those powers so I was familiar enough with them to get them back."

"Perhaps that's something going in our favor then," the Murderer responded. "Just in case this fellow's playmates decide to pop in on us." He spread the pile of ashes with a foot.

Logan sheathed his sword as he looked down at the grey-brown remains of the Demon. Somewhere, not physically, and then again very physically, Logan could feel the soft touch of the three sprites as they giggled their congratulations. The stillness of Greenwoods remained, and the threat the other Demons posed still hovered above their heads, yet the strength and vitality of Sparrill's Nature had not yet given up. That meant that somewhere the Heart still pulsed with life and magic . . . perhaps enough magic to get Logan home and back to a normal way of life.

An arctic breeze broke through the night and scattered the Demon's remnants across the forest floor.

Black eyes flared into being on the boxlike mass of flesh compressed in the center of the large marble chamber.

"A Demon," the deep, accented voice rumbled. "I have lost a Demon."

Groathit looked up from the yellowed Darklight grimoire as Gangrorz unfolded, expanding his pliable bulk upward.

"The creature called Matthew Logan has used the Pureness of this land as a weapon," the Worm said, its eyes flaming. "And he has slain a Demon."

Groathit's good eye blinked, and his hands clenched tightly about the volume in his lap. "That is because you did not listen to me, beast," the spellcaster snapped. "I warned you of the danger Matthew Logan posed, yet you ignored me. Now you see what magic that whelp is capable of."

The maggotlike shape of the Worm twisted downward, a disjointed arm burbling up from the pulsating, oozing pillar of protoplasm. "I told you once before, inferior organism, there exists no one other than the three sisters capable of stopping my task."

"And what of the Purity you sensed earlier?" Groathit snarled, narrowing his right eye at the *Deil* while his left eye, sickeningly, remained wide open and unblinking. "Does this not threaten your existence and your task?"

"I have a great hatred toward all that is Pure and Untainted, for that is why I was created," the Worm responded, its arm bubbling back into its body. "I was formed to destroy all that is Pure, but so is that my only weakness. Whatever magicks aid the creature called Matthew Logan are drawn from this source, yet there can be no way any such forces would threaten my Being. Therefore, it would expand my Knowledge if I could study the Purity that aids this Matthew Logan. Unable to harm me, the accursed Purity may hold some key to the destruction of all such Purity . . . including the object I was sent to destroy."

A malevolent frown crossed Groathit's face as he returned his gaze to the leatherbound volume in his lap. "You are allowing Matthew Logan to live," he sneered. "You will never survive to accomplish your task."

Gangrorz shifted, fixing his coal-black eyes on the wizard. "On the level you struggle, Matthew Logan can cause your downfall. On my level, he is nothing."

"He is the sole heir to the magic of Sparrill," Groathit replied, his voice strained and his knuckles white. "He is to be the next Smythe. He is to be the single most powerful spellcaster in all the land and you would let him attain that position!"

"On my level that means nothing . . ."

"On your level that means he shall be a vessel for the very object you seek!" screamed Groathit, jumping to his feet. "He shall be the magic of the Heart and of Sparrill! He will control and command the very Nature you so violently loathe! And he will kill you in much the same way the sprites did beforehand!"

The Worm was silent, a row of misshapen teeth spreading

across his glistening, featureless face. "Then I was not mistaken when I assumed he was the source of power I had earlier sensed," the _Deil_ grumbled.

Groathit sat back down, turning once again to the Darklight volume. "Perhaps he is, perhaps he is not," the spellcaster declared. "To be entirely certain, one should dispose of any threat—immediately."

"And rid myself of the only chance to study the magicks that may banish me to the Sleep of Death?" the creature questioned, eyes flickering. "You do not understand, inferior one. This is my only chance to learn how to fend off my own destruction should the Forces of Purity strike at me again.

"My Masters shall not tolerate a second failure."

A small smile raised one corner of Groathit's mouth as he looked up from the book in his hands. "Yes," he rasped, "tell me of your Masters. What names do some of them have?"

The Worm coiled about gracefully, folds of dark flesh shifting and rotating like fabric. "They have no names," the monster replied, a lingering tone of deep respect in its accented voice. "Nor any shapes to be spoken of. They are the Darkness and the Voices that speak in that Darkness. They are my Masters, and they are All. No names, no forms . . . no mind such as yours can comprehend just _what_ they are."

Groathit's smile widened. "They are Power," he whispered.

The _Deil_'s ebony eyes gleamed. "Yes, in Darkness there is great Power." The creature abruptly trained its eyes on the Reakthi spellcaster and a distorted beak formed out of its shifting mass. "But why do you ask such questions? What purpose do these questions serve? And what of that tome you continuously stoop over? I sense it houses secrets of eons ago that eyes of one such as you should not be allowed to gaze upon."

The wizard rose out of his seat and started out of the marble chamber. "One day soon the world will know, beast," Groathit enigmatically answered. "You, unfortunately, will have been slain by Matthew Logan by then." The Reakthi sorcerer halted his brisk stride and cast a quick glance over his shoulder at the dark shape pulsating in the center of the room. "Enjoy what little time you have left on this plane," the wizard croaked. "I shall not be seeking your aid any longer."

A low chuckle escaped Groathit's throat as he hurried out of the chamber and made his way down a narrow corridor.

*   *   *

Logan tore off a bit of jerky and chewed vigorously at the bland-tasting meat. His feet were sore, he stank of sweat, he wanted to sleep, and he was eating meat that tasted like cardboard! Throughout the last two days, the four had continued to walk their horses through the thickness of Greenwoods. They only stopped for brief rests during the night, plagued by the sounds of the remaining Demons hovering over the trees. Occasionally, claws would rake at the leaves, yet none of the creatures attempted to teleport in and confront the group. Maybe, as Moknay surmised, they were waiting for the open spaces east of Greenwoods.

"My feet hurt," Logan complained, clutching his Nikes.

Mara agreed: "So do mine."

"I can certainly say mine have felt better," Thromar put in.

"They've certainly smelled better," Moknay retorted. "That's probably why the Demons haven't gotten up the nerve to fight us—they'd fear Thromar might take his boots off!"

Thromar boomed a good-natured laugh as Logan looked upward at the roof of greenery overhead. There was no humor in the young man's eyes as he peered at the trees, narrow slits between leaves allowing bright sunlight to peek in on the four. And yet, there still remained the awful silence. No power could dampen the beauty of Sparrill, yet with an all-consuming quiet, the air held a thick, foreboding odor. More than just the reminder that a horde of Demons awaited the quartet somewhere outside the protection of Greenwoods.

Worrying, Logan pulled himself to his feet by leaning heavily on Launce's staff. Close by, or so Thromar hoped, was the Roana River. The river posed another threat to the small band, and Logan could not help but feel the twinge of guilt that struck his nerves when he rested his eyes on the oaken staff in his hands. Druid Launce had died at the Roana, regardless of how beautiful the riverbank was. The Roana would be open space, just what the magically endowed Demons were longing for. In order to cross the river, the four had to come out into the open. Trees, the young man sourly mused to himself, did not grow in the middle of rivers.

Leading their horses through the labyrinth of foliage, the four continued as the sun drew westward. Gradually, Logan could make out the sound of gurgling water breaking the uneasy and unnatural silence of the forest. His trepidation concerning the river crossing mounted as they came closer, yet, through the tight mesh of trees, Logan's contact-covered eyes could not see the crystal-clear stream.

Blackness began to spread across the land as the sun dipped behind the Hills and an icy wind heralded the coming of night. Unexpectedly, Logan felt a searing jolt of nausea course through his numbed system as the darkness took form and came alive. Trees warped and mutated about them, coiling inward and sprouting black, brittle leaves. Healthy bark turned black, and green leaves spilled to the ground in a hail of foliage. Branches shuddered and another convulsion of sickness gripped Logan's stomach as Launce's staff flared an emerald hue as if in protest to the distortion of nature about them.

Startled cries went up from Logan's companions as they watched the thick vegetation of Greenwoods writhe in agony at the Worm's distorting magic. In a macabre dance, the closely knit trees drew inward, becoming shriveled and bent like aged men. The darkening sky loomed overhead as the healthy roof of greenery dropped away under Gangrorz's corrupting sorcery.

"The trees!" Thromar bellowed. "By Brolark! The trees!"

Moknay drew his steel-grey eyes away from the transforming patch of forest around them and glanced upward. "Forget about the trees," he warned. "Worry about them!"

Still hurting from the magical attack, Logan cast his gaze skyward and saw the collection of dark shapes swooping down at them from above. Flares and sparks leapt from the many clawed hands, and large, bulbous eyes glittered evilly in the dusk as the Demons attacked.

Mara jerked her Binalbow off her shoulder and fired. One of the creatures veered off sharply, the twin bolts lodged in its chest. With a curt screech, the wounded Demon crashed into an untouched portion of forest. Its companions, however, ignored their brethren's altered course and did not swerve from their dive.

"Agellic!" Moknay cursed. "We can't fight! Logan and I aren't healed!"

"We can't run, either, Murderer!" Thromar shouted back.

His vision blurred by pain-caused tears, Logan spied the oncoming Demons ready their magic. Faint, piercing barbs of sensation made their way into Logan's frame as he pulled himself erect and withdrew his sword.

"Matthew!" Mara cried out. "Run! It's you they want! We'll try to keep them back!"

The young man shook his head violently, trying to clear the pain misting his thoughts. Run? he asked himself. Where? Alone? No.

A blinding burst of energy struck the ground beside Logan and erupted in a massive sheet of flame. Forced back by the heat, Logan stumbled sideways, still trying to blink the confusion from his eyes.

Silver flashed from Moknay's bloodied right glove and struck a Demon squarely in the eye. The wounded monster screamed, furiously plucking the blade from its face and glaring down at the grey-garbed Murderer. Sorcery spat from its hands and seared the grass as Moknay rolled out of the way and dived behind a mutated tree.

"Damn Demons! Damn magic! Damn! Damn! Damn!" he swore, rolling to his feet and extracting another dagger.

Thromar fended off a magical blow with his sword and flinched as sorcerous sparks leapt into the night air. "By Harmeer's War Axe!" the huge fighter boomed. "There's too many of them!"

"Brilliant observation," Moknay jeered, evading another bolt from the hovering creatures.

Mara pulled back the lever on her Binalbow and released two more shafts that speared a second Demon's wings. Screaming, the beast momentarily lost control yet righted itself before crashing to the earth.

"They keep healing!" the priestess shouted in angered frustration.

A red-blue explosion ripped the distorted turf at her feet.

Logan staggered to his right, trying desperately to keep his balance. A blast of magic shook the trees behind him and Logan careened to his left, planting his staff in the ground to help hold him up. Fighting his unfocused vision and the muted feelings of warped magic, Logan tried to look up at his enemies and narrowly avoided another shrieking whip of sorcery.

Shit! the young man cursed, diving. I can't even think straight!

Thromar launched himself forward, skewering a Demon on his heavy sword. Yellow-white blood squirted as the fighter released a triumphant laugh that was quickly cut short as the spitted Demon swung at him.

"Brolark!" the fighter yelled. "Doesn't a clean blow count anymore?"

Moknay darted out from behind a protective tree, launching two daggers in rapid succession from his right hand. "Does anybody see Nightwalker yet?" he queried sardonically. "I think it's about time he showed up to save us poor, pathetic creatures."

Logan wheeled about when he heard Mara shout. A Demon

crashed into the dark-haired priestess, knocking her to the ground and her Binalbow out of her hands. Instantly, her dagger was out, yet the slim blade looked so useless before the Demon's magical strength.

"Mara!" Logan cried out, lunging blindly for the downed priestess.

Oak cracked across the Demon's fragile skull and it glared up at Logan, hatred glowering in its amphibian eyes as blood dribbled down its face. Logan's own eyes went wide as he recognized the small cuts and abrasions that criss-crossed the creature's face. This was the same Demon that had stolen the medallion from him, the young man realized. This was probably the leader!

A blue-white blast of magic spumed from the Demon's claws and caught Logan in the midsection. The young man flew backwards, stunned. His sword spilled from his grasp, yet he still clung tightly to the staff in his left hand. An abrupt jolt of pain told Logan he had landed, and a thunderous rush sounded in his ears.

Blinking the lights from behind his eyelids away, Logan turned and spied the Roana at his back.

An airborne Demon emitted a victorious yowl and launched itself for the dazed Logan. Hearing the scream, Logan glanced up, bringing his staff out before him. Magic crackled as the Demon rammed into the oaken pole and was mystically thrown over Logan. Limbs thrashed in bewildered pain as the creature tried to right itself, yet it splashed into the crystal waters of the river.

Almost overwhelmed by the collection of pain and numbness bombarding his senses, Logan turned about to confront the Demon, and his eyebrows raised. The beautiful waters of the Roana had turned a milky grey, and churning, violent bubbles broke the surface. Steam hissed skyward as if the river were boiling, and, from the tortured shriek of the drowning Demon, Logan surmised he may have guessed right.

Moknay's voice cut through the young man's surprise: "Logan! Your back!"

The young man pivoted, drawing up Launce's staff for protection. Green energy erupted from the wooden pole, catching the oncoming Demon full in the face. Jagged, lime-colored streaks arced up and down the gangly creature as it writhed in agony. Logan gaped at his staff when the Demon crumpled to the ground, looking at the blunt end as if it should hold a secret pistol or sword point.

Remember. A soft voice reached Logan's mind. *Remember us, Matthew.*

The sprites! the young man thought. So close to Roana's river, they were able to offer help even without his asking!

A sudden shout from Mara pulled Logan away from his thoughts and back toward the battle. Bone-chilling fear gripped the young man's throat when he saw the priestess struggling with the scarred Demon, its bony hands entwined in her long, dark hair. A malicious smile was smeared across its rounded mouth, and magicks stolen from Logan's medallion sparked in its eyes.

Logan kicked himself to his feet, dirt spewing into the air beneath his tennis shoes. "Let her go, you sonuvabitch!" he screamed in fury, driving forward with Launce's staff.

Emerald light flickered in the early evening darkness, spearing the scarred Demon with oak and theurgy. A garbled shriek escaped the Demon's throat, and it released its hold upon Mara, yet it did not die. With a malevolent smirk, the creature pulled itself off Logan's staff and allowed the young man to watch its rapid regeneration of sinew and tissue—an event which reminded Logan of his first encounter with Groathit.

Logan, however, gritted his teeth as he saw the flow of yellow-white blood stop. All right, he growled. You want a magic fight, I'll give you a magic fight!

The hands of phantom sprites touched Logan's temples, and discomfort flashed briefly through his nerves. When he blinked his eyes clear of the nausea, every conceivable mote of magic surrounding him was his. Undaunted, the Demon towered before the young man, flickers of magical force leaping from its talons. Another Demon—answering an unspoken command— spread its leathery wings and dove downward, claws directed for Logan's face.

Logan looked up, eyes narrowing. Controlled by a surge of anger, the young man gripped the oncoming Demon by its millions of molecular parts and pulled. A scream of misery split the unnatural silence of Greenwoods as the lean monster dissolved, torn asunder by Logan's fury.

The lead Demon took a cautious step back, its large eyes flicking back to where its brother had disintegrated in mid-flight. The Unbalance meant to fight, the creature's mind informed it. Surely the Creator would not want his Children destroyed by the Unbalance? Surely the Unbalance must be the one to die!

Calling upon the hideously Natural sorcery swirling in its body, the Demon reached into the dimension of rays and plucked forth a stream of bolts. Still focused in the molecular plane, Logan easily took each blast and scattered its atoms across the night sky.

"What in Imogen's name are they doing?" Moknay wondered, feeling helpless in the face of such a conflict.

"Dueling, Murderer," Thromar answered without really needing to. "Come on, friend-Logan! Soup-bowl the damn thing over!"

Caught up in the myriad configurations of energy, Logan did not hear the fighter's encouraging cries. He only felt the magic flowing through him, numbed, yet powerful. And Logan seethed with anger at the monster facing him. Anger made up of fear, confusion, and the demanding need to go home.

Flames roared from the Demon's hands and Logan popped momentarily out of existence. A sudden control of natural forces introduced itself to Logan's body when he reappeared, and the young man struck with his newfound powers.

A vicious wave of water rushed upward from the Roana and swamped the lead Demon, its clear liquid still frothing venomously. Touched by the active waters, the scarred monster screamed, using its own magicks to teleport away.

Teeth clenched, Logan called upon the same teleporting energies yet did not use them. Instead, he squinted and peered through multiple layers of energy and space to see the Demon shifting instantaneously to another area. Reacting, the young man summoned the natural magicks at his command and directed a blue-white flare of power at where the Demon would reappear.

Air exploded outward as the scarred Demon teleported in, and an agonized scream fled its circular mouth. A slash of magic as cold as liquid nitrogen struck the beast on the right side, turning the flesh of its frail right arm a sickening blue. Like a loosely packed snowball, the limb splintered and broke as the Demon clutched at it, severing its own arm at the shoulder.

The horde of remaining Demons watched in stupefaction as their leader gazed down at its maimed right side.

Logan still boiled with intense hatred and rage.

As if by another mental order, all the Demons fled, screaming at the pale moon that hung in the dark sky.

The ire and power gradually leaked free of Logan. With an exhausted sigh, he dropped to his knees. Mara came instantly to his side, trailed by Moknay and Thromar.

"By Brolark, what a show!" Thromar bellowed. "And you keep saying you're not a spellcaster!" The large fighter grinned with yellowing teeth. "I think you should have taken out your eye, friend-Logan; that would have sent them running!"

I am *not* a damn spellcaster! the young man wanted to scream, yet he was too weak. I am not a damn spellcaster nor do I want to be! I don't know why I used that magic! Maybe because I had to! Maybe because I thought it would speed things up! Maybe because we would all be dead if I didn't! What does it matter? I am not a spellcaster and I am not planning on sticking around long enough to become one! It's bad enough I take in magic just being here, let alone how much I take in when I use the damn stuff!

Don't you understand? the young man pleaded to his friends silently. I don't want to be here . . . I just want to go home.

Imploringly, Logan accidentally looked into Mara's green eyes and found the mental plea answered. The priestess seemed to understand the young man's paradoxical plight—his reluctance to use magic, yet the necessity of it.

Logan sighed: caught between a rock and a hard place again.

The young man noticed Moknay's grim stare at the star-filled sky and tried to follow the Murderer's gaze.

"You've scared them away for now," the grave-faced man remarked, noting Logan's perplexed look, "yet we're still nowhere near Agasilaus's stronghold. We have at least a good four leagues between Greenwoods and the castle. And they'll be back." The Murderer faced the heavens again. "They'll be back, and next time they'll be much more cautious."

"And we'll be ready for them!" boasted Thromar, tugging at his sheath and sword.

Logan frowned at the sureness in the fighter's voice as he glimpsed the river behind him. Victory belonged to the four only because of the help Logan received, the young man decided. Next time, there'll be no river at his back and no sprite to help him win. Next time—in addition to the Demons' added caution—Logan would be without any magic.

A pair of ebony eyes seemed to form out of the shadows that danced upon the Roana's surface before fading into the night.

·13·

Fortress

A dull, spattering sound tolled in Logan's ears as droplets of rain struck the heavy robe he had worn in Debarnian. Mara, similarly clad in her heavy robe, held tightly to the young man's waist, trying to shield her body from the pelting rain. Moknay and Thromar rode before the pair, blankets draped over them in an attempt to stay dry. A musty smell hung heavy in the air as the three horses plodded through the marshy soil, their hooves sloshing in the mud.

"This is *not* helping us get to Agasilaus's castle any faster," Thromar grunted, his beard beaded by raindrops.

"Maybe . . . maybe not," Moknay retorted, tugging the blanket around his neck so his strap of daggers did not get wet. "This rain certainly keeps the Demons out of the air and well behind us."

"Unless they use that teleportation spell," Mara remarked.

"I've a feeling they won't be relying too heavily on the magic of Logan's medallion," the Murderer replied. "It got their leader's arm lopped off, so I think they'll be both wary of it and of us. We've been out of Greenwoods for two days now and haven't seen any sign of them."

"That's not to say they're not out there," Thromar grumbled.

Listening to his friends' conversation, Logan blinked his contacts clean and peered into the rainy forest. Two days out of Greenwoods, he mused, and still no attack. Okay, maybe I did worry the Demons a little, but that was because Sparrill is still trying to fight off Gangrorz. Somehow, the closer I am to the sprites' rivers, the more chance they have of helping me. Now, however, everybody thinks I'm the one conjuring magic and that—should the Demons attack—I'll be the one to fight them off. And all the while we're getting farther and farther from the Roana!

Logan gave a backward glance at the forest and accidentally peered into Mara's eyes. The priestess flashed the young man a reassuring smile and Logan felt his stomach knot. Even Mara, he moaned to himself. When the Demons attack, even Mara's going to look to me for magical help. Oh, God! I'm going to look like a fool!

The young man frowned gravely. A dead fool! he added.

There was a sputter of thunder in the clouds above Sparrill as the four continued clinging to their mounts, rainwater dribbling off their protective coverings. A wintery chill pervaded the air, and white mist hissed free from the horses' nostrils. Every now and then, Smeea released a perturbed snort and shook her wet mane with discomfort, splattering her rider who glared down at her with beady eyes.

The odor of wet leather began to seep into Logan's nose from his drenched saddle and saddlebags, and the robes he wore started to become weighed down with water. The young man forced his head and hood up as a growing rumble sounded in the forest ahead of them. Through the sheets of rain, Logan could make out the dim outline of a winding river, its waters a darker green than the surrounding forest. Perplexed, he turned to his companions.

"Dung," Moknay cursed. "I'd forgotten about the Demonry."

"We could always go around it," suggested Mara.

"And lose more time." The Murderer shook his head. "If we're to find some kind of weapon to battle Gangrorz, we've got to find it quickly. Thromar, do you have any rope?"

The fighter nodded, water dribbling down his face. "Some, why? What are you thinking?"

Moknay grimaced, eyeing the green river as they steadily approached. "If one of us can get across and secure the rope, the others won't have such a hard time. Imogen knows how deep it is; I've never known anyone foolhardy enough to want to cross the Demonry."

"I suppose there's always a fool to try anything first," Thromar replied. "I'll do it."

"Your rope," Moknay said with a shrug, "and I can't say that I envy you."

The three horses neared the overflowing banks of the Demonry and halted, the rain pattering about them. Thromar pulled free the neatly coiled rope from Smeea's side and began to unravel it. Logan, however, could not take his eyes away from the rushing river before him. A sour, fetid odor arose from the water, unbroken even by the musty smell of the rain. The gurgling waters were a hideous stagnant green, yet the river rushed with the ferocity of the Jenovian River. How in the world could a rushing river carry stagnant water?

Moknay leapt from his horse and managed to keep his footing in the mud. "Logan and I will hold this end of the rope should you get swept off Smeea."

Thromar glanced up as he tied the rope around his vest of chainmail. "Believe me, Murderer, I've no intention of taking a swim down *that* river."

Moknay replied with a grim frown as his gloved hands sought a firm hold upon the rope. He winced as a tingle of numbness made its way up his unfeeling left side and seemed to sap the strength from half his body. Logan came up behind him, his Nikes slipping in the wet soil. Mara also dismounted, watching from the bank.

With a snort, Smeea started into the hideously green river, her rider holding tightly to her reins. The sweet-sour smelling waters instantly engulfed the pair, almost sweeping the mare off her feet. Thunder filled the sky as the red-and-black horse cautiously made her way across the river, rain pelting them from above. Thromar released a startled shout when a vicious wave of water almost knocked him out of his saddle and threatened to drown Smeea.

Logan cursed, his tennis shoes failing to find any traction in the mud. Before him, Moknay struggled with the rope, favoring his right side while Logan favored his left. Mara watched them anxiously as Thromar and Smeea reached the middle of the Demonry.

"Thromar!" Moknay called out. "The current's too strong! We'll have to try again later! Maybe in the morning!"

Water trickling down his heavily bearded face, Thromar nodded and began to turn Smeea back. Unexpectedly, the riverbank gave way, soft, marshy ground crashing into the stagnant waters. Logan clenched his teeth as Moknay fell in, his hands still wrapped tightly around the rope. More brackish water sprayed as Mara pitched sideways and was instantly swept away by the current.

"Mara!" Logan screamed, helpless to release the rope and lose Moknay as well.

Thromar jerked his rain-spattered head up and saw the priestess shoot toward him on the green waves. With a hurried command to Smeea, the fighter slipped free of the rope around his waist and splashed into the dark waters. Moknay and Logan toppled over backwards as the weight on the other end of the rope vanished.

"Thromar!" Moknay yelled.

"I can reach her!" the fighter shouted back, battling the overpowering rush of liquid.

Smeea clambered to the opposite bank, unburdened by the weight of a rider. She tossed her mane and began to trot along the muddy bank, following the pair that spiraled down the murky river.

By the time Logan had gotten to his feet, Moknay was already trailing the two along the bank. Thinking rapidly, Logan sprinted back to his horse and leapt astride. The familiar twinge of numbness sparked through his right side, yet the young man ignored it as he dug his heels into his horse's flanks. A frenzied shout escaped Logan's lips as his yellow-and-green mount bolted forward, mud spewing up into the air.

The rope trailed uselessly in Moknay's hands as he watched the two forms pulled farther downstream. Rain soaked the Murderer's dark hair, and he had lost his protective blanket somewhere down the river. His grey eyes flickered momentarily as they caught sight of gnarled trees grouping on either side of the Demonry, their twisted branches and roots drooping into the brackish waters. Like the waters, even the plant life of the Demonry was warped and unnatural, which made perfect sense for a river created by a *Deil*'s fatal plunge from the heavens.

Semi-fatal plunge, Moknay corrected himself.

A green-and-yellow blur swept through the rain past Moknay as Logan thundered insanely downstream. Rain plastered his hair to his head and sent streams of water racing down his face, but the young man's eyes never lost sight of his two companions struggling against the mighty current. Oddly twisted trees began to surround the river and the young man, their barks emitting an unpleasant, rain-soaked odor. Logan abruptly saw Mara snag one of the drooping tree limbs, clinging desperately to the branch as the waters sucked at her lithe frame.

In a frenzy, Logan dismounted, almost lost his footing in the mud, and hurried to the banks. The roots of the odd trees were above ground, stretching obscenely out into the green and rancid river. In some places, root and branch seemed to connect, like warped, wooden stalactites and columns.

Blinking rainwater away from his contact lenses, Logan found a lengthy root and began to creep out along it, his feet dangling into the stagnant water. He halted as the root sloped down-ward, vanishing into the dark waters. Mara glanced up, her long, dark hair soaked and streaked with filth. She reached vainly for Logan's outstretched hand, using as much of her strength as she could muster without losing her grip on the branch.

"Reach!" Logan urged her.

The priestess swallowed water. "I can't!" she choked.

Logan pulled his hand away, glancing back toward the shore. He was still too far from her, he realized, and Moknay hadn't arrived with the rope yet.

The young man's blue eyes suddenly fell upon Launce's staff strapped to his horse's side and he quickly scuttled back to shore. He returned to the root with the pole in one hand, leaning out over the river and the disappearing root as he extended the staff toward Mara.

Come on, the young man coaxed himself. You've got to reach her! You've got to!

There was an emerald spark from the tip of Launce's staff and Mara felt the branch she held come alive. The roots and limbs of the oddly distorted trees became living creatures, snaking out and grasping one another to form a gnarled, oaken bridge spanning the Demonry. Mara swiftly clambered onto the mesh of roots and branches, coughing. There was a shout as Thromar rammed into the magically formed bridge, his meaty hands reflexively gripping the side. Sputtering, the fighter pulled himself from the river and sat heavily on the bridge. He spat water from his lungs before he realized what had saved him.

"By Brolark!" the fighter exclaimed, glancing at the tree-formed bridge in sudden—if belated—amazement. "Friend-Logan, did you do this?"

Logan looked away from the oak staff in his hands and gave the fighter half a nod. There's still some magic on your side, he informed himself. Launce's staff. It worked outside Plestenah when the Jewel had caused the river to swell; it had flared when the sprites had been captured; and Munuc had told the young man it was worth holding onto. Why didn't he think of it before? The staff's magic was responding to Logan's subconscious commands all along since the young man was not directly thinking of using the staff.

Moknay skidded to a halt in the mud, his grey-and-black horse trotting behind him. Smeea watched the four from the opposite bank, her red eyes flaming indignantly at the muck that covered her from the Demonry. The mare seemed to accuse them of sending her across when there was a bridge farther down the river.

Logan replaced Launce's staff on his horse and glanced southward through the rain. Vaguely, he could make out the hazy outline of Lake Atricrix, its shores overflowing with dark, foul waters. Such trees as the ones surrounding the river also lined the lake's shores.

Thromar wrung out a pant leg. "As if I wasn't wet beforehand," he muttered, throwing his companions a yellowing grin.

Mara shivered despite the fact that she wore Logan's robe.

"We'll camp on the other side of the river," Moknay stated, "and build a large fire. Hopefully, no one will be able to see it through the rain."

Using the sorcery-born bridge, the four made their way across the green and turgid Demonry River and found a dry spot a few yards into a copse of trees. They could still see the river and the distant lake, but they were far enough away so that they were not threatened by a sudden flood. The fire Thromar soon had blazing relayed some warmth back to Logan as he huddled nearby, the others in a tight ring around the flames. Wet and bedraggled, the quartet sat around the blaze as the rain-filled sky grew darker, and blackness began to cover the land beneath the clouds. The patter of rain continued about him as Logan's body grew numb to the cold and the wetness of his clothes, and he drifted off to sleep.

For some unexplained reason, Logan knew the darkness surrounding him would not go away. Everything was made up of a living blackness—a writhing, coiling mass of ebony that coated the world like dust. In the darkness, Logan peered through the forest and spied a massive building looming up from where Lake Atricrix had been earlier that night. The rains had stopped, but the musty smell of moisture still densely filled the night sky.

Tentatively, Logan got to his feet, hearing the damp earth squelch grotesquely beneath his shoes. That building had not been there before, Logan's mind repeated. Even through the rain you would have been able to see it, and what the devil was it doing out in the middle of where the lake had been?

The living darkness of the night swirled about the young man as Logan started for the massive structure. His eyes only pierced the veil of blackness in parts—perhaps only where it deemed him worthy to see through it. There were no stars or sky present . . .

only the overall enveloping blackness.

A faint tingle of fear crept up Logan's spine and he threw his sleeping companions a backward glance. Better not wake them, he decided. I'll just see what this thing is and then tell them. No sense in burdening them with unnecessary fears.

His Nikes making soft, squishing sounds across the swampy ground, Logan carefully made his way toward the building. He stopped once, eyeing the structure through the moving blackness and placing his numb, right hand on his sword hilt before continuing. Whatever it was, the building seemed to radiate a sensation that unnerved Logan moreso than the usage of magic. Maybe even the gelatinous darkness writhing through the air around him was caused by this mysterious piece of architecture. Whatever power lurked within fed Logan's deprived senses with an aura of terror and foreboding. Nonetheless, the young man strode onward, beads of perspiration beginning to dot his brow.

Logan took a cautious step toward the double doors and halted. The entire building was made up of marble, elegantly carved without the slightest trace of weathering. Golden handles adorned the twin portals, a strand of damp riverweed choking the left one. Shaking, Logan reached out a hand and pulled the doors open. A disorienting feeling of death arose in the young man's mind, and he recognized the building as resembling a small structure he had once visited in a graveyard. Urns had covered the walls, filled with the ashes of the dead. Was this building a shrine of some sort? Was the young man going to find nothing more than the cindered remains of the dead?

The logical speculations running through the young man's brain did not dampen the icy feeling of fear that settled in his stomach. Death was here, another portion of his mind worried. Death lingers everywhere within this place.

An eerie, unseen source of light gleamed dimly off a winding marble corridor that beckoned the young man forward. Smooth, almost glassy pillars of marble stood sentry along the hall, their tops reaching up to a roof that did not exist. Only that same, living blackness thrived above, obscuring any ceiling that may—or may not—have existed.

Logan's mud-smeared shoes made faint squeaking noises as he started down the marble corridor, his sweaty palm grasping his sword hilt fearfully. An unsettling feeling of desolation accompanied the young man's fear as he walked farther into the marble structure. The hallway was widening, he saw, and the unexplained light source flickered malevolently off clumps of water plants that lay strewn about the floor.

His sword drawn, Logan poked his head into the massive chamber at the corridor's end. A box was situated in a corner and an elegant coffin stood in the center of the square room. His mind recalled the shrine of cremated bodies but another portion of his brain told him this marble structure could not be a funeral home. It was too empty . . . too ominous.

Curiosity quelled the horror brewing inside the young man as Logan approached the bronze coffin. It certainly didn't look like anything from Sparrill, he noted, and some anxiety seeped back into his body. It was a coffin straight from Earth . . . so what was it doing here? What was this whole building doing here?

Logan sheathed his sword and went to lift the coffin lid. Like a swarm of bees, his fears descended, freezing his muscles. Dracula! his mind screamed. Vampires! Don't open the lid! He'll jump out at you and bite your neck!

Logan hesitated a moment, eyeing the casket suspiciously. He hadn't heard of any rumors of vampirism while in Sparrill, but he had encountered creatures like that reptile-dragon thing outside of Eadarus when he first arrived, and all the Demons. Who's to say vampires didn't exist in Sparrill?

Then again, the young man mused, who's to say they'd have coffins from Earth and buildings that take the place of entire lakes?

His muscles free of his fear, Logan went to lift the lid and halted again. As an afterthought, the young man freed his sword and then proceeded to raise the cover. The bronze lid flipped back and locked into place, revealing white pillows and a white mattress. In the flickering glow of the marble building, Logan couldn't be sure, but the coffin looked used—as if someone had been lying in it not all that long ago.

See! I told you! his terror shouted once more. Vampires! It's night, so he's not here right now! You'd better get out of here before he comes back! You opened his coffin and he might get mad! Run! Run away!

This time it was Logan who froze his muscles, refusing to let his legs carry him away from the Earthly coffin. Frightening or not, this empty—but used—casket meant something, the young man understood. What it meant, he wasn't quite sure, but, then again, throughout this entire quest things were happening that never seemed to have any sense behind them.

There was a sudden feeling in the air, and Logan felt the hairs on the back of his neck prickle. His eyes left the empty coffin and looked up, but there was nothing else in the chamber. Then he remembered the box in the far corner and turned around to face it.

The box was no longer a box but a towering mass of dark, oozing flesh that peered down at the young man with flaming black eyes. Nostrils flared across the otherwise featureless face and then submerged, like the snout of some animal coming to the surface of the water to breathe. Unable to move, Logan gaped at the massive form behind him, his sword and arm frozen at his side.

"You are the one they call Matthew Logan?" a deep, hideously evil voice echoed about the marble walls.

A fanged frown of befuddlement spread across the creature's face and swiftly vanished. "You are not what I sensed either . . . perhaps the danger lies within your staff, for it is not in you."

Blackness flared in the monster's eyes.

"You are nothing."

Two serpentine arms shot out from the hulking pillar of dark protoplasm as Logan tried to bring his sword up to protect himself. Each arm glistened with a thin sheen of mucus, and blue-grey claws glinted upon each of the three fingers. Logan's horror amplified as razor-sharp beaks suddenly grew out of the palms, lashing out for the young man's chest.

Logan screamed, and blood sprayed, as the twin beaks pierced his breast and bit into his rib cage, severing bone. Intense agony flooded Logan's brain as he started to pitch forward, the beaks cruelly wrenching at a part of the young man that would not yield. Unexpectedly, the arms tore away, and Logan felt an immense emptiness swell and replace the hole in his chest.

"My . . . heart," the young man rasped, staring in horror at the lump of muscle held tightly in the beaks' grasp. "My heart."

Logan crashed forward . . . filled with emptiness at where his heart had once been.

"My . . . heart," Logan murmured pitifully. "My heart."

Mara wrapped her arms tighter about Logan, turning her eyes toward Moknay and Thromar. Unexpectedly, Logan went rigid, his own eyes popping open. He pulled himself out of Mara's embrace and swung around to face the southern forest. Lake Atricrix lurked just beyond the trees, half-obscured by the slight drizzle of rain that continued.

A dream! his mind sighed. It was just a dream!

"Matthew," Mara said softly, "are you all right?"

The young man glanced up at the priestess, his numb right hand feeling his chest and the subconscious reminder of what had happened to it. "My heart," he breathed, the nightmare still vivid. "The bastard ripped out my heart."

"What?" Thromar blurted out. "What are you saying, friend-Logan?"

Logan shook his head, trying to decipher reality from dream. Out of all my dreams here, he thought, that was the most real. There was no red sky or silver stars . . . nothing to indicate that it might have been a dream except for that building suddenly in place of the lake. That was why I saw an Earthly coffin . . . I haven't seen a Sparrillian coffin yet, so I stuck in one I have seen. But why? Who's going to need a coffin? Better yet . . . who no longer needs a coffin?

"Gangrorz!" the young man exclaimed out loud. "The son of a bitch is right out there!"

"If you're referring to Atricrix," Moknay stated, "that goes with the myth. Lake Atricrix is the crater Gangrorz created when he fell back to Sparrill from Roana's blast."

"From the Heart's blast, actually." Mara corrected the Murderer. "Roana was just attempting to control it."

"Gangrorz's Tomb," Logan recalled. "Thromar called something Gangrorz's Tomb . . ."

"Lake Atricrix," Thromar answered, nodding. "Gangrorz landed there and the sea poured in on him. That's why the water's so foul."

As the dream slowly faded, Logan tried to piece together the information his subconscious had relayed to him. "He said something about me," he mumbled to himself. "I'm not the one . . . or something like that." The young man blinked. "No! My staff! He sensed my staff, not me! That's probably why he was after me! He thought Launce's staff was me!" Logan hurriedly got to his feet. "We've got to get out of here! We're too damn close! He'll have his Demons here in no time!"

"Matthew, what are you talking about?" Mara inquired.

Logan threw his arms into the air. "I don't know!" he exclaimed. "Launce's staff is magic . . . Natural magic. Enough so that Gangrorz wants to get rid of it or something. What he thought was me was actually the staff! That must be why he had the Demons after us! Now that he knows it's just another object like my medallion, he'll send them swarming in after it! And they already got the medallion from me easily!"

"Wait!" Moknay cried, trying to stop the young man's frantic actions. "What do you mean, Gangrorz knows it's just another object? How do you know what Gangrorz knows?"

Logan paused, teeth clenched. "I think I just met the son of a bitch," he snarled.

The expressions on his three companions all read the same. A jumbled collection of shock, horror, and concern etched their features. Somehow, through his sleep, Logan had come face to face with their enemy, who—according to the young man—lurked close by.

They did not need much more encouraging to leave.

"He wants your staff, friend-Logan?" Thromar wondered as he mounted Smeea. "Why?"

"I don't know," admitted Logan. "I don't even know if he *wants* my staff. I just keep remembering what that Blackbody told us about the natural Balancing the unnatural. Launce's medallion was Natural and Gangrorz took that. I know damn well that the staff is too. It freaked out when that first wind hit and the sprites were captured. I just never added it all up before. Gangrorz obviously wants my weapons *because* they're weapons. Nightwalker told us we needed a Natural weapon to fight Gangrorz—Gangrorz isn't even letting me keep the ones I've already got!"

The three horses broke through their protective copse of trees and thundered back into the light drizzle of rain. A common fear churned in all four members of the group as they rode eastward, knowing the Worm lurked at their backs. Mara held fast to Logan's waist as they rode, and the young man could not fight the conflicting sensations about his middle. Mara's arms were warm and pleasureable, yet that same dream-felt emptiness throbbed only inches above in his chest.

Logan wiped rainwater from his eyes, gritting his teeth as he tried to remember the nightmare. How could he meet Gangrorz? he pondered. It was his dream . . . would the Worm actually participate? Of course he would! Somehow my subconscious is much more in tune with Sparrill and magic. The Smythe warned me through my subconscious . . . so did Nightwalker. Who's to say Gangrorz can't do that? Christ, who's to say I can't pop around in my sleep? I've been using enough goddamn magic! Without that feeling of disagreement always bothering me, sometimes I forget that using too much magic will stick me here for good!

The young man frowned. So what the hell are you going to do, Matthew? Fight the Wreaker of Havoc with your sword? Might as well use a toothpick against a grizzly bear!

Four rain-muffled explosions reverberated throughout the trees as the three mounts forged onward. Questioningly, Logan swung about in his crude saddle, trying to pierce the curtain of light rain. No flames, he noted. No smoke. What exploded?

Soul-twisting shrieks split the darkness, and the hollowness in Logan's breast seemed to expand. Reflexively, the young man's heels dug into his horse's flanks, realizing the horde of Demons had teleported close by. Then he had been right. The Worm was trying to dispose of some threat that he had . . . and knowing the threat was not Logan, the creatures were attacking once more.

"They're behind us," Mara said into Logan's ear.

The young man nodded frantically, catching the frenzied rustle of wet shrubbery echoing at his back. "Let's keep it that way," he replied.

The rain-drenched soil splashed high into the air as the yellow-and-green mount hurried through the woods, its eyes wide as it scented the pursuing Demons. Smeea and Moknay's horse flanked it on either side, hooves slicing the marshy earth. There was a large frown scrawled beneath Thromar's dripping beard as his dark eyes stared far into the forest.

"If luck is with us—and we can keep the Demons behind us— we might just be able to reach Agasilaus's castle," the fighter declared.

The drizzling rain ceased, leaving the sky empty. The scrabbling of the Demons through the underbrush stopped, as well, as the gangly creatures took to the air.

"Luck isn't with us," Moknay sneered.

Chestplate gleaming blue-grey, the Reakthi soldier made his way across the damp grounds and entered the large tent brightly lit with lanterns. Although the sun slowly rose above the Lathyn Mountains, every now and then peeking through the clouds, the lanterns continued to burn, illuminating the tent with an orange-yellow glow. A white-chestplated Reakmor looked up as the soldier stepped in.

"You have news for the Imperator?" the Reakmor queried, running a hand across his clean-shaven face.

"Yes, sir," the Reakthi answered. "Scouts returning from the south have spotted three or four people fleeing what appears to be a horde of magically endowed Demons."

There was a sudden silence in the tent as a man stood up behind the Reakmor, his black chestplate gleaming in the light of the many lanterns. He held a large book in one hand and, with the other hand, stroked a trim goatee of silver hair.

"Magically endowed Demons, you say?" the Imperator questioned.

The Reakthi swallowed. "Yes, sir."

Imperator Quarn turned his light blue eyes on the Reakmor beside him and then returned his gaze to the grey-chestplated Reakthi. "And you said people," the Imperator remarked. "What people?"

"Three or four, sir," the soldier responded. "Three men and, we think, one woman."

The Imperator set down his book and clasped his hands behind his back. "Of Sparrill or of Denzil?" he interrogated.

"Three appear to be Sparrillian," the Reakthi reported, uneasily fidgeting under the scrutiny of the Imperator's light-colored eyes. "The last is neither. We thought at first he may have come from Droth, but then saw how closely he fit the reports of Imperator Vaugen concerning the stranger."

Quarn's light blue eyes sparked with interest. "The stranger *and* magically endowed Demons?" he said, the pleasure in his voice recognizable. He turned to the Reakmor. "Well, Osirik, it looks as if we're going to be able to reap the harvest and fight the war with the same scythe."

Reakmor Osirik nodded curtly, dismissing the Reakthi scout. "Yes, sir, I'll have the camp thrown and the men ready by midday."

"Sooner than that," came Quarn's reply. "We have both magical Demons *and* the stranger. This is our one chance to regain the power that was once ours!"

Logan squinted through the cloud-filtered sunlight at the black mound of stones that stood atop a small slope overlooking Lake Xenois. There had once been a wide clearing all around the fortress, only now it was littered with weeds and saplings. The horses easily galloped across the wide expanse of ground, their hooves still sloshing through the rain-soaked dirt.

"Open space!" warned Moknay, giving the pursuing Demons a backward glance. "Watch yourselves!"

Logan risked a glimpse down at Launce's staff strapped to his horse's side and urged the yellow-and-green stallion on faster. The Demons would not hesitate to kill him, Mara, or his horse in order to get the staff. If Logan's dream had informed Gangrorz as it had informed him, the Worm knew the threat was in the young man's staff and wanted it as he had wanted the medallion.

His shaggy, red-brown mane of hair blown dry by the wind, Thromar looked at the abandoned castle nearing them and swiveled about to glare at the Demons. "There's only four of them," he boomed. "Why don't we kill them?"

"Because," Moknay retorted. The Murderer eyed the looming black structure warily. "You aren't balking, are you, Thromar?"

Thromar pulled himself up in his saddle, chest out. "Who? Me? Thromar the Fearless?" He patted his worn and stained sword appreciatively. "I was the one who killed that Reakthi bastard!" he reminded his companions.

Moknay wore a secret grin as they rode onward. "So I remember," he jeered, "but I also remember our bet, Thromar the Not-Quite-So-Fearless."

Glancing over his shoulder, Logan thought he saw some color drain out of Thromar's bearded face. "An unfair wager, Murderer," the Rebel argued. "Circumstances force us to run from your part of the bargain."

"And run toward your part of the bargain," Moknay replied. "I've withstood my fair share of sorcery, Thromar. Now it's your turn."

Inquisitively, Logan threw his companions a glance, but neither man explained their discussion. Something, the young man guessed, had happened to Thromar in Agasilaus's castle. What, he couldn't begin to imagine, unless it had to do with Thromar's phobia of tight spaces.

As the trio of horses raced closer, Mara drew herself closer behind Logan and said into his ear: "There's only four of them. Why?"

Logan shrugged and almost hit the priestess on the jaw. "Don't know," he called back. "Gangrorz probably thought four was enough to steal the staff. He only needed two to get the medallion."

Mara started to look back at the trailing Demons yet caught the bitterness in Logan's voice. "You can't blame yourself," she stated.

"Why not?" the young man demanded. "It's my fault they got

the damn thing. My fault they've got magic on their side now."

"You're not Agellic," Mara said. "You don't have the power to change or alter events in our lives. What happens happens!"

"And it all happens bad," Logan pessimistically added.

Mara's arms about his waist squeezed tighter, and Logan knew it wasn't because the priestess was losing her grip. "Bad or good," she told him, "you can't put the blame on yourself."

Logan found himself without words as the quick—not even real—embrace left his tongue in knots. Bad, his mind moaned. Everything goes bad. Here I am in the middle of a cosmic war—Christ! Being chased by Demons!—and I can't get Mara out of my mind! What a lousy time to fall in love.

The young man blinked. Love? Did I just say that? Do I? Does she? How much? Wait a minute! This isn't even my world! Oh, forget it! It's no use trying to make sense out of the unsensible! I might as well just kick back and think about four Demons who want to rip my throat open and eat my head.

As the group charged recklessly closer to the bleak, deserted fortress, the Demons kept up their steady pace, leathery wings cutting through the cloudy sky. The one-armed Demon was not among the four pursuing the group, yet one of the creatures had been appointed leader, its bulbous eyes locked on the colorful horses and their riders.

The Natural magic, the Creator had ordered. Get the Natural magic from the Unbalance. Only the magicks matter ... the Unbalance and those with him must not be harmed. They are no threat to us without the Natural magicks and the unbalancing effect of the Unbalance himself is of no concern.

A victorious cry wrenched itself from the lead Demon's round mouth as its large eyes spotted the oaken staff strapped to the green-and-yellow horse. That was the object the Creator sought, its dim mind understood. Now it was time to spring the trap that awaited the Human creatures so patiently.

The Demon's slender tongue forked through its jagged teeth in anticipation as it watched the three horses bolt into the abandoned courtyard of Agasilaus's castle.

Logan gave the castle courtyard a brief glance as he directed his mount for the massive doors marking the front entrance. Weeds still speckled by the previous night's rainfall cluttered the once-grand courtyard, and the dark stones that made up the fortress glistened with the same sheen of moisture. For a castle that had been deserted, the fortress certainly didn't look desolate.

Thromar leapt off Smeea, his heavy boots sinking into the mire of the yard as he fought to push open the doors. Moknay also dismounted, two daggers instantly in his hands. Logan caught the flinch of discomfort as a flash of numbness must have raced through Moknay's left side and looked down at his own right side. Nightwalker's spells still hadn't worn off, he thought, and my wound was less severe than Moknay's. He probably has little feeling in his left hand at all.

With a groan that gave away the castle's loneliness, the double doors swung inward and the three horses darted inside. A titanic boom resounded off the stone walls as Thromar heaved the doors shut, leaning up against them as he inspected the deserted foyer.

"Hasn't changed all that much," the fighter grunted sardonically. "It's only lacking a few thousand Reakthi maggots."

"Thank Imogen for that," Moknay quipped, replacing the dagger he held in his left hand. The Murderer turned to study the empty castle. "We don't have much time, Thromar. Those Demons will be teleporting in soon enough—a pair of castle doors isn't going to stop them for long."

Thromar scratched his thick beard, and his face paled once more as memories came flooding down upon him. "Agasilaus's chambers were on the fourth floor, I believe," the fighter murmured. He walked to a wall where an elegant lantern coated with dust hung and took it down. In a moment, the fighter had lit the first lantern and was lighting a second. "A gloomy place if ever I saw one," the Rebel muttered uneasily to himself.

Moknay took the second lantern. "Then you've never been in a back alley in Eadarus," he joked, the light in his hands dancing across the stone walls.

Logan gave the dark castle a disturbed glance, eyeing Launce's staff. "You guys had better go," he instructed. "I'll stay here."

"What?" Moknay wondered. "Why?"

Logan unstrapped the staff at his horse's side and grasped it tightly. "Launce's staff," he reminded the Murderer. "We can't just leave it here for the Demons to take while we go to the fourth floor. We might not find anything up there."

Moknay threw the massive flight of stairs on his right a swift glance. "Can't you take the staff with you?" he queried.

"And let the Demons kill the horses?" Mara put in. "No, Matthew's right. We need someone to stay and look after the mounts." The priestess unslung her Binalbow. "I'll do it."

"No," protested Logan. "You go with Thromar and Moknay."

"They can take care of themselves," Mara replied, "and they certainly wouldn't need my help to pick out a magical item."

"Two and two, huh?" Thromar snorted, swinging his lantern toward the stairs. "Sounds good to me. After all, how long can it take to climb four flights of steps?"

Moknay frowned. "Quite a bit longer than it takes to teleport," he remarked. Shadows pranced about his grey form as the Murderer set the second lantern at Logan's feet. "Here, friend, you might want this to keep some of the darkness away." Moknay turned to follow Thromar up the stairs. "Why is it fortresses lack windows on the lower levels?" he grumbled in disapproval.

"Effect, Murderer," returned Thromar. "Just for the effect."

Unexpectedly, there was a series of eruptions from the left-hand corner of the foyer as the four Demons magically appeared. Claws glinted with sorcerous might as the lithe monsters charged the four, high-pitched screams of triumph splitting the stillness of the castle.

"Finally worked up the courage?" Thromar roared, tossing aside his lantern and unsheathing his sword.

Mara stepped out in front of Logan, Binalbow raised. "Matthew, get behind me!" she commanded.

The weapon twanged in her slim hands, and one of the Demons toppled, twin quarrels lodged in its throat. Yellow-white blood stained the dust-laden floor of Agasilaus's fortress, yet the Demon staggered back to its feet, glaring malevolently at the priestess.

Logan looked about. He was holding the very item the Demons wanted, and Mara was trying to protect him. With his hands full, how could he make sure *she* wasn't harmed? I'd rather something happened to me than to her, the young man concluded, wishing he could set down the staff and fight.

Moknay released two blades from his hands. One of the daggers sliced a Demon's shoulder open; the other—thrown by his left hand—veered off sharply and clattered against a wall.

"Dung!" the Murderer spat, leaping back down the stairs, his cape swirling through the gloom about him. "Looks as if close quarters is the only way I'm going to be any help!"

An echoing roar of fury escaped Thromar as his mighty sword cut the stale castle air. One of the Demons emitted a cry as the blade bit deep into its neck, cutting through flesh, muscle, and bone. With a weak sigh, the Demon's head spilled one way while its body careened the other. Even so, the decapitated body

continued to clutch frantically to life before its helpless quiverings
gave out, and it died.

"Hack! Slash! Tear!" the fighter thundered in exaltation. "Even
magical these things are puny!"

With an enraged scream, the lead Demon pointed a taloned
hand at the Rebel and released a shaft of power that spat shards
of rubble from the surrounding walls. Mara's Binalbow fixed on
the creature and sent two bolts tearing through its bowels, but
the monster only staggered. Fury and magic flared in the beast's
toadlike eyes as it glared at the priestess.

The Creator wishes for none of the Human creatures to be
harmed, a soft voice whispered in the Demon's mind.

Saliva sprayed around the circular mouth. The Creator no longer
mattered! This was Pain! Humans caused Pain even without
Natural magicks! The Demon would see this Pain stopped! Even
if it meant going against the Creator's wishes!

Moknay jumped to one side as the leading Demon slashed at
him in its wild lunge for Mara and Thromar. "If these damn things
are going to keep healing, we're never going to be able to kill
them all!" the Murderer swore.

Logan watched from behind Mara, a feeling of helplessness
overpowering him. Okay, he reasoned, if the Demons can heal
because of something magical in the medallion, why can't the
staff do anything about it?

The young man looked down at the shaft of oak in his grasp and
frowned. I don't know what this thing does, he groaned to himself.
It controls nature, I guess. It stopped a river from overflowing—
unnaturally—and it formed a bridge out of trees, also unnatural.
What else does it do? Launce had it control regular plants. Can it
cancel the medallion's magic? Naw, that's asking for too much.
So how the hell are we going to stop these things? Like Moknay
said, if we can't figure out a way to kill them, we're never going
to get out of here alive.

Mara backed into Logan as the lead Demon made a frenzied
dive for her, sorcery leaping from its claws. Taken by surprise,
Logan also backed up, his left foot almost tipping over the lantern
on the ground.

Logan froze. Fire? he wondered. Only a really fatal blow is
killing these things and keeping them dead. If we can burn them
to ashes like I did the first one . . .

Without another thought, Logan scooped up the lantern and
hurled it at the lead Demon. Glass fragmented and oil splashed the

grotesque creature across the shoulder and face. Flames instantly caught and leapt upward, feasting merrily upon the Demon's oil-spattered flesh. A painful shriek escaped the beast's mouth as it turned to flee. In its agony, it failed to remember where it was and flew directly into a wall. With a crunch of bones, the Demon flopped to the ground, blazing orange and red as it burned to death.

The last two Demons gaped as their newly appointed leader died. A sword tip suddenly pierced the back of one's neck, and it screamed in surprise and pain. Its spinal cord was severed and it pitched forward, yellow-white blood pooling around it. Thromar, however, was not satisfied and sent a second blow into the monster's skull, cleaving the head wide open.

The surviving Demon screamed in panic and teleported.

"Go!" Logan ordered Moknay and Thromar. "Get up there and then get back! There's no telling if the others are going to join in!"

Moknay threw the Demon corpses a glance before scurrying up the stone stairs, Thromar behind him. Logan watched them go until the light of Thromar's lantern faded into the surrounding gloom. Mara lit a third lantern, and the two led the nervous horses away from the Demonic cadavers. An uneasy silence once more filled the deserted castle hall, broken only by an anxious snort from Logan's mount.

"Do you think they'll find anything?" Mara queried.

Logan shrugged, and his right side did not tingle with sensation. "I hope so," he responded, "but I don't know. Nightwalker suggested a Natural weapon, but he's not even here."

"I don't trust him," Mara said. "He knows too much about what's going on . . . or what will go on."

Logan grumbled, "At least it makes sense to somebody."

"He wants something out of all this," Mara went on seriously. "He's making sure everything goes about in a certain way so he can get something, and I can't tell what."

"And he won't tell you either," Logan quipped. "That much he makes very clear."

"In his own cryptic way," returned Mara, smiling.

The couple grew silent, throwing expectant glances at the gloomy staircase on their right. No sounds traveled through the stone castle, and the feeling of emptiness and desolation struck a subconscious chord in Logan's heart. Abruptly, there was a feeling of warmth on the back of Logan's neck, as if he were being watched from behind. Quizzically, the young man looked behind him but could not pierce the curtain of shadows that hung throughout Agasilaus's fortress. Hand on sword and gripping Launce's staff, Logan took a cautious step toward the far end of the foyer.

"What is it?" Mara questioned, noting his rigid stance.

Logan shook his head.

Blinking, the one-armed Demon receded back into the shadows. The Unbalance had sensed him, the creature realized. The plan had gone awry. How could one of his Brethren even consider going against the Creator's wishes? Only that which reeked of Natural magicks was to be taken—not the Unbalance's lifeforce. Now the ambush was delayed all because of one rash move by a fellow Demon who had been justly punished.

Logan turned away from the darkness, frowning. Probably just nerves, he thought, trying to console himself. Questioningly, Mara watched the young man settle himself against the stone floor, Launce's staff across his knees. The stench of burnt Demon wafted through the stale castle air.

After a moment, Mara lifted her head. "What was that?"

"What?" Logan asked back.

"I heard a horse."

Logan listened, leaning forward as if in an attempt to aid his hearing. Just as he was about to tell Mara she had imagined it, he too heard the snort of a horse. Voices as well, and footsteps muffled by the castle doors and the mud outside.

"Too many footsteps to be Nightwalker," Mara stated. She looked at Logan. "Go tell the others."

Logan hesitated. "What about . . ."

"Go tell the others!" Mara commanded.

Torn between warning his friends and leaving Mara, Logan hesitated a moment longer before turning for the stone steps. That was when the one-armed Demon sprang.

Thromar pounded a fist on a dust-covered table and sent clouds of greyish smoke into the air. "Damn!" the fighter cursed. "Every single one of them! Gone! Every last one!"

Moknay grimly inspected the empty walls and cupboards. "It seems the other Imperators weren't so choosy in what they wanted. Unless somebody else ransacked this place."

"Who would want to come here?" Thromar grunted, fury

bubbling within his massive frame. "Had to have been those Reakthi bastards—or else Groathit and his fellow scumcasters took everything!"

"Unfortunate," mused Moknay, trailing a gloved hand along the stone wall. "He must have had some collection."

"Largest damn collection I've ever seen!" Thromar boomed. "Should've taken it when I left this accursed place!"

"You wouldn't have been able to carry it all," the Murderer commented. He faced his heavily bearded companion. "And besides, you were slightly cooped up for the next few weeks, if I so recall."

The anger brewing in Thromar decreased as the fighter shuddered involuntarily. "Don't remind me, Murderer," the warrior growled. "I'm having a hard enough time as it is just standing here." A meaty finger pointed to an adjacent room. "Right in there's where I killed the whoreson. Got him while he was trying to make some more nefarious plans for the conquest of our land. Bent over his table like a damn scribe, he was!"

The fighter stepped into Agasilaus's private bedroom and sneered. The table was still there, Thromar noted. Even the half-finished papers the Imperator had been writing at the time of his death. Hah! I wonder if there's any of the bastard's Reakthi blood dotting the pages?

Like a grey shadow, Moknay flowed past his war-sibling and curiously glanced down at the dusty tabletop. A sudden spark of interest flared in his steel-grey eyes as he lifted a sheet of parchment, sneering in admiration.

"Agasilaus had quite a grasp on magical items, didn't he?" the Murderer remarked, smoothing his mustache.

Thromar nodded. "I suppose he *had* to know something with all the ones he had stolen and brought with him," he grumbled. The fighter caught the gleam in Moknay's eyes. "Why? What did you find there?"

"I believe it's one of Agasilaus's plans for conquest," Moknay answered.

Curious, Thromar reached out to take the paper, but Moknay swept it away from him. The fighter's beady eyes filled with a sort of indignant anger at his friend's selfish act, but there was still an overriding puzzlement on his bearded face.

"For the love of Lelah, Murderer," Thromar exclaimed, "what's so startling?"

Moknay looked up, eyebrows narrowed. "It would have worked," he said softly.

Thromar was silent before blurting, "What? What would have worked? By Harmeer's War Axe, what in Imogen's name did the bastard want to do?"

"Use the Heart against us," Moknay read. "Somehow Agasilaus learned about the Heart and tried to find it—hoping that, by controlling Sparrill's Heart, he would control Sparrill. And he would have."

"That's why the Reakthi-slime were so well organized!" Thromar boomed. "Friend-Logan made me see that earlier— like they were looking for something . . ."

Moknay gave the fighter a curt nod. "And they were." The Murderer frowned. "And Vaugen's intense pursuit of Logan is beginning to make more sense as well. Logan could—just as he was doing earlier—track down the Heart with his ability. With the Heart, Sparrill would have become Vaugen's. Even if the Heart turned out to be just a myth, Logan's ability would have been enough to find Vaugen a multitude of magical items with perhaps enough power to defeat Eadarus and the rest of our lands."

"So maybe Vaugen did take the weapons that were here?" Thromar contemplated.

"Perhaps," Moknay answered, "but why hasn't he been using them? If not against Sparrill, why not against us?"

The Murderer's keen senses abruptly picked up a faint noise echoing upward from the lower levels of the castle and he sprang to a nearby window slit in the stone wall. Outside in the muddy courtyard he could see a massive sea of chestplated men making their way toward the supposedly empty fortress. All were battle-ready, and a black chestplate gleamed among them.

"Demon dung!" the Murderer spat. "Reakthi . . . a whole swarm of them! There's an Imperator down there as well!"

"Vaugen?" Thromar snarled in question.

"I can't be sure," Moknay replied. He began to leave the bedroom but halted, eyes flickering. "Thromar, we've got to warn Logan and Mara. Without windows they won't know what's going on outside."

The large fighter nodded his agreement. "Then let's be off . . ." he began.

Moknay's hand caught his companion's thick arm. "That way's too long," he declared. "We need a short cut." His expression held no hint of jest or mockery. "Thromar, we need to use the passages."

The fighter blanched, his face going white as he threw a terrified glance over his brawny shoulder at what appeared to be a solid wall. "The . . ." he tried to force out. "Ummm . . . my . . ." A sigh escaped his lips. "My friend . . . I can't."

The desperation still blazed in Moknay's eyes. "You've got to! Only you know where they go! We've got to use them . . . for Logan's sake!"

Thromar could not stop his hands from shaking. "I spent twenty days cramped up in those infernal passages!" the warrior roared. "I wasn't able to leave this damn fortress until after the search for Agasilaus's killer was given up! No one but Agasilaus and the builders of his castle knew about those routes . . . except me! Probably thought that having a series of secret passages installed would save his life if his castle was ever attacked! Cost him his life more or less!"

Moknay was nodding impatiently. "I wouldn't ask you to do this unless it was truly necessary, friend, but I can't fight—this blasted magical healing throws off my timing! We need to warn Logan and Mara and hope we're not discovered! The passages are the only way!"

Uncertainty and terror ran rampant in Thromar's tiny eyes as he struggled internally with his phobia caused by the dark, cramped panels hidden within the stone walls of Agasilaus's castle. At the time, the passages had been the ideal route to infiltrate the fortress, slay the Imperator, and hide until the moment came to flee. Thromar had had no idea the hiding would last nearly a month, and, in that time, he grew to loathe and fear dark, tight spaces. If it hadn't been for his own stealth and the fortunate aid of a rebellious servant, the fighter probably would have starved to death in those black, rat-infested panels!

Still trembling, Thromar bobbed his bearded head up and down in silence. Respect flashed in Moknay's eyes as he watched the fighter walk to the wall he had glanced at earlier and slide it inward. Beyond was a tight corridor that reeked of decay and mildew.

Thromar froze as he lifted a foot to enter the panel. He threw his friend an imploring gaze and Moknay swiftly came up behind him. The urgency still flamed in the Murderer's grey eyes, and Thromar turned his thoughts away from the hellish days he had spent in darkness and constriction and thought of Mara and Logan.

In order to save them from the Reakthi horde, the two had to be informed of the passages that wound their way through Agasilaus's abandoned castle.

His face pale, Thromar stepped into the dark passage and ran to aid his friends.

·14·

Thorns

Hot, fetid breath struck Logan full in the face as he grappled with the Demon for possession of Launce's staff. Three hands locked around the pole, the two spilled backwards, bouncing down the stone steps. Hard, cruel rock slapped the back of Logan's skull, and stars went supernova behind his eyelids. His muscles forgot their commands and relaxed, allowing his fingers to uncurl around the piece of oak in his grasp. With a triumphant yowl, the one-armed Demon jerked the staff away from the young man and fluttered to ground level.

Yellow-white blood splashed across the creature's chest as Mara's Binalbow drilled twin bolts through its rib cage. The Demon staggered, its one-handed grip faltering, and it dropped the staff to the ground.

"Matthew! The staff!" Mara shouted encouragingly.

Dazed, Logan swung around. The deserted castle foyer was swirling around him like someone had placed a kaleidoscope in front of his contacts, and the young man could not properly orient on the staff. His blurred vision caught the pale form that sat up somewhere nearby, two crossbow bolts protruding from its breast. In desperation, Logan heaved himself forward, landing across Launce's staff. Unexpectedly, there was a sudden rush of wind, and Logan rolled toward the front doors, the staff still in his possession. Mara watched as the last four Demons teleported in, flanking their one-armed leader.

Logan stopped his roll and tried to sit up. Jesus! he cursed. I haven't felt this bad since I got whacked over the head at Barthol's!

Trying to fight the constant pounding in his skull, Logan glanced up and spied the blurry line of Demons. His fingers tightened about the staff until sweat seeped in between them, but the young man knew what it was that the Demons wanted—and so long as he had it, the Demons had not won.

Using the staff to clamber to his feet, Logan backed up alongside Mara. The double doors were behind them, urging the couple to run away, but Logan decided it unwise. The odds were five against two, unfair no matter which way you looked at it. So where the hell were Moknay and Thromar? Four against five at least sounded better—even if the Demons *did* have magic on their side.

Half a grin spread across Logan's lips as he set his hazy vision on the oaken shaft in his hands. The staff was Natural magic, he pondered, like the medallion. Maybe that meant it could do similar things.

"We need to stall," Logan whispered to Mara. "I'm going to try something."

The priestess answered with a curt nod and the leveling of her Binalbow. The flank of Demons didn't even acknowledge her, knowing the wooden quarrels could not do any permanent damage to their magically endowed bodies.

Fighting the dull hammering in his brain, Logan tried to concentrate on Launce's staff. The plane of rays, he thought over and over. The rays. Take me to the rays. Anxiously, the young man waited for the gut-churning flash that would accompany his interdimensional vision, yet none came.

Mara looked away from the Demons and trained her green eyes on Logan. She didn't know what he was up to, but, from the expression on his face, he wasn't faring too well. The Demons had come to consider her a nuisance—like she might consider a biting insect a bothersome pest. Still, there might be some way she could help Matthew in whatever he was trying. The Demons kept healing—aided by the medallion—and yet, they could only heal up to a certain point. Once dead, they had no magical control, and, therefore, no magic stayed within their bodies. That left them dead for good. Also, the more serious the wound, the longer it took for them to heal—that made sense. So that meant a series of well-placed blows might be enough to wound a Demon, keep it wounded, then deliver the killing blow.

Mara turned back to the five Demons. It was worth trying, she thought with a shrug.

Just as one of the Demons took a step forward, the Binalbow twanged. With a skilled hand, Mara threw the lever forward and pulled back, releasing more shafts. Yellow-white blood fountained through the stale air as a Demon crashed to its knees, needled with wooden bolts from head to toe. Even as the first wounds began to heal, Mara placed four more bolts into the Demon's body. With a helpless quiver, the Demon pitched forward. A low "thwock" echoed throughout the empty foyer as two bolts speared the Demon's skull and snuffed out the magical life brewing within it.

The creature died.

The one-armed Demon emitted a high-pitched scream of fury, silently commanding two Demons to charge the priestess. Logan jerked up his head and instantly regretted it as the throbbing in his skull increased. Mara! his brain shouted at him through the pain. Mara's in danger!

One of the Demons screamed as a red streak of magic erupted from the tip of Launce's staff and burned through the top of its skull. The Demonic corpse slid to the floor, yellow-white blood and brains mingling with the dust of past years. With a confused blink, the other Demon charging Mara stopped, looking back at its leader with uncertainty in its large eyes. Natural magicks! the monster thought, flinching. The Unbalance uses more Natural magicks!

Logan winced at the combination of pain and numbness coursing through his body. That ray had been quite similar to the rays he had used in the other plane, but his attempt to get there had failed. So how . . . ?

An understanding began to formulate within his mind as Logan pointed the oak shaft at another Demon. A blistering flash of red energy spat from the tip of the staff, blasting off the Demon's kneecap. A sardonic smirk appeared on Logan's face as he mentally congratulated himself. Unlike the medallion, the staff didn't take the user to the plane, the young man mused. Only the staff went, and it plucked out the rays you wanted and directed them.

With an infuriated shriek, the one-armed Demon ducked to one side, narrowly avoiding the beams that exploded from the knoblike handle atop the staff. One of its Brethren wasn't so fortunate and twin shafts of energy sliced its head off its shoulders. Only two Demons remained, one already wounded. The creature without a kneecap on its left leg hobbled into a corner, yet Mara's Binalbow fixed on it and sent two quarrels into the back of its neck. With a pitiful wail, the Demon started to pitch forward, and more yellow-white blood spurted as powerful hooves connected

with the beast's face. In its fear, the Demon had limped to where
the horses were, and Smeea had instinctively lashed out at the
monster.

The bloodied Demon toppled backwards and lay still; Mara sent
a last pair of quarrels into its face and turned to help Logan.

The one-armed Demon turned its amphibian eyes momentarily to where its Brethren had fallen. Dead, the creature's mind
observed. All its Brethren dead. The Unbalance and the Human
WoMan had killed them all—even though Demons were their
superior.

The monster shrieked as a sizzling blast of sorcery splintered
the stones of the castle walls. Must succeed, the Demon concluded. The Creator will be most displeased with failure.

Without recalling what had happened to it the last time it
had engaged Logan in mystical combat, the one-armed Demon
teleported. Logan let out a startled shout as the toad-eyed beast
reappeared directly in front of him, its taloned hand grabbing
the staff.

A flaming burst of energy sent both Demon and Logan crashing through the heavy wooden doors. Already dazed by his fall
down the stairs, Logan felt himself momentarily blacking out as
a clawed hand tried to pry the staff from his grasp. Mud squished
beneath the young man as he slid out into the courtyard, and he
sensed a large crowd around him, but it was probably just his
mind confronted by all that pain. Abruptly, the Demon looked
away, spraying saliva that dripped onto Logan. Magic burst from
its hand, and it released a warning scream at something beyond
them. Then a million bees struck.

Logan was spattered by yellow-white blood as a dozen arrows
suddenly materialized in the Demon's chest. The blinding throb
continued to pound at his skull, and the young man felt an
unexplainable anger swell in his breast. He's bleeding on me!
his befuddled mind snarled. The son of a bitch is bleeding all
over me!

Controlled by a brain benumbed with pain and confusion,
Logan drove Launce's staff directly into the rounded mouth and
watched in grim satisfaction as brains and blood splattered across
the courtyard. Twitching spasmodically, the one-armed corpse
toppled to the mud.

Logan fought his spiraling brain and pulled himself up, grinning
foolishly at Mara. He couldn't understand why the priestess was
gaping at him—why there was such a look of horror in her

beautiful eyes. It wasn't *his* blood spattered all over him, it was the Demon's. I may be a little mixed up right now, but . . .

A muddy footstep sounded like a gong in Logan's ears, and the young man looked over his numb right shoulder. A vast armada of blurry forms filled the courtyard, and a white-vested figure stalked toward the young man.

Maybe they were coming to congratulate him, the young man's chaotic mind suggested. Maybe they were going to make him an official Demon-slayer.

Logan flashed the blurred figures the same foolish grin he had given Mara. I accept this award on behalf of the Academy . . .

Unconsciousness freed him from all the pain and turmoil, and Logan spilled into the mud.

Like an infant learning how to walk, Thromar found great difficulty in moving his own legs through the narrow passages. There was a part of his mind that refused to go any farther—a portion of his brain that had not even admitted to itself that the fighter had actually entered the secret panels. Each step Thromar took was forced by a determination and loyalty that struggled against a fear that was almost insurmountable.

Behind the fighter—itchy with impatience—Moknay coaxed his companion on. "We've got to hurry, Thromar," the Murderer urged. "Logan and Mara won't know what's out there."

Thromar lost his concentration and his legs halted in mid-step. "Confound it, Murderer! I know that!" the fighter barked, his fear easily changing to anger. "I just can't move any faster!"

"Then tell me which way to go," Moknay suggested. "I'll run ahead and find . . ."

"No!" Thromar cried, terrified. "For the love of Lelah, don't leave me here!"

"But I'd just . . ." Moknay inhaled deeply. "Don't worry, friend," he said. "I won't leave you."

The fighter succeeded in moving another foot forward and cringed when his hand accidentally brushed against a spider web. "I feel like a damn fool," Thromar grumbled softly.

Moknay smirked. "You look like a damn fool," he commented.

"Don't try to ruffle my beard, Murderer," Thromar growled, taking a second step. "It won't work. I'm afraid even your insults can't take my mind off where I am."

The Murderer shrugged, and his daggers gleamed in the light of the lantern. "You can't say I didn't try," he remarked.

The two proceeded on in silence, Thromar leading the way. From the fighter's slow and cautious pace, it seemed they trod upon treacherous ground, yet the floors within the passages were as sturdy and as solid as the rest of Agasilaus's fortress. Only Thromar's claustrophobia robbed them of the speed they were capable of . . . and in dire need of.

Dust swirled under Thromar's boot as he shuffled forward. "I don't know how in Imogen's name I let you talk me into this," the fighter rumbled nervously to himself. "Small, cramped places are one thing—but these . . . this place . . . that's another thing altogether!"

Moknay winced as something that may have been an explosion reverberated through the stones. "Something's going on down there," he declared.

"Surely not a battle," Thromar worried. "Friend-Logan and Mara would be no match for the Reakthi we . . ."

"Be that as it may," interrupted Moknay, "something's going on down there."

"Then we'd better hurry," Thromar proclaimed.

The fighter tricked himself into hurrying three steps farther, then his fear returned and resumed control of his muscles. The slowness retained its hold, keeping the two locked in the enclosed space of the secret passages. Darkness and gloom swallowed them whole, and perspiration wound its way down Thromar's face. His meaty hand grasped tightly to his sword hilt, but he knew this foe was unable to be slain by his weapon. Thromar had to rely on his courage to save him from these infernal walls—here, his sword did little good.

Moknay felt the rock floor slope downward as he trailed Thromar through the narrow halls. Various other routes branched off from the one they followed, yet Thromar ignored them. Moknay hoped the fighter's fear had not thrown off his sense of direction but followed on without comment.

Unable to judge the length of time, Moknay breathed a sigh of relief when Thromar stopped and inspected something on his left. Dust spumed upward as the fighter smacked a brawny fist against the hidden panel, breaking its cobwebbed locks. On the other side was a faintly lit chamber, a winding hallway leading back out into the foyer. Hurriedly, Moknay pushed his way past Thromar and dissolved into the gloom. The fighter watched him go, leaning heavily against the wall. His complexion was still white, and he breathed with a great deal of effort. Then, forcing aside the terror he had just faced, Thromar jogged back to the foyer to save Logan and Mara.

A gloved hand pushed the fighter back, indicating for him to be silent. "We're too late," Moknay whispered, grey eyes flaming.

Thromar looked beyond the gloom and saw the castle doors splintered and destroyed. A number of men stood outside, clustered around Mara who sat on Logan's yellow and green horse. The young man himself was not to be seen.

"What did they do to friend-Logan?" Thromar snarled quietly.

Moknay shrugged.

In silence, the pair watched as the Reakthi troops started away, Mara riding among them. There was a hushed snort nearby and Thromar whipped about, grinning broadly as Smeea stepped free of the shadows. Behind her was Moknay's grey-and-black mount.

"Mara must have lied," the Murderer decided, his voice still hushed. "The Reakthi didn't know we were here. Must not have seen the other horses."

"And I think I know why," Thromar replied, pointing toward a Demonic cadaver. "But what I don't get is why they're letting her ride her own horse . . . and where's friend-Logan?"

Moknay frowned. "Chances are they have Logan too," he answered. "And you're right about the horse. Unless she had had it with her, they wouldn't have let Mara go back to get the horse, so she couldn't have chased our horses farther into the castle. But if some Reakthi retrieved her horse, they would have seen our horses and started asking questions."

"And somehow Mara convinced them that we weren't here even though our horses were?" the fighter queried, shaking his head. "Reakthi are too suspicious to be that stupid. They would have searched the castle from top to bottom."

"Maybe they did," Moknay put in, "while we were in the passages."

Thromar shook his head again. "It's a big castle, Murderer," he said. "They wouldn't have gotten past the first floor."

Grey eyes flashing, Moknay straightened his strap of daggers and took his horse by the reins. "Do we attack or trail?" he questioned.

"Neither," another voice ordered.

Thromar and Moknay wheeled about to see a form step free of the darkness, and Darkling Nightwalker stood beside them. His white eyes shined dully in the faint light of their lantern and of the open doors.

"Look who's decided to show up," sneered Moknay. "Things going so badly that you felt you should come straighten us out?"

Nightwalker ignored the insult—or didn't even hear it—and stalked past the two men. "You must not attack or follow," the ebon-skinned stranger advised. "We must let things take their course."

"Friend-Logan's just been carted off by Reakthi and you tell us to sit around and wait?" Thromar bellowed. "Listen, Nightcreeper, we of Sparrill have a certain kinship with those we fight beside. Friend-Logan and I are just as much war-siblings as Moknay and I are! I'll be damned if I don't do something to aid him!"

Nightwalker slowly cocked his head to face Thromar. There was no expression on the strange man's face—only the unsettling gleam of his black skin reflecting the light. "You do not understand," Nightwalker rasped. "It is of the utmost importance that Matthew Logan go with these soldiers. It will become clear to you in time."

With a sneer distorting his upper lip, Moknay stalked forward and threateningly grabbed Nightwalker about his cowl. Grey eyes blazing, the Murderer glared directly into Nightwalker's white eyes and growled: "It will become clear to us right now or else I'll inform you of an engraver I know who doesn't charge much to chisel out a name as long as yours on a gravestone."

Darkling Nightwalker's face remained impassive, but a sort of tension filled the air. Moknay knew Nightwalker loathed to be touched—he could sense it—but the Murderer would not release the stranger. Finally, some of the enigma dropped away from the dark-skinned Nightwalker.

"These are important events, Murderer," Nightwalker vaguely explained. "The Reakthi who have escorted your friends away are under the command of Imperator Quarn. There are two reasons why you and the Rebel must not interfere."

"Quarn?" Thromar exclaimed. "What's he doing out of his fortress? I thought he wasn't interested in conquest any longer."

"He is not," Nightwalker replied, smoothing his cape when Moknay released him. "Something was taken from him and he went to recover it. Instead he found Matthew Logan. Over the years, Imperator Quarn has turned his interest to knowledge rather than the conquest of your world. Matthew Logan will expand the knowledge Quarn seeks, for Quarn has become quite intrigued with the workings of magic."

"He's the one who took Agasilaus's collection!" Moknay understood.

Darkling Nightwalker nodded. "So now you know why it is imperative Matthew Logan stay with Quarn and his men."

The Murderer raised a suspicious eyebrow. "But no Reakthi Imperator is going to help us . . . or even an outsider like Logan."

Nightwalker allowed a brief, somewhat sardonic, smile to cross his face. "Quarn has become a very learned man," the ebon-skinned creature stated. "He knows when something foul pervades the air. He may sense when the clouds build overhead to spill their rain of Darkness. If they are allowed the time, Matthew Logan and Imperator Quarn may reach some compromise."

Thromar and Moknay were silent a moment, watching the troops fade down the side of a hill. Abruptly, Thromar fixed his beady eyes on Nightwalker. "You said there were two reasons," he remembered. "What's the other one?"

Darkling Nightwalker stepped up to the shattered castle doors, the sunlight playing off his brilliant white hair. "That I may not reveal," he said, "for it has not yet come to pass. And if I mention it, it may never be. All you need know is that Imperator Quarn is your only hope in fulfilling your task and destroying He who is the Wreaker of Havoc. Other than that, you must wait on the doorstep of Gangrorz's Tomb."

"What?" Moknay demanded.

Nightwalker stepped outside. "On the shores of what you call Lake Atricrix," he explained as he turned around the corner and was lost from view.

Halting just as he started to move, Moknay turned a sarcastic smirk on Thromar and shrugged. "Why do I have the feeling that if we chase after him, he won't be there?" the Murderer inquired.

"Probably because he won't be," the fighter agreed. Smeea snorted uneasily as her rider mounted up. "I can't say I like the idea of friend-Logan and Mara in *any* Imperator's clutches," he remarked. "What say we trail them anyway?"

Moknay nodded, grinning. "Sounds acceptable to me."

Thromar suddenly threw the Murderer a yellowing grin. "Oh, by the way, pay up."

Moknay pulled on his horse's reins and steered it toward the broken doors. "Excuse me?"

"Pay up," Thromar repeated. "We had a bet and I won."

The colorful horses both headed westward as their riders quarreled. "You did not," Moknay retorted. "The bet was that if I went back to fighting magic, you'd get over your fear of tight spaces."

"And I did! Pay up!"

"Ah, ha! But I fought magic first."

"That's only because there's a lot more of it around than tight spaces!"

"Doesn't matter," sneered the Murderer. "Technically, that makes me the winner."

Thromar scratched his beard in thought. "But you never had to actually go *into* a magical burst," he argued. "I had to go *into* a tight space."

"If I had to go into a magical burst, I'd be dead."

"Doesn't matter," Thromar said with a shrug. "I'd still adhere to the rules and pay up . . . not like some people."

Squabbling, the pair let their horses lead, following the massive force of Reakthi as they made their way toward Quarn's fortress. Neither man noticed the faint flicker of movement in the one-armed corpse that lay half-submerged in the mud of the abandoned courtyard.

A soft, orange-red glow filled the room as Matthew Logan felt sensations returning to his body. There was no pain, only a very relaxed, peaceful feeling that stirred warm emotions inside him. He lay upon a soft bed, and warm blankets covered him. He felt cleaner than he had in weeks and realized he wore only a pair of silken slacks. Still, the tender fabric soothed whatever sores lingered in his legs and backside—man was not meant to ride horseback for as many days straight as he had done.

With a startled shout, the young man bolted upright, realizing he had no idea where he was. There was a momentary flinch of pain from the back of his skull, and numbness tingled up his right side, but there was nothing in the sensations to remind him of the abuse his body had taken as of late.

A door creaked open and Mara entered, a silky white robe draping her supple form. As with Logan, the grime and dirt had been washed from her skin and hair and she looked more ravishing than ever. Nonetheless, confusion ran rampant in Logan's brain as he glanced from the priestess to his strange surroundings.

"Mara?" he sputtered. "What . . . ? Where are we?"

"Reakthi," the priestess explained, sitting on the edge of Logan's bed.

The young man could not help the feeling of déjà vu that roiled to life within him. This was so close to how Mara and he had first met—him in bed, her at his side. Huh? What was that she said? *Reakthi?*

Softly, Mara touched Logan's hand. "Imperator Quarn got word of our whereabouts," she said, noting his alarmed expression. "We're at his castle right now."

"Castle?" the young man exclaimed. He started to get up but Mara held him back. "We've got to get out of here! What about Moknay? Thromar? Are they all right?"

"They're safe," the priestess nodded. "When they let me get your horse, I was able to hide the other two. Moknay and Thromar hadn't come down yet, anyway." Mara pursed her lips, her green eyes looking to one side. "And I think we're relatively safe, too," she added.

"Safe?" Logan cried out. "We're prisoners! Reakthi prisoners!"

Mara smiled faintly, touching the silk robe she wore. "I was given this while my own clothes are being washed and mended; they let me bathe and gave me my own room. You were treated with similar respect—probably more because you were wounded. The Reakmor even made some comment about an elixir for that blow you took. That doesn't sound like we're prisoners to me." A soft hand touched the back of Logan's head. "How do you feel?"

"Fine," Logan tartly responded, wondering how the priestess could be asking questions as meaningless as that.

The young man suddenly stopped, touching the back of his neck. There was no pain, he realized. After falling down a flight of stairs and being blasted out of a castle door, he felt no pain! Something screwy *was* going on here!

"I don't like it," he muttered.

"They seem to be treating us nicely enough," Mara shrugged, and her robe parted slightly.

Logan forced himself to look away. "Yeah," he grumbled, "so I'll work for them."

"But that's the really odd thing," Mara stated. "Quarn gave up all his plans for conquest sometime around the death of Agasilaus."

"Sure, and now he's going to bring them all back 'cause he's got a magic-detector working for him!" sneered Logan.

The priestess got to her feet, tugging closed the partially open robe. "I don't think that's necessarily true, Matthew," she said.

"From what I learned on the way here, the men were out because of another hunt. Something to do with Demons."

Logan raised his eyebrows. "Why?" he asked.

Mara shrugged once more. "That's all I know right now," she apologized.

A door opposite the one Mara had come in through opened and a trim girl entered, timidly setting down the couple's clothing. She flashed the two a smile before hurrying back out, cringing slightly as she passed the Reakmor who stood behind her.

"I trust you are feeling better?" The Reakmor directed his question at Logan.

The young man nodded.

Reakmor Osirik nodded, rubbing his chin. "Good." He hesitated a moment. "We mended your clothes the best we could. I'm afraid we didn't do very well on the blue garments—they're made of an odd substance . . ."

"It's a sweat suit," Logan informed the Reakmor, eyeing him warily.

Osirik nodded curtly. "Ah . . . yes. Well, the seamstress did her best at repairing your clothes and I hope they'll be to your liking." The Reakmor abruptly straightened, resuming his military posture. "Now, there is a matter of business Imperator Quarn wishes to discuss with the two of you, so if you'll get dressed and meet me in the Grand Hall." The man in the white chestplate started to leave but remembered something and stopped. "Two flights down and to the right," he told them, shutting the door.

Logan threw Mara a nervous glance as he pulled himself out of bed.

The grey, bleary walls of Quarn's castle were covered with fine tapestries and paintings, giving the entire fortress a very compact feeling. Unlike Agasilaus's abandoned structure, Quarn's castle rang with noise and overflowed with servants and soldiers. Many occupants stopped to stare as the newly arrived couple made their way down the stone steps, their clothing clean and only slightly telling of their wear.

"I don't like this," Logan whispered into Mara's ear, catching another soldier watching him.

"You're overly cautious," the priestess whispered back.

Logan jerked about as a trio of Reakthi halted and gaped at the newcomers, exchanging whispers among themselves. "Better overly cautious than overly dead," the young man quipped.

Their footsteps only echoing for short distances around them, Mara and Logan made their way down the corridor on their right and continued forward. A curious eyebrow raised on Mara's brow as she noted the odd implements decorating the walls. There were some pictures and tapestries here and there, but strange devices began to adorn the hallway in greater numbers. Some were oddly shaped weapons or staffs; a cloak even hung near-by from the sculptured skull of some make-believe monstros-ity.

The pair stepped into a room and Logan knew this was the Grand Hall. Hardly a hall at all, the chamber was immense in size with large, triangular windows of stained glass filling the room with daylight. A mighty oak table filled much of the room. More of the bizarre items covered the stone walls, each one of them polished and kept amazingly clean—another contrast to Agasilaus's dust-enshrouded home.

Through the sunlight, Logan could see the Reakmor at the front of the table. A fourth figure was in the room, his back to them as he stared at a window. Even in the glare of the stained glass, Logan saw the evil gleam of black armor covering the man's torso.

The Imperator slowly turned, the multicolored sunlight playing across his neatly groomed silver hair. A trim goatee and mustache covered the lower regions of his lean face, and pale, light blue eyes fixed on the priestess and young man.

"It is an honor to have you two as my guests," the Reakthi commander said.

Logan muttered something inaudible.

Imperator Quarn smiled fleetingly. "While I am not surprised by your mistrust, you also do me a great injustice by it," he remarked. "I am not your enemy nor have I ever been, while I know my . . . um . . . fellow associates have not been the least bit kind to you or your land."

"So why are you?" Logan snapped, unnerved by the docile tone of the Imperator.

Quarn approached the table, hands clasped behind his back. "I have grown older," he replied. "I've gained what you might call a realistic eye. In the end, conquest gives us nothing. No satisfaction, no new land . . . only discontent that there are oth-er lands to conquer and more wars to fight and more ways to die. I understood some time ago that this was not what I wanted. These lands are beautiful—why ravage them with war and killing? Why burn them to ashes and proclaim yourself master of a smoking ruin? After my fortress was complete, I turned away from our original plans to conquer your world. Those who didn't saw things the way I did a bit too late." The Imperator smiled grimly. "I hear they never caught Agasilaus's assassin."

"No, they never did," Mara agreed, nodding.

The silver-haired Reakthi pulled up a chair and sat down; he motioned for Mara and Logan to do the same. "I turned toward knowledge," the Imperator went on. "I found myself fascinated by many of the things around us. I've read any book I could get my hands on, studied any tool or weapon that I could uncover." A pale eye fixed rigidly on Logan. "Tell me, is that costume you're wearing *really* made up of sweat?"

The young man blinked. "What?" he exclaimed.

Quarn smiled amicably. "Osirik here tells me you called it a sweat suit," the Imperator declared. "I've never heard of clothing made from perspiration."

"That's because it isn't," Logan sputtered, forgetting all about where he was and wondering just how in the world anybody could not know what a sweat suit was. "It's just a jogging outfit. Sort of made for *when* I sweat."

Quarn cocked back his head. "Ah!" he exclaimed in understanding.

Reakmor Osirik cleared his throat and shuffled his feet with embarrassment.

"I'm very interested to know all about you and your treks," Quarn addressed the couple once more. "Undoubtedly, you've had some grand adventures! But, the real reason you're here is that I have a few questions I need to ask you."

Uh-oh, Logan breathed. Here it comes.

The Imperator stood up, his black chestplate glaring in the Grand Hall's light. "About those Demons," he started. "Any idea where they gained their magic?"

Logan and Mara blinked. There was a moment of initial surprise before Logan queried, "Why should that interest you?"

"Well, it really is somewhat embarrassing to tell, but, you see, a while back a Demon ambushed some of my men while they were returning with provisions from the stronghold. They happened to have a magical item with them—a new addition to my collection." He waved a hand at the odd objects lining the walls. "Most of these originally belonged to Agasilaus, but he's no further use for them. I felt quite justified in taking them since nobody else wanted them, and I've expanded the collection quite a bit if I may say so myself.

"Anyway, these men were attacked by a Demon. Snatched the ring and made off with it even before I had a chance to study it." The Imperator leaned upon the table, eyes boring into the back of Logan's skull. "That's why I'm curious as to why you were fighting those Demons endowed with magic."

Logan frowned, running a hand through his black hair. He didn't know what to say to the Imperator. He couldn't just blurt out that it was his own magical item that the Demons had stolen; the Imperator might want to know why. Quarn might even try to keep Logan's staff if he found out the young man was carrying around a fistful of sorcerous goodies. Shit! If he finds out I can attract magical items like a magnet can attract iron, I'm never going to get out of here—whether he wants to use them to conquer Sparrill or just study them!

"Matthew," Mara suddenly cried out. "The Demon at the Roana! We had no idea where it had gotten its magic . . ."

Logan nodded, slowly at first and then more enthusiastically. "Yeah, the first one we bumped into," he agreed. "That makes sense." He faced the Imperator. "How long ago was this ring stolen?"

"Weeks, at least," Quarn replied.

Logan continued nodding. "It fits," he decided.

"Then you did find the Demon who stole my ring?" Quarn wondered.

"It found us," Logan muttered in reply.

The Reakthi commander narrowed his eyes at the two. "What became of it?"

"We killed it," Mara answered.

There was silence in the Grand Hall, and Logan began to grow fidgety. Those pale blue eyes seemed to be looking everywhere, and Logan didn't know whether or not Mara had said something wrong by telling the truth.

"So," Quarn finally declared, "we're even."

"Excuse me?" asked Mara.

"You killed the beast that stole from me, I killed the beast bothering you," the Imperator explained. "I'd say that just about evens things out."

Logan gave Mara a bewildered glance. "Yeah," he murmured, "I guess that evens us out."

"Your horse is in the stables," Quarn told them, "and I've taken the liberty of giving you fresh supplies. You may leave any time you like."

Footsteps resounded as the black-chestplated Imperator strode out of the Grand Hall and disappeared down a corridor. Reakmor Osirik was directly behind him.

Logan blinked and felt his contact lenses almost pop free from lack of moisture. A similar stunned expression was on Mara's face. They were actually free to go! The Imperator wasn't holding them prisoner or torturing them or anything! For a moment Logan was suspicious again. Okay, he pondered. What the hell does this guy want? He can't really be letting us go . . . can he?

The young man clenched his teeth. Well, I'm not about to let him change his mind. "Come on," he told Mara. "Let's get out of here."

The priestess lashed out an arm and held Logan back, halting him in mid-turn. "Matthew," she urgently said, "we can't leave. Didn't you hear what he said? *He's* got Agasilaus's collection. That means there was nothing back there for Moknay and Thromar to find."

"So?" the young man retorted. "What can we do about it? Ask him politely to take any Natural weapon he might have?"

"We can try," Mara responded. "I used to be a priestess of Lelah—maybe I can . . ."

"No!" snapped Logan, jealousy foaming within him at even the mere thought of Mara and another man. "I mean, no," he repeated, trying to regain his composure. "We don't need to go . . . uh . . . quite so far. Maybe we can steal it from him."

"Steal it?" Mara returned. "Matthew, we've been treated quite fairly and now you're suggesting robbery?"

"Lousy idea anyway," he grumbled. "We'd never know which item did which."

"Maybe if we came out and told him the truth," suggested Mara.

Logan snorted. "Oh, sure! He's really going to believe there's a resurrected *Deil* out there who's working for a Reakthi wizard who wants me dead but isn't going to kill me 'cause his real task is killing the land and the only way we can fight him is if we find an item of enough Natural magicks to kill him a second time! Even if he believes all that, why would he care?"

"Because he lives here now," Mara urged; her green eyes were imploring. "We need a weapon, Matthew. Without one, the land dies."

Logan inhaled, looking up at one of the strange items hanging from the castle wall. What if they could trust Quarn? What if they did tell him what was happening? Would he help? Would he believe them? Or would he just shrug them both off as lunatics?

The young man shrugged diffidently. Oh, well, won't be the first time somebody's thought I was crazy.

An almost fluid blackness escaped from around the sides of the tent, carrying with it a sickly-sweet odor that hung heavy in the air. Clusters of unarmored Reakthi gathered away from the dark tent, passing hushed comments among themselves. Sporadic bursts of color would illuminate the interior of the tent, revealing the writhing darkness that languished within it. Sometimes a gnarled form could be seen, arms outstretched, robe aswirl. Then the blackness would move back in and obscure the scene, releasing its pungent smell.

Vaugen watched with a distasteful scowl on his half-closed mouth. A flicker of anxiety sparked within his drab grey eyes, and his maimed hand twitched nervously upon the hilt of his blade.

"Perhaps it was a mistake to allow him back?" a soldier voiced, fearful more of the concealed actions inside the tent than of his mutilated Imperator.

Vaugen whirled on the man, his uncertainty tinged with fury. "Mistake?" he tried to roar, his voice barely a rasp. "I make no mistakes!" A charred and burned hand clenched into a tight fist, and pain registered across the Imperator's distorted features. "I have allowed him back because he claims he can find a means to more power than anything Matthew Logan could give us. If he succeeds, I will rule this land and many others. If he fails, I have one less sorcerer to worry over."

The Reakthi at his side shifted, eyes glued to the glowing tent. "But if the rumors are true," he said, "he's already conjured up some kind of creature that was said to have died . . ."

"Ridiculous Sparrillian blather!" Vaugen snapped. "If Groathit has indeed summoned up such a beast, why has he so faithfully returned? He attempted to strike out on his own, failed, and has come crawling back to us." A warped smile tried to pull across the Imperator's face and his fused flesh stretched like raw dough. "If he does well, I may reward him with his life."

"But if he succeeds, he may try to turn . . ."

The Imperator's eyes flamed. *"You dare?"* he choked, spinning on the soldier. "You dare imply that I have need to fear a spellcaster? *You* may fear! *You* may cringe! But I am your Imperator! You bow to me while I bow to no one . . . not even some mystic! Do I make myself clear?"

The Reakthi backed away. "Yes, sir," he apologized. "I'm sorry, sir."

Vaugen pivoted, returning his gaze to Groathit's tent. "As well you should be," he snarled.

Another tendril of blackness seeped free of the wizard's tent and curled gracefully skyward. Like thick, dark liquid, the strand of blackness wound its way upward before reaching a certain height, then dispersed into a thousand tiny globes of darkness.

Imperator Vaugen felt an icy chill crawl down the back of his chestplate and reach in between his vertebrae. Perhaps there was danger in what the wizard attempted, he mused, but the danger was not directed at him. He knew Groathit too well for that. The danger would be centered around the spellcaster himself . . . and Matthew Logan.

Imperator Quarn set four wooden spikes on the table while he trained his pale blue eyes on the two across from him. "I had had an idea things were bad," he said. "A scouting party spotted something like those distortions of nature you mentioned—but I had no idea things were this bad." He lightly touched the green-brown stakes. "I think perhaps these might be what you're looking for."

Logan quizzically lifted one of the shafts, turning it over in his hands as he examined it. "What are they?" he questioned.

"They're called thorns," Quarn responded, "or so I'm told. They're the most potent Natural artifact Agasilaus had in his collection. Got them from somewhere in Denzil, I believe. How they work I was never quite able to figure out."

Logan raised suspicious eyebrows. "Then how do you know how powerful they are?"

"My own studies," the Imperator assured him.

"But what good are they if I don't know how to work them?" the young man pressed.

Quarn stroked his beard. "You didn't know how to use your medallion or staff," he stated, "but you learned."

"That's different," Logan protested.

Quarn lifted a silver eyebrow. "Is it?"

"Hell, yes! I wasn't facing a *Deil* at the time!"

The Imperator frowned. "I can see your point," he nodded. "Still, that's the best I can do for you. I'm not very knowledgeable on Natural magicks . . . on some aspects, yes, but the pure Natural stuff is strictly Sparrillian."

A sudden touch on his arm from Mara drew Logan's attention away from the Reakthi commander. "Maybe we can ask Nightwalker," the priestess suggested.

Logan's frown matched Quarn's. "Good idea," he said, "but can we find him first?"

Mara pursed her lips and responded, "Maybe he'll find us."

"Yeah," Logan gravely retorted, "before or after the fight?"

Silence filled the Grand Hall as the trio stood poised around the table, the four thorns lying across its surface. Grimly, Logan stared down at the shoots of green-brown wood, his mind focused on the upcoming battle.

Why am I doing this? he asked himself. This isn't my world. I didn't even want to come here. So why the hell am I risking my neck for a world that isn't even mine?

So you can get back to a world that is yours, was his answer. You can't go home with Gangrorz around, and you know that. You need the Heart to get home, and Gangrorz'll take that away from you the minute you find it. Besides, you just can't pop out of here and leave everyone behind with Gangrorz, can you? Like it or not, you've got ties with this world now.

The young man glanced over at Mara, and his frown increased. Why do good things always happen at bad times?

Logan returned his gaze to the four stakes spread out across the table. From the way the thorns were crafted, Logan was vaguely reminded of a knobkerrie. The Hottentots and Kaffirs of South Africa used them, making them generally from wood, and, sometimes, from a rhinoceros horn. But knobkerries had spherical or elliptical knobs on the top—the thorns had none. In fact, the thorns were actually nothing more than a handle for such a weapon. With no knob, what good would throwing the stick be? There'd be nothing to whack your opponent across the head with. Unless these thorns were meant to be wooden daggers of some sort. The pointed tip certainly seemed sharp, but it lacked a handle in this case. As a knobkerrie it lacked a knob—as a dagger it lacked a handle. So just what the hell did these things do?

The young man gathered up the four shafts and nodded his thanks. "I guess these will have to do," he sighed, as if resigning himself to an early death.

Mara watched with a concerned expression on her face as Logan started to head out of the Grand Hall. Solemnly, Quarn gazed downward, peering at the tabletop.

"Where are you off to now?" the Imperator wondered.

Logan halted and shrugged. "Don't know," he admitted. "Probably to try to stop this mess." The young man chuckled darkly. "Matthew Logan, Cosmic champion to a world he never wanted to be a part of!"

There was a momentary flash of eye contact between Mara and Quarn as Logan resumed his dejected pace. The priestess started after the young man, leaving the Reakthi Imperator to stroke his beard in thought. The two were hardly out of the Grand Hall when Quarn called after them.

"Would you care for an escort of men?" he queried. "It goes against my principles to send out men for a nonpersonal reason, but I . . ."

Logan looked down at the four thorns and shook his head. "No," he murmured. "I'm already in your debt."

The young man shivered when a small door to his subconscious opened and released the deep, accented voice of Gangrorz from his dream:

You are the one they call Matthew Logan? You are nothing.

Logan gave himself a malicious smirk. Yeah, he berated himself, tell me something I don't already know.

·15·

Tomb

Thromar threw a quick glance over his shoulder as Quarn's fortress faded into the distance behind them. He wasn't quite sure what had happened inside, but friend-Logan had been very silent since he and Mara had left. That was another thing that surprised the large fighter. No Reakthi hounded his friends; no troop chased after them. The yellow-and-green horse had very simply walked out the front gates and had headed directly toward the area where he and Moknay had concealed themselves. Mara had tried to explain what Quarn had offered and how he had treated them, but somehow Thromar just couldn't see a Reakthi Imperator—or any Reakthi, for that matter—being nice to a Sparrillian priestess and a young man who could take out his eye. Perhaps that was it, the Rebel mused. Friend-Logan—although he keeps saying he isn't a spellcaster—cast a spell on Quarn to aid him. Imogen knew they were going to need all the help they could get.

That grim mien so constant on Moknay's face was there now. "I don't know, friend," the Murderer stated. "It might have been better if you had accepted Quarn's offer. The more men on our side, the better our chances."

Thromar snorted a laugh, spotting that there was no visible reaction from Logan. "Nonsense, Murderer!" the Rebel jeered. "Friend-Logan did the right thing! Who needs Reakthi tagging along? Not us, certainly!" A beady eye saw the young man still did not respond to the fighter's good-natured compliments.

Mara looked at the two. "You say Nightwalker told you to wait by Lake Atricrix?" she questioned.

Moknay nodded, silent.

"Any idea why?" the priestess asked.

"None whatsoever!" boomed Thromar cheerfully.

"Does he ever say why?" Moknay asked back.

There was silence between the four as the three horses made their way southward toward the stagnant lake. Already Thromar could smell the wretched perfume that stank of decay, but the fighter's mind was more concerned with the quiet that radiated from his young friend. He had seen Logan become despondent before—indeed, the young man tried to bear the burden of an army's supplies!—yet there was such an aura of doom surrounding him now. Things looked grim, the Rebel mentally agreed, but things had been certainly worse! The Jewel had almost tilted the Wheel, but friend-Logan stopped that. Moknay had almost been cut down by a Reakthi crossbowman, yet he pulled through. Why, the fighter himself had almost fallen off a cliff and had braved the hideous tortures of reliving his agony in Agasilaus's castle. No, things had indeed been worse.

Thromar's eyes widened as Smeea slowed her pace, nervously sniffing at the air. The trees and plant life around them suddenly began to betray traces of distortion, vague at first. Leaf structure and bark color were altered, and, the farther south they continued, the greater the deformity became. Green blades of grass were replaced by malformed black weeds, and trees were bent and twisted, filling the air with silent cries of pain. Bushes were contorted, their leaves unable to grow, and even stones had changed hue, taking on a sickly bluish tint.

"Agellic's Gates," Moknay breathed, grey eyes aswirl with his distrust of sorcery.

"He's killing the land," Mara choked, horrified by what she saw but unable to turn her face away. "The Heart must be failing."

Logan flinched at Mara's words as a subconscious pulse of emptiness filled his own heart and sent a shudder of fear through his nervous system. I'm really going to try to fight this thing? he asked himself incredulously. I'm going to go up against a creature with enough power to do *this*, and all I've got are four sticks of wood?

There was no answer for the young man as his horse proceeded southward, winding its way through the warped and twisted foliage. The brackish Atricrix gradually poked its way through the perverted shrubbery, its black waters calm and tranquil. The Demonry was a branch of that darkness, blemishing the land as it writhed its way across Sparrill before spewing itself into the sea many leagues northwest of them. This eyesore does not belong, Logan told himself. The lake and river are grotesque mockeries of the beauty that Sparrill holds. They do not belong in this world.

Like Logan himself, they should not have been there.

A garbled, unrecognizable sound split the stillness between the four, and Logan's horse reared up in terror at the disfigured beast that rose before it. A startled shout escaped the young man's lips as he tried to get his horse under control, and he felt Mara slip off the back of the stallion and fall to the ground. A shout echoed from Thromar's direction, but Logan's heavy depression made it impossible for him to react immediately to the danger present.

Something that could have been a clawed hand raked the air near the green-and-yellow horse's throat, and the stallion swerved, throwing off its second rider. Logan landed with a thump among the distorted vegetation, too startled to still see straight. There was obviously a pale form attacking them, but the young man could not recognize the outline of his opponent.

A numb hand extracted the young man's Reakthi sword from its scabbard and slashed blindly at the figure confronting him. There was resistance, and Logan knew he had hit, but his weapon suddenly spiraled out of his untrusting grasp. He saw steel flash and pale flesh give way, and watched as Thromar's heavy sword bit into the shoulder of his Demonic attacker.

Demonic? the young man's brain registered. This wasn't a Demon! Demons didn't look like this and . . .

Sudden revulsion tightened Logan's stomach as he realized the back of the Demon's skull had been blown wide open like a half-opened pomegranate. Dried blood congealed across the creature's blank, staring eyes and trailed in hardened streams down to the stump of its missing arm. No flickers of magic sparked from its remaining hand, nor did any life kindle behind its toadlike eyes. It was simply animated by its own stolen magicks—an already-dead guardian for Gangrorz's Tomb.

Logan went for Launce's staff and cursed himself when he remembered it was strapped to his horse's side. His sword had been torn from his grasp, and his dagger was too small to thrust with without getting his neck slashed back. The only remaining defense was the slender shoots of green-brown wood at his side.

As Thromar's arm swung down, Logan scrambled for the thorns. What might have been a high-pitched scream forced its way out of the Demon's gaping mouth, pushing its way up a windpipe and vocal cords half burned away by Logan's magic. Instinctively, the young man shut his ears to the sound, made more terrifying by the horrible mutilation of its face and head. Logan's numb fingers of his right hand curled around the nearest thorn and he

propelled himself forward, only briefly remembering he did not
know how to use them. At the moment, the thorns were the only
weapon available to the young man and he was going to use them
in the simplest way he knew.

Logan plunged the wooden shaft daggerlike into the one-armed
Demon's breast. No blood flowed from the wound, yet an eerie
luminescence filled the forest. The Demon's rounded mouth gaped
at Logan, and the young man felt bile rise in his throat as he saw the
forest behind the Demon through its opened mouth and shattered
skull. Unexpectedly, there was a resonating wail from the misshapen plant life around them as the embedded thorn flashed.

The Demon collapsed, its magicks taken from it; it smelled like
it had been dead for two weeks.

"What a stink!" Thromar grunted. "I'd forgotten how bad these
things smell!"

"And this one's been dead a day already," Moknay commented,
replacing two daggers he had withdrawn but not thrown. "It seems
that medallion had more power than any of us suspected."

Logan tore free the thorn and was surprised to see no blood
at all had collected on its point. "I don't think so," he replied,
somewhat detached. "The medallion healed, but not this much."
He glanced down at the thorns and tightened his grip. "This was
Gangrorz's work."

Mara stopped brushing dirt off her recently cleaned clothes.
"How do you know?" she inquired.

Logan started to shrug when another voice answered for him:
"There was a time once before when Darkness reared its foul
head above the waves of our Cosmic ocean, caring not of the
damage and havoc they wreaked. Their only purpose to destroy
that which they loathed. And now that time has come again."

Darkling Nightwalker's white horse stepped around an irregular
bush, its rider a human shape of darkness. Slow, casual movements
drew the hood away from the dark-skinned face, and Nightwalker's
white eyes trained on Mara. "What Matthew Logan says is true,"
he said. "The Worm knew you would be coming."

A dagger was in Moknay's gloved hand. "And you knew he
knew," he snarled, mouth and mustache twisted above a sneer.

The white-haired figure nodded.

"You didn't tell us," the Murderer accused.

"You did not wait as I said," came the matter-of-fact reply.
Nightwalker faced Logan. "You have the weapons you will need,"
he declared. "You must face the Shatterer now."

The young man tore his gaze away from the thorns. "But I don't know how to use them," he protested.

"I had hoped you would learn here," the strange man explained, waving an ebon hand at the dead Demon. "Interference has made that impossible." He shot Thromar and Moknay a malevolent glare.

"Now just hold . . ." Thromar began.

"This ring of distortion you see around you stretches out all around the Tomb equally on every side," Nightwalker went on. "The Worm draws on much of his Power to seek out the Heart, hoping that a deformation of Nature in its vicinity will draw it out. We must put a stop to him now before he does much more damage. As it is, the Heart already suffers much under this unnatural onslaught." A brief smile flashed across the black lips. "A pity the *Deil* still thinks this a battle between two Forces."

Logan blinked in confusion. "But where . . . ?" he started.

Nightwalker cut him off with an extended arm toward Lake Atricrix. "The battlefield is there," he remarked, "at the Worm's own burial. You have been there once before."

Logan saw a swift flashback of his dream sweep across his conscious mind before he was interrupted by Thromar. "We've got to go in there?" the Rebel exclaimed, screwing up his face. "It was bad enough fording the Demonry, now we've got to swim Atricrix?"

Nightwalker dismounted and led his horse through the warped forest. "We will not be swimming." And that was all he said.

In a dubious silence, the quartet followed their black-cowled guide through the remaining circle of gnarled brush and came to the shores of the lake. A cold, arctic wind moaned across the surface of the Atricrix, yet the dark waters did not stir or ripple. The chill of the wind knifed through the clothing of the four behind Nightwalker, sending tingles of cold through their bodies. Still, the frigid gale left the dark waters untouched, and Logan thought foully that the lake might have been made up of green-black pudding for all its fluidity.

Darkling Nightwalker released his mount and set his blank eyes on the group at his back. "We will not need our horses," he informed them, voice low and ominous. "Take whatever weapons you feel you will need."

The white-eyed stranger watched as Thromar tethered Smeea to a tree and set his hand on his sword hilt. Moknay tied his horse to a tree as well, his dagger-strap glinting in the fading sunlight.

Mara checked the amount of quarrels in her Binalbow as Logan tethered their horse and turned to face the others. A thought abruptly popped into his mind and the young man unstrapped the staff at his horse's side. Without a word, he handed Mara the oaken shaft as he juggled the thorns nervously in his right hand.

A vague smirk drew across the ebony hue of Nightwalker's face as he took a step into the green-black lake. The quartet expressed their surprise when the water did not part or ripple but swallowed Nightwalker whole.

Thromar set a tentative foot upon the surface of the lake. "I just hope it doesn't lead to a narrow corridor," he muttered, faking a yellow grin.

Logan watched as the bearded fighter disappeared beneath the unmoving waves and started forward himself. Mara's hand suddenly grasped hold of his and she followed him into the Atricrix, hands clasped. Moknay trailed them.

Perplexity scuttled about Logan's mind as his Nike sank through the dark lake and did not become wet. The surface of the lake neatly sucked up his shoe, leaving no trace or indication in the water. It was like walking into a stationary patch of pitch blackness, the young man thought, watching as his other foot vanished into the gloom.

Perhaps it was habit, but Logan took a breath of air just before his head disappeared beneath the Atricrix. Eyes shut tight and cheeks puffed up with air, the young man made his way down what felt like stone steps, his hand still tightly attached to Mara's. No moisture or water seeped through his clothes, and, when a freezing wind whistled past him, Logan's eyes automatically popped open.

Living, writhing darkness surrounded him. Thromar walked in front of him, dimly perceived through the churning blackness. Gloom and void embraced them, but Logan could see the stone stairs at his feet leading farther into the sable surroundings. What appeared to be a large structure lurked below them, the black-swathed steps leading down to its double doors. The young man knew immediately what the building was and accidentally lost the breath he had been saving.

Panicked, Logan gasped for air and found he could breathe through the gelatinous darkness. He shot Mara a bewildered glance, but the priestess had already learned what he had just discovered. From the uneasy glint in Moknay's eyes, the Murderer also knew they were not in anything that resembled water.

Terror crawled its way up Logan's spine as he neared the marble mausoleum. Sweat coated his and Mara's palms as they walked onward, his subconscious screaming warnings by flashing scenes of his nightmare through his brain. Determinedly, the young man forced these pictures aside, knowing he had to go inside. He had to confront the Worm. But what of Groathit? What would the Reakthi spellcaster do to him? He had a means of fighting Gangrorz, but what about Groathit?

Horror and foreboding sending his body into a state of utter turmoil, Logan trudged onward. The ominous architecture of Gangrorz's Tomb grew larger, every gleam of marble identical with Logan's dream. There was even a drooping strand of riverweed covering the left handle as Nightwalker threw open the doors and walked defiantly inside.

Mara tightened her grip on Logan's hand and his staff as she followed the young man into the Tomb. She was glad to be free of that hideous darkness, but her green eyes soon noted the blackness remained. There was no roof to this building, she noted. Although from the outside there had appeared to be one, from inside the ceiling was more of that churning blackness of Lake Atricrix. A convulsion of dread worked its way through the priestess's frame as she tried to fight it by biting on her lower lip.

The hallway the five were in gradually widened out, leading into a larger chamber lit with an eerie, unnatural glimmer. Darkling Nightwalker hesitated a moment, and, for the first time, Logan thought he caught a sense of indecision in the strange man's actions.

"He knows we have come," the ebon-skinned man declared, his voice hushed, "but he does not know what we have." Although pupilless, his eyes singled out the thorns. "It is up to you, Matthew Logan, to defeat him. You have that ability because of your inconsistency. You are an Unbalance, Matthew Logan. You are not controlled by the tilting and swaying of the Wheel—*you* may, in fact, cause those changes. This is our greatest asset in this battle."

Nightwalker resumed his pace but Logan whispered, "Wait! What about Groathit? I can't fight him."

"He is no longer here," Nightwalker said, stopping but not turning around. "Our only concern is the Worm and his overall destruction."

The fluid, agile stride of the darkly clad man commenced, and the four behind him trailed, lacking the urgency of his gait. At least, Logan thought, I'm not getting that feeling of death like in my dream.

The hallway ended and Nightwalker stepped into a massive, squarish chamber glistening from the mysterious light source. Thromar, sword extracted, followed quickly, tiny eyes flicking from side to side. Logan and Mara entered as a pair, Moknay a single shadow for the two.

The stillness urged the sensations of horror and doom to grow within Logan's gut as he glanced across the chamber. Unlike his dream, the room was empty, yet an abrupt gurgling echoed in his ears and sent streams of perspiration racing down his face.

Logan wheeled around to see a massive form burble up from nowhere, flashing black eyes fixing on the five. Tentacles, fangs, nostrils, and ears all briefly decorated the pillar of glittering flesh before sinking back into the protoplasm and reshaping into something else.

"I welcome you to my home," a deep, accented voice rumbled, shaking the marble walls and awakening a terror deep within Logan's brain. "It is not often I receive guests."

"We are not guests," Nightwalker snapped, surprising the four by displaying fury. "We have come to spell your downfall, Shatterer."

An antler momentarily grew from the right side of Gangrorz's shifting form. "Indeed, inferior organism?" the monster grumbled, amused. "I fear only one thing—that which I was created to destroy."

"You fear Nature!" shouted Nightwalker. "For the natural Balances the unnatural!"

Logan raised his eyebrows, recalling the similar comment made by the Blackbody he had encountered.

Gangrorz looked down at Nightwalker and an alien type of puzzlement filled the darkness of his eyes. "Who are you, little one?" the Worm queried. "I sense you are not one of these inferior beings." A slimy, wormlike arm pointed at the quartet gathered behind Nightwalker.

A malicious smirk crossed Darkling Nightwalker's sable features. "You realize now, Shatterer?" he mocked. "You see now that this is no longer a struggle between two Forces. More have come into play."

A low, jeering laugh boomed throughout the chamber. "You are filled with delusions, inferior organism," Gangrorz declared. "Whatever you may be, only the Forces of Light and Dark are in combat here. There are no others . . ." The night-filled eyes shifted on the featureless face to fix on Logan. " . . . except, perhaps, one."

Logan swallowed hard as the coal-black eyes robbed him of his courage.

"I welcome you, you who are called Matthew Logan." The Worm's deep voice resounded about him. "I have heard much about you and you kept true to your fame. You have slain many of my Beloved and tried to rally the Forces of Purity. I applaud your efforts."

Logan felt a chuckle slip free of his lips. Applaud? his mind sniggered. This thing doesn't even have hands! Applaud?

An uncertain flare deepened the darkness in the Worm's eyes. "How is this?" the creature's voice murmured, filling the marble room. "The other holds the staff, yet no magicks stem from it. Still, I sense that stench of Purity all about you."

The voiced ignorance pulled Logan free of the insanity that he had almost slipped into and he looked back at Mara. Gangrorz wasn't sensing the staff now at all? the young man pondered. He must be sensing the thorns I've got, but why isn't he sensing the staff?

An agonized howl split the silence of the chamber as Darkling Nightwalker plunged a grey spear of energy into the pliable flesh of the Worm. "Now, Matthew Logan!" the dark-skinned stranger yelled. "Strike! Slay the Worm!"

Black energy exploded, dissolving the shaft of power that had been embedded in the *Deil*'s glistening skin. Twin mouths stretched across the mucus-coated flesh, fangs dripping with saliva. "That hurt," the Worm bellowed in rage. "What manner of being are you to dare strike He who is the Wreaker of Havoc?"

Grey energy leapt from Nightwalker's black fingers, sending shadows streaking across his white hair. "You came before my Birth, Worm," the ebon-skinned stranger snarled. "You came when there *were* but two Forces opposing the Wheel, but now there is a third. Now there is a Force *because* of the Wheel to oppose you and your Foes.

"You are of Dark, Worm, while your enemies are of Light. I was Created between your War to safeguard the worlds that formed and were trapped between! Light and Dark merge in this dimension to form Shadow, and through the spinning of the Wheel I was Created to be its Guardian! No longer will you or your Masters dare to take advantage of the multiverses caught between you and your adversaries. Although I am the Child of Darkness and Light, I have allegiance to neither!"

An angry roar came from Gangrorz's shifting form as he lunged for the dark figure of Nightwalker. Things made sense, Logan thought as he tried to piece together information frantically. Nightwalker's magic was not of Sparrill, so Logan didn't feel the disagreement he generally did whenever Nightwalker said he used magic. Nightwalker's magic was the magic of an entire universe . . . universe? Multiverse! But how did two Forces meet in a third dimension to create another Force that was loyal to the hybrid mixture of the twin powers? Probably the same way the Blackbodies had been formed to keep the Balance of the Wheel.

Logan tore his hand away from Mara and dived at the glossy dark *Deil* towering in the center of the chamber. Green power crackled up the length of the young man's arm as he drove a thorn into the thick hide, acting out of horror rather than bravery. Gangrorz didn't even look back at him as an invisible fist crashed into Logan's stomach and knocked the young man backwards. Stars exploded behind his eyelids as he rammed up against a marble wall, the thorns clattering around him.

"Natural magicks," Gangrorz's low voice growled, his black eyes shifting about on his body so that they were actually on the back of his head and glaring at Logan. "You have brought more Natural magicks into my home."

"Matthew Logan!" Nightwalker's voice rang out through the din. "You have used them incorrectly! As a whole! They work as a whole!"

Black tendrils of thaumaturgy started to seep through the cracks of the marble mausoleum, piecing themselves together to form fluid, ichorous shapes—tiny caricatures of Gangrorz. With an agonized shout, Thromar clutched at his arm where one of the black maggots touched him, burning his flesh with an invisible flame.

Two daggers launched from Moknay's hands, slicing two of the dark worms in half. "They're solid enough," the Murderer noted, releasing more daggers.

Thromar rubbed his burned arm. "I could have told you that, Murderer," he snorted, sword ready.

Mara pulled Logan to his feet, lending him the staff. Dazed, the young man leaned on Launce's oak pole and looked at the battle between Gangrorz and Nightwalker. Once again the dark eyes rotated, focusing on Logan while the fight with Nightwalker went on.

"The staff," the Worm rasped. "It was neither the staff nor you that I detected." A furious sneer appeared on the creature's body. "The threat was the two of you together!" The eyes turned back to Nightwalker. "Away from me, Shadow-spawn!" the *Deil* thundered, blasting the darkly hued man across the chamber.

Terror rushed through Logan's veins like blood as he spied the massive serpent of dark flesh squirming in his direction, still upright so that the beast resembled a pillar. Limbs, claws, and tails spumed from the shifting, bubbling frame as it lumbered for the young man and priestess, black energy flashing in its eyes.

Logan tried to think. The staff and me, he repeated. It wasn't the staff Gangrorz sensed, and it wasn't me. It was the combination of the two. But it isn't enough to kill him. If it was, Nightwalker would have said so (and I guess we can trust him now). Somehow the thorns are what I've got to use. But as a whole? *As a whole?* What the hell did that mean?

Fingers trembling with fear, Logan tried to fit the slender shafts of green-brown wood together, but the thorns would not connect. Each was identically carved with no opening or slit in which to slip another. As a whole? The young man's mind screamed again in panic. Just what the fuck did Nightwalker want him to do with them?

"Friend-Logan!" Thromar shouted, hacking at dark maggots that filled the room. "Gangrorz!"

Logan glanced up from the thorns, and his blue eyes went wide as he saw how near the *Deil* had gotten. Nightwalker swayed dizzily in an opposite corner, a stream of blood trickling down one side of his face. Glistening flesh was almost upon Logan when he recalled his main source of power. I'm an X-factor, he remembered. If I do things out of the ordinary, no one's going to expect them.

Logan touched a thorn to the ball-like top of Launce's staff and felt a wave of red-hot disagreement wash over him as the shaft of wood adhered to the larger shaft. Hurriedly, Logan magically set a second thorn in place, grinning in self-proclaimed victory as a turgid green glare began to radiate outward from the two thorns already in place.

As a whole, Logan beamed to himself. I'll use 'em as a whole all right!

A sudden scream rang in Logan's ears.

"Matthew!" Mara cried out. "Look out!"

Shock, terror, confusion all crashed into Logan as Mara shoved the young man aside. Three of the thorns coruscated atop the oak staff, filling the young man with hopes of success that were instantly dashed as he fell to the ground and dropped the remaining thorn. In befuddlement, he glanced up to see twin arms of dark flesh shoot out overhead, razor-sharp beaks protruding from the palms of three-fingered hands. There was a splash of blood as the beaks pierced Mara's breast instead of Logan's, pelting the young man with droplets of the priestess's lifefluid. Mara released a scream as she crumpled to the ground, her black tunic already soaked crimson. A portion of cloth had been shredded, revealing soft flesh that was also slick with blood.

Logan remained on the floor, frozen, staring in disbelief at the priestess as more blood pooled around her slim form. An unexplainable, unstoppable rage built up in the young man's chest so that he strangled the staff with such ferocity that the oak groaned in protest. A painful emptiness accompanied the fury—a deep, hurting sense of loss that originated directly from his heart. All time seemed to stop as the young man fought the overwhelming grief and anger and instinctively reached out for the last thorn, magically gluing it to the top of Launce's staff.

Logan pulled himself to his feet, staring down at Mara as desolation swelled in his breast. "My heart," he murmured. He glanced up at the dark form with more shapes threateningly sprouting from its bulk. "You bastard," Logan howled, "you ripped out my heart!"

Green-brown sorcery rocketed from the oaken staff as the young man lunged straight at the *Deil*. The four thorns exploded with green energy, becoming mere outlines of emerald light. Launce's entire staff gleamed with a brilliant green aurora of color as Logan thrust the spiked end toward Gangrorz's face, Natural powers crackling throughout the marble chamber.

An explosion that reminded Logan of what might happen should matter and antimatter collide rocked the mausoleum. The Worm's upper half reeled backwards, arms and tentacles grabbing for its featureless face. Blood, black and sizzling like ebony lava, geysered from a savage wound that ripped across the Shatterer's body. Piteous bellows of agony wracked the dark, hulking monstrosity as it toppled to one side, its boiling lifefluid hissing like acid around it.

Logan watched in sadistic satisfaction as the *Deil* coiled in on itself across the marble floor, squirming in agony at the Natural energies that had torn open its flesh. The staff remained flaming in the young man's hands, but he stood back, observing the creature's pain with a grim smile. Abruptly, the Worm's howls died, and its dark eyes flicked back into being on the compressed, bloody bulk.

"Do not stop!" Darkling Nightwalker screamed from across the chamber. "Slay him! Slay him!"

Logan looked up, staff flaring. Gangrorz glared at him from the ground, dark blood trickling down one eye like black syrup. Half a smile formed on the *Deil*'s pain-distorted face as it fixed its eyes on the young man.

"You have injured me, Unbalance," the Worm gritted, its accented voice tinged with agony. "You have injured me but you have not killed me." The *Deil* flashed with Dark sorceries. "That was where you erred!"

Lightless Power radiated outward from the shifting, maggotlike shape on the floor. Logan heard the staff snap like a twig in his grasp just seconds before the blast struck him.

The Tomb exploded.

·16·

Worm

Matthew Logan painfully lifted his head up out of the sand, wiping blood and water out of his eyes. A muted, rhythmic roar sounded in the young man's ears, and cold, icy waters swirled around his body. The smell of salt hung heavy in the darkening sky, and Logan turned his blurred vision behind him to see grey waves lapping at bleak shores. To his right were the mouths of two rivers merging with one another to become one cascading stream that flowed out into the Sea of Hedelva. Silver-white bubbles flecked the surface of the ocean, churning and mixing the waters with the sea. Logan's sweatsuit was damp and heavy, bloated with the foul waters of the Demonry, and strings of black waterplants were tangled in his hair. The salt from the ocean sent a throbbing pain through an open wound on the young man's forehead, and he spat brine from his mouth in disgust.

Staggering weakly to his feet—finding it difficult to find his balance in the sand—Logan spied a dark form on his right, white hair slick with water. A portion of Darkling Nightwalker's cape had been torn, and beads of moisture trickled down his ebon skin like miniature pearls. Memories gradually materialized within Logan's perplexed mind and he half stumbled, half ran to the dark Guardian of Shadow.

"What happened?" the young man cried, his balance almost deserting him as he reached Nightwalker's side. "Where are we?"

Nightwalker looked up slowly, the beads of salt water that ran down his sable features resembling tears. "We have lost," the deep voice murmured. "We confronted the Worm and were defeated."

Logan threw a frantic glance at the Sea of Hedelva. "No!" he protested. "We've got to get back! We've got to save Mara and the others!"

Nightwalker's empty eyes filled with a genuine pity. "We are undone, Matthew Logan," he declared softly. "Our weapon was destroyed; we were cast helplessly out into the sea." The wet head of hair shook gravely back and forth. "There is nothing to go back for. Your friends are surely dead, and the reign of the Worm is upon us."

"No!" Logan screamed, clenching his fists in impotent rage. "There's got to be something we can do!"

Nightwalker blinked slowly. "We have done all we could," he explained. "And we have failed."

Frustrated anger burned deep in Logan's chest as he swung around and faced the grey ocean, blue eyes narrowed. Mara! his mind cried out. She was injured! Hurt! Dying, maybe! And Moknay and Thromar! Alone with that thing! He had to get back and save his friends! He had to!

"We'll run," the young man said, desperately searching for a way back. "We couldn't be that far."

"We were sent down the length of the Demonry River, Matthew Logan," Nightwalker stated. A dark hand motioned toward the sky. "The dusk has already descended. Much time has passed since our defeat. There would be no purpose to return."

"To save my friends!" Logan cried. "To save the Heart!"

"It is useless, Matthew Logan," the white-eyed stranger sighed. "We did what we could, and it was unsatisfactory."

Logan kicked a furious foot into the surf, spraying sand and water. "Bullshit!" he barked. "I've still got my sword! I've still got my dagger!" A tear came to the young man's eye, which he hurriedly wiped away, hoping Nightwalker thought it to be the spray of the sea. "I wounded the bastard! I hurt him! He's weak now! We can't give him the chance to recover!"

"Mere weapons alone cannot quench the horror of what is happening," Nightwalker responded, using the exact words of the Blackbody once again.

"Then we'll go to Quarn," the young man tried again. "We can get another weapon and go back!" He failed to stifle a sob that half choked his words. "Dammit! We just can't sit here!"

Darkling Nightwalker rose slowly to his feet, his black cowl glistening with salt water. "No," he agreed grimly, "we can get up and dare attack the Worm once more and be the first of millions to die. We would be fortunate. We would not see the Heart burst under the Shatterer's Power nor the land twist and reshape itself like Gangrorz's own foul, formless Evil."

Logan glared for a long time at the dark form of Nightwalker, trying to keep his anger blazing or else he knew he would break down and cry. He was helpless, he admitted. He had been beaten and was completely useless now to do anything about the Worm's ultimate domination and fulfillment of his task.

A grey wave washed a foot-long fragment of oak at Logan's feet as if in silent mockery of the young man's failure. Dimly, Logan watched the piece of wood bob and sway in the surf, roiling inward with the waves and being drawn back out only to sweep in once more. With each returning crash of the sea, the splinter of staff returned to plague the young man, reminding him of his defeat and the friends that he had left to die.

While his conscious mind was lost in the turmoil of his thoughts, Logan reached down and lifted the fragment of Launce's staff, peering at it with a sorrowful swirl in his eyes. Broken . . . destroyed, his brain noted. Like you. Like Mara. Like the land.

The raging ire erupted back into life, and Logan hurled the remnant of staff far into shore. As the fury broiled inside him, he watched as the section of wood spiraled out over the twin rivers and disappeared with an inaudible bump somewhere near the junction.

A blood-red gleam half-obscured by moist earth caught Logan's eye.

The young man squinted at the mouth of the two rivers that became one. He couldn't be sure, but it looked like there was something buried directly in the center of the two streams, lodged firmly in the piece of ground that made up the V of the joining rivers.

Logan looked back at Nightwalker, who was gazing morosely out over the sea. The ebon-skinned Guardian was lost in his own thoughts of despair, the young man decided. He'd be no help, so Logan turned back around and fixed his eyes on the rivers.

Crimson light winked at the young man through the earth.

Surprise blocked out the dampness and cold enfolding Logan as a distant, yet familiar feeling made its way into his deprived senses. He almost found himself smiling when he recognized the disconcerting buzz as the sensation of disharmony that had pestered him constantly since his arrival. It had been so long since he had felt the twinge of disagreement, Logan wished he could run up to it and embrace it like a long-lost friend.

Nightwalker turned his head around as he heard Logan run up the sloping shore back toward the rivers. The young man had withdrawn his sword, but there was no enemy in sight. Too disheartened to feel any emotion more than just idle curiosity, Nightwalker watched as Logan charged the river junction and hacked at the loose dirt with his Reakthi blade. Dirt clods tumbled into the mingled waters of the Roana and the Demonry as Logan worked at the soil, the sense of discordance growing stronger with each scooping motion. Pupilless eyes widened on Darkling Nightwalker's features when he glimpsed the flickering red light that gleamed from within the land, and a skull-sized stone of blazing crimson suddenly splashed out into the sea.

Logan's hands tingled with disagreement and numbness as he hefted the massive Bloodstone out of the waves and held it triumphantly overhead. "Hey!" he exclaimed. "I found it! I found it!"

Nightwalker realized he was gaping but found it difficult to stop. "Between the combatants," he murmured. "Lost directly between the Forces that had been battling—it makes sense."

Logan grinned. "Sense?" he shouted. "Who cares if it makes sense? I found the damn thing! Does it matter where?"

"I suppose it does not," Nightwalker agreed, but his tone was serious. "Yet we must be cautious. Should the Shatterer learn what you have uncovered, he will instantly snatch it from your grasp."

"I'd like to see him try it!" Logan snapped, his face set in an expression of determination made all the more powerful by the red glare radiating from his hands. "I'm going to kill that son of a bitch!"

Darkling Nightwalker took a step toward the young man, his black skin reflecting the Heart's crimson light in odd, rosy shades. "We have a day's journey on foot ahead of us," he stated. "We must think of some way to hide the Heart's magicks."

Logan tore the skull-sized gemstone away from Nightwalker, scarlet fire reflecting in his eyes. "Bullshit!" he spat. "By that time Moknay and Thromar will be dead! And so will Mara! We've got to get back now!"

The young man's urgency overpowered Nightwalker's shield of mystery, and the Shadow-spawn cocked his head to one side. "You would risk the life of the land and of yourself to rescue your friends?" he queried.

"Damn right I would!" Logan smirked, liking the ability to tell Nightwalker what to do. "I owe that beast something for everything he's done to me! For everything he's done to Mara!"

Nightwalker's eyes flickered, and a hint of sympathy flashed in their pure white emptiness. "You know in your heart she is beyond rescuing," he said. "So, too, must your other friends be slain."

Logan howled, refusing to believe what somewhere in his mind he knew was true. "*No!*" he screamed. "I've got the Heart! I can win now! They're not dead! Not yet!"

"And if they were not," Nightwalker went on, his voice calm and steady and oh-so logical, "how would we reach them in time? We are a good two leagues from the Tomb."

The logic struck at the very center of Logan's determination and caused a frown to stretch across his face. Teleport? his mind suggested. Maybe it wasn't possible. The Heart controlled the land's magic—did that necessarily include the overlapping dimensions that smaller, less powerful items intertwined with? And, besides, teleporting was limited. A few yards at a time was the maximum—not a few miles.

The glittering Bloodstone in the young man's hands flashed in silent response to a thought that had—for some odd reason— forced its way into his skull. Logan had no idea why the phrase crossed his mind. Phrase? It was just a word. Something some-body had said, the young man couldn't even remember who.

Waterfoals.

Logan caught the snicker that arose from the memory. Waterfoals had made him think of large sea horses saddled and ready for riding, looking awkward and unbalanced with a man riding its sloping back. Why the word had popped back into mind was beyond his understanding.

A bubbling whinny sounded at his back and Logan whipped around. A herd of frothing waves churned toward the mouth of the twin rivers, a delicate, pale blue. Bright, gemlike eyes adorned each single wave, and Logan could barely make out the separate structure of each creature until they split apart.

Waterfoals! his mind registered.

Two of the watery beasts pulled up alongside the shore, training their bright eyes on the blood-red Heart in Logan's hands. One of them released a snort, relaying to the young man in unspo-ken words that there was a task that needed fulfilling. In awe, Logan paused. The waterfoals were all a shade of blue, their manes frothing, silver bubbles that gurgled and sprayed like real hair tossed by a breeze. The shape of each creature resembled a horse's upper half, except the similarities ended at the legs. Instead of legs, the waterfoals bobbed upon sleds of whirling foam, as much a part of them as their white-water manes. How any creature made up of water could support him, Logan did not know, but the waterfoals certainly seemed to indicate they wanted him to mount up.

Nightwalker drew his empty eyes from the herd of sea horses. "You have . . . caused this?" he wondered, hesitating.

Logan nodded, then shrugged. "Yeah, well . . . I don't know." He stepped into the waves and stared at the liquid horses. "Are they safe to ride?" he questioned.

Nightwalker cast his empty eyes upon the young man. "You wield the Bloodstone," he replied. "You tell me."

Logan glanced down at the pulsating red globe in his grasp and swiftly concluded that any risk was worth taking to rescue his friends. With a doubt-riddled leap, the young man jumped astride the nearest waterfoal. At first he felt uncomfortable, as if he had sat in a chair too soft and too yielding; then the horse surged forward. A massive, rushing tide of creatures swarmed up out of the Sea of Hedelva and leapt into the mouth of the twin rivers, forging their way upstream with an ease that defied reason. The foul water of the Demonry seemed to shrink back in horror, its stagnant, algae-coated surface recoiling in disgust as the sparkling beasts crashed through. Beads of salt water filled the air, and the lingering rays of day struck each waterfoal and turned it into a transparent splendor.

Logan leaned forward on his mount, the fear gone from his system. The smell of the sea was thick in his nostrils, and the light spray of water from his horse's mane and body sprinkled his face and revitalized him. He became oblivious of the wound in his forehead or the lack of sensation on his right side. All that mattered was the glistening crimson weapon in his arms, and the safety of his friends.

They can't be dead, he thought, trying to convince himself. I've got the single most powerful item I can use against Gangrorz. Moknay and Thromar can't be dead! And Mara . . . The young man had to force away the sight of her bloodstained tunic and her soft flesh sticky with red. No! his mind rebelled. She can't be dead either! She can't be! Not now! Not when I can win! Things don't happen like that! The good guys are supposed to win! They're supposed to!

A gut-wrenching anxiety began to gnaw at the young man's innards as the pouring wave of waterfoals made their way up the brackish stream of the Demonry. My ability found the Heart, he continued to himself. I "accidentally" bumped into something again. I have the greatest luck with mistakes—that's probably the most unusual paradox of this whole place. The more accidental the incident, the more powerful the item or calamity. I find the most things when I'm not even looking for them!

Another portion of the young man's mind pushed through. Yeah, paradox, it sneered. Remember that word, Matthew. Remember that in order to win you need to use magic, and, in order to go home again, you need to win, but, in order to go home, you can't take in any magic because no such thing exists in your world. So now what are you going to do? You've got a chance to go home . . . use it.

Logan shook his head, tightly closing his eyes as if to ward off the temptation. It's not a quick process! he snapped at himself. The Smythe said so! It takes time to soak up magic.

But you haven't been soaking it up, that section of mind rasped. You've been using it—willingly. You were wounded, you turned to magic. You were outnumbered, you turned to magic. Now you've been defeated once and you're returning to use more magic. Don't you see you're going to get stuck here?

No, I'm not! Logan shouted mentally. I'm saving people who have helped me! I'm rescuing my friends! That alone is not going to condemn me here!

A low voice sounded in Logan's ear as Nightwalker's mount splashed its way alongside him. "Matthew Logan," the Guardian called out over the rush of water, "I sense a great disturbance in the Wheel's rotation—the Equilibrium is being sorely distorted!"

"Is it Gangrorz?" Logan called back.

"I do not think so," Nightwalker responded, "but what are your plans? How do we confront the Shatterer before he steals the Heart from us?"

Logan screwed up his face. "I don't know," he admitted.

"You do not know?" repeated Nightwalker.

"Yeah!" Logan retorted. "I don't know! Now back off! You said yourself one of my greatest assets was my ability to cause the unexpected! So I'm going to do that! And I won't know what I do until I do it!"

The young man dug his heels into his horse's flanks and felt water fly. Nonetheless, the waterfoal responded to the command and suddenly plunged below the surface. The Heart glared scarlet in Logan's hands as he plummeted through the murky darkness of Lake Atricrix. Reach inside it, the young man told himself, peering into the depths of the Heart. Reach inside it like you did with the Jewel. Grab hold of an iota of energy . . . no . . .

grab a handful. Make this bastard sorry for what he did. Make this bastard pay for hurting Mara!

The tide of waterfoals halted in the mysterious blackness that was not water and the majority of the herd charged ahead, Logan's and Nightwalker's beasts staying behind. In an explosion of pale blue and marble, the force of waterfoals threw themselves against the side of the mausoleum, sacrificing their watery bodies to tear a hole in the Tomb wall. Logan and his mount propelled inward, weaving precariously close to shards of marble and debris. Unexpectedly, the horse beneath Logan dissolved, and the young man rolled to a stop within the main chamber of Gangrorz's Tomb. Nightwalker righted himself beside him. The dark shaft of protoplasm that was the Worm slowly unfolded, writhing around in unspoken agony from the wound on its body.

Logan panicked as he realized he had dropped the Bloodstone.

"*You!*" Gangrorz roared, a thousand teeth flashing across his pliable features. "You live still? And you dare return?"

"We have not yet been sensed," Nightwalker exclaimed in surprise. "Strike now, Matthew Logan! Strike!"

Logan muttered something unintelligent in Nightwalker's direction as he lunged for the fallen Heart. He didn't see any of his friends in the chamber, and it was possible the same explosion that had knocked him and Nightwalker to the sea had knocked his companions in the opposite direction. Or, then again, Gangrorz could have utterly destroyed them . . .

The Worm's ebony eyes trailed Logan's desperate lunge and went wide with a sudden terror as ruby flames sparked in their blackness. "Purity!" the *Deil* screamed in panic. "The Heart of the land! You seek to destroy me!" Tentacles, arms, and wings swelled outward on the monster's ever-changing shape as he grabbed for the Bloodstone. "You shall not return me to the Slumber of Death!" the creature swore. "I shall be triumphant! My Masters are returning! When they arrive, I shall not have failed them!"

"Buster, you already have," Logan snarled, allowing a warm, almost sentient power to course through his arms from the Heart and fill his body.

The buzz of disagreement went silent as raw magic filled Logan's frame and he felt it swirl and strengthen within him, fueled by his own anger and hatred for the Worm. Crimson energy abruptly sliced the air, pouring forth from the tips of Logan's fingers, sending tingling barbs of numbness up the length of his nerves.

Gangrorz screamed in fury and pain as scarlet power ripped into his tractile flesh, releasing waves of brackish ichor that sizzled the marble floor where it splattered. An echoing cacophony of agony overwhelmed the chamber as the Tomb itself seemed to mimic Gangrorz's wail of misery and rage, and Logan watched with a blazing smirk of victory as the black eyes blinked out of existence, and the slab of protoplasm careened forward and lay still.

Matthew Logan looked down at the bloody, unmoving bulk and grinned. Gangrorz was dead . . . again . . . and he had been the one to do it. He had won, just like it was supposed to be. The good guys triumphed—through whatever botched-up way Logan had caused this time around.

A sudden seizure of pain exploded in Logan's skull, and the young man felt vertigo grip him about the throat. Whatever powers he had used, they had the same disorienting after-effect as those mental powers from the medallion. Unsteadily, Logan leaned against a wall, inhaling deeply. He felt flushed and feverish, and the wound in his forehead pulsed in an agonizing harmony with the throbbing in his head.

Nightwalker's hand was on the young man's shoulder. "You are unwell?" he queried.

Logan started to shake his head but found that only unbalanced him even more. "I'm just . . . woozy," he made out. "Go see if you can find . . . Find the others."

The darkly cowled stranger hesitated, an ebon hand wavering near Logan should the young man need to be propped up. Then, somewhat reluctantly, the Guardian of Shadow turned on his heel and left the main chamber.

Logan slid down the wall and breathed deeply. He set the Heart beside him and gave the gemstone a sardonic stare. Jesus! he cursed the Bloodstone. You pack one helluva wallop, don't you?

As the young man relaxed back and closed his eyes, a scream split the silence of the Tomb and chilled the young man to the bone. It was a single scream of three voices. Three people screaming as one. An absolutely terrifying chord of horror that startled Logan awake and alert, and his blue eyes widened when he saw what lay beside him.

A dripping, oozing tendril of flesh had entwined itself about the Heart. In shock, Logan trailed the limb back to Gangrorz's corpse and felt a paralyzing fear heave in his stomach as he saw the malevolent black eyes had reappeared on the dark flesh. The Worm's eyes glittered in unholy glee as the *Deil*'s mucus-smeared tentacle squeezed the life from the Heart.

"You are indeed a fool, Unbalance," the deep voice boomed around him. "You have unwittingly handed the victory over to me. Did you not know the blast that delivered me to Death was so great that not even the sprite Roana could control it? It was a thousand times greater than the paltry blow you dealt me, yet it was enough to suffer the pain of your impudent attacks knowing that they have resulted in my triumph."

Logan lunged for the glistening red gem lost within the bubbling, shifting limb. "No!" he screamed.

The first tentacle drew away, taking the Heart with it; a second limb shot forward, barbed and pointed. Searing agony banished Logan's headache as the lance of flesh speared his chest, burrowing through flesh and muscle. Logan was knocked backwards, warm blood trickling down the inside of his sweatsuit. Blinded by pain, Logan's hand tore the dagger from his belt and severed the pointed limb plunging for his heart. Ichor splashed the marble floor as the tentacle dropped away, squirming with a hideous, gelatinous life of its own. A snort of discomfort came from the *Deil*'s accented voice as its limb was cut off, yet its other tentacle remained firmly wrapped around the Bloodstone, more flesh flowing over the gem and thickening the limb.

Gangrorz yowled as a blade bit deep into his fluid flesh, spitting black blood across the chamber. The Heart spilled from the Worm's obscene grasp as the beast thrashed its maimed limb, mouths appearing and screaming and then vanishing. In amazement, Logan looked up to see Thromar before him, his bearded face bespattered by the foul blood of the Worm.

"I thought you surely dead, friend-Logan," the fighter declared, grinning with yellowing teeth at seeing that he had been mistaken.

Logan clamped a hand over his wounded chest and shook his head in confusion and pain. "Wait," he gasped. "Where's Moknay?"

"Right beside you, friend."

Logan turned to see the Murderer on his right side, holding the ichor-splashed Heart in his gloved hands. There was a hint of nervousness in Moknay's grey eyes, but revenge cancelled out the unease. Both Murderer and Rebel held small wounds that showed they had suffered from Gangrorz's miniature self-shapes; the latter walked with a slight limp. These small signs told Logan his friends had a score they wished settled with the pliable, malicious being facing them. Nightwalker stood behind the two, his black features a mixture of doom and wonder.

Logan took the Heart from Moknay and peered into its sanguine blaze. "Mara?" he asked, almost unable to voice her name.

There was quiet in the Tomb.

"I'm sorry," Thromar finally replied. "She's dead."

"Dead, yes," Gangrorz interrupted, pulling his wounded form erect. "So shall you all be for injuring me . . . for harming a Servant to Darkness. You will learn that there are Powers insignificant creatures such as yourselves were never meant to become involved with. What say you to that, Shadow-spawn? For all your talk, you and your Unbalance are nothing! Light and Dark are the Forces at work, and the tilting of your precious Wheel has little influence on Beings as great as we." The black eyes flamed. "Yes, I see you sensed the disruption earlier. That was why I did not know what you had uncovered—I was too busy trying to decipher what could have caused some unrest in this frail little multiverse of yours. Have you guessed? Have you come to comprehend what you face? Even I was not expecting it, but it has come to pass. My Masters are preparing to grace your petty dimension with their Presence. I know not for what purpose, nor how, but they are coming. They shall rule this land, and I shall sit at their side. But I need to show my worth by preparing this world for their entry, and I may only do that by wrenching the life from the accursed Heart which beats with such numbing Purity!"

Logan gradually lifted his head, turning his eyes away from the Bloodstone. Mara was dead, his mind repeated. Mara was gone. He fixed his blue eyes on the towering bulk of darkness before him. This was the cause, his mind whispered. This monster caused her death—caused the young man's misery. My heart . . . this is the bastard that's ripped out my heart.

Like a blossoming flower, petals of scarlet energy forked out across the chamber. Gangrorz released a shriek that shook the walls, withdrawing the limbs he had sent out to steal the Heart from Logan's benumbed grasp. Blood-red fire crackled, and pliable flesh exploded as the outstretched tentacles burst, raining ichor. The Worm bellowed, lurching backwards and crashing to the ground, his maimed limbs whipping around him. Ruby light flooded the mausoleum, sweltering up around Logan like a personal aura of power, arcing and spitting like electricity gone wild.

The *Deil*'s black eyes burst in a grotesque spray of writhing blackness as shafts of crimson force lashed out from the Heart. Needled by rays of sorcery, the dark shape coiled inward, attempting to escape the pain by retreating in on itself. Black, acrid blood spumed from its wounds, and the pulsating flesh expanded outward like a balloon on the verge of popping. Frantic limbs and appendages flailed from the bloated form as a last, garbled screech reverberated throughout the Tomb. Both the Heart and Logan flashed with a blinding sheet of red magic that spiraled, shrieked, and plunged straight into the black interior of the swollen monster.

Gangrorz the Worm exploded.

Matthew Logan felt a deep, hurtful emptiness thriving within him as he looked down at the still form of Mara. I'll never talk to her again, he realized, eyes filled with tears. Never hold her. Never tell her just what I felt. I had something and I lost it—even though I won, I lost. It's not supposed to happen that way. Dammit! Why is life so damn unfair? It doesn't matter what world I'm in, life is just as cruel! The young man cradled the priestess's head, stroking her long, dark hair. I loved you, Mara. I think I always will.

A delicate hand touched Logan's shoulder and the young man looked up into Roana's violet eyes. "Matthew Logan," the sprite said solemnly, "you have done us and the land a great favor."

Logan nodded impatiently, wiping away the tears. He gave the Bloodstone a distasteful glare and hung his head in sorrow. Life isn't easy, his mind reminded him. Never said it was—never said it would be. Cyrene, Launce, the ogre, the Smythe . . . they all found that out. And now Mara. Oh, God, why Mara? Why? Why the only thing good to ever happen to me in *any* world?

"You mustn't blame yourself, friend-Logan," Thromar advised, his expression as saddened as Logan's own.

Logan shook his head helplessly, choking back a sob. "Why not?" he asked. "There's no one else to blame."

"To turn the blame inward is self-destructive," Nightwalker commented. "You do yourself great harm."

"So what?" Logan snapped. "Maybe I should hurt. Maybe I should know something about pain. I caused this! No matter how much Mara said she did on her own, when it comes right down to it, the fault lies with me."

Silence filled the Tomb as Logan fought with the tears that tried to flee his eyes once more and blur his contact lenses. I've lost you, Mara, he cried. I wish I could dream. I wish there was some way I could get you back. Keep you. Hold you. Love you. Tell you about my world.

"We've won," Glorana said, hands on hips. "We should be rejoicing, not grieving."

Thromar faced the sprite. "We've lost one of our band," he explained.

"It doesn't have to be that way," Glorana retorted, pouting.

Logan jerked his head up. "What?" he demanded. "What did you say?"

"You possess the Heart, Matthew Logan," Roana stepped in, explaining for her younger sister. "With it you wield all Natural magicks that are a part of the land. That includes the Forces of Natural Laws. You have a limited Power to bend them . . . alter them."

Logan reached out for the glimmering Bloodstone, his hands trembling. "Are you saying . . ." he started. "You mean . . . I can bring Mara back?"

Roana nodded, smiling faintly. "If it is not too late for even the Heart's Powers."

The young man gripped the Bloodstone with shaking hands, staring down in awe at the pulsing red gem. Faint humming vibrations dimly reminiscent of the buzz of disagreement filled his ears, and blood-red sparks of light danced across his fingertips. He gave Mara a glance, the desolation lurking within him howling in its agony. No thoughts entered his mind concerning the usage of magic. He didn't consider the power he would be calling upon voluntarily. He didn't stop to think that he had just destroyed the Worm with a blast more powerful than the original one Roana herself had used to slay the *Deil*. He didn't recall that he had mentally protected himself and his companions from any sorcerous back-lash which had lost the Heart once before. He didn't worry himself with the realization that this one, last act might strand him forever in Sparrill. All he thought of was the possibility of having Mara again—the ability to hold her and love her as he longed to do.

Soft ruby traces of magic scaled across Mara's body, and Logan lightly touched her forehead. He sensed a stillness within her—an emptiness almost similar to his own which had taken possession of her form. Swiftly, Logan dispelled the intruding vacuum, urging life back into the young priestess. With the Heart's radiance, the young man touched her mind, sent oxygen to her brain, resurrected cells that had withered and died. He moved to her wounded chest, knitting together flesh and sinew, piecing together veins and arteries, magically restarting her heart, sending oxygen-rich blood pumping through her slim frame.

Delicately, Logan begged the Heart to search out and recover the magic that had made the priestess what she was. He asked the Bloodstone to defy the Law of Death, to pull Mara back from whatever had taken her from him. To return her to her body that Logan had so meticulously pieced back together. Bring Mara back to me, he pleaded. Don't let it be too late. I restored everything I could—had any magic heal whatever could be healed within her. Please, just bring her back.

Dark eyelids fluttered open and eyes greener than any Logan had seen in either of his two worlds peered out at him. For a moment, cold fear filled Logan's throat until he saw the intelligence behind those emerald eyes, and a smile drew across Mara's lips. Somehow, *magically*, Mara had come back. She had been returned.

Logan and Mara embraced; Thromar released a thunderous sniff.

"By Brolark," the fighter remarked, his tiny eyes damp, "it's been far too long since I've seen a truly happy ending."

Moknay sneered grimly. "Take a good long look, friend," he quipped. "Things never stay happy long enough."

"Indeed, Murderer," Nightwalker agreed, his empty eyes foretelling doom, "already this moment is past. The priestess has been returned, but I fear another matter arises. There is something else I am disturbed over."

"But Matthew's done what was needed to be done," Mara argued. "He's slain the Worm. Can't he go home?"

"Perhaps," Nightwalker responded, "but, then again, perhaps not. Both the Shatterer and I sensed a disruption in the Wheel . . . a perversion of its rotation."

"Someone attempts to contact the Voices," Salena stated, nodding her green locks of hair. "They are close to succeeding."

"Then my fears are confirmed," answered Nightwalker. The ebon-skinned Guardian faced Logan. "We need to ask you once more for your aid, Matthew Logan. Only you as an Unbalance and the Heart's magicks may stop this invasion from another plane of Force. I only pray to whatever gods may exist in this dimension that we may prevail."

Logan got up, helping Mara to her feet and keeping a steady hold around her. His mind was filled with happy thoughts, yet he heard what Darkling Nightwalker told him. Mutely, he nodded his head in acceptance, his grip on Mara tightening. The Heart glistened in his other hand. He knew his leaving had to be postponed until the cause of his troubles ended, and that meant slaying Groathit. All along the fight had been between him and the Reakthi wizard, and the young man was now intent on ending that conflict before his voyage home.

"So much for happy endings," Thromar snorted, shuffling out of the Tomb.

"I hate to say so, Thromar," Moknay remarked, "but I did say so."

Matthew Logan locked his eyes with Mara's as the two made their way up the stone steps and back into the Sparrillian night. Behind them the green-black decay of Lake Atricrix was dispersing, magically eating itself away as the *Deil*'s eon-old hold finally gave way.

Logan smiled inwardly to himself. So there's a fight impending, he shrugged carelessly. I've got the Heart and I've got Mara; I can go home any time I want. So maybe things weren't ending, but— at least for a little while—things would be happier.

A warm, natural breeze rustled the trees, and, somewhere, a cricket chirped.